Max Blaze:
Re:Generation

Steven M. Gondré-Lewis

to my mother and father

"The most beautiful pictures have the brightest lights, the darkest darks, and every subtlety in between."

CONTENTS

1 WELCOME TO THE UPA

5015 FD (Final Destination): His eyes opened. He found himself back in the car where he belonged. He looked up and saw a man driving. The man looked back to check on him. There was a girl who glanced at him from the other side of the seat. He rubbed his eyes and began to stir. There was a boy in the passenger's seat in front of him.

"Max always was one to doze off in a car." The boy chuckled. The car continued to whiz through the sky. The sun reflected off the buildings as cars soared by. The trees stood tall as their colors blended on the cloud-like canvas. The buildings were even taller, unchallenged in height, with docking bays ready to service. Below, people hustled about by the thousands in stores and restaurants, keeping money moving and everyone content.

In front of them stood the largest tower that overlooked the city, reaching for the twin suns orbiting in the sky. Directly in front of it was a large green pasture that remained untouched. On the other side of this field was a series of large, tall and shiny buildings, like a campus. The car descended onto a parking platform near one of the buildings.

"Well, he couldn't have picked a better time to wake up. Zack, Max, Tyra, I officially welcome you to the Universal Protection Agency headquarters!"

The three kids got out of the car, awestruck at the structure in front of them. It seemed to never stop rising. There were starships chasing each other miles above their heads while they could hear the sounds of machines being tested behind the doors. Voices over the PA announced the next missions for the agency's members.

Max stretched his arms and legs, still trying to wake up from his nap. He had on a necklace he never seemed to take off and some worn-out jeans. His T-shirt was faded, and he wore a fleece vest over it with gloves to hide his ashy skin.

He looked over to Tyra, but she seemed not to pay any attention to him. She had red hair, a short black T-shirt, and a black skirt with tights. She seemed determined not to look back at him. Zack put his arm around Max's shoulder in excitement.

"Dude, we finally made it! We're here!" Max smiled at him and was really excited. Zack looked back at the man. "Thanks for the lift, Dad."

The man smiled and waved back as the kids walked forward to join the group standing at the door waiting to enter. "No problem, kiddo," he shouted back. "Don't lose the gear I gave you, Zack. The family has used it for years. Oh, that reminds me. Max, come back here for a second."

Max turned around and ran back to Zack's dad. "What's up?"

"Yeah, before you go, I know I'm probably not going to see you guys for a long time, and I know your old man wanted me to give you this." He pulled out what looked like a hilt to a sword connected to a sword's case, but it had no blade. Max took the gift, not really knowing what to do with it.

"I know how much you and Zack played with your swords, so I thought when you grew up a bit, I could give you your father's Blade."

"So my old man used this?"

"That's right. Got him out of a lot of jams," he said, chuckling.

"How does it work? It doesn't even have a blade."

"Well, that's something you'll figure out soon enough."

"Why not just tell me now?"

"Because I know you can figure it out." The man smiled and looked into Max's eyes. "You look so much like him, you know."

Max showed a hint of a smile. It was followed closely by slight worry and anticipation.

"I know how hard you three have been training for this day. You have grown a lot together. You'll have each other's backs and you'll prevail. I believe in you three."

Max smiled as the man patted his head and walked back to the car to soar off into the sky's oncoming traffic. Max held his Blade, clipped it onto his person, and joined the others.

They found themselves on a balcony looking over a giant lobby. There was a massive staircase in front of them with teleports and tubes leading to different locations around the base. The kids were amazed simply at how much was going on in this one room. A man in a uniform approached, greeting them with sickeningly rehearsed enthusiasm.

"Hey there, everybody! My name is Craig. Welcome to the UPA training facility. This is where all the new recruits are broken in, schooled, and trained into eventually becoming soldiers who will be deployed for missions. You guys are all informed about what's going on out there in the sky, aren't you?"

The children shook their heads to indicate 'no', while Max just rolled his eyes.

"Well, let me explain everything to you." A giant hologram appeared behind him. "We are the Universal Protection Agency. As suggested by our name, we are the defense for planetary, galactic, and intergalactic systems against catastrophic anomalies. We have several million stations spread throughout the universe, but the one right here on Zapheraizia is the big one. This is where all the plans are initiated and managed. Now, for the past five thousand years, we've been at war with a very destructive force known as the 'Negatives.' These creatures are Negative matter formed into soldiers. They seek to latch onto Positives, like you and me, and feed off of us to enslave the universe. The whole of the enemy is led by a vicious tyrant named Xaldoruks. The name has been passed down from one man to another. This battle all started when the first Xaldoruks attacked this base five thousand years ago, beginning the war. That was our first victory. As a symbol, we built the Final Destination Tower standing opposite the base. It also stands for our one-thousand-year journey from our old home, Earth, to here—hence the name. Since then, this war has caused incredible destruction and chaos, spreading darkness throughout the universe. It is our responsibility to bring the Universe back into the light.

"That's why we need operatives like you. If you are in this group that means your special powers have activated. In addition, it means you have some manner of control over them. Here, your superpowers will be honed and perfected so that you can do more than simple tricks. You'll be able to give them purpose. I know that at twelve to fourteen years old, some of you probably don't care about refinement, but when you all are Sandsharks leading soldiers onto the battlefield, you'll be glad you started training young.

"Now, there are twelve types of Sandsharks that parallel the twelve basic powers: fire, pyroshark; water, aquashark; electricity, voltshark; nature, vineshark; wind, ventushark; physical traits, anatoshark; ground, terrashark; psychic, mentoshark; sound, sonicshark; time, temposhark; space, spatioshark; and light, lumoshark. It's important to know all of these classifications now because you need to make sure you are working under a Sandshark that will allow you to be the most productive and advance faster."

"Wait a minute," Max spoke out. "Weren't there thirteen basic powers? Why aren't there thirteen Sandshark types?"

"Well, someone's been reading up. Yes, the UPA used to have thirteen sharks, the last one being dark, or necroshark. As I am sure all of you know, dark powers have been made illegal in this system. With that, the necrosharks were exiled or eliminated."

"Wait—how come?"

"After advanced studies on the subject, we found that Negative Matter's main component was dark energy – a huge amount. With this discovery and the knowledge that dark energy is naturally unpredictable, the Sandshark Council agreed that it would be exiled or purified from the population to protect all of you. Dark users are far rarer now, so hopefully we'll never see others like the first Xaldoruks emerge ever again."

"But what if they did? What would happen then?"

"Well, first off, it wouldn't even be able to get near us. This planet is protected. We have dark energy sensors orbiting the planet. Nothing will get in or near this base—not for lack of trying, though. This base has been attacked before, but that was eons ago, back at the Final Destination Tower that's facing us. No force has ever dared to attack us since."

"What is that tower?" a child asked.

"That tower was actually built out of the very rocket that took the Terrascopians from Earth to Zapheraizia five thousand years ago. Since this was determined as the place to re-settle for good, it was named Final Destination Tower. It's also from that day that we started our current dating system."

The hologram disappeared, and Craig moved to the door. "I think it's time you saw some of the fun stuff."

The building was huge. The entirety of the base itself could be a small town. Structures they thought were buildings flew into the sky. UPA operatives with magnificent powers were displaying their strength all around them. The more Max and Zack looked around, the more excited they became to be a part of this world.

"Over to your right you'll see our hangar. This is where all the airships and Intergalactic ships are housed. Part of your training here involves your learning how to use each of these ships. Each one is capable of traveling at sonic light speed; the speed of light to the power of the speed of sound. Needless to say, we have the best equipment to help our operatives on their missions." They walked into a building with two sword pillars standing in front of it.

"This is the combat training building. As you can see, the building is locked to all but members of the agency. You guys will spend most of your time today here. Today, you will be classified into appropriate rankings that will allow you to flourish most. For your training, this is where you will work at improving both yourself and your team. Follow me."

As they snaked their way through the building, Craig stopped at a room and turned on the light. Suddenly the children stood in awe, facing a seemingly endless supply of weapons and gear.

"Here is the armory. Every weapon you've ever seen on TV and its cousin are here right now. Eventually you'll have the opportunity to train with these – your skills will be assessed."

The kids ran inside and took a closer look at each one.

"Don't pick a favorite now. You need to be flexible in your weapons. The first piece of advice I can give you about these is that what the battlefield gives you is what you get. You are able to pull out five weapons at a time and only when in the training room or on missions. You have a choice between guns, Blades, cannons, armor, and any weapon of your choosing or design, as long as our Sandshark Council approves it. Any questions?"

A number of kids raised their hands.

"Geez! Yes, you in the back. What's your name?" A kid who was hiding behind another put his hand down and crept into view.

"Um…my name is…Robert," he said with a stutter. "I was wondering…what is the Sandshark Council?"

"Do any of you want to answer that question?"

Tyra raised her hand. "The Sandshark Council leads the UPA, right? It sets all the missions, gets reports on the status of the entire universe, and ultimately is the one fighting this war against Negative Matter."

"That's right. There are ranks among Sandsharks as well. There are Sandshark, Elite Sandshark, Sandshark Council members, and then the Supreme Elite Sandshark, who heads the council. He is ultimately the president of the planet. Our current leader is named Luand."

He moved the group to the next area. They entered a wide room with a large window that looks down on a number of empty steel rooms.

"These are the training rooms. Right now you're in the control center for them. You're about to take your test in here. These rooms are designed to test your abilities and push you above your limits."

They all looked out one of the windows and saw a woman kneeling behind a shield. She had a sniper rifle, but three turrets were targeting her. She shot over her shield at one of the turrets, and the bullet ricocheted off that turret and hit the other two, disabling them. The kids gasped, completely amazed.

"As you can see, we expect excellence from all of you. Skills must improve always." They moved to another window and looked out of it. "Here, you may also battle one another in sparring matches, as these two are about to do. At the end of each battle, you must explain the weaknesses, if any, of your opponent."

They observed as two soldiers engaged each other in combat. One seemed able to launch small hooks from his hands while the other let the hooks cut him. As he bled, he manipulated his blood to form into spears he used to retaliate. "These battles can be excellent for determining where you stand against your fellow members."

The group moved from the control room into one of the training rooms.

"Alright, kiddos, welcome to the training room! This is where your preliminary exam will take place. So any two of you step up, and we'll get started."

Without missing a beat, Max and Zack ran into the arena, ready to do whatever they needed.

Craig smiled and then laughed. "Well, we have our victims. Be prepared to have an exhibition match and display your best work." He moved the group back to the wall while the two stood facing each other, bursting with anticipation.

"Max, you know this isn't going to be like our normal chess game, right?"

"Unfortunately for you, this is going to be one quick checkmate." A red flame began to ignite around his hands while sparks of electricity crackled around Zack's. Just as the battle was about to begin, an alarm sounded. It sounded not just in their room but also throughout the entire base. There was a device on the side of the guide's head. He tapped it, and a small screen appeared in front of his right eye. A lady appeared.

"Attention, all members of the UPA. Our intelligence has informed us that we have located ground zero. Repeat, we have located ground zero! Everyone, mobilize and prepare for a full assault. More briefings shall be given upon convening above the planet."

Craig gathered the kids and rushed them out of the building. Max and Zack, disappointed that they didn't get to fight, followed the group.

Looking around, they saw that the whole base was different. Everyone was moving quickly and gearing up. The place stopped being magical and started feeling militarized. Craig escorted them back to the main building and dropped them off at the teen lounge. He posted two guards at the door. Max turned to him just before he left.

"Wait! What's going on?"

Craig answered in a more serious and less friendly tone. "Look, guys, we have a chance to end this war. So you don't have to fight, we will! I'm setting up security around the base; there are guards right outside the door if you ever need anything. With any luck, this war will be over before you have to witness any of its bloodshed."

He sprinted out of the lounge and locked the door behind him.

There was a stillness that haunted the base. It was a quiet that held the entire room in suspense. No one moved. The kids listened through the silence for any kind of signal of what was happening. All of the sounds that had stimulated them before had vanished. Instead they heard large ships launching from the hangars all around the facility. After the ships left, there was silence. No one moved or made a sound.

The tension only started to release after a few minutes. The kids started to relax around the lounge and managed to entertain themselves with games and other things. Max sat on the couch with his feet on the table in front of him and his body limp. His fingers kept tapping on his legs. Tyra sat close to him.

"What's wrong with you two?" Zack asked.

"Nothing," Max said, almost cutting him off.

"No, I've lived with you for a good long time, and I know when something is on your mind...Something's got you all annoyed."

"Come on, Zack; you know me. I don't like being idle. I get all fidgety."

"Don't worry, dude. They'll be back soon enough, and then we really get to have our battle! It's going to be so sweet!"

"That's not totally what I'm worried about," Max said, sighing. "What about after this when we get into the UPA! There will be nothing to do after that!"

"What do you mean?"

"It's just...I feel like we came in at the end of the biggest event in Terrascopian history, you know?"

Zack paused and looked at Max with a disapproving frown. "Max," he said, "are you disappointed that the war's going to end?"

Max just looked back at Zack. Tyra turned and looked at Max, too. Suddenly, the power shut off. The room went completely dark for a few moments. Then a red glow lit the floor. Max shot up and put his ear to the door. Nobody moved. He heard nothing on the other side. The silence held their breath. Then Max heard something collapse onto the floor. Confused and curious, he cracked the door a bit to see what had fallen. He looked down and saw the bodies of the guards. Max backed away from the door. The rest of the room was silent.

"The two guards outside," he said, his voice shaking with fear. "They're down. I don't know what's happening, but they're not getting up."

The group of kids started to panic, wondering who was going to guard them or what would happen next.

Then a boy stood on a couch and yelled at the group. "*You idiots!*"

The kids stopped in their tracks.

"Don't you see? This is the real test. This is what they are looking for: how we react in dire situations. Will we run around pathetically panicking or take initiative proudly like Sandsharks? We need to be ready."

Max stood up and confronted the boy. "I don't think that's what's going on! You didn't see them. Their bodies look so real. This is definitely not a simulation. I'm sure."

"What makes you so sure about it, kid?"

"I don't know; I just have a feeling about it."

"This is the greatest military training facility in the universe. I'm sure their illusion program can deceive the likes of a twelve-year-old."

"And what authority do you claim to have? What makes you so special?"

"My name is Sardax, and I'm probably the only hope you morons have of making it here. So this is the plan..."

Zack stepped out of the room and over the bodies parked at the door, followed by a few other people who made a small group. He looked back at them and ran down a hall as the rest of his team followed. Another group emerged from the room and proceeded down another hall. Sardax had his group exit and sneak down a different hallway, leaving only a few kids in the room. Max swiftly rushed to the end of the line as the last team left.

Zack and his team ran out of the main building and across the campus. He found it odd that the place was completely deserted. Security seemed to be completely down throughout the campus. The feeling of unease only worsened when they found that the training building was not locked.

He and his crew made their way to the armory and picked up as many weapons as they could. When they'd gathered all that they could carry, they made their way to the door. Just as they were opening the door, a shadowy figure blocked their path. Reacting on instinct, Zack pushed the group back into the room and shut the door. His heart was racing, and adrenaline rushed through his body, paralyzing it with both fear and excitement. However, there was an unmistakable sense of danger running through him. Unable to fight his curiosity, he cracked open the door to take a peek at what was out there. It was in the shape of a soldier, but it didn't have a face—just glowing eyes that emitted a purple radiance. All that could be felt was darkness and shadows. The creature didn't seem to notice the door behind him. Zack closed the door, trapped in the shadows.

"Sardax," he reported into the communicator. "We have a situation." Sardax picked up the communicator and halted his team.

"Make multiple trips if you can't carry them all in one!" Sardax said, dismissing him.

"No, it's not that! There's something here!"

"What thing?"

"I don't know. It's dark and gives off some really weird vibes. It looks like the creatures from the war that they show on TV. The group and I are stuck! It's definitely not a UPA member!"

"Dude, grow up! It's just a simulation. Just get the weapons back to the lounge, and we'll meet you there soon, okay?"

"But wait—"

Sardax hung up the line before Zack could say anything. From the back, Max recognized his friend's voice, and he recognized that he was in danger. He ran up to the front of the pack.

"He's obviously in trouble!"

"Hey," Sardax said, completely surprised. "What the hell are you doing here? Get back to the room."

"He needs help! He can't get to the lounge without some backup. We should go to his position and fight!"

"What? Now all of a sudden you want to make plans? Sorry, you had your shot, and I'm in control."

"That's my best friend out there, I know when he needs help!" Max said, starting to get louder.

"Then you go and get him!"

Suddenly something appeared in front of them. Max pulled Sardax back down, covering his mouth, but Sardax pushed him off. The whole group looked at the creature traveling by.

"Look, it's almost exactly like Zack described," Max said to Sardax.

"I've never seen one up close…"

16

One of the kids in the group spoke up. "What is it?"

"It's a Negative."

Max was sparked with excitement all over again. He grabbed the Blade's hilt and prepared to launch at the creature, hoping that the actual blade would appear.

"Step back—I'm taking this!" Max said, excited.

"No way! We need to examine it. We can learn its patterns and then attack." Sardax pulled Max back.

"Let go of me!"

"No, we have to be smart!"

"I am smart. I'm going!"

"Don't be a moron!"

As the two struggled to get in front of each other, they fell out of their hiding place right behind the Negative. The creature turned around and looked at the two boys. They looked back and saw that there were a bunch of the same creatures lined up behind them. The other kids in the group ran away, but the Negative's arms stretched out and grabbed them all.

They started to seep into the creature. They struggled all they could, but its grip tightened, and their pain intensified. They felt the creature start to walk again. Max felt powerless swirling around in the belly of this monster. He tried to look around but couldn't determine where the thing was going. The creature stopped and pushed them out of its body. They were all in one of the hangars, standing in front of an unfamiliar alien ship.

Max continued to struggle while in the monster's hold. Sardax kept rolling his eyes at him. Max then felt a pressure in the air that stopped his movement in his tracks. He felt he was suffocating as it pressed down on him and practically sucked all of his energy from his body. Fear was the only emotion running though him—unbearable fear, though he didn't know why. A figure walked out of the ship wearing a black cloak with odd writings on it. The only thing that could be seen of his head was his white hair. The man walked up to the children and examined them. His eyes glowed a sinful yellow, and his smile reeked of deceit.

"Take them to the ship. Put them in the stasis tubes."

Just as they started off, the figure got a glimpse of Max and stopped for a second. Shrugging it off, he walked away.

Each captive was put in a cylindrical glass container on the sides of the hall within the alien ship. Once they were inside, it released a gas that filled the chamber. Everyone coughed and eventually was knocked out. Sardax sat with his arms crossed. He looked at Max, who was trying to fight the gas.

"So this is your brilliant plan?" Sardax snarled.

"Shut up."

"Interesting fix. This must have been according to plan. So well done."

"Would you shut up?" Max snapped.

"No, because my plan was brilliant, flawless."

"Are you kidding? Your plan was what got us in this mess."

"You screwed my plan up! This is entirely your fault. We are all going to be kicked out of the program thanks to you."

Max stayed quiet. Sardax's words kept piercing him. Though he wanted to deny it, he knew he was responsible. He started to question his ability to be a part of the UPA. He started to release the tension and began to breathe in the gas. He heard a knock on his glass container. He looked. The smoke of the gas prevented him from seeing who it was. Suddenly it opened, and Zack appeared in front of him, waving the smoke away.

"Rise and shine, scuz bucket!"

"Zack!" he said, surprised. He looked around and saw Zack's crew opening the other pods as well. "Never thought you'd show up! What happened to you?"

"Well, after I called you guys, the creature found us and took us here."

"How'd you escape?"

"Well, you know how sometimes I sneeze and my electricity ends up doing that thing…"

"Oh…cool!"

"Then I let my team out, and we started searching for a way out. Then we found you. Now that we have, do you know exactly what's going on? Seems a bit unorthodox for an initial skill simulation."

"It's real, everything. The creatures that brought us here are Negatives, like the ones on TV."

"Stop being an idiot," Sardax said. "It can't be real. These creatures only look like Negatives, but they can't be since the whole planet is on dark energy lockdown!"

"I'm not too sure," Zack said. "My team went to the armory, and everything was shut down. It didn't look like it was just us. The entire city was out of power. None of the sensors were working."

"Sardax, I felt powerful and weird vibes off of that guy too. That presence was not anything positive. This was something evil. This can't be simulated."

"The people who are still in the lounge are in danger."

"We can't worry about them right now," Sardax said, dismissing it. "You mentioned trying to find an exit. Did you find one?"

"No. We've been going around in circles."

"Then we can't relax. Follow me." He started walking off. Nobody seemed to follow him.

"Oh no!" Max spoke up. "Not this time."

"What was that?"

"You're just going to leave the people in the lounge without any heads-up? No, I can't leave them in the dark."

"Need I remind you that if you stayed in the lounge like I told you, we wouldn't have been caught, the mission would have succeeded, and we would be there by now?" Sardax said, shaming Max.

"Don't project this on me. Your arrogance is really what's destroying this," Max said a little bit too loudly.

"You're giving me a lecture on arrogance, Mister 'Let me at 'em'?"

"You know what? Just stay here and make sure everyone wakes up okay."

Max turned back to Zack, and the two started off. Sardax looked back at everyone still lying around, knocked out. He felt disgusted looking at them and joined Max and Zack.

The three boys walked around the ship, searching for an exit. The ship seemed to be like a labyrinth. They kept making turns but not finding anyone or anything behind them.

"Is it me, or do you think there would be more security in a ship like this?"

"What experience would you have to tell how much security would be in this kind of ship? You need to stop referencing your movies and grow up." Sardax pushed Max forward. When he did, a floor panel in front of him opened. Zack reached out and caught

Max just before he could fall through.

"That's why we walk carefully, Sardax," Zack said, berating him.

They all continued watching out for various traps and springs. They turned the next corner and found the room that contained the weapons Zack had picked up.

"Well, look at this!"

"Awesome! Zack, Sardax, head back to the group with these in hand. Make as many trips as you need in order to get ourselves armed up." Max grabbed one of the rifles and started off.

"Wait, dude! Where are you going?" Zack called out.

"We still need to find our way out."

"So you're going by yourself? Makes perfect sense."

"Don't worry, man! I have a mental map ready to go whenever I need it. Remember when I figured out the way back to our parents when we were lost on Organos?"

"Oh, please, if we're trusting you with finding our way out, we'll never get there," Sardax said. "Here, I'll go!"

"Step back, dude!" Max retaliated.

"I don't trust you with my life."

"Well you're going to have to if we're going to work together here." Sardax tossed the rifles to Zack and followed Max. The two shoved each other down the hall. Zack was left alone in the room holding an armful of rifles, struggling to keep them in his arms.

"Okay, then I'll just make the trips by myself! No problem."

Max and Sardax competed down the hallways, turning the corners and not really keeping track of where they were or where they were going. They were focused on being better than the other. As Max ran out of energy, he stopped to catch his breath. He looked over and saw that he was in front of the first door they'd seen for a while. Sardax walked back and opened it.

"So this is the engine room," Sardax assessed.

"We can blow it up with the weapons."

"Move." Sardax sprinted off into the next room. Max started to run, but then he saw what looked like blueprints. He walked into the room and had a closer look. He picked up a map sitting next to a bunch of controls and ran off to catch up to Sardax.

When Max and Sardax got back to the group, all of the kids

were awake and prepping the firearms that Zack had brought for them to defend themselves.

"You all right, Max?" Zack asked.

"Yeah, I'm fine. Found a map to get us out of here."

"Where'd you find a map?" Sardax asked.

"Amazing what you find when you look for a split second." He turned to the joined groups. "Okay, listen. Once we get out of the ship, the base will be filled with Negatives all around. We need to make sure that they are all eliminated. Next thing we should probably do is head back to the lounge and make sure everyone is safe. Zack, you're going to lead a party of four back to the weapons room in the base to pick up some more weapons and give them to the people in the lounge to see if we can get some more hands on board." Zack promptly started moving. Sardax twisted his face and moved with the group.

The plan began to go as expected. They escaped the ship and were greeted by rows of Negatives right outside the door. Their nerves collectively locked them up as they fragilely aimed their guns. Max fired the first shot and attracted the attention of the other Negatives. The other children, still scared out of their minds, fired and eliminated their first targets. After feeling the adrenaline rush of their first success they moved out of the ship and rode their energy high throughout the base. Maneuvering though the chaos and the battles, Max and Zack reached the lounge with a bunch of weapons. Tyra ran up to them and gave them a hug. Then she hit Max on the side of his head.

"Don't leave me with these guys alone again," she said.

"Bigger problems, Ty." She looked out the door and saw that the Negatives were moving in.

"Oh my god, what are those things?"

"Shoot first. Explanation later." He gave her a rifle, and she started shooting with the rest of the group. The Negatives kept marching down the hall, getting increasingly closer to them. Both Max and Zack eventually ran out of ammunition. Hiding behind separate walls, the two looked at each other and smiled. They both threw their guns away. Max rubbed his hands together. There were light sparks coming from his skin. Suddenly his hands caught fire, and the flame formed into a ball in the palm of his hand. Zack rubbed his hands together, and the sparks started to fly around him.

21

Electricity circled him and gathered at his hands. Max threw his fireballs down the hall and Zack launched his electricity, leaving a gaping hole in the Negatives' attack.

Max looked and saw an opportunity. "Zack, I'm going to head back to that ship. I need you guys to cover me down this hall." He looked back.

"Wait—why?"

"I need to take care of the leader that's in charge of all of this."

Tyra pulled him back as he started to go. "No, Max, stay here; we'll take care of this together. Just finish this battle and we'll take him."

"But he might get away if I don't go now!"

"But you don't have to do this alone!"

"Guys, we are the only ones protecting this base now. We have to take out the leader in order to win. It's just like chess. If we secure the leader, it's checkmate. Nobody gets hurt." Max looked at Tyra and saw this weird look in her eyes, almost concern. He smiled at her. He saw something he recognized as that look from every other time he did something stupid growing up. Somehow it reminded him of the sense of comfort she always gave him. "Relax; I'm coming back. I'm going to end this battle."

"I suppose you want me to let you go and kill yourself."

"Yeah, some help would be great."

She sighed and placed her hand on the floor. Its temperature suddenly started to drop rapidly. Ice started to form on the floor and froze the Negatives in their tracks. Zack and the group attacked their frozen targets and watched them shatter.

They all celebrated their victory. "That was great thinking, Max," she said, surprised the plan worked. When she turned around, he was nowhere to be found. She sighed and looked back down the hall. The shattered pieces of the Negatives had started to move again. The creatures were rebuilding themselves. Tyra alerted Zack and the others, and they prepared desperately for round two.

The battle continued for several hours. The kids were surviving and fighting back with more force and power than they ever thought they had.

The cloaked figure was in the library, completely ransacking it. He noticed that his forces were being destroyed throughout the base. He quickly inserted a thumb drive and uploaded a virus into the library's database and made his way back to his ship. When he got to the hangar where his ship was, he was surprised to see that someone was waiting for him. He chuckled a bit.

"You've got some serious guts, kid."

Max sat at the foot of the steps to the ship. He stood up with a gun in hand, ready for a fight. The man's eyes widened, almost as if he were impressed. He heard someone coming down the hallway and created a force field surrounding both of them and the ship. Tyra and Zack emerged from the hallway. Zack ran to Max but hit his face on the force field. Max looked at Tyra, and he knew that he had to follow through with what he had gotten himself into.

"Show yourself!" Max demanded.

"Look at you, trying to act all high and mighty." He removed his cloak. He looked like a young man, possibly in his thirties, with long white hair and a smug look on his face. "You know that this is an act, right?"

"What? This attack?"

"No, not what I'm doing. What you are. That's the act. You know it, and I know it."

"This is checkmate. Tell your forces to retreat and put your hands on your head."

"Look at you: so desperate to be a hero, so afraid of having your name lost with the wind as another casualty of war."

"Stop it."

"The reality is you lack the nerve. You have no guts to do dangerous and risky things. You just want things easily; you're too fragile to jump without a net."

"I said stop."

"Proof enough. You're no hero, just playing one."

"Enough!" Max yelled at him.

"Oh, you want to shoot? Go for it, boy!"

Max's arm was shaking violently. He looked at his arm holding the gun and realized what he was doing. The reality of him being able to kill someone started to settle in, and his mind began to race.

"Oh, seriously kid, if you pulled the trigger, I would be impressed. You would prove to me that maybe this whole 'I will kill you' act isn't an act! You'll prove to yourself that you really are ready to fight me."

Max still panicked. He kept thinking to himself that he couldn't possibly do it. He looked back at Tyra and Zack. Everyone eventually showed up around the force field, watching the confrontation. With all of them watching, he gritted his teeth, determined to fight for them and thinking no one else could do it. A black and purple glow surrounded his body. He felt a burst of anger through his eyes as he saw the smug look on his opponent's face. He pulled the trigger. Everyone that watched it, most of all Max, couldn't believe what he had done. The man was shocked. He stared at his bullet wound. His face changed. He fixed the boy with a menacing glare.

"You're brave. But you should know, bravery is the kindest word for stupidity."

The man walked toward Max. Max was petrified, seeing him not damaged. He tried shooting his gun again, but nothing came out. He threw it off to the side and picked up his Blade and tried to bring out the blade itself. However, he didn't know how to use it. He kept shaking it, hoping it would work, but to no avail. He looked up and saw the man above him. The man picked him up by the shirt and held him against the ship.

"Now that I know you have the grit of a Sandshark, I might as well treat you like a Sandshark!" He threw him to the opposite side. "Come on! Stand up! You want to be one so badly, why don't you fight me like one? See if you're really ready for the fight!"

Max struggled to his feet, still driven to fight back.

"You don't realize who I am yet, do you?" He pulled him closer and whispered, "I am Xaldoruks."

Max's eyes widened. His body was paralyzed with dread. He realized how outclassed he was.

"W-what?"

"Oh, you should really learn how to pick your fights, kid. Because you just signed your death warrant." He materialized a sword in his hand and raised it, ready to strike. Max closed his eyes and prayed that he would be saved. He felt pressure on his Blade. He looked up and saw that the blade of the sword had appeared just in time to block the attack.

Xaldoruks looked at the Blade. "This sword…why does it

look familiar?" he said, puzzled.

Max stood up and just gazed at his Blade.

Xaldoruks began his approach again. "So you lucked out. Let's see how lucky you really are."

Max, amazed with his summoning of his sword, felt incredibly comfortable dispelling his fear in exchange for confidence. He aimed his sword at Xaldoruks with an inflated sense of pride in his skills. He looked at his friends and tried to think of a heroic line.

"It isn't luck, evildoer. It's the power of justice!" he said gleefully. With his cheesy line delivered perfectly, he was ready to live out his fantasy. He launched at Xaldoruks and swung his sword. Xaldoruks analyzed his attack pattern, and all of it seemed too familiar to him. Max kept up, with the warmonger blocking and countering swiftly. All the while he couldn't understand how a small boy could fight with a sword like that. Max was filled with new determination to defeat his opponent. He felt the adrenaline rushing through his body as if he could go on for days. Nothing seemed to be able to stop him.

With an unexpected lunge, Max managed to cut a bit of Xaldoruks's cheek. Max backed off with confidence. "Let that be a lesson to you."

The crowd cheered. Xaldoruks roared, unleashing large amounts of his sickening energy from his body. Max saw the dark auras pulsing from him. Great waves of darkness chilled him and everyone observing the fight. There was nothing in Xaldoruks's face but pure, unadulterated rage. He appeared in front of the boy instantly and hit Max's Blade so hard it fell out of his hand. Then he launched him to the force-field wall and grabbed his head. He continuously smashed his head on the invisible wall, watching more and more of the child's blood being painted on it. He tossed the boy to the center of the arena and choked him.

"You think this is all a game, don't you?" he yelled at him. "You're just loving this whole thing! Grow up, kid!"

Xaldoruks pounded the boy's body with punch after punch. He didn't stop. "I guess you'll never get the chance to." With one blow after another, the boy became more broken, and tears fell from his eyes—the tears of a mere child. This didn't cause Xaldoruks to pause. He only continued to assault the boy's body. The crowd watching him did nothing but cringe, certain of the boy's imminent death. Zack kept pounding the force field's wall, trying to break in and help him. Xaldoruks paused once and then punched Max's gut, pushing him so hard that the floor started to cave in. He kicked Max to his stomach, placed his foot on his back, and grabbed his right arm.

"You wanted to be a part of this fight. You wanted to defy me." He started to pull his arm. Max screamed in pain, unable to do anything to stop it. He kept pulling the arm slowly. The pain kept surging through Max's entire body, and there was nothing he could do. Max was dying. He felt his arm loosening from its socket. All of his muscles started to tear, all of the tendons were released, and with a final tug and a mass of blood, Max's arm flew off his body. Max screamed even louder. He held his remaining hand to the armless socket. He felt his nerves yelling at him in sheer agony. Xaldoruks walked away from the boy's writhing body and held the dismembered arm in his fist as he turned to address the crowd. He looked at them all, quaking in their shoes, disgusted by what he saw.

"Do you fear me?" he asked quietly. He got no response. "Do you fear me? The human race, God's perfect imperfections. Please, look at you all. Scared stiff. This is the reality of the war in which you have decided to partake. Get used to it, because this is the price of the status quo. Death and destruction is the only way to reach your true final destination. But because you're too stupid to see that, you prolong your suffering, plaguing this universe with your stasis. You humans sicken me."

He walked over to Max, who was still cringing with unbearable agony, and crouched to whisper to him. "And you...Do you see the price of arrogance? Your confidence will get you in trouble. When you least expect it, you'll always be doomed by your own personal devils."

At that moment Max opened his eyes, screaming again, but his pupils glowed a combination of red, blue, and yellow. Xaldoruks looked into them for a split second and went flying to the other side of the arena. Max closed his eyes, holding his hand to his face. The crowd looked up and saw that Xaldoruks, out of nowhere, had been attacked. He stood up and his body was on fire. His flesh was burning off. He quickly began to regenerate his skin cells. Just as the scarred man started back at Max, he looked out the window and saw that ships were docking at the hangar. The UPA had returned to headquarters. He picked up the arm and lowered the force field. People started coming out of the ship, and Xaldoruks just looked at them as he disappeared into his shadow.

One man ran to Max in the middle of the room. Max was still dazed and could barely see the man's face. He couldn't hear anything. All he remembered was lights flashing on him as he closed his eyes and lost consciousness.

Max screamed at the top of his lungs when he opened his eyes. He saw he was in a room that was mostly white, with beds all around the walls. He looked to his right and saw that there was a holographic arm attached to his body. He had bandages and a mechanical device on his head. He was in the hospital. Max relaxed his head and gave a big sigh of relief.

"Now that you're done screaming…"

He heard a voice. He turned to see a man sitting there who wasn't there before.

"Maybe you're up for some actual conversation."

Max just looked at him. "Uncle Luand?"

"You can't call me that anymore, kid. Now that I'm your superior, you have to call me Supreme Elite Sandshark."

"Oh, right." Max sat up and tried to comprehend his right arm.

"Hey, what's up with this arm?"

"Concrete holographics. It's hooked up to your brain so that it moves like you still have your arm. It's able to pick up and move and support you until you get your replacement arm."

"Yeah, that's great and all, but where is my other arm?"

"We couldn't find it."

"What do you mean?"

"When we arrived on the scene, it wasn't anywhere to be found. My guess is that the guy who took it from you kept it."

"The guy? What happened to him? What about my friends, and the mission? And you guys? What happened?"

"Jeez, slow your roll; one thing at a time. Your friends are okay. The Negatives were neutralized once we got back to the base. Unfortunately, the man you faced vanished. We're searching for him now, but he's not likely to be anywhere around here. The whole thing was a setup. He gathered enough of his forces to distract us far enough away to attack our home in a much more powerful way."

"He was terrifying."

"I can imagine he was. He doesn't go into the field often. He must have wanted something pretty badly if he came to get it personally. You did pretty well against him, though, I must say. Not many well-trained Sandsharks have the nerve to face him, much less bring the fight to him. Hell, I couldn't beat him if I tried."

"You've fought him?"

"Oh yeah, more than once. Stalemate every time."

"I was way over my head."

"I don't know about that. Eons of Sandsharks have tried to fight him and couldn't last a fraction of a second, yet you show up and not only last against him, but also manage to damage him. Only I've been able to do that. You may have nearly died, but you still got farther than most people have against him."

"What does that mean?"

"It means this fight may be destined to repeat itself. You made the most progress against him, and it would be a crime not to further hone your abilities. If you increase and better yourself…then maybe, just maybe…"

"Maybe what?"

"Oh, never mind; it's just speculation. I hope you know, you and all of your comrades made it into the highest-level program the agency can offer as gratitude for your service to us. Once you're out of the hospital, you'll be deployed on missions and begin your training."

Luand got up and started walking around. Max looked at his right bedside table and saw a strange cube with multiple colors. He picked it up.

"What's this?"

"Oh yeah, it's a Koratoric cube. It's a puzzle. The idea is that you need to solve all the sides by twisting and shifting the colors so that each side is one color."

"Sounds easy enough."

"But there's a catch. With this cube the colors change every thirty seconds. Even worse the cube learns how close you are to solving it. You have to outsmart the cube's changes and solve the puzzle."

"I take it back; that's impossible."

"Not impossible, just a bit unlikely." Max kept looking at it and then he looked at his holographic arm. Luand made his way to the door of the room and then stopped.

"Oh, wait! There's one other person who did fight Xaldoruks and gave him a run for his money."

"Who?"

Luand smiled. "Your old man."

"My father?"

"Yeah, he and that Blade were undefeatable."

"I was using his Blade during the fight. It protected me."

"Yeah, that Blade is unique. It's called the Chaos Blade. It can give the user large amounts of power to conquer his enemies. I think you let that power go to your head."

"I have to learn how to use it. Do you think you can make sure that it's all right?

"No problem, kid. Now, you rest up." Max lay back down in his bed and picked up his Koratoric cube, trying to solve it.

Luand exited the hospital hallway and went to the security rooms.

"What do we have?"

One of the attendants responded. "All security was down for most of the invasion. It's like what the Roark kid said: the whole city was powered down, including all the sensors. They planned for this."

"Damn it. Made us look like idiots." He saw that one camera had a blurry feed. "What about that one? What can we get from that?"

He zoomed in and watched the moment Xaldoruks burst into flames away from Max during the final fight.

"What was that?" the attendant asked. "It looks like he just spontaneously combusted."

"That wasn't spontaneous." He looked closer. "That was the Xylonite."

2 REALITY

Max became driven. Every moment he spent in that bed only made him more eager to sharpen his fighting skills so he could someday get another shot at Xaldoruks. After they outfitted him with the latest in mechanical limb technology and he recovered from the hospital, Max and the rest of his group started their careers at the UPA as official soldiers. He was given a room and access to the high-tech training facilities, weapons rooms, and extensive libraries—everything he could possibly need for top-notch training. Their education advanced, and they were deployed on missions often.

Max was assigned to an Elite Sandshark who would be his commander on missions. Though Max was not particularly fond of his commanding officer, he knew he couldn't let it show if he wanted to advance in the ranks. He always showed initiative and adaptive qualities in his missions. Although his solutions to unexpected problems were hasty and not communicated to the rest of his squad, his superior officer could not argue with Max's results. Any challenge that arose, he faced with ease. He was rapidly elevated to more advanced squads that could better challenge his abilities. He found that Tyra and Zack managed to make their way up the ranks at record speed as well. He was overjoyed to be reunited with his best friends, and the three of them on the same missions seemed unbeatable. They compensated for each other's weaknesses and were uniquely able to handle each other's egoes, specifically Max's. Their well-oiled machine was getting recognized.

Their higher-ups couldn't deny their aptitude. At the age of nineteen, Max, Zack, and Tyra were almost complete in training to become leaders in this ancient war. There were a few members of their old squads who also excelled in their training. Max saw them as competition and was determined to outshine them. Their final Master class would test their mental prowess, their physical skills, and their ability to command teams.

Before they knew it, the test for their Sandshark certification had arrived. Known to everyone as the hardest test in the universe, this was the one thing Max didn't underestimate. Through a series of demanding, endurance-challenging, and potentially fatal tests, the trio managed to make their way to the final round of examinations, where their physical skill was tested against each other. In the end, only Max and Zack remained on the field. The two fought harder than they ever had before. Their Blades clashed against each other with great energy sparking from each blow. Fire and lightning danced around them as they used their powers to take the other down. They both relished the all-out fight they had so desperately yearned for their entire lives to see who was the best. Despite Max's best efforts, Zack was the victor. Though they lost, Max, Tyra, and a number of their fellow classmates advanced to Sandshark status, and Zack was placed in the position of Elite Sandshark. Each Sandshark was given a specific squad to man with every mission along with a special code name. Max was sore about losing but glad that he lost to someone he respected and considered a brother. With his new status and advanced skills, he thought no mission, task, or person could challenge him. Until he led his first mission as a Sandshark.

Zack strutted around the base with his Elite Sandshark badge shining, freshly polished and bright. He strolled with a completely inflated sense of confidence and swagger.

Max stood in the middle of the training room with his eyes closed, sensing his surroundings. He looked up and saw Tyra waving her arms in the air. She summoned soldiers made of pure ice, controlling them like puppets. Max ran toward Tyra, taking down all of the pawns she set up. Tyra jumped high over Max and trapped him in an ice prison dome. Max released thin Blades of fire that cut the dome. As the dome collapsed, he ran toward Tyra and tackled her onto the mat.

"What the hell, Tyra?" he said, frustrated. "I was in the middle of training."

"Well, I had to make sure you're on your toes, right?"

Max got up and walked back to the center of the room. The training program materialized a jump rope into his hand, which he started to use.

"So I like your new room," Tyra teased. "Very big and spacious. Are your bed and desk coming this afternoon?"

"So you're just here to mock me? Great."

"Well, you spend all your time in here. I'm surprised you don't have your meals sent here, too. Feel like telling me why you're so obsessed with this?"

"Because I'm not the best yet."

"Oh, of course. So you're just going to keep bashing your head into a wall until you are?"

"Yep."

"Max, you just became a Sandshark. You're not going to get there any time soon. You realize that, don't you?"

He stopped jumping and walked to her. "Who's going to defeat Xaldoruks? I'm the only one who can do it. It's my destiny. Don't you see? I'm the only one who can end this war, and it's not going to happen while there are people who are better than me."

"Oh geez, you're more egotistical than Zack. He thinks he's the bomb just because he won the exam, but *you* think this war is all about you! You know, this is why we broke—" she stopped. Max looked at her, hurt, while she tried to avoid eye contact. Max turned around and started jumping again.

"I'm sorry."

"No, no, it's fine," he said, denying any facial expression.

"You know what I meant by that, right? It wasn't to bring up any scars."

Max stopped jumping again. "Do you remember the night by the waterfall?"

"Max, don't."

"On that mission to Hydraplaux. You and I were sitting at the edge of the river and looking at a moon trying to hide its size behind the midnight trees."

"Max, stop it!"

"You held my hand, and we didn't care if we got in trouble,

and you know what I think? I think you miss it. Somewhere in there, you miss what we had."

She smacked him across the face. "Not enough to want to go back." She began to storm off. "You need to get a reality check, Max. You can't always live in your fantasy world."

As she left, a small smile appeared on Max's face.

Zack strutted back to his room. When he entered, he found there were two giant books on his desk. The grin he wore all day disappeared from his face. Just the sight of the massive books overwhelmed him. He walked up to them and saw there was a holo-message on top of them. He picked it up, and suddenly a hologram of Supreme Elite Sandshark Luand appeared.

"Congratulations, Zactavious Roark! You have successfully become an Elite Sandshark. Now you must be unaware of the meat between the bread since you advanced in the ranks so quickly. So you unfortunately are required to read both the Sandshark manual and the Elite Sandshark guide. Due to your higher level, more will be expected of you, so you will need to read both of the books in the week that remains so you may accept your first mission. I suggest that you start with the Sandshark manual first, because that's where information relevant to the next mission can be found. Happy reading, and once again, congratulations. Supreme Elite Sandshark Luand."

Zack sighed. "Well, that's just great," he said to himself. "They make it so that I can't just skip the Sandshark manual and just go to the Elite Sandshark stuff." He opened the book's first page and saw that inside the cover was written "Property of the Virus Sandshark." It had a list of page numbers written under it as well. Zack flipped to each of these pages and saw a bunch of military strategies along with vast and extensive notes on each one. Zack studied the notes into the early morning hours of each night.

While each Sandshark read his or her book, Zack was not seen outside his room for a while. He kept his head inside the books, feeling his mind numb as he struggled to understand the material. He realized that on the next mission people would be looking to him for guidance. They needed a reliable leader, someone who understood what to do at any given time. Zack wanted to make sure that he was that Sandshark.

Max and Tyra finished studying the Sandshark manual by the end of the week. Upon completion of the manual, a card slid out of the book's back. It had the details on where to meet for their first mission as Sandsharks.

The next day, Max went out of the main base to the official mission center. He located his assigned room and went inside only to find just three people there: Sardax, Robert, and Zack. He sat next to Zack, who was being talked at by Robert while he was reading the last pages in his Elite Sandshark guide.

"I'm just saying that if they could survive in space, ducks would have a serious advantage over us in battle."

"Oh my God, Rob, I do not care!"

"I'm just saying! Oh hi, Max. I didn't see you come in!" Max looked at him, trying to tell him not to drag him into it. "Don't you agree that if ducks could survive in space…"

"Okay, Robert, I'm going to stop you right there and save me the trouble of listening to what I'm sure would be a great waste of time."

Robert retreated back in his chair and began annoying Sardax instead. Tyra walked in and Sardax struggled to ignore Robert.

Another Sandshark walked into the room, but he didn't seem very well put together. He only wore a tank shirt and his pajama pants, with a beer in his right hand. His face wasn't clean, his eyes were barely open, and he looked a bit hung over. When he got to the podium at the front of the room, he slammed his beer can down on it. Tyra twisted her face, annoyed at how unprofessional this seemed.

"Attention, *now!*" he yelled.

The five Sandsharks stood up and didn't move.

"Zactavious: Volt Storm Sandshark. Tyra: Crimson Winter Sandshark. Sardax: Terra Breaker Sandshark. Max: Chaos Flame Sandshark. Robert: Bladed Skull Sandshark. All present. My name is Elite Sandshark Staniu. I'm from the Karosean side of the planet. I just woke up, so any questions or stupid commentary will not be tolerated. I'm only going to say it once."

They all sat down together and looked at the holograms that appeared.

"All right, the Plasian people: very proud and fine, but not very forgiving. You see, a couple of years after the very first of the human race, the Terrascopians, landed on Zapheraizia, they were more power-hungry than we are today. They wanted more land and more planets. They figured that if they could move from Earth to Zapheraizia with little difficulty, why couldn't they populate other planets? So the greedy and power-hungry people went to the first planet that seemed weak enough, in an attempt to take it over. Ultimately we failed, and the people are still touchy about that. Now the Plasian people can live far longer than us average terrascopians with our lifespan of two hundred to three hundred years. The Plasians on the other hand—let's just say that they still have the scars from the battle with the first terrascopians."

"You mean the Plasians can live up to five thousand years?" Tyra asked in shock.

"Longer, as it turns out. So the Plasian Council plans to take its revenge on us. This mission is two in one. Our foreseeing mentosharks have informed us that their high council is planning on attacking Zapheraizia as a form of revenge. Your first priority is to persuade the council not to attack. Next, you need to disable the Negative volcano."

"What Negative volcano?" Zack asked.

"This Negative volcano." He hit a button on his remote, and a hologram of the entire village near a volcano appeared. "This volcano is filled with Negative Matter. At its base, they installed an erupter that stirs up the matter and blows it onto not just the city but onto the entire planet. Your second job is to make sure this volcano doesn't erupt and turn that planet into a Negative haven. Sardax, Maximilian, Zactavious, and Tyrishana—you will have to do all the dirty work. You will have a fresh battalion of troops that will follow your commands. The battalions trust you know what you're doing. Now, Robert, you will create the exit conditions. You will fly in with a ship. Stay cloaked until they are ready. Be ready to pick them up in a moment's notice. Prepare for the worst. Just don't get blown up." He checked his papers. "Since this is the first mission for all of you, Zack, the highest ranking Sandshark here, will be in charge of its proper execution. Uh, you guys have a maximum of two days to complete this mission, as the volcano could erupt at any moment. Standard mission protocols are in effect, which means refer to each other only by code name. All right. Beat it!"

As he left, Max was filled to the brim with joy and grew impatient to jump into the fray. Overflowing with excitement, he shot out of his chair to meet with his team. Robert enthusiastically followed. Sardax glared at Zack and walked out begrudgingly. Tyra started off but noticed Zack hadn't moved. She walked back and sat next to him.

"Organos," she said. Zack looked up, confused. "Remember that time we all went on that trip to the Organos swamps? Max took Genesis off into the woods to find some artifact he had read about in a bedtime story, and he ended up getting lost for a few hours. You didn't want him getting in trouble, so you went out to find them yourself. Even when you found them and Max insisted on blindly leading, you managed to find your way back to us before our parents found out!"

"Well, you know how reliable Max's sense of direction is."

"My point is I know how leading can be a bit scary. You've spent a lot of time following, even when it comes to Max. But you have done it before. It's in you somewhere. Just remember and find it. You'll be fine."

"But what if I..."

"No 'what ifs.' You can. We trust you and your judgment."

She stepped up and headed for the door. "Organos! Remember."

As she left, Zack smiled, reminiscing about that moment in his past. With a new sense of determination, he jumped up and met with his team in the hangar.

There were three ships ready for them. Tyra and Zack got their own while Max ended up reluctantly sharing one with Sardax and his squad. The ships launched out of the building and out of the atmosphere one by one. Once they were in position, they made engaged sonic light speed and soared across the galaxy to their first mission.

On the way, Max was twitchy, overloaded with anticipation. He knew he wanted to charge in, guns blazing, to save the day. He kept telling himself that this was his moment to shine and prove himself. He proudly looked at the stars on his gear, but remembered that Zack was the one assigned to be in charge of the mission. His excitement dwindled when he knew he couldn't steal the moment from his best friend. The thought of outshining a higher-ranked operative was entertaining for Max. He struggled back and forth with these thoughts for a long while during the trip. He looked up to find Sardax staring at him. Max stared back. Neither one backed down for a long, solid moment. Finally, Sardax scoffed and turned around. Max turned as well but found he was more annoyed than excited.

The ships came out of sonic light speed and approached the planet Plasia. Upon entering the atmosphere, the ships rattled violently. The turbulence and atmospheric density shuffled the ships around more than expected. They were unequipped to handle the entry. They all came hurtling toward the surface, none landing where they were meant to.

Max, Sardax, and their squads hopped out of their crashed ship into a large ditch in the ground surrounded by alien plant life. They looked over to find a city glowing in the distance.

"Well, that almost sucked!" Max said with a chuckle.

"Well, I'm glad you can make jokes, Chaos."

"Well, you know I'd hate to have a stick up my butt as far as yours."

Sardax rolled his eyes and turned on his headset. A small screen appeared in front of his right eye, and he called his teammates. "This is Terra Breaker with Chaos Flame. Locate Volt Storm and Crimson Winter."

An AI's voice responded. "Crimson Winter and her squad are approaching. Volt Storm, however, is seven miles west from your position."

"Typical."

"What is?" Tyra asked, joining the group.

"Volt Storm is nowhere close to us. We are going to have to move now without him if we're going to finish the mission in time."

Max and Tyra didn't budge with their squads.

Sardax turned back and sighed. "Problem?"

"Protocol states we have to follow the highest-ranking officer in the case of a mission improvisation," Max answered.

"So you're going to be the type of Sandsharks who can't think for themselves?" Sardax said, challenging Max. "And since when did you decide to follow the rules, Chaos? You're normally the first one to break them."

"Since I'm now responsible for an entire team's safety."

"You were always responsible for it, Chaos. When you're part of a team, each one of you is responsible for each other. That's something you never understood. You focus on the glory, and to hell with everyone else."

"Volt Storm is the Elite Sandshark for this mission. He earned that, and we have to respect him for it."

"Oh, that's bullshit! You know Volt hasn't earned that title. He hasn't any more experience than any one of us. *We* could easily take this mission and do it ten times faster."

"Quit dissing my best friend," Max said, shoving Sardax back.

"You know you want it to be you! You try to be a good friend and follow the rules to let him have his moment, but deep down you wanted that victory...oh, to have that taken away!"

Sardax walked away and sat on the edge of the crash zone while they all waited for Zack to arrive.

Zack's squad emerged from the ship. A bit disoriented, Zack looked around, trying to figure out in which direction to go. He looked to his team, who eagerly awaited his command. Zack grew more nervous, sweating up a small pond around his feet. He stood with his chest forward and his head up so he could maintain a confident façade. He saw some smoke in the distance and thought that was a good place to start. A smile snuck onto his face, and he moved his squad toward the smoke.

After several hours even Max and Tyra were growing impatient. Max felt the temptation to get up and lead the rest of the mission. He kept reminding himself that he wouldn't ever do that to Zack, and if he did, he'd be proving Sardax right, which to him was almost worse.

A rustling in the leaves behind them put the soldiers on alert. However, they all relaxed when Zack and his squad finally appeared. Sardax jumped off his giant rock and rounded up his squad.

"Finally, our wayward leader. Shall we get started since we're already down six hours?" he asked, moving toward the city.

Zack remained still for a moment, uneasy and shifting his weight.

"Actually," he called out. "I think we're going to stay."

"What?" Sardax paused.

"It's dangerous to roam the planet's surface at night, and our destination is close. This area is easily defendable; we may not find another location like this for us to squat, so we're going to stay here."

"And in the morning, you expect us to travel the whole way to the city?"

"I'm just saying..."

"No, I'm just saying, because of you, we've already lost hours, and now you want to lose the entire day? Unlike you, I'm not trying to fail this mission!"

"Back up, Terra," Max said, defending his friend. "Remember who's in charge."

"Even you have to know this mission is going to fail with this peon in charge."

"You have to respect the authority he's been given."

"What authority? The only difference between him and me is he doesn't have the nerve to command any of us!"

"The council thought so. We'll respect their decision. And *his*!"

Sardax backed up and laughed a bit. "It hurt you to say that, didn't it, Chaos?" He walked away and ordered his squad to begin setting up camp.

Zack stepped away and walked to the edge of the area. Max followed him. They looked toward the city. The surface of the planet was bountiful and full of plant life. The light from the Zacore Star hanging in the sky glistened atop the forest leaves. The light reflected back, pouring onto the city.

"Beautiful, isn't it?"

"Volt, don't let Terra get to you."

"This planet manipulates light so beautifully."

"You know how he is. He's just trying to push you!"

"This is my mission, Chaos. I'm going to stand by my decisions firmly."

"Good. But trust me, I wouldn't say this if it wasn't really imperative, but Terra is right. At least on one count. We do need to move. We can't make that run in one day. If we're going to make the mission deadline, then we need to move now."

"I don't want to find out what specific dangers the planet has to kill the men I'm responsible for."

"Oh, but that's half the fun—the danger, the challenge, taking on anything. We're not exactly defenseless."

"This isn't a game, Chaos!"

"I know! This is real! This isn't some strategy game where

you can just hope this is danger free. You need to find some guts and take risks!"

"I'm not endangering my men just to do a rush job!"

"It's not a rush job. It's time sensitive." The two remained quiet. Zack turned around and looked Max in the eye. "You don't think I can do this, do you?"

Max remained quiet and steady in his position.

"We're staying," Zack said, leaving Max behind on the rock.

The day transformed into night rather quickly. The trees stored in the sunlight from the daytime and radiated it in a glowing cascade across the surface of the planet. Sardax roamed with his squad around the perimeter, keeping watch and fighting the temptation to just leave. Max sat among his squad boasting about his adventures when he was at their rank, grossly exaggerating as he talked. Tyra was sitting in the back of the group, shaking her head and challenging the stories as Max told them.

"And that's how I got out of the belly of the beast," Max said, concluding his tale.

"Are you sure that it wasn't a cute little angel fish?" Tyra mocked. "Maybe a small cobra?"

"Hey, both of those at some point in history were scary...I think."

"Oh, I'm sure. Don't worry, boys, he's drastically exaggerating."

"Am not."

"Are too."

"Am not."

"Are too."

"Either way, it was a great story," one of the soldiers said.

"Yeah. Are we going to have any missions like that?" asked another.

"Oh sure," Max said, jumping in excitement. "Trust me, guys. We just need an awesome name and a badass stack of cards to pass the time. Stick with me, and we'll go amazing places. I promise we'll be an unstoppable force. They'll send us in to kill Xaldoruks himself."

Tyra leaned over to a soldier in the back. "He's going to keep on this for a couple of hours. It'll get worse if he starts summarizing his tenets of battle."

"Chaos Flame's tenet number one!"

"Here we go!"

They all laughed and bonded throughout the night.

Zack stayed in his tent, keeping his head in the Elite Sandsharks handbook. Even after everyone had fallen asleep, Zack remained vigilant, looking for answers.

Early the next morning as the trees' light began to dim and the sun ascended, Zack brusquely woke his forces. They stirred, emerged from their tents, and Zack addressed them all.

"Gather your gear and prepare yourselves. Today we arrive at the city and complete the mission."

"I think you're the one who needs to be woken up because you're dreaming if you think we can make it to the city in time."

"Did I ask for your comments, Sardax?"

"Please, what are—"

"That's right; I didn't. Don't you dare forget who's in charge of this mission, so if you have any more comments, keep them to yourself, or I can authorize any hardship I see fit. And seeing as how you have been a pain in the ass since the day we joined the UPA, I wouldn't count on me being lenient in any way. Understand?"

Sardax, with no comeback, stayed quiet.

"Good. Now let's go!"

Several hours passed. The squads were making progress. However, for as long as they were running, they felt they weren't getting any closer. They slowly grew sluggish and sweaty as their energy started to fade. In a flash, an obscenely large wolf with a third pair of limbs and six tentacles jumped out and tackled one of the soldiers. Before the creature could kill him, a lightning bolt jetted out of Zack's hand, pierced its heart like a Blade, causing the beast to fall and splash into a nearby river.

Zack continued on the path. "Keep moving! Let's go!"

The soldiers started to march again, but still with a low energy. Max ran ahead and caught up with Zack.

"Volt, we have to stop."

He didn't respond.

"Dude, we've been running for hours; we need to rest. *You* need to rest."

He still said nothing.

"What are you trying to prove?"

Zack looked at him and ran faster.

Finally, as the day turned to evening, they arrived at the gates of the capital city. It was booming and teeming with life. The people zoomed by in flying tubes across towering buildings that emitted glorious shades of color that complemented each other wonderfully as if they were all working together to keep its people satisfied and happy. In the center of the city was a chapel that glowed blue and teal, blessing the city with its presence. The gates opened, and they were greeted by one of its citizens. They were an orange-colored people who had a light protruding from the top of their heads like a lamp. They wore homemade pants with intricate details at the bottom of the pant leg that varied depending on their name and history. All the women wore ponchos, while the men wore half-made T-shirts. Most of them had braids in their hair in many different shapes, and their tails wrapped around them like sashes.

"Welcome to the capital! May I be the first to show you around?" the Plasian greeted them. He looked at them closer and saw they weren't ordinary travelers. "You guys don't look like you're from around here," he said politely, still holding that friendly face. "Where are you from?"

Zack walked up to him carefully, knowing he didn't want to accidentally upset these people.

"We've come to speak to this planet's council."

"Interesting," he replied. "You don't look like you are of this world. Where are you from?"

"The soldiers are merely for protection against this world's terrain. We're not accustomed to it and needed to defend ourselves. We mean no harm."

"Good to hear, but still I must know—where are you from?"

They all remained quiet until Sardax gave a large sigh. "For God's sake, we're from Zapheraizia!"

The friendly smile immediately disappeared from his face. Everyone who heard Sardax scowled at the group.

"Follow me." He reluctantly turned around, got into a tube, and led them to the city chapel. As they passed through, citizens glared at them. Their murmurs turned into loud cries, and they started throwing junk at them.

They got to the chapel and were led in. The troops were ordered to stay out of the temple so as not to arouse any hostile reaction. The walls were painted with intricate paintings and detail, and the dome was so high that they had a hard time seeing the designs on the walls. He went over to their guide.

"What are all the engravings along the walls of the dome?"

"They are of my people's history. From the biggest events to the small things like our kindness to each other, our history makes us who we are. It stretches back three hundred thousand years."

The Plasian knelt at the altar and prayed in his language. Everyone remained quiet and still so as to not interrupt the ceremony. Suddenly from the top of the dome clouds began to form, and lightning materialized from these clouds. The fog of the clouds started to encircle the group. Wind blew in their faces, and jolts of lightning rose from different parts of the chain. Eventually the lightning made a closed loop from which the council members sprouted.

They were enormous. Six giant beings sat in their thrones around the room. The staffs they held were covered in technology they had acquired through the millennia.

"I am Shinanjig, the head of this council," one said. He turned to the Plasian who had led them to the room. "Trukkuib, why did you bring the scum Terrascopians before us?"

"They demanded that they meet with you, my lords. They say they mean us no harm and wish to talk of peace."

"Terrascopians have no reason to be on this planet. They come with weapons and soldiers, and they say they're here to talk of peace?"

"With all due respect, sirs, we do," Zack said sternly. "Just hear us out."

"We take no commands from you scum."

Zack retreated to his group as they all stood in silence, waiting for the next course of action.

"What is it that you want, Terrascopians?"

Zack stepped forward slightly, still a bit shaken by the being's tone of voice.

"Sir, I am Elite Sandshark Zactavious Roark, codename, Volt Storm. We have come as ambassadors of the UPA. Our intelligence has informed us that you have intentions to attack Zapheraizia. We have come to discuss this course of action and hopefully persuade you otherwise."

"It is too late to change our minds," he said in a deep voice. "The act to attack Zapheraizia has been argued over for thousands of years. We will not have outsiders, much less the likes of you, altering our decision."

"Yes, but you see—"

"Get this scum off our planet."

"No, but wait," Zack replied, as the guards surrounded them and pushed them toward the door.

Max finally spoke up. "We aren't the ones who did it," he yelled.

The guards stopped and the council started to listen.

Zack leaned over to Max. "Dude, what the hell are you doing?"

"Improvising." Max walked up to them. "What our people did to yours was indeed wrong, but we aren't those people. Your people outlive us for a couple of generations. While you guys contemplate whether or not to attack us, the people you wanted to attack are gone. We Terrascopians can and have changed for the better. If we were all evil like the ones who attacked you, by now we would've attacked many times more. If you attack us, you would attack an innocent people. We want what you want—peace. Right now fighting us would not be peaceful. There is a sense of what's fair, but the ones who attacked you are long dead with the guilt of trying and failing to capture your world. Isn't that enough?"

There was silence. No one spoke or moved for fear that anything they did would offend them further.

"The vermin's request has been heard. It seems our information is outdated. In order to make informed decisions for the future, we may need to gather new information. We will open communications again to the outside worlds. We will no longer live in a shadow."

Max smiled. "That's all we ask, oh great ones!"

Tyra burst past Max and addressed the council. "Wait! You're saying all this time you've had no communication with the universe? Completely disconnected for five thousand years?"

"We care and provide for the people on our own world. The matters of other worlds are not our concern."

"Then you don't know?"

"What do you speak of, vermin?"

Zack walked up to them. "Sirs, for the past five thousand years, the universe has been at war with a man known as Xaldoruks. He commands a limitless army of soldiers known as Negatives. They are known for taking living beings and using their materials, components, and energy to make more. Their intention is to enslave the universe."

"This was a big part of our mission," Tyra added. "But our intelligence sensors inform us that Negatives have been spotted at a nearby volcano. We can only assume that with the amount of potential energy it contains, they intend to use it to make the entire planet Negative, allowing Negatives to flow endlessly from your planet."

"How about this?" Max said in a more casual tone. "To prove we are of benevolent intent, we can investigate and neutralize the volcano for you if it presents any hostile threat to the planet. Let it be the first kindness of the new race of Terrascopians."

"The Terrascopian plague will stay away from the sacred volcano!" The council said in unison.

Sardax had had enough. He burst in front of his comrades in a fit of rage. "You idiots! They're going to make it happen. Negatives are trying to destroy you. Don't be stupid. Let us do our job and neutralize the damn thing."

"They are too insistent on going to the volcano. The scum may plan to set espionage equipment on it."

Tyra whispered to him to shut up, but he ignored her. "And stop calling us scum and vermin! We're helping you!" He summoned his Buster Blade, and the guards prepared to take action. The council didn't flinch.

"Disrespect, hostility, deception—the characteristics of the Terrascopians of old. Your deception has failed. Zapheraizia must be destroyed. Dismiss them." The tails on the guards extended and pulled them all out the door of the chapel. Max got up and furiously pushed Sardax back to the floor when he tried to get up.

"This is ridiculous. We were so close! Why? Why did you lose your head?"

"I don't let anyone disrespect me like that, and they clearly weren't getting it!" Sardax responded.

"He was disrespecting me, too, and you didn't see me going ballistic. I kept control. I kept my cool. But now you've guaranteed another unnecessary battle!"

Sardax looked up in the distance at the rock formation behind the city.

"Not necessarily."

"What do you mean?"

"The volcano! What if we didn't stop it?"

"What?"

"The Negative Matter would stop this threat before it becomes one."

"They may be hostile, but we are not sacrificing a planet for your failure. Besides, if we didn't do anything, we would completely fail the mission."

"Not exactly. Failing to stop the volcano would destroy the planet no matter what the council's official decision was. Who's to say they weren't convinced? Either way the Plasian threat is neutralized. Or we stop the volcano but have to worry about Plasians coming home with us. It's one objective or the other at this point."

"Enough," Zack yelled. He walked up to the Plasian who was sitting on a rock a distance away from them. "What is your name again?"

He looked up at Zack and responded, "Trukkuib."

"I want to thank you for taking us to your council. You've been a great help. Do you think we can bother you further in taking us to the volcano?"

"The council has forbidden it."

"I know you would be breaking some big rules, but whether the council believes it or not, that volcano is going to erupt. We have an obligation as living beings of this universe to assist in saving your people."

Trukkuib examined Zack, trying to figure him out. "I will guide you."

"This is a mistake," Sardax said.

"Hey, Sardax, remember what I said about your words and how much I don't need them?" Zack turned to Trukkuib and let him lead.

After having had a good long break, the troops moved with more energy than before. Sardax and his men carried the rear while

Max's and Tyra's groups handled the sides. Zack walked directly behind Trukkuib.

"I'm sure you already have a negative view of us Terrascopians, so I'd like to express how much this means to us."

"Actually, my view is not so negative as you may assume. I heard your points presented to the council. I too have made those same statements to them a while ago. The Terrascopian race on Zapheraizia may be different than we assumed. But they still confuse and intrigue me. They are capable of so much violence and carnage, and monstrous levels of destruction."

"Well, that's a comforting view."

"But studying your history, you are also capable of great knowledge, skill, and love, growing more powerful as the millennia roll by. Your evolution makes you formidable. Like us, you are a mixture of both hostility and benevolence. At least I would like to believe so. But every race, whether it is good or evil, has a base nature that is revealed in the most sinister of circumstances. I'd like to believe that your people are good and full of light like you, but even other warriors of light contain darkness in them—especially him." He turned around and looked behind Zack.

"Yeah, Sardax is a bit hot-headed, but he means well...I think. I don't know; he—"

"No, I mean the dark-shaded one."

Zack looked and saw he was pointing to Max. "Max? No he's just a type of Terrascopian whose skin color is darker than ours. That doesn't mean he's dark. He is literally no different than me in that respect."

"This may be. But I refer to his heart. His heart emits an unnatural darkness unseen."

Trukkuib turned around and continued. Zack kept looking back at Max, trying to see what might have been so dark in his best friend.

They all finally arrived at the volcano's base and stood in awe of its size.

"Thank god we don't have to walk the whole thing," Zack said. He turned to the Plasian. "What do you think we're looking for?"

"There is a shed around here that we thought benign. It's over in that corner if you wish to take a look."

Exactly where he said, there was a tiny shed hiding in the forest. The structure was too small for all of the soldiers to fit into, so only the Sandsharks and Trukkuib entered. They investigated for a while but found nothing.

"We may need to move stuff around to find a lever or a door or something." Zack spotted a giant container of tools. He and the rest of the team worked together to move the giant paperweight. They removed the rug from under it and found a door with the Negative symbol on it.

Max felt a shiver run through his spine as he thought back to when Xaldoruks was killing him on his first day. He shook his head and snapped himself out of it.

"Um...Volt Storm, would you like to do the honors?" He cleared a space for Zack and the rest of the Sandsharks to jump into the lair. He walked outside and addressed the squads.

"Listen, create a perimeter around this shed. We'll call in and report on what we need to have done."

"Sir," a soldier called out. "I just remembered this great cheesecake place where we all have to celebrate after this is over."

"Roger that, kid! Looking forward to it. Extraction should be super easy. We go in, stop the volcano, come out; extraction comes and picks us up; then cheesecake! Okay?" his soldiers saluted him and got into formation. Max went back into the shed and down the ladder, following his fellow Sandsharks.

Everyone stared down a long hallway. Max looked back at Trukkuib.

"Now this is what we were talking about. When we succeed in our mission here, you have to go to your council and say we were truthful in our story."

Trukkuib stared at him for a moment and reluctantly nodded. They walked down the hall and saw that only two tunnels were in front of them. Just as Max was about to start down the one hall, Sardax called him out.

"Now hold on, Chaos," he said. "Wasn't it you who said earlier, 'Because Volt Storm is in charge, we need to wait for him to figure out what to do next'?"

Max twisted his face. "Right," he said, painfully agreeing with Sardax. "Okay, Volt, what are we going to do?"

Zack's stern voice became choppy. "Um...Crimson Winter,

you are with me, and…Chaos Flame will go with Terra Breaker. Trukkuib, go with them." Max's whole body sunk in his gear. Sardax rolled his eyes and walked down the tunnel. Trukkuib just looked at Zack and walked. Zack and Tyra went down the right tunnel while the rest went down the left.

Max, Sardax, and Trukkuib marched down the tunnel, each desperately trying to escape the tension in the air. Trukkuib followed closely and studied his companions. They found a door that led to a control room. Max walked around and looked out the window in the front of the room. They only saw lava that had no color.

"What is this?" Max asked. Sardax rolled his eyes. He looked at the material.

"Well, we're inside the volcano. So this must be the Negative lava. The large concentration of Negative Matter can make itself into any form it desires. So let's find this terminal and end this, I guess."

Max looked at the computer on his left. "Terra," he called out. Sardax turned around. "Do you think that you could hack into the computer to see if there are any files that could help us?"

Sardax scoffed, refusing to admit that it actually seemed like a good idea.

"Move over," he said, pushing Max aside. "Alright, you work with the main panel and try to shut the volcano down. I'll work on hacking this thing."

Max went to another computer and started searching for the controls to the volcano's erupter. He couldn't help but notice that even though they were in enemy territory, nobody seemed to be stopping them. Max knew something was wrong.

Zack and Tyra walked down the passageway but didn't find anything—not a door, vent, or outlet. They started to get tired, and Zack turned to her.

"Tyra, how do you think I'm doing as a leader?"

"What?"

"How am I doing? Use some of that brutal Tyra-brand honesty you love."

"What—you named it? Fine, I'll be honest. You suck at it."

"Well, you could have sugarcoated it a little."

"No, Zack, I couldn't. You are extremely inconsistent. You fear conflict, and because of it, you let Terra shape who you become. You let him ruin the first part of the mission. But guess what? That wasn't his fault; that was yours. You need more conviction to stand up to your bullies. But most of all you need to be yourself. Didn't I tell you this before we left?" She hit him behind the head. They were both quiet for a bit, and then they both started laughing.

"Thanks, Ty."

They turned the corner and found a dead end, but something was different.

"What's this?" Zack asked.

"Don't know. A container of some kind? Some liquid. I can feel it." She touched it then immediately pulled her hand back. "Lava."

"Well, can you freeze it?"

"I can try. It should respond just like normal lava."

"Can you take that much heat?"

She looked at him. "Oh, you know I can." She called Max. "Crimson Winter with Volt Storm to Chaos Flame. We've found a vat of negative matter. Attempting to neutralize.

"*No*," Max responded. "It's too hot!"

"Flame, I'm able to handle you! I think I can take a vat of fire rock."

"It's not just a vat. It's a tube. It's connected to the whole volcanic supply. You can attempt to freeze it, but you will overheat and potentially combust in a matter of seconds."

"Okay, so what do we do?"

"Nothing. Just get out of there and go."

"What? Why?"

"I found the countdown for the eruption, and we have less than fifteen minutes."

"No!" Zack yelled. "We can't fail this mission! Tell me we can shut it down!"

"Hold on; let me see what I can do!"

Max hung up and stared back into the computer. Looking through he found the off switch in the computer.

"Did you find it?" Sardax asked.

"Yeah," Max said with a heavy heart.

"Great! End it."

"If I do, we'll die."

"What?"

"If I hit this button, it puts a lid on the volcano, but it

wouldn't stop the eruption. The volcano would erupt, and it would redirect itself through the facility. We'd all get caught and die in it. All the troops surrounding us would die as well."

Sardax backed up and sighed. "You know what you have to do, right?"

Max nodded and twisted his face. "I have to stop the volcano."

"No!" Sardax yelled, pushing him against the wall. "Are you insane? I'm not dying here!"

"I'm not sacrificing innocent people, Terra!"

"They aren't innocent; they were going to attack Zapheraizia, our home, no matter what happens here!"

"They haven't yet; maybe we can change their mind again!"

"Not if we are dead!"

"I can't condemn an entire planet to burn in Negative Matter."

"What about your friends, Zack and Tyra? Condemn them to death for a planet whose only thanks will be to destroy your home. What about you? This is only your first mission. I guess it's all about how you want the legendary story of Max Blaze to end." He backed off and went back to the download.

"Flame," Zack said over the communicator. "Any word on stopping it?"

"Whatever the answer is, it seems he wants to know right about now."

There was a moment of silence. Max took a deep breath and responded. "No, I can't stop it. We have to get out of here."

"Damn it. All right. Volt Storm out."

Max looked at Sardax holding a sickening grin on his face.

"You made the right decision," he said. "And just in time for me to finish the download, so this was not a completely fruitless endeavor."

He made his way to the door. Max hung his head, feeling the weight of the decision he had just made. He looked up and saw Trukkuib, standing in awe of what had happened.

"You've just damned my entire people. How could you?"

Max said nothing, ashamed of his decision. He saw Trukkuib look at the panel. Just as he was about to make a break for it, Max grabbed his arm and pulled him with him to make the escape.

Tyra and Zack were running around frantically, trying to find a way out and feeling the clock chasing them.

Zack called in. "Chaos, Terra, we are extremely lost right now. How do we get back to our squads?"

"Forget the squads for now," Sardax shouted. "I'll take care of it. Just head up."

"What?"

"Find a set of stairs and head up!"

"Understood."

They continued up their own stairs until Max stopped him. "How do we save the squads?"

"We don't." Sardax continued up. Max followed as he tried to catch him and yelled at him for deceiving everyone. Before they knew it, they opened a door leading to the mouth of the volcano.

"Great! Where do go from here, genius?" Max demanded.

"Shut up, will you?" he yelled. "Bladed Skull, are you in position?"

"Affirmative," Robert replied.

"Take the ship off surveillance mode."

The ship appeared above the volcano. Tyra and Zack showed up on the opposite end of the mouth. Sardax linked everyone together.

"Okay, we have three minutes before this thing erupts. The ship can't get any lower than that, so we're going to use the volcano to launch ourselves onto the ship. First, we jump in and turn our shields on. When the volcano erupts, we'll be launched into the air, and Skull will catch us with the ship."

"What about our troops?"

"Do you really want to go back for them now?"

Reluctant and annoyed, they all prepared themselves to jump into the volcano. Max grabbed Trukkuib close to him. With one more rumble, they all jumped into the volcano. They each activated the force field built into their equipment and bobbed in the lava. Immediately the surface of the barrier got hot. They knew they wouldn't last much longer. Then a huge explosion propelled them high into the sky. Robert moved the ship quickly in order to catch them. They bounced into the docking bay and fell to the wall. Robert met up with them and made sure they were all right. They all breathed deeply now that their lungs were taking in clean air. Tyra looked around and saw that Max was nowhere to be found. She looked at the open bay door and saw him dangling with his left hand while his right was holding onto Trukkuib. She reached out her hand to grab him, but Max struggled to pull him up. His mechanical arm started to break because of the weight.

"Trukkuib, you have to pull yourself up! Grab her hand. I can't hold on to you for much longer!"

"You would forsake me as well, Terrascopian?"

"My arm can't handle this much weight! Hurry!"

"So you destroy me to save yourself? Like you did my people?"

"No, I'm trying to…"

"You are all monsters! The council was right. First my people, then your own men! All of you…selfish monsters! I hope another race sees you for the beasts that you are and destroys you for it."

Max shook his head. He was determined to prove him wrong. Another explosion from the volcano erupted, even more powerful than the last, and it hit the ship. The bump shifted everyone suddenly, and Max's arm broke a bit more, cutting off the connection to the nerves in his hand. He lost his grip on Trukkuib and let him fall into the burning volcano. Max shouted, trying to grab him back. He watched as the Plasian's flesh was burned off his body.

Tyra and Zack pulled him up and into the docking bay. They closed the bay doors and flew into the sky—heading home far more damaged then when they arrived. With a final explosion, Negative Matter flooded the planet, consuming the cities nearby. The shining jungle burned and the surface was decimated, leaving nothing but a Negative haven.

They all sat at the table in silence. One look around the room and they all sensed what was on everyone's mind: failure. Their first-ever mission had fallen apart right before their eyes. Zack thought about all of his shortcomings as a leader on this mission and sighed, heavily disappointed. He walked away from the group and went into a corner.

"Final report: Mission Z7503K. Leading operative: Elite Sandshark Volt Storm. Mission objective: neutralize volcano—failed. Mission objective: persuade Plasian Council to cancel their planned attack…" He paused for a moment, thinking really hard about what he was going to say next. "Failed. Casualties: all members of all squads are dead. Only the Sandsharks on the mission survived. Additional details: Sandshark Terra Breaker managed to gather intelligence from the enemy's software. The information will be relayed directly to data analysis teams upon arrival headquarters. No further reports."

Max walked up to the window. Tyra followed him.

"What are you thinking about?" she asked.

"Everything. The failure at the council, losing Trukkuib, the volcano…"

"Don't keep beating yourself up, Max."

Max's breath grew more heavy and pained until finally he blurted out, "We could have stopped the volcano."

"What?"

"Sardax and I…It could have been stopped. But if we had, the lava would have flooded the facility and killed all of us. I couldn't do that. I couldn't make the sacrifice play. I was too scared."

There was a moment of silence. Tyra couldn't immediately figure out what to say. Finally, she found the words.

"Max, don't regret your decisions. That's not what you need to do. I won't lie to you; I don't think there was a better move you could have made. It may have been costly but it may be better in the long run. Either way as leaders in this war, we have to learn how to live with our choices."

"Live with our choice?" Max scoffed. "How am I expected to live with this, Tyra? How am I supposed to be okay with this? We just committed genocide. All of those people are burning right now! And I am expected to live with this choice?"

"That's exactly right. We knew what we were getting into when we signed up for this—to be Sandsharks, leading this war. We try to save as many people as we can. We won't succeed every time. You're cranky right now because you didn't win. It wasn't a fairy tale ending the way it was when we were kids. Welcome to war."

"I don't get you. How can you stand there and be okay with all of this?"

"Okay?" Tyra scoffed. "Max, what are you talking about? I'm anything but okay right now. You're right. We're responsible…and we'll have to pay for our failure someday but I can't let this ruin me. Don't let it ruin you."

"You said I needed a reality check," Max said somberly. "Well I sure as hell got one." Max cradled his head into her as she wrapped her arms around him. All she felt was wetness on her shirt followed by a sound she hadn't heard Max make since his first day at the UPA. Faintly she could hear him repeating a small phrase.

"So many people…"

3 DRASTIC MEASURES

"Okay," Max started. Four Sandsharks sat in the briefing room on a carrier ship en route to their latest mission. Zack and Tyra sat at the far end. Next to them was Patrick Phantomwing, also known as the Aero Tempest Sandshark. He was one of the few to finish the Sandshark test with relatively remarkable scores and advance with his class. Dressed in the highest quality of gear, he stood out as one of the most mobile of the graduates specializing in aerial combat.

On the far end of the bench was a large man by the name of Leroy Lewis. He was an old veteran of the Sandshark program. He had a mask over his mouth and one over his left eye which housed containing a targeting system. His long hair covered it most of the time.

After getting a good look at his new comrades, Max began his presentation. He turned on the holograms in the room that illustrated his points.

"Our target is a planet by the name of Darod, a desert planet in the Zeta sector. The Negatives managed to grab it under the radar a few weeks ago."

"Why is this sand ball worth dying for?" Patrick blurted out.

Max looked at him with a stern expression. "No interruptions during the presentation please! The planet has few inhabitants and scorching temperatures making it hard for Negatives to find hosts to take over and to sustain themselves in the sunlight. Once we take it, it will be easy to defend."

"You still haven't answered the question: why is it worth…"

"I'm getting to it, damn it. The planet is actually in a very operative location. It can be easy to fortify as a supply facility. It can send medical aid as well as reinforcements to any location. So here's the plan to take it."

"Oh boy, this ought to be good," Lewis scoffed.

Max tried to ignore him.

"The planet has a Negative blockade defending it. Luckily there's only one and it doesn't cover the entire planet. What we are going to do is head through the asteroid field to cover our tracks and sneak around it."

"Because that always works."

"Trust me. It will."

"Trust you? Please."

"What do you mean by that?"

"This mission is a joke. You're just trying to prove you're not a failure since the three of you failed your first mission. The whole of headquarters heard about it. 'Best five of the graduates' my ass. None of your soldiers survived. God forbid you lead more to their death."

"Well, trust me, I won't let that happen. I'm making sure of it," Max said in a stern voice, silencing Patrick. Glaring at him, Max went back to his presentation. "We'll head to the surface, where Crit Bullet Sandshark will meet us near the base. He and Tyra will create a seventy-kilometer perimeter and deal with any Negatives that may come out. Aero Tempest, Short Fuse, Volt Storm, and I will enter the base. Our intelligence shows that there is a large concentrated amount of radioactive Negative Matter that is too unstable to neutralize or contain, so our only option is to destroy it. We'll have explosives rigged to blow. Once one of us finds the generator of the matter, call it in. The rest will set the explosives down wherever they are and evacuate. Also we are on the clock. I'm giving us two hours."

"Why are you giving us so little time?" Patrick asked.

"Oh, because that's when the bombs go off."

"I know, but why only two hours?"

"That's when the bombs explode! Oh, I forgot to mention this. The bombs are on a timer that's already started. And can't be stopped."

The entire room went quiet.

"Tell me you're kidding."

"The bombs are set. You have a little over two hours from

the moment we arrive at the planet to complete the mission. The bombs will go off whether you've planted them or not." The whole room echoed silence. "Oh, now you all don't have anything clever to say?"

"You're insane!"

"Maybe, but that's too bad. You'll have to hustle more now. This mission will be completed. And you will follow my command. Now find your squads and brief them on your part of the mission." They all walked off, staring at him in disbelief. Tyra walked up to him and pulled him aside.

"Have you lost your damn mind? Are you trying to kill us?"

"I knew they wouldn't listen to me. You saw them in there. I'm not letting the first mission I'm assigned to lead go down the gutter because of insubordination. We've lost our credibility, Ty. We have to show that we deserve it back."

"This is how you do it? By saying 'follow me or die'?"

"Tyra, relax. I know what I'm doing. Go brief your squad." Max walked away to the bridge. Tyra just watched him, fighting the urge to smack his head off.

The ship approached Darod's asteroid field. The planet glowed orange with two suns on either side of it. There was a belt of shadows tracing it. The asteroid field stretched in front of them. They saw a few ships monitoring the rocks. Leroy walked up to Max as they watched the ships approach.

"Couple more than one ship. What do we do? We don't have the firepower for a full frontal attack."

"Go into stealth mode," Max said to the pilot.

The ship slowly vanished as it moved through the asteroids and empty space. The ship blended in as it flew slowly under the enemy ships. Nobody spoke for fear that the enemy might pick up some stray transmission. A light tap sounded from the top of the ship. Max jumped up to the pilot again.

"Shut the ship down."

"What?"

"Shut down! Let the ship drift for a while."

"In an asteroid field?"

"Just do it!"

"I'm sorry, but I can't do…" Max pushed the pilot aside and

clicked on the panel.

"Command override. Chaos Flame, Delta status: shut down all systems!"

The ship immediately shut down and floated aimlessly through space. The enemy ships continued to move by. After a few minutes, when they thought they were safe, the Negative ship turned toward them and aimed its guns.

"Oh my god! Turn it back on! Now!" Patrick screamed. The ship started to warm up but not fast enough. "Damn it, we're sitting ducks!"

"Don't worry," Max said, calming his teammates. "I planned for this. Crit Bullet, you ready?"

"Affirmative," a voice said over the communicator.

"Activate contingency: Arachnid Spring Trap."

"Got it."

Behind them, electric generators from the asteroids caught the enemy ships in a web. Other asteroids turned around, revealing several tanks moving on their surfaces. They all began bombarding the enemy ships. Max watched from the ship's back camera and smiled.

"I told you, I planned for this. Now let's head down to the surface; we don't have all day."

"Yeah, we barely have two hours," Tyra said under her breath. The ship then bolted to the planet.

There was a small building in the middle of an ocean of sand. The ship arrived and hovered within a two kilometer radius and dropped soldiers to circle the building. Each Sandshark jumped out with their squads. A few vehicles were driven out to the perimeter. Crit Bullet's ship flew down just in time for them to get started.

"Nice shot, Crit," Patrick complimented.

"Always is," he said with pride. He was covered in incredible numbers of weapons and gear, even a bow and arrow. "So what's the plan?"

"Winter and Crit, stay here. Crit, you will have a great view of any incoming attacks. I'm putting you on attack duty. Winter, you're the only one we have with medical training, so you're on medical duty."

"Oh, hell no!" Tyra shouted. "You are not making me a nurse

on this mission."

"Winter, this isn't an option. It's only two hours; it can get real ugly real fast if you're not out here. I need you here."

"Chaos!"

"Please." He reached for her hand, and she pulled it away, marching off to the ship to grab the medical supplies.

"Right...uh, Volt Storm, change of plans. Put your squad on the perimeter as well. I have a feeling it's going to be uglier out here than in there."

"Roger that."

"Also," he whispered, "watch out for Tyra for me. Make sure she doesn't, you know, despise me by the end of this."

"You don't intend to make that job easy, do you?" Zack walked away to his team.

"The rest of you, we're leaving. We should have a total of twenty-four troops—three commanders, six bombers, and fifteen field troops." After he checked, they each got on their vehicles and traveled to the base. Upon entering, they were faced with several corridors to pass through.

"Okay, there is a core, and we have to find it. We will divide into three groups of eight. Okay, so find the generator, bomb it—literally blow the top—and get out. Simple, right?"

"You're going to get us killed," Patrick protested.

"Well, prove me wrong. Get it done so you don't have to worry about it."

Patrick, Leroy, and Max left in different directions with their squads.

Patrick walked down the hall very cautiously. He walked to the left passageway and kept searching. He found nothing. He looked at his watch, and before he knew it, an hour had already passed. The labyrinth had spun its web around him. His men were tired, and he grew angrier with Max for endangering everyone. Getting nervous, he started to move faster until he came upon a door. Hopeful that this was his final destination, he gently opened the door and found a room filled with paintings.

"Check them!" Patrick commanded. Each walked up to a painting and thoroughly examined it. The eyes of the pictures followed them around the room. Slowly, the eyes became more active until they came out of their frames and turned into Negative spawn.

"Get ready for an attack, guys," Patrick said.

Max ran as fast as he could around the corners. He felt like he wasn't getting anywhere. Just when he was about to give up and call for help, he found a door. He opened it and nothing was behind it. He looked down the hall at a seemingly endless valley of doors to choose from. Each soldier picked a door and started looking. For each one opened, more doors appeared—not just on the walls but on the ceiling and floor as well. When Max opened a door on the floor, gravity changed. There was another hallway. He went through the door and walked down the hall. He heard some commotion further down, and he started running towards it. When he reached the source of the sound, he saw the bunch of opened doors he and his troops had just searched. He gave a great sigh, thinking this would be endless and ran further down the hall. Then to his surprise he reached a wall. There was a door, but it was heavier. It seemed like he had found what he was looking for. Max tried opening the door, but it wouldn't move.

"Chaos Flame, we are under attack!" said one of the troops. Max whipped around.

"What?" he said. "Great. Alright, you two bombers try to open the door while the rest of us cover you by taking care of these shadows." He snapped his hands, and fire sparked at the ends of them. He threw fireballs at the Negatives left and right.

Leroy moved quickly and efficiently. He acted like he knew exactly where he was going. His troops didn't question him. They struggled to keep up. Leroy knew there was no time to waste, especially since he had explosives that would blow at any second. He heard something as he went further into the base. He stopped his troops and listened. It sounded like crossfire. Leroy ran to the source of the sound with his troops, and soon enough he found Max and his team completely pinned down by Negative spawn. Taking advantage of the element of surprise, he charged at them with a powerful scream while his soldiers fired at the Negative spawn.

Patrick was pinned down in the paintings room as well. He was running out of firepower and running out of soldiers. He set off a flash bomb and threw it at them. The Negatives were all stunned. Then all of the troops fired at them, and they all disintegrated. His communicator started to ring.

"Chaos Flame to Aero Tempest. I'm pinned down by a ton

of Negatives. I need backup. Oh Jeez!" There was a crash in the background. "Looks like Short Fuse found me. Still could use your help!"

"I can barely navigate this place; how the hell am I supposed to figure out how to get to you?"

"I'll send you my position."

"Like that'll do much good."

"Would you shut up and help me?"

Patrick looked up at the paintings and saw there were far more eyes than there were before. The door to the room shut and then disappeared.

"Chaos Flame…I have a bit of trouble myself."

The creatures came flooding out of the paintings more than ever before.

Outside the troops were waiting for a signal. They quickly grew tired under the hot sun. Tyra was able to supply everyone with water, but even she was getting tired.

Crit Bullet was wiping off his weapons while keeping an eye on the base and the area around it. Tyra leaned heavily on the supplies. Crit looked up at her.

"What's up with you?" he asked.

"The heat," she said, exhausted. "It's not compatible with my biology."

"How come?"

"I am ice. That's my power. Heat weighs me down, weakens me. I'm not exactly happy out here."

Crit opened one of the supply canisters and gave her a blue pill. She popped it in her mouth and immediately started to feel cooler. She smiled and thanked him.

"So you're not the biggest fan of heat, yet one of your best friends is one of the most hot-headed people we know."

"I honestly don't know how I got through a childhood with him."

"Yet you make an exception for him. How come?"

"Because the idiot's lost without me."

"Are you sure it's not the other way around?"

"Please, I don't need a man, much less a child."

"I'm just saying not all fire is the same. This planet, for instance, is harsh. This heat is meant to test the inhabitants and weed out those who cannot survive. But some heat is more passionate, not to be cliché. It burns for something other than them, burns for something they know they can nurture and make better. It's a benevolent flame."

"Well, that's definitely not him. He's very focused on himself. He can't handle another person."

"Maybe that's why he needs you. I know that under this entire snappy attitude you have toward him, you respect him. And really that's the most valuable thing you can give, at the moment." He got up from the boxes and walked off.

The ground started to shake. Everyone stood on guard. Out of the sand, red Negatives appeared and started crawling from all directions toward them. Suddenly they were the ones surrounded. Crit happily loaded his multiple guns and turned them on the Negatives. The soldiers stood ready for battle. They waited for Crit to give the command. With the snap of his fingers, the troops charged at the Negatives, and the battle began.

Patrick kept fighting against the ocean of Negatives trying to claim his ammunition. Leroy kept charging at as many Negatives as possible, and Max's field troops and bombers were getting shot down.

"Short Fuse!" he yelled. "I need you to distract them!"

"What?"

"I don't have soldiers left to defend me anymore! I need your help!"

"Damn it!" Leroy ran up to the Negatives. He attempted to attack and destroy them with his bare hands. They all started to converge on him. He then grabbed his men and ran the other way. The Negatives started chasing after them. Max resumed working on the door from where his dead colleagues left off. After a few minutes of aimless tinkering, he gave up and melted the door down. There was an elevator on the other side this time. He walked inside and descended to the bottom floor.

Outside Tyra, Crit, and Zack were barely holding on as an ever-increasing number of Negatives came out and wore them down. None of them were sure how much longer this battle would last.

Finally, Max called in. "Chaos Flame to Crit Bullet: come in!"

"What!" he yelled.

"We're running low on time. Call in the shuttle for

evacuation."

"Well, we would be willing to do that if we weren't being ambushed by Negatives with a lot more firepower than we anticipated! They seem to have adapted to the heat on this planet."

"What? That's important. Capture one of them and then use a cosmic bomb! End that battle and call the shuttle. We're going to need a quick exit!"

"Roger that." He turned to Tyra. "Winter, finish this battle once and for all. I got to go call the shuttle. We're almost done here."

She nodded. Crit left and Tyra picked up her communicator. "Commander, set up the force field around the enemy base and call all the men to retreat." The carrier ship launched into the air and hovered above the base. Crit picked up a special gun from his arsenal and fired a stun pulse at one of the red Negatives. The electricity around the creature shrunk it down. Crit's soldiers managed to pick it up and rush it out of there.

The commanders each pushed a button on their belts, and a giant shield was raised on their side of the base. Tyra was running away with the troops as the Negatives chased after them. Tyra called in to the main ship. "Fire the cosmic bomb, *now!*"

The ship fired a shining ball right onto the planet. There was a giant flash, then the sound of the explosion. Suddenly all of the Negatives were sucked into the light. Then in a flash, it was all gone, leaving the landscape dingy and Negative-free. And the base, even though it was at the explosion's center, was untouched.

Max got to the bottom floor. It was just a wide room with a window on the ceiling that let the blazing sun shine through. The room was empty aside from a generator in the center. Once he walked in, he got a call from both of his colleagues at the base.

"Chaos, we're running out of time."

"I know. Don't worry. I found the generator."

"We're not getting out of this alive."

Max looked at the clock and saw they had thirty seconds left. Patrick gave a huge sigh as he saw Negatives swarm his men. Short Fuse stopped running away from the Negatives following him.

"Gentlemen," he said solemnly. "It's been an honor fighting with you."

"You as well," Short Fuse agreed. They all looked at the clock and flinched. When the clock hit zero, nothing happened. They looked around, and they were still in the situation. Patrick, infuriated, yelled! "Chaos!" Max was giggling a bit. "What the hell is this?"

"Yeah, I forgot to tell you those timers were just timers. The bombs are remotely detonated, and once you're all clear I'll set them off, okay?"

"*Damn it, Max?*"

"Easy. Code names, buddy."

"I'm about to get swarmed by Negatives right now."

"Oh, you'll be fine. Just make sure you're away from your bombs soon, though, because I did legitimately find the generator. Short Fuse, you're alright, right?"

He heard no response but an end to the transmission. Max felt a bit of a heavy heart, but he put it out of his mind for the moment. He walked over to the generator to set the explosives. Once he set the actual detonator on a timer and was about to head out, he saw a giant mirror on one side of the wall. He stared at it for a moment, unsure of what he saw.

He walked closer, and the mirror showed him his reflection as a Negative. It had no face but the same clothes. He waited for something to happen. A few seconds later, it seemed like an ordinary reflection again. He started gesturing in front of it to test it. He concluded that there was nothing odd about this mirror, so he moved back to the generator. When he got a few steps away, he felt uncomfortable for another moment. He felt that something was watching him. He stopped in his tracks and turned around to the mirror again. His reflection was still copying him without fail. He still felt odd, as if there was another entity in front of him. He kept moving around the room. He stopped in front of the generator and looked at his reflection again. Something ominous was coming from it that he couldn't explain. There was a sense of fear that told him to run, but he quickly dismissed it. He turned back around and felt a rock hit his shoulder. He looked up, and his reflection wasn't following him anymore. Max stood up and stayed in the light. The reflection moved on its own out of the mirror toward him. Max pulled out his Chaos Blade, ready for a fight.

"What is this?" Max asked it. It stayed silent. Max looked around it. "Are you a Negative?"

It still didn't respond. It kept following his movements. "Now you're back to mimicking me?" It stayed silent. Max started moving more rapidly. "What is that? Copying? No, are you learning? Absorbing perhaps? Adapting?" Max took out his gun and pointed it at it. The creature swatted it out of his hand, grabbed his arm, and flipped him over its shoulder and to the ground.

"Okay, you know how to defend yourself now?"

The creature's face moved. Max understood that it was smiling at him. It kicked him away. The creature's face started to emerge out of its head. One feature after another kept popping out like moles. It turned around, and Max saw that it was wearing his face.

"Oh now really?" the creature said. "That's your response? Must not be all that great if you're throwing up at the sight of your own face."

Max still looked in amazement. Everything about what was in front of him was exactly like him. His voice sounded exactly the same, and his eyes, nose, ears, and even the scars, looked the same. The only thing that was different was that his right arm was flesh. Max got up and started walking around the room.

"Incredible, right? I'm quite the incredible anomaly. Don't get too taken with me. I'm only here to convey a message." In the blink of an eye, the creature appeared right in front of him and whispered. "This war is coming to an end. Very soon this will finally be over. Exciting, isn't it? The end of the war. That's what you've been fighting to bring—the end of an era. But wait. You're fighting to prevent chaos and destruction, right? You want to return the universe to a time of peace and retain the status quo. But there's only one problem with your little plan."

He got really close to his face and pulled him by his hair. "You see, this war has been going on for ages. All the universe has ever known for centuries is chaos and destruction. It's become the status quo. Many of your ancestors have gone their whole lives not knowing what exactly it was they were fighting for. So really, would breaking the status quo be a good thing? I mean, what would the UPA even be for? After all, it's why you joined in the first place, right? Oh yes, I have your memories as well. I remember how you felt at that moment, at every moment in battle. It felt good, the thrill of winning. You were built for battle, Max. You can't live without it. The missions you get are what drive you. Commanding a fleet, destroying a Negative generator, being a hero—all of that will be dead, along with this war. You're a weapon, Max. You weren't made for idle periods of peace. As a matter of fact, none of your ancestors were. This is the Terrascopian race. Seems like Trukkuib was right." He took out a digital file and threw it to Max. "If you don't believe me, look at it for yourself." He walked back toward the wall. Max started after him.

"Hold on; I'm not done with you yet."

The creature smiled. "Oh, I wouldn't try doing that if I were you. Oh wait, I am." He paused and turned back to the wall. "We'll see each other again very soon." He snapped his fingers and the generator exploded next to Max. Max went flying to the other wall. He looked back, and his clone was gone.

Outside on the battlefield, a huge explosion erupted from the base.

"That's our cue, guys. Let's move!" Everyone ran back to the shuttles that had brought them there, and they launched into the sky.

"Chaos," Zack called in. "You've got to get out of there! Where the hell are you?"

Max looked back at the elevator that had taken him down only to find it crushed by a bunch of debris.

"Uh, yeah! I'll be right there." He looked up at the window above his head.

As portions of the building exploded and the smoke rose into the air, Patrick flew out with shimmering white eagle wings into the sky, firing at the building, and soared away to the carrier. Leroy smashed through the wall of the building, holding a few of his members on his shoulders, and rushed to where everyone was gathered. One final large explosion destroyed the remainder of the base. Max managed to barely make it out of the blaze on his team's vehicle as the only survivor. On his way back, he looked up and saw multiple UPA carrier ships from headquarters arriving on site. When he met up with everyone, a member of the Sandshark Council stood waiting for him. Max stood up and greeted him.

"Chaos Flame Sandshark reporting in. It's an honor to have you here to oversee the transition."

"Sandshark Council member Iramint. Thank you. We'll prepare to convert this to a supply station. Not only will we be able to send aid to our troops, but the surrounding civilizations will be able to get the supplies they need."

"The building does mess with your head. I'll put it in my report as a warning before any serious construction takes place."

"Very good work. We'll take over from here. I'm impressed, though. You managed to complete this mission in record time for a task of this level. All objectives were met, and you even managed to catch a Negative that has adapted to natural light. I expect great things from you, Chaos Flame. Your mission has been accomplished."

He walked away. Max smiled and turned around and saw his colleagues staring at him.

"What? Am I supposed to be scared of a few glares and hurt feelings?"

"You lied to your entire team," Patrick complained.

"Oh, grow up, will you? The end result is what's important. We finished the mission in record time—even got some extra points for capturing the Negative. My methods may be unorthodox, but they work."

"Your 'methods' killed almost everyone in my team."

"You can't blame that on me. They needed to be prepared. You needed to help them and never give up on them. Don't get me wrong. That doesn't mean I'm not sorry for their deaths. This was supposed to be simple. No one was supposed to die."

"You're out of control."

"You can tell that to the council member who just commended me for my work."

Leroy marched toward him and grabbed him by the neck, contemplating squeezing. Max remained calm and unbothered.

"I know you want to. But you won't. You're not just brawn, Leroy. You're smart enough to know what would happen to you if you killed another Sandshark." Leroy put him down and walked back to the ship. Crit, Patrick, and Zack followed. Tyra just stood with her arms crossed, shaking her head.

"You want to choke me, too? That's nothing new."

"You have a very curious way of getting to the top, you know that?"

"What do you mean?"

"You immediately decide to make enemies once you get in a position of power, then proceed to use that power to dangle in front of their faces. You know you're not ahead of them, right? The method you use when you are in charge of a mission is what they will model when they are in charge, and some day they will put you on the front lines, hoping you die."

"And I'll prove them wrong so gloriously."

"What was the point of all of this? You're trying to prove something, but for the life of me, I can't see it."

"We messed up, Tyra. On our first mission, we messed up badly. We were gods among mortals at the UPA, and we lost all of that. Our credibility drained away, leaving a huge hole in our pride. No one respected us anymore. That's what this whole stunt was about."

"So you kept us in the dark, thinking our lives were at risk?"

"They followed me for as long as I needed them to, and they did it in amazing time. Fear pulls out the best in all of us. When our lives are at stake, we show the most potential to save them. It proves my point."

"What point?"

"That it's better to be feared than respected."

"Well, I'm glad you think so because I lost all respect for you."

She walked away from this stranger in front of her and into the ship. Max sighed and walked on as well with Zack following behind.

"I told you she wouldn't like the plan."

"Zack, it's not even like she was in any danger."

"That's not the point. She doesn't care if she's in danger. She can take care of herself, and you know that. She's more worried about you."

"I set it up; none of us were in danger from me."

"It's not that part of you she's worried about."

The two hopped onto the ship. As it departed, Max sulked at a nearby table, sticking his hands in his pocket. He pulled out the data file the Negative gave him. He then kept thinking about the entire experience, so confused as to what to make of it. All he knew was that he was abnormally scared of the data file. He felt unprepared for whatever was in it. Paralyzed by fear, he slipped it back in his pocket.

Deep in a secluded area somewhere in the universe, a man in

a black-and-purple coat looked at his holograms, moving them like toy soldiers around the universe. He could hear footsteps in the background getting closer to him. He stopped and addressed the entity. "Well?"

"The message has been sent, my lord."

"And the data file?"

"Delivered. He'll seek him out and fall into place soon enough."

"You've done well, Zamx."

"I still don't understand why I couldn't just take him down when I had the chance."

"You don't fully grasp the power that you have over him. You wouldn't be able to control it yet. We need both of you alive for the end."

"And what happens in the end?"

"Patience, boy. You'll have your moment soon enough."

"Really? You're going to lecture me on patience? You, of all people? You almost sound like your father." Zamx looked back and found himself with his back against the wall and being held by the neck.

"Your arrogance makes you forget whom you're addressing. Remember, I am allowing you to live. So compare me to my father again, and I shall revoke your allowance."

He released him and Zamx fell to the floor. Zamx knelt to him.

"Yes, master."

"Now, get back to work."

Zamx turned to leave. The man took out a Blade from his coat and continued sharpening it.

4 MISCALCULATION

A young black girl zipped from one building of the base to the other. She had brown eyes, and her black hair was pulled back in a ponytail that whipped through the air as she ran. She seemed to be looking for someone. She looked everywhere that he could possibly be and was still unable to find him. As she looked around in the mission hangars, she finally spotted him walking off to another ship. She sprinted to him and tackled him to the floor.

"Max!" she screamed. "Guess what?"

"What? You're crushing my baby-maker? Oh, fascinating." He pushed her off with a groan and stumbled back up again.

"You should show me some more respect. I just became a Sandshark not a few moments ago! So tonight we celebrate, and you are paying." As she started to walk away, Max caught her attention.

"Yeah, sorry, sis. I'm heading out on another mission right now."

"What? Why?"

"It's kind of my job and apparently yours now, too. Which reminds me, I need to talk to you about the whole tackling me thing."

"Can I come with you?"

"What?"

"I want to come with you!"

"Okay. One, it's not even my call. Two, you haven't even been briefed on it yet. Three, regulations state that you need to read the handbook before going on any missions."

"Oh, come on. I've already read your version of the book without you looking, so it's fine."

"It doesn't matter; you have to…wait—you did what?"

"Well, you owe me something."

"Says who?"

"I don't know. Says you. I'm pretty sure you promised me that every time I do something amazing you take me out to something fun."

"No, I didn't."

"Yes, you did."

"No, I didn't."

"Yes, you did."

"Okay, I'm going to have to take a rain check on that."

"Max, come on. I've always wanted to be on a real mission with you. Please get me on this mission."

"The thing is that I don't necessarily have the most influence with this guy. I sort of messed him up on the last mission we were on. I'm actually surprised I'm on this one."

"Has that ever stopped you from going after what you want?" Max sighed and grabbed her hand. He walked up to Patrick, who was talking his plan through to his soldiers.

"Patrick!" Max called. Patrick rolled his eyes at him.

"What?"

"This is my sister, Genesis. She's a new Sandshark, and she thinks she can just hop onto your mission because I'm on it. I told her no, but she insisted I run it by you. Now, before you make your decision, I know you hate me, but I have to tell you this now: she is a nightmare. She will ruin this mission, and frankly she is a pain. She will mess this up! I'm asking you as one Sandshark to another— please do not let her on the mission."

He looked at Genesis as she looked at Max like he was crazy.

Patrick smiled. "Miss Genesis, welcome to the mission. You can shadow Max and see what he does."

"Thank you so much," Genesis said, smiling. Max threw his hands up in disbelief. Both of them walked away to their ship. Max leaned over to Genesis.

"You're welcome."

Genesis skipped excitedly onto the ship. Max looked over and saw Tyra entering the ship with her crew through another door.

Their eyes met, and he turned away into the ship.

Max sat at a table across from Genesis, who was jumping up and down in her seat. Max smiled at his sister's excitement. Then, out of nowhere, he felt jolts of pain pulsing through to the back of his eyes. Each one delivered some image that he couldn't make out. All he could see was Genesis on the floor screaming, with her hands over her eyes. The pain and the image subsided quickly. He looked up to see Genesis asking what was wrong. Max smiled and shook his head. He suddenly wasn't so comfortable with Genesis on the mission. But before anything could be done about it, the ships soared off one by one into the sky.

They soared through space. While Max was resting, Genesis went to explore the architecture of the ship when she ran into Tyra, who was training in the simulation room. Tyra turned around, shocked to find her on the ship.

"Genesis," she exclaimed. "What are you doing here?"

"I'm a shadow on this mission. I made it to Sandshark status, so I'm getting a look at a mission."

"Oh my god, that's great! Why didn't anyone tell us?"

"It was a kind of last-minute thing. Max hooked it up."

"Really? I'm surprised, he normally would...Never mind."

"What?"

"It's nothing, sweetie. I'm just glad you're here."

"So, tell me. What are you called? Your code name."

Tyra smiled and leaned in closely to her ear and whispered, "Crimson Winter."

"Oh, I love it when you whisper in my ear."

"What are you?"

"I'm Fusion Ember."

"Aw, cute!"

"You'll see how cute I am later."

"Only if you're good."

"Oh yes, mistress." Both of them giggled. "You know, my brother is just over there." Tyra grabbed her hand and pulled her back. Genesis looked confused until she saw the look on her face. "Oh god, what did he do?"

"Nothing, I just...don't want to see him right now."

"Tyra, tell me. What did he do?"

"He's just changed. That's all."

"How so?"

"I don't know. He just…wasn't ready for it, I guess."

"Well whatever you mean by that, you know he's going to need your help."

"No, this is something he has to figure out. I can't keep bailing his ass out of his internal problems. This time he's on his own."

"You know, losing you is probably going to send him spiraling into something worse."

Tyra sat down. "I just want him to be…I don't know. I just want him…back."

Genesis sat down with her. "Maybe he's in the process of changing for the better. You just have to be patient. Wait for him. He always gets better."

Tyra smiled, gave her a kiss, and hugged her.

The ships had finally reached their target planet, Tronk. Max, Tyra, and Genesis all gathered at the bridge to receive a briefing from Patrick. Another Sandshark named Kevin joined them. Quiet and enigmatic, he stood in the corner with a hood over his head as they all stood around the holo-imager waiting for Patrick to start explaining the mission.

"Tronk. The whole planet is as close to one hundred percent water as you can get. It's the same size as Zapheraizia. The only solid rock here is one boulder at the center of the planet. Its gravitational pull is greatly out of proportion to its size—so much so that it is stronger than any other known rock in the universe. It also sends out a positive-energy pulse in tandem with the force of gravity that sustains life and keeps the water habitable for all the life forms. Now, there are three rings of cities that surround the planet in air bubbles. The UPA base we are heading to is on the bottom of the lowest ring. So gravity will end up being strongest there. We are going to take the shuttles and tow some of the other vehicles with us down there."

"What exactly is the point of the spare vehicles?" Max asked. "And you haven't exactly told us the plan."

"Be patient, Chaos," Patrick snapped. "I warn you I will not have this mission screwed up because you're too hasty." Max stood back with a still-combative look on his face. Genesis looked and saw the discomfort between the two. "Now let's head down and meet up with the other members of the team down at the base."

They started to move out. Patrick signaled to Genesis. "Actually, Fusion Ember, isn't it? Why don't you join me on my trip down and ride in style?"

Max grabbed her hand. "Sorry, sir, but she's my shadow for this mission."

"With all due respect, Chaos, she isn't even supposed to be here. I only allowed her on this mission for her educational benefit. Besides, I'm sure she would much rather see a mission from a point of command. Wouldn't you?"

"Before she can learn that, she needs to learn how to take orders from leaders who are at her rank as well, no matter how depraved their ulterior motives may be. She's coming with me." Patrick and Max glared at each other. Max turned away with Genesis and put her on the ship.

The shuttles were deployed into the water, and tethered to them were the spare vehicles. The trip took quite some time. Max studied up on the biology of the planet while Genesis looked out the window and saw various life forms she had never seen before. She turned to Max and hesitantly tried talking to him.

"So, are you going to tell me what's up with you and Patrick?"

Max just rolled his eyes. "We're just teammates, that's all."

"Oh, come on, you can't even pretend that there's no tension between you two after that battle of testosterone you displayed."

"It's nothing that you need to worry about. Just try to keep your eye on him."

"As a Sandshark it's my responsibility to take in all information about my surroundings. This includes anything that may inhibit the success of the mission. That's rule sixty-eight of the handbook, remember?"

Max sighed. "We just don't work too well together."

"Why is that?"

He put the data file down and gave his full attention to Genesis. "Look, a few months ago, we had a mission to this planet called Darod. It was technically the first mission that I had command of, and I had him on my team. I knew he wouldn't follow any of my plan, so as a contingency, I, uh, threatened all of my teammates' lives. I thought at the time that the only way they would listen to me was if I put their lives in danger, and the only way for them to get out was by following my plan. Ever since then he doesn't trust me, and I frankly don't blame him."

"Doesn't sound like you at all. What happened?"

Max paused and sighed again. With a heavy heart, he mustered the energy it took to tell her. "The first mission I had, I failed miserably. Nothing went right; the plan failed and a local citizen of the planet saw me as a monster—one who would sacrifice his own men for the sake of the mission. I knew that that wasn't me, and I was determined to prove him wrong and regain the respect I had earned before, but it turns out the whole time I was proving him right. On the two missions I've been on, none of my men have survived. I have to take responsibility for it. All of that blood will take its toll, Gen. I just hope you're prepared for it."

"Is that why Tyra is mad at you, too?"

"Have you been talking to her?"

"She's hopeful for you. But she wants you to figure it out by yourself."

"Typical. When I need her the most, she's leaving me be."

"When you figure it out, tell her. I don't like you two fighting."

"Thanks, Gen."

"Now tell me more about this scumbag, Aero Tempest."

"Oh well, it's not that hard to hate on the guy. He's just so pretentious that it just pisses me off. He thinks that just because he's got money that he's the coolest guy there is."

"Now that sounds like you."

"Okay, there's a difference between being pretentious and being confident."

"And you don't like the way he looks at me, either, obviously."

"And he knows it, too. He purposefully does it to get to me."

"But you missed an important detail." She looked at him, waiting for him, and said what she knew he didn't want to hear. "You both have feelings for Tyra."

Max just looked at her for a second. "What? Feelings for Ty? He doesn't have feelings for...and I don't have...I wouldn't care who she likes, anyway."

"I never said anything about who she likes."

"Genesis, I don't care for her like that. I care for her like I care for you."

"I certainly hope you don't care for me that way!"

"My point is that Tyra and I are just friends. We tried it once and...I'm just watching out for her, okay? She's a close friend that I just happen to desperately need. Besides she's too dark and feisty for me."

Genesis rolled her eyes. "Do you know why she's never been friends with any of the girls you've ever dated? It's because, one, the girls you date tend to be 'dark and feisty.' Two, she feels like you're replacing her. And three, she likes you back."

"Genesis, I've been friends with her for a long time. She would tell me if any of that was true."

"Oh, you'll never understand the power of a girls' night out."

"I understand a lot about girls, thank you very much!"

"Max, you may understand the mechanics and techniques of a lot of things, but the one thing you will never understand is girls."

They were approaching the rings of the different cities surrounding the planet's core. Lights glittered all around as different bubbles held the cities. Circuits connected them like arteries, sending waves of citizens from one to another. The whole planet looked like it was alive. There were tubes that traveled from the surface of the planet to the rings below it. As they delved deeper into the planet's body, the layers started to thicken. Each layer surrounding the planet's core was thicker and more clustered.

Max turned back to the captain's chair, took the ship off autopilot, and navigated through the city. When they arrived at the third ring, they went into the hangars and landed the ships along with their cargo. One by one the ships opened, and the battalions, along with the Sandsharks, exited. Tyra looked over at the door of the hangar. There was a woman there in her early forties with red hair, wearing a Tronkian uniform. Tyra smiled and ran toward the woman and gave her a hug.

"Auntie Karen!" she said in a squeal.

"Tyrishana! How's my favorite niece?"

"I'm just fine! I didn't know that you'd be stationed here right now. Is Mom here too?"

"No, she got moved to another system just last week. You should've told me you were coming!"

"I didn't know until last night! But I'm not here for pleasure.

I'm actually on a mission right now."

"With me," Patrick said, interrupting. "Patrick Phantomwing, the Aero Tempest Sandshark at your service, Madame." He grabbed her hand, bowed, and kissed it.

"Well, I'll say I'm glad that you are the team that was called for this assignment," she said, flattered.

"Allow me to introduce also the Ora Kinetic Sandshark, and you already know Crimson Winter. They will be assisting me on this mission. Also shadowing the mission will be the Fusion Ember Sandshark. She hopefully won't get in the way of the mission too much."

"Very nice to meet you all. Now that introductions are done, let's get down to work."

The group walked to a big holo-imager in a dimmed room. Once everyone was in, she began the mission briefing.

"As you may know, this planet has a single boulder holding all of the water together. It also pushes a positive energy force supplying life for all of the organisms in the planet. Unfortunately, we have received reports that there have been sightings of Negative forces at the planet's core. They've built a network all around the core, blocking any of our forces from getting to it. We can only assume that they are trying to tap into the core's gravitational force."

"What for?" Max asked. "If they try to destroy the planet's pull, sure they destroy the planet and the UPA, but would they really work so hard on a barrier only to have it destroyed?"

"That is why we believe that the planet's pull isn't what they're after, but rather, the positive energy. We believe that they are after that force in an attempt to make that positive life force into a negative one. They will set off a generator that will end up corrupting the planet. This would change every atom on this planet into a Negative, creating an impenetrable Negative factory able to tip the war in their favor." Max thought back to what the Negative on Darod said about the end of the war.

"Is what it said happening now?" he wondered to himself.

"So here's how we are going to attack this situation," Patrick said, stepping in. "There will be several groups diving down into the grid, penetrating the barrier with a few well-placed missiles in several weak spots in its structure. Now we can safely assume that the structure is going to repair itself relatively quickly, so we will launch pods into the holes made as soon as possible. They should be prepared for a fight, so we have to fight our way to the support system of the grid. First, we set explosives on the supports, and our men will set them on the generator. Once we destroy the generator, the explosives on the supports will blow as well, and the base should crush itself due to the weight of gravity. Then we will teleport back to the sub and make our escape. Now, Ora Kinetic and Winter, you and your battalions will come with me in carrying out the mission. Now, we do have an issue of the water pressure down there damaging and crushing the subs. Chaos, this is where you come in. While we prepare for the fight, you and your team will take apart the materials from the spare vehicles that we brought to fit the sub to maintain the pressure for three to five hours. Once that's done, we'll move out."

The holograms turned off and they all exited the room.

"Wait—the maintenance man? That's my job here?" Max called out.

"If you want to give yourself that label, sure." Patrick kept walking and Max followed behind him.

"Even though I have a strong skill set and would be more effective in the field?"

"My battle plan was made specifically for the people I decided to bring with me. Kevin can use his telekinetic powers to sweep large groups of opponents while Tyra has swiftness in her attacks. To add you I would have to rethink the whole route. That, and are you forgetting you are a pyroshark? Your powers don't work well underwater, do they? You'd be dead weight."

"But this is barely anything. You're not giving me anything to do."

"And you should be grateful. You'll still get the credit for the mission, and all you have to do is sit back and relax. Besides, you have a second mission, after all. You have to watch out for your shadow."

Max stood there because he knew he couldn't say anything back to him. Patrick walked away again and turned back to Max.

"Don't worry, Chaos, I'll take good care of Tyra for you."

Max tried to contain his anger. He walked away slowly, trying to not let him bother him. Genesis followed Max off into the hangar to get started on the work.

Several hours went by. Genesis helped Max and the rest of

his team suit up the submarine. Kevin sat in his corner quietly. Tyra went to Patrick, who was briefing his battalion on the mission. She pulled him aside and slammed him in a corner.

"Oh my, Tyra, I never knew you were so forward."

"Shut up! What the hell was that in the briefing room?"

"I'm sure I don't know what you mean."

"I swear to god, if you don't start talking straight to me, I will give you frost bite right here and now."

"I love it when you use your teeth. Where this time? My fingers or…"

Tyra swiftly kicked him in the groin, and Patrick started cringing but laughing as well. "Thank you, ma'am; may I have another?"

"Patrick!"

"There was a time when I would dream that you would fight for me the way you do for him."

"If you're trying to belittle him to impress someone, it's not going to work."

"I'm trying to teach him a lesson."

"A lesson taught by a guy who needs to learn it himself—real smart."

"Maybe you can teach me tonight."

She grabbed his neck and brought him close. "Listen, you and I were never going to work. You were just a rebound."

"And you still can't let him go. How adorable. The stone cold wall of ice she puts up around her heart melted by a mediocre flame."

She kneed him in the gut and walked away. "Hope you are ready to go soon," she said in an innocent voice. "Looks like Max will be done soon."

Patrick crawled back up to his feet and saw his battalion staring at him trying to get up. "What the hell are you looking at?" he yelled at them.

The soldiers turned around and went back to reading the mission objectives.

Max angrily continued tweaking the submarine's enhancements. Genesis at this point was sitting nearby, reading her manual slowly and feeling her mind numbing after every page. She climbed back up on the sub to see if she could help Max at all.

"Anything I can help with?"

"No, Genesis."

"Are you sure? Because the fin doesn't look too secure."

"I'm fine, Genesis."

"Well, you don't have to talk to me like you're angry with me."

"Would you just go back and read your manual?"

"I don't feel like it right now."

"Frankly, my dear, I don't give a damn."

"Do you think the shields are going to hold off the gravitational forces down there?"

"Genesis, do your reading."

"It doesn't look secure."

"Genesis," he screamed. "Would you please read your damn manual?"

"Don't yell at me like you're my father!"

"It's not like anyone else will."

There was a moment of silence. Max stopped what he was doing and looked up at Genesis, who started to tear up. She turned around, wiped the tears from her face, slid to the floor, and stormed off.

Max jumped up and followed her. "Genesis, I'm sorry."

She didn't respond and just marched off. Once he caught up with her, he pulled her in for a hug.

"That was mean. I forgot for a moment, okay?"

"How could you forget?"

"I don't know. After not thinking about it for a while, you just do."

"I miss them so much."

"I know you do, sis. I do, too."

They stood together in that embrace for a couple of moments. Genesis muttered something quietly.

"We're the only two left, aren't we?"

"We don't know that for sure."

"But we do, don't we? Last seven years, we haven't found anyone. We don't have any way of knowing if any other Blaze is alive. And the fact that no one in the UPA can find our family's data file doesn't help!"

"I know. I know. But we can't give up, can we? We have to

81

stay strong, not just for us but for them, too. Can we do that?"

Genesis nodded. Max kissed her forehead, and they walked back to the submarine.

Max completed the submarine and sat in a chair watching everyone get into it. Genesis stood behind him, watching them as well. The battalion climbed in one by one, followed by the Sandsharks. Patrick looked back at Max and Genesis, who smiled and gave a huge wave and a thumbs-up. Patrick then jumped into the sub. As soon as Max couldn't see Patrick anymore, he jumped out of the chair and stormed off. Tyra looked back and saw him walk off. She looked at Genesis, and they nodded to each other. Genesis then ran after Max.

Once everyone was in the sub, the hatch below the sub opened and it dropped into the water. The ship went through a tube, out of the bubbles of the city, and straight to the center of the planet. As they plunged deeper into the planet, the ship and its passengers felt heavier. The ship began to creak as the water pressure built on top of it. Eventually they started to see hexagonal structures in front of them. As they got closer, it started to become clearer. There were Negatives swimming around, still building the structure connected to it. Kevin turned off the lights to the submarine.

"Did they see us?" Tyra asked.

"I don't think so," Patrick replied. "We may have lucked out. We still have the element of surprise. You see those parts connecting it to the center? That's what we need to get rid of." He moved the ship to one of the weak spots he had indicated earlier.

"Troops, get into the jet pods. Prepare for launch."

The troops moved down into several escape pods. Kevin and Tyra started to make their way down, too. "The ship is going to have to retreat as soon as the pods are shot and come back around for extraction. I'm going to have to set it to autopilot, but it'll have to be on low power so it isn't detected."

"If only we had someone who isn't doing anything right now for this job," Tyra said, poking her head out.

"What was that?"

"Oh, I'm sorry. I said, if only we had a professional leader to assign appropriate jobs to everyone instead of being juvenile about it."

Patrick looked back at her and turned back to the controls. He launched the missiles and ran to one of the pods. The assault had begun.

Max was working on another submarine and messing with the spare parts he had just to keep himself busy. He kept rolling from under it to grab a new piece to play with. Genesis sat on top of the sub, bored. She slid down to Max, who was taking out his anger on the machine.

"So this is the life of a Sandshark, is it?" she said, teasing him. "You've really hit your stride."

"Like I said, Genesis, you have to learn how to deal with commands of the same rank as you…no matter how depraved their ulterior motives may be."

"This must really kill you—sitting here, not really doing anything."

"No, you think?" Max said sarcastically.

"Why can't you just go on a 'stroll' and just 'happen' upon a Negative base at the center of the planet?"

"Because no one's actually going to believe that, and it's unprofessional."

"Professionalism? Really?"

"Despite the laid-back nature of the UPA, on missions we are expected to perform as professionals—people who can be counted on thoroughly to come up with a plan and take care of any and all mistakes or mishaps. That's also what it means to be a Sandshark."

"I've never seen you be so chained by the rules. You're so boring."

"Oh, don't think that those rules have ever stopped me from doing something ridiculously fun during a mission."

"That's why this needs to happen. Just for me."

"Well, you see it's not all bad up here."

"How so?"

"I get to keep an eye on you, and I don't have to worry that you're in trouble. It's the easiest way to protect you on this mission."

Genesis frowned and pulled Max out from under the machine. "Answer me this, Max. Why do you always feel the need to protect me?"

"What do you mean? It's my job. I'm your older brother.

You're all the family I've got."

"Max you have to face it. I'm not your little gem that you are responsible for guarding. I'm not some delicate flower that needs to be nurtured or anything. I'm my own person."

"That doesn't mean I have to stop looking out for you."

"But that doesn't mean you have to breathe down my neck. You don't have to look out for me. I can watch out for myself, anyway."

Max stood up and walked to the side of the sub. He paused then looked at his sister. "We can't be on the same missions anymore."

Genesis looked up at him and saw the solemn look on his face.

"Because you know what? I'm never going to stop defending you. I can't help it. It's how I'm built as your brother. You're stuck with me whether you like it or not."

Genesis smiled a bit.

"And the second reason is that if you say something stupid and unprofessional that I probably shouldn't do but thought about…I'm crazy enough to start doing it." He snapped his fingers and the submarine turned on.

"Oh my god, Max. Are we going after them?"

"Why do you think I was working on a second submarine? For fun?"

"Well, yeah, kind of."

"Okay, stay here. I'll be back soon."

"What? No, I'm going with you."

"What? No, you're not."

"I have to. I'm your shadow."

"Uh, no, you're my sister. You're staying here."

"What happened to professionalism, Chaos Flame?"

"Do you really want me to pull the 'you haven't finished reading your manual' card, Fusion Ember? Because if you had read it, you'd know you couldn't actually be in the field until it's complete—no matter if you're my shadow."

"Max, come on! What was the point in bringing me along, then?"

Max twisted his face. He sighed and signaled for her to get into the submarine.

"This is a personal test for you. If you can take care of yourself, I'll start to ease up, okay?"

"Yes!" she exclaimed. Genesis giggled and jumped into the sub. "You know Patrick's going to be even more mad with you once he knows you're following him."

"Are you kidding me? That punk couldn't live without me. They are probably going to need some backup."

"How come?"

"Ha, ha! Call it Sandshark's intuition."

Max deployed the second submarine through the tubes and straight down to the center of the planet to follow his teammates.

They were pinned down. Tyra and Kevin were camping behind a corner while Patrick sat crouched behind a stack of blocks in the hallway, hiding from a myriad of bullets that were preventing them from moving forward. Tyra kept putting up ice shields to try to gain some ground, but they kept shattering before they could move forward. Kevin sat down and meditated.

"What the hell do we do now, Captain?" Tyra yelled at Patrick.

"Kevin, we need you to do another burst."

"He can't do anything since the last one he did. He has to recharge."

"So we are ultimately pinned." He called into his communicator. "Alpha, Beta, and Gamma squad, where are you?" There was no response. "Alpha, Beta, and Gamma! Respond!" There was nothing. Patrick saw that more Negatives were coming from the hall behind him. Kevin broke his meditation and put up a force field before they could attack them.

"This wouldn't have happened if you had put your damn pride aside and used Max as backup."

"My plan was made for only the three of us and our battalions!"

"Then maybe you shouldn't have been the one to make the plan!"

Patrick sighed, put his gun down, and sat against the wall. He closed his eyes and muttered words quietly. Soon they got louder.

"Silent Feather Dance!"

His wings expanded and several feathers appeared and drifted through the air, pointing at the Negatives in front of them. They all launched at them and drilled through each one of the Negatives. One by one they disappeared.

"Okay," he said, a bit out of breath. "Let's move."

The three of them ran around the corner and kept running from the swarm of Negatives rushing behind them. They found a door ahead of them. Kevin put up another force field to block them while Tyra and Patrick got the door open. The Negatives kept pushing on him, slowly pushing him back. It took a few seconds, but Patrick eventually got the door open. Tyra jumped through and called for Kevin to join them, but he didn't budge. Patrick jumped through and started closing the door. Tyra kept screaming for him to come through, but he didn't move. The door shut in front of her and left Kevin on the other side.

Tyra started hitting Patrick. "Why did you do that? Why did you leave him on the other side?"

"He was trying to let us go."

"What if he was going to come through? You can't just sacrifice people like that!"

"Oh please, do you know how many soldiers your little boyfriend has sacrificed in the last two missions alone? Don't talk to me about sacrifice. Besides, there's nothing we can do now! He's dead. We have to continue on with the mission."

"His blood is on your hands. You know you're responsible for him."

"And I'm perfectly okay with accepting that responsibility as long as the mission succeeds. Besides it's not like he's got people missing him back home. It'll be okay." He turned around to continue and saw Kevin standing in front of him against the wall. Patrick jumped back. Tyra gave a sigh of relief and continued down the hall with him. Patrick followed behind.

"Hey, Kevin," Patrick said, trying to greet him. "Glad you could make it. I knew you could use the teleport from your belt. No hard feelings, right?"

Kevin remained quiet.

"Come on Crimson, you know I was kidding, right?"

"Just shut up and do your job for the rest of the mission, and I'll make sure it's completed. Otherwise, we may just 'sacrifice' you. We take out the support beams; he'll take out the generator."

"Okay, sounds good. Whatever you say," Patrick said spinelessly. "Wait a minute—who's 'he'?"

In the base command center several security cameras were broadcasting their video feeds. There was a man standing in the center of the room, taking in all the information. One of the cameras projected a hologram of three people walking in a hallway.

"Well, well," he said, chuckling. "Looks like there are a few viruses in my system. We'll have to deal with that." Just as he was about to flood the hall, he heard a voice behind him.

"Report the situation." Immediately the man turned around and addressed the figure.

"Ah, my lord. It is nothing. There were three intruders in the west third hallway, and I was just about to get rid of them for you."

"Please don't even worry about them. What you should be worrying about is the ship that's coming in on your blind side."

The man looked at the security cameras and saw there was nothing there. "Sir, I do believe you're mistaken."

"Of course you'd think so; you're blind. The point is there is a second submarine coming where the base is still under construction. If you hadn't seen it, your sight must be inhibited."

"Oh no, my lord. You've shown me such beautiful things about the universe. I've seen the building blocks of its creation. I understand the Truth. I see perfectly well. I will follow your power anywhere."

The voice behind him walked forward. The man shuddered and looked at him.

"And you have been a very faithful student, Minocraz. Your loyalty will be rewarded, I promise you. The Truth that you see is only the beginning. I will share everything with you at my side as my partner."

He knelt down. "Thank you, Lord Zamx."

"But before we do that, there is one thing we have to do. I need your help in preparing something for my master. Can I trust you with that?"

"Yes, sir. Your will is my command, and it shall be done."

"Good. Now head to the generator and wait for me there."

Max and Genesis were approaching the base. They started to

circle it, looking for an opening. They found an open entrance where they could land and dove into it. Once they landed they got out of the ship and tried to find an entrance to the generator.

"Hey, quick question," Genesis said. "Why are we not super heavy right now?"

"Their antigravity is probably on high. It's the only way to keep anyone from being crushed from their own weight this close to the core. But based on the status of the place, we can only guess that they won't last forever. We have to be quick. Tyra said to take out the generator?"

"Right. They take out the support beams; we take out the generator."

Max twisted his face. "Something still seems off with this whole charade. Anyway, come on. Let's move."

Tyra, Kevin, and Patrick reached one of the halls that had an elevator that led to the center of the planet. There were twelve in total, and each elevator had a teleport attached to its base.

"I still can't believe you called him in for backup," Patrick said, astounded.

"Really? You realize we're out of time, right?" Tyra yelled back. "We can take out the support beams, but if the generator supplying power to the station is still operational, they'll just rebuild it, and nothing would be done. Now, we're going to have to use our teleports to each elevator in order to do it in time. However, we can't use our teleports too much or we won't be able to teleport back to the ship. So we each take four support beams. Once they're out, we teleport back to the ship. We only have three teleportations before we scramble our sub's connection to us for extraction. Move out."

They all ran around in the one tube and found the different elevators, setting the explosives as they descended and then teleporting to a new elevator. Tyra reported in after finishing her bombs.

"Heading out; my part is completed." She teleported and ended up in the passenger seat of the sub. Kevin finished his set and tried to teleport as well, but the teleports couldn't figure it out. He kept pressing the button, but it couldn't find where it needed to go. Kevin looked up and just sat down next to the elevator. Patrick ran around the ring about to set his last charge when he passed by Kevin.

"Dude, what are you doing? If you're done, get back to the ship." Kevin just stayed quiet. "Come on, man, teleport out of here." Kevin still didn't respond. "What's wrong? Can you not or something?" Then Patrick remembered why he couldn't. "It was the door. You used one of your teleports to get past the door and now you're connection to the ship is fried."

Kevin looked at him.

Patrick looked at his teleport and paused for a moment.

Tyra kept speaking into the communicator, but no one responded.

"Hello? Anyone? You guys going to talk to me, or am I talking to dead space?" She turned off the communicator and rolled her eyes. "Typical." Suddenly, someone teleported to the captain's chair. "Finally, Aero. Next time I call you I expect you to answer." She turned around and saw Kevin sitting next to her. She looked back at the controls and spoke into the communicator again. "Aero Tempest, report your position." There was no reply. "Patrick, where the hell are you?"

"Sorry, Crimson," he responded. "Looks like you're heading home without me."

"Don't be stupid; just teleport back."

"I can't. Kevin's teleport couldn't find the ship, so I gave him mine. I'll finish the job here. You guys head back to the Tronk HQ."

"No, I'm not going to do that."

"I'm not giving you a choice. That's a direct order. Kevin, drive her home okay?" There was silence on the communicator. Patrick laughed a bit. "Still as stone silent as always, I see. I'll see you guys later…"

The line went cold. There was nothing after that. Tyra just sat quietly in her chair. Kevin drove the submarine away from the web and to the base, leaving Patrick behind.

Max walked through the halls, Blade in hand and ready for anything. Genesis followed closely behind with her twin katana Blades ready. They crept quietly through the halls, listening for any possible attacks coming from in front or behind. Max suddenly stopped. Afraid to breathe loudly, Genesis held the air in her body, holding all the tension in her feet.

Max turned to her. "Okay, I think we are really close now,

but I need to check if it's clear. Stay here and don't move. I'll be back in a split second."

Max moved and Genesis stayed behind. He turned the corner and saw the massive generator sparking and making a lot of noise, with blue lighting surging out through its top. Max went back to get Genesis, but she had disappeared. He called out for her, but there was no response. Then he heard a voice from behind him.

"You know, you really shouldn't leave your valuables unattended. Something may happen to them." It was the same creature that he had seen on Darod. Max remembered all the fear and the terror of that day all at once. As it shivered every fiber he had, he gripped his Blade harder and pointed it at him.

"Zamx," he said. The creature paused. "That's it, isn't it? Your name?"

"You know it. That's impressive—actually incredibly impressive. How the hell did you know that?"

"Lucky guess."

"No, you and I know you don't believe in luck. Hell, you never need it, do you? It just gets in your way."

"Tell me—what's up with this generator?"

"Why does anything have to be up with the generator?"

"It's not just the generator; it's this whole base. It's concentrated on the bolder of Tronk to turn all the positive life energy it emits to negative energy, turning every atom on the planet into a negative particle, giving you a planet full of new Negatives to fight and end this war faster. But this isn't it. This isn't how the war's ending, right?"

"Ah, you still remember what I said that day."

"I can't get it out of my head. That's all I see. Just you. You're always talking to somebody. That's how I know your name. Those aren't dreams, are they? I'm in your head. It's always ringing and taunting me."

"Well, certainly sounds like me. But how do you know this isn't going be the end?"

"Look at the generator. That thing is barely supporting enough power to hold this base in place and just barely keeping the gravity intact. It doesn't have nearly enough power to convert the base of this planet's energy. That implies this whole attempt is a trap."

"You're a lot smarter than you look."

"Hey, don't talk about yourself that way. You're a handsome guy."

"I will say, you have most of your logic correct. But unfortunately, with that, I've already told you more than I am allowed to."

"Allowed to by whom? Xaldoruks? Who is he? Who preceded him? How is the next one chosen?"

"I'm sorry, but at this point in the conversation, all I can hear is 'Please, Zamx; please hit me!'"

He summoned his Blade and got into a fighting stance. Max got into the same one. The two charged at each other, swords clashing with energy sparking off with every blow.

Genesis was screaming with her hands bound behind her while being carried away. Minocraz held her from behind while she kept moving and fidgeting, making it hard for him. She head-butted him and broke free from his grasp, summoning her twin Blades and rushing her captor immediately. He summoned a dark cannon completely marked up with writing from an unknown language. When she charged at him, he fired a large burst of dark energy that blew a hole in the wall as it missed her. She tried attacking again, but he maneuvered with the cannon so quickly that she didn't have a chance to get close.

Max pulled no punches. He fought Zamx with fierce energy and power. However, Zamx had a counterattack for every attack he had. His fighting skill was exactly like Max's. His fireballs burned black and always canceled out Max's own flame. Max heard the sounds of a cannon being fired during his fight with Zamx. Immediately thinking it was Genesis, he ran to her aid, completely forgetting Zamx. However, Zamx just chuckled a bit. He took out a communicator.

"He's on his way. Finish her now." He threw his sword at the nearest window and set a bomb near the generator. He made the sword disappear in a dark flame and then vanished himself into his own shadow.

Genesis kept running around, dodging the attacks from Minocraz's hand cannon. Her attack strategy was speed. She kept running around him and attempting to attack. Every time, Minocraz would hold up his cannon to her, and she would vanish in midair and try again. He shot at where she would end up running, slowing her movements. She vanished again. Minocraz turned his back to her. Taking advantage, she jumped from behind a crate and launched at him with her Blades, ready to attack. He skillfully dodged the attack and grabbed her head, holding it in the air with one hand. He held the other to her face and sent dark aura straight to his palm. Genesis started screaming in pain as her face was being mutilated. There was no way for her to escape.

Max got to the room just in time to see Minocraz drop Genesis with her face bloodied. In a fit of unimaginable rage, Max yelled, shaking the whole structure. A dark aura surrounded him, and his eyes turned yellow. Red markings suddenly glowed on his Chaos Blade. He charged at Minocraz and stabbed him in the gut, pinning him to a wall behind him. He then repeatedly punched him in the face until his face was also covered in blood. Max took the Blade off the wall and threw him off to the side. He walked up to him and stabbed him in the chest repeatedly. He then stabbed him in the head and stood back. He looked at his work, put his hands together, and disintegrated him into nothing but ashes with a flame that had never burned hotter.

Max was panting as he started to calm down. The dark aura surrounding him vanished, the red markings disappeared from his Blade, and his eyes returned to their normal brown color. He looked at his hands and realized that it wasn't a Negative that he had killed. It was an actual human being. He looked over to Genesis and crawled over to her. He held her in his arms, sobbing and crying and muttering to God to bring her back. He listened to her heart and heard a faint heartbeat.

He just sat there with his half-dead sister in his arms, her blood dripping onto his fingers. Suddenly he felt a pat on his back. He looked up and saw Patrick standing there offering to help him. He looked back to his sister, who was barely breathing. There was a huge explosion near the generator. Max took off his teleport and gave it to Patrick.

"Patrick, use the teleport to head back to my ship. Get back to headquarters and take Genesis to a hospital, okay?"

"What about you?"

"There is one more person I have to find."

"What do you mean?"

"Just go! I need to end this once and for all."

Max picked up his Blade and ran away. Patrick picked up Genesis, looked at Max, and teleported back to the second sub with her. Max walked around the exploding base, and his weight started getting heavy. He kept stumbling, screaming out Zamx's name, demanding that he come out and face him. But he was nowhere to be found. He felt the base start to crumble down to the planet's core. As his body could barely hold his own weight, he looked out to the window. He saw something hurtling toward him. With a loud burst the sub crashed through the window. The door opened, and Patrick stumbled out. As the place started to flood with water, he mustered all his strength to pick Max up and put him in the back seat. With both Blazes on the ship, Patrick rushed out of there and drove the ship away from the collapsing base as it met its final destruction in the planet's core.

Tyra and Kevin sat waiting for some sign that their mission was a success. Suddenly a second submarine surfaced at the base. The medics rushed to the ship and picked up Genesis and Max, put them on stretchers, and rushed them to the infirmary. She looked back and saw Patrick walking out of the ship. Tyra looked at him and turned away. As she did, Patrick could just barely see the end of a smile.

A couple of hours passed, and Max had his legs bandaged. He sat up in the hospital bed and looked over to the door and saw Tyra standing there with her arms crossed.

"Well?" she said, expecting an answer.

"Well, where should I begin?"

"How about where you know I want you to."

"Okay, well thank you for using Genesis to call me into action."

"Oh, you're welcome...but you know that's not what I was talking about."

"Right." He laughed a bit and then looked back up to her. "I'm sorry. I know what was happening to me. Trukkuib's death haunted me, not just because I was trying to prove him wrong about us Terrascopians, which I only ended up proving true anyway, but it was my own personal failure. I went into that first mission with the childish idea that no one would die. Not only did all of our men die but the one person I had the chance to save I couldn't even pull up to the ship. I was so desperate to bury those failures with successes that I sacrificed the quality of the success and thought I needed to do it by any means necessary. I'm still working on dealing with those losses, but I'm on a better track."

Tyra looked at him and grunted ambiguously.

"That's it? A cryptic grunt?" Max joked.

She smiled and walked away.

"So are we good?"

She didn't say anything but walked away with an embarrassing smile.

A while later, Max sat outside Genesis's room with a bunch of bandages around his legs and face. Patrick walked up to the same hallway and sat on the other side of the door from him. The two were silent for a bit, not sharing any words. Then Patrick glanced at Max and saw all his bandages.

"How bad was it?" he asked.

"Not too bad. They said that considering I was that close to the planet's core with a failing antigravity, I'm lucky to be alive."

"Ha, yeah. What about Genesis?"

"She's getting repairs. Right now they're repairing her facial tissue, so her face will be back to normal soon, but the damage to her retinas is too severe. Some sort of dark force is covering her eyes. They say she may not be able to see for a while, if ever again. And even that would be very lucky…"

"Yeah, I'm sorry about that."

The two were quiet again. Max sighed.

"Thank you," Max said, slightly under his breath.

"What?" Patrick said in disbelief.

"I just want to say thank you for coming back for me."

"Oh…you're welcome." Patrick kept tapping his wrist. "I guess I should say thank you, too."

Max laughed a bit. "For what?"

"For completing the mission."

Max looked back at him. "What?"

"You blew up the generator, especially when we didn't have time to find it and escape. You completed the mission."

Max shuffled through his memory but couldn't remember doing it. "Uh…yeah…I must've. No problem, then."

Patrick turned to Max. "We're cool, right?"

Max turned back to him and nodded. "There's nothing to

disagree over."

"Yeah, I was just thinking the same thing."

The two sat in silence.

5 LEGENDS

One month had passed, and Genesis was still comatose. Max had her moved from Tronk to Zapheraizia's main branch in order to keep a better eye on her. Every day he would visit her and simply hold her hand. Sometimes he wouldn't leave her side for days. He finished his missions just so he could sit by her and help in the only way he could. He stayed there, hoping she knew she wasn't alone.

It was late one night; the whole base was nearly shut down. The nurse came in occasionally to check her charts.

"You've been here all day. Don't you have things to do?"

Max sat there with a blank face, holding Genesis's hand.

"She's going to be fine. You need to go home at least for tonight."

The nurse left, and Max remained. A tear left his eye and dripped to his right hand.

"I'm sorry, Genesis," Max whispered. "I didn't come in time." He let go of her hand and walked out the door to his room.

He walked in and leaned on the door, putting his hand in his pockets. The red light in his room flickered as if it were weeping. He wished there was some way to at least make Genesis feel better. He went to his desk drawer to start researching anything he could do when, fumbling around, he found a thin, cylindrical item that he didn't recognize. He pulled it out and saw that it was the data file that Zamx had tossed him on Darod. He still felt the strong fear and uncertainty that he had when he first received it. Suddenly all of the memories associated with him came rushing back. He remembered

Darod, the fight at Tronk, and the monster that caused Genesis's injury. He remembered there was a part of the mission after Genesis was hurt that he still couldn't remember. The memories plagued him like an incurable disease that kept returning after he thought it was gone. However scared he was, he felt that there was a possibility that somewhere in the file there could be a way to help Genesis.

He clicked the side button and it separated, showing a holographic screen that read: Data file—Blaze Legacy.

Max's couldn't believe it. It was his family's data file that went missing from the UPA archives. He first thought it was a prank, but he couldn't help but grow more excited. What he and his sister were looking for was right before him after being lost for so long. Every question about his family's history was right in front of him. He scrolled through, and found it had every story from every family member during the war. The first thing he did was search the stories related to his father. He scrolled down and found the generation just before his own. He clicked on one, Marcus Alangocux Blaze. There was nothing there. His father's biography was completely blank. Disappointed, he looked up other members of his father's generation, reading about his aunts' and uncles' adventures but also how they unfortunately ended.

He scrolled down to his own generation. He found his history since joining the UPA as well as Genesis's history. It was even updated to the point where she was in the hospital. It was almost unsettling how accurate and precise it was.

He kept scrolling down and, curiously, found a third entry in his generation under his father's and mother's names. There was no picture, just a name: Codysseus Blaze. Max started to read the file slowly, coming to terms with what he had never dreamed of. He scrolled to the bottom of the page. His was the only one that was still being written. Max put the file down and sat on his bed, still overwhelmed by the information he'd happened upon. He looked up the last couple of paragraphs to find out where Codysseus Blaze was located. It said he had landed on a planet somewhere in the V-Nebula. Once he started scrolling again, the file started to malfunction and flashed a message: DATA CORRUPTED.

He heard a knock on the door. He jumped out of his bed and hid the file under his pillow. He opened the door to find Zack standing there.

"How's she doing?"

Max sighed as his excitement turned back into despair and sat back on his bed. "Not so good. The nurse tried to make it sound like she'll make a full recovery, but I read her charts. She's definitely not going to be able to see after the surgery. They've healed all the damage on her face, but her eyes…That bastard did something to them with that dark power of his—so much so she's permanently blind."

"Really?" Zack sighed in disbelief. "Wow, is there anything we can do?"

Max shook his head. "Nothing we can do…But I may have just met someone who can."

"What do you mean?"

"Okay, first: Brotherhood Pact."

"Right."

Max put fire in his hand while Zack gave his hand a strong electric charge. The two grabbed hands and stared each other down while speaking together:

"May it be known that Maximilian Xerxes Blaze and Zactavious Andreas Roark swear to the deepest level of secrecy among brothers. May no soul apart from us know the words about to be released between us…except for Tyra."

"Wow, this secret better be good," Zack said, his anticipation rising. "We haven't done one of those in like five years!"

"Oh, trust me, it is. Remember how my family's data file was the only one in the archives that was missing?"

"Yeah, the first day we were here, we had people looking for it, and it didn't turn up."

"And since Genesis joined the UPA, we've both been looking for anyone who may know someone who is related to us. Well, I found it!"

"What?"

Max pulled the data file out from under his pillow and held it up to Zack. "This is it. This is my family's data file. I found it on Darod, on my mission."

"Wait—what? What the hell was it doing there? Where did you find it?"

Max hesitated. He knew that if he told how he'd found it he'd have to tell Zack about Zamx.

"All right, this is another secret I need to keep between us. On Darod, in the generator room, I encountered this Negative. It was different than most. It could think and talk as if it was human, but…it also took my face, my likeness, my entire physical form. It didn't manage to copy my right arm, which I thought was weird. It was discolored compared to the rest of it, but it was me. It gave me the data file."

"So you are taking information from the enemy now? What are you, insane? What makes you think you can trust any of it?"

"It works just like the rest of the files here do. It has my file, and it's up-to-date."

"Maybe, but it's supposed to be impossible to take anything from these vaults without the council knowing. This went missing, and no one had known about it until someone asked. Whoever stole it can hack UPA security. What makes you think they couldn't tamper with this and leave no trace? What if giving you this file was just a trap and they intend to use you for something?"

"I can't just leave this. This is real—I know it!"

Zack sighed. "Why haven't you told anyone about this Zamx character? Sounds like a prick."

"Did you not hear me say that it was me?"

"Like I said, sounds like a prick."

"I don't need the UPA setting me up as some lab rat trying to find him. I don't want to be associated with darkness. I'll be decommissioned so fast! I'm trying to stay as deep inside the light as I possibly can."

"You still think that this is a good idea?"

"It couldn't hurt, and here is why: I found someone, someone alive! He's in my generation. It looks like it could be my brother. I read his talents, and he's good at pretty much everything, including medicine. All we need to do is find him and have him heal Genesis's eyes."

"So you want to drag your long-lost brother, whom you haven't met yet, back here to heal your hospitalized sister, purely based on the family angle."

"Don't talk to me like I'm crazy. He's been an Elite Sandshark for years. He reached that status within the first couple months of joining. And he's led several of the battles that could've potentially won the war until he disappeared, apparently. He's the closest thing we've got." Max stood up and started for the door. Zack stopped him before he got there.

"Max, calm down. You're being very impulsive right now. You can't go out looking for him."

"I'm not looking; I'm finding. I already know exactly where he is. I just need to go out and rescue him."

"Did you ever think that maybe he doesn't want to be found or maybe he's a traitor who's trying to destroy the UPA?"

"I highly doubt that."

"How do you know? You're acting like you know this guy when you haven't even met him. I bet you haven't even finished reading his file entry."

"I totally would but the data got corrupted when I was in the middle of reading it."

"You are putting faith in a very unstable plan with too many variables, dude."

"Zack, you're not making any progress in changing my mind by lecturing me, so either come along or get out of the way."

Zack twisted his face. "I can't let you go without any backup, not to mention someone to bail you out when things blows up in your face."

Max smiled. "Still glad I can thoroughly rely on you, Zack."

"So where is this guy, anyway?"

"Some lost planet in the V-Nebula."

Zack stopped again. "The V-Nebula?"

"Yeah?"

"The reason why they call it the V-Nebula is because everything vanishes there. That ring of planets makes things disappear forever, and you're thinking, 'Let's dive right into that'?"

"Zack, he's the only other person I've got. I at least have to meet him."

Zack sighed again. "So how are we getting there?"

Max and Zack crept into the ship hangars across the base. They hid against the wall and walked along it to get to the door.

"Max, you are insane!" Zack whispered.

"I prefer the term 'ambitious' or 'brave.'"

A camera turned in their direction, and they ran back around the corner.

"There are cameras all around the door."

"Remember what we were taught in our espionage lectures? Every camera has a blind spot."

"Yeah, except ours. Otherwise they wouldn't be very good, now would they?" Zack turned back to Max and saw that he wasn't there. He looked up and saw Max waving to him from the roof of the hangar. Zack scaled the wall and joined Max on the roof.

"Okay, short circuit the roof doors. We need them open to get the ship out."

Zack rolled his eyes. "This is the king of bad ideas."

"Therefore, one of the best stories should come out of it."

"You know that theory of yours isn't very airtight." He sent a shock wave though the system, sending a surge of energy to open the door. Max and Zack fell in and landed quietly. They ran to one of the ships and got on board.

"Max, have you even thought of what you're going to say to the council when they find out about this?"

"Oh, right," Max replied. "I got it all planned out. We'll just say that there was a cry for help near the V-Nebula, and we took the liberty to go check it out." Max took a second to think about that story. "Yeah, that works."

Zack rolled his eyes.

The ship lifted from the ground and flew out into the night sky.

"We ready?" Max asked.

Zack checked all the instruments. "Coordinates are locked. We're clear."

"Now, sonic light speed, engaged," Max commanded. The ship flew out of sight into the depths of space.

Deep within the base, Luand sat in his council chair in the meeting room. There was a light shining in another chair. Another member of the council joined the room.

"Aenlan," he said quietly. "What a surprise. You have news, I trust."

"It's as you said. They're hunting them. The one you hid on Gemini is gone."

"And the one on Rasalon?"

"Gone as well, sir. They're picking them off one by one."

"Then it's as I feared."

"My question is, who else knows of their existence? We spent so long hiding it in folklore and fairy tale that it should've stayed just a story."

"Well, you know how mortals are—so afraid of their own mortality they'll do anything to escape it, even seek mythical objects."

"Well, we're all in danger. If they manage to get them all, it's game over."

"I know. That's why I'm not worried. Someone I trust completely is employing a countermeasure. We can only assume that whatever our adversary is planning, they need all thirteen in order to set their plan in motion. If we reclaim at least one, their plan is halted—probably bringing the fight to us."

"So what do we do?"

"The only thing we can do. Let events unfold and defend what we can. I don't think the crystals should be too much of an issue."

"Well, I guess you can't do too much with ten or eleven of them, right?"

Luand's face dimmed. "Don't misunderstand me, Aenlan. A single one can destroy a planet if uncontrolled. Ten of them can destroy a galaxy. But it would be ridiculously unstable to control, and there are very few who are brave enough to attempt to use them like that."

"Except..."

"Except him."

The ship had come out of sonic light speed. In front of Max and Zack was a cloud mixed with red and green colors cascaded with a yellow hue in the background and a star peering out from behind them. The clouds looked so vibrant and detailed, it seemed like they were in a dream.

"So this is it? The V-Nebula?" Zack asked.

"Seems like it. It's incredible to look at."

"So where is this Cody character?"

Max checked the data file, but the screen hadn't changed. "The data's still corrupted."

"So now what?"

"Well, we know he's here; all we need to do is find the

planet."

"In this cloud? I'm not sure how we're supposed to get out."

"It's simple. We fly in in one direction, then fly out in another."

"You're so confident this is going to work, aren't you?"

"That's why I get the women, Zack; that's why I get the women."

Max flew this ship into the cloud in search of his missing planet. The two flew straight for a bit, but soon after entering the nebula, their radars started to fail. Zack looked at Max with worry, and Max tried to stay positive. The two flew for hours with no idea where they were or where they were heading. With their scanners and maps down, they didn't even know how wide and vast the nebula was. The two started to feel tired and started to lose hope that they would find this planet or even get out alive. Without warning, Max had the sudden impulse to move to the left. He flew the ship in that direction violently and traveled in that direction for a bit. Emerging from the clouds was a planet.

"And behold, the planet that we seek."

Zack laughed in excitement. "Max, how did you know it was here?"

"I don't really know. I just did. Let's go meet a Blaze." The ship descended into the atmosphere of the planet.

Upon their arrival they discovered the air on the planet was full of smoke and not very breathable. In the lower levels the jungles were thick with plants that seemed to have been dead for centuries. The water that flowed from the river was a golden-brown color that had junk floating all through it. The sky covering the whole planet was a murky brown and yellow. There didn't seem to be any life around at all.

Max and Zack walked out of the ship and the wind's stench hit them hard. Zack's face twisted at the smell.

"What would this guy be doing in a place like this?"

Max stepped out further and tried one of his radars.

"Scanners seem to work down here. I think it's just the nebula that prevents any systems from working. Looks like there aren't a lot of life signs; not even bacteria seem to grow here. This planet must be naturally polluted. Look—everything's dying."

"Well, enough about that. Where do we go next? I don't want

to stay here any longer than I have to."

Max looked around, a bit lost and disoriented. He tried to act like he knew where he was going but he hadn't the slightest idea.

"I think you're finally starting to see the holes in your plan," Zack said.

"What do you mean?"

"Well, we may be on the same planet as your relative, but guess what? We don't know where the hell he is. He could be on the other side of the planet for all we know. Second, we have no idea where he's heading. Third, we don't know if he's actually on *this* planet. We're just assuming he is. And fourth, the data file said he was in the V-Nebula, not a planet in the V-Nebula; for all we know, he's on a ship in the middle of the damn cloud. You see, there are so many variables you didn't account for. You've been pretty impulsive over the years, but this stunt takes the cake. And guess what? We're stuck here chasing what might as well be a myth. So, how's the great Maximilian Blaze going to get us out of this one?"

Max covered his mouth. "We go that way," he said. He pointed in a seemingly random direction then started walking.

"How exactly do you know?"

"I don't. I'm being impulsive."

Zack gritted his teeth and followed him anyway.

Max led the way fearlessly, pretending to have a clue of where he was going. He would never let Zack see that he was really going on nothing but an idea and a gut feeling to lead him through the polluted thicket. Day quickly turned to night as the burnt-orange nebula sky turned into a green shade, and Max quickly grew tired. He found an area with a green tree hanging over it. It was next to the dead river and a cliff with the path still ahead of them.

"Let's rest here for the night."

"Why now?"

"Well, it's never a good idea to travel at night since we wouldn't be able to see anything, and we haven't gotten sleep for a long time." Max set a flame on the ground to start a fire.

A couple of minutes later, Zack had set up some resting areas and handed Max some food and water. The two sat around the fire, watching it flicker back and forth around the trees. Max looked at Zack and smiled a bit.

"Thanks, dude," he said quietly.

"For what?"

"You're the only person I know that, despite all the criticism of my logic, would actually go along with me on this."

Zack smiled. "Yeah, well, what are friends for?"

"No, what are brothers for?" The two laughed.

"I'm still worried about Genesis, though," Zack said.

"Yeah, I know. Me too. Hopefully this guy will help us."

"I'm sure he will in the end. He's got to be a nice guy."

"Here's hoping, right?"

The two toasted the notion and drank their jugs of water. Zack kept tapping his fingers against his cup.

"Can I ask you something, Max?"

"Anything, bro. Shoot."

"Well, Genesis…have you ever heard her say anything about me?"

"Wait, that's the question people ask when they…Do you like my little sister?"

"Well, when you put it that way, it sounds awful."

"Well…not awful, just…something I never pictured. Just imagine how I see it. It's my brother having the hots for my sister. It's kind of weird in my setting."

"Yeah, well she grew up, and I never noticed her until now."

"Fair enough. Well, I will tell you this: if she had to date anyone, as her brother I would allow her to date you."

"Why thank you, sir. I'll have her home by midnight. Ha!"

Max chuckled with him. "Yeah, but she's way out of your league, dude."

"Wait—what?"

"Zack, Genesis attracts some of the more impressive men at the base. I have to fend them off every time she makes a milkshake at the cafeteria."

"So? I'm rather impressive. I'm an Elite Sandshark."

"Dude, a private can walk in and totally out-league you. It's not about rank at all. It's about social value. That's what she'll initially see."

"What do you mean by social value?"

"Confidence. You are an Elite Sandshark, but you haven't grown into yourself yet. The first mission was a wake-up call, and you have gotten better, but there needs to be a full change to be an effective leader. In the end, that's all that matters. It's all in you. You just need to grow into it."

"You still think I can't do this."

"No, *you* still think you can't do this. You're doubting yourself. You don't believe you're important enough to do this. Zack, confidence isn't something necessarily set by birth. It's something that grows from within. You need to give it chances to do just that."

Max sensed something watching them from the cliff. He didn't look up, but he felt the presence. He looked at Zack and tapped his finger twice on his cup. Zack tapped once on his. The two continued their conversation.

"Confidence?"

"That's it. I'm telling you, the key to the universe is in fact confidence."

Max jumped up and threw a fireball at the top of the cliff, and Zack threw a lightning bolt in the same place. Two shadows jumped and dove toward them. Max got out his Chaos Blade and blocked some sword that seemed to come near him that he couldn't see, but sensed. He moved from defense to offense and swung at his unseen opponent who blocked each attack and jumped away. The other shadow came down in a thud. Zack put a shock wave in the ground and kept him sitting there. The big guy was being electrocuted as the surge of lightning flowed through his body. However, he powered through it and mustered enough strength to try to crush Zack with his gigantic bare hands. Max and the other shadow clashed Blades one more time. The two jumped back and stood in front of each other. Max squinted, trying to get a good look at him.

"Cody?" he asked, still trying to see his face. "Codysseus Blaze?"

Just as the big guy fighting Zack was about to attack, the shadow put his hand up, and he stopped. He walked toward Max and took off his hood. He was a black male with dreads tied up in a ponytail.

"Who are you?" he said in a rough voice.

Max took a nervous gulp and cleared his throat. "My name is Max Blaze. I'm your brother."

The man looked stone-faced and turned to the big guy. "Jacques, sit down." The huge lug slammed his butt to the ground.

The two stared at each other for a while.

They all sat down near the fire, eating with an awkward silence. Max kept looking at Cody, and Cody kept looking back at him. He kept a flame floating around his hand as if it were a habit. Max looked at it, amazed at how easy it was for him. Jacques sat there mindlessly, waiting for something to do.

Max spoke up. "I have so many questions. I have to ask, where have you been all this time? All our lives?"

"What do you mean?"

"Where were you when I was born? I've never seen you before."

Cody just stared at him for a moment. "You've never seen me before."

"No, you've been gone, essentially erased from all existence at the UPA. I've gone nineteen years without so much as hearing your name."

"Nineteen years. That begs the question, how did you find me?"

"Well, the family data file at the UPA had been missing the whole time. But I found it, and I used it to find you. It said you're the only other living Blaze."

A slight smile crept onto Cody's face.

"What?"

"Nothing."

There was silence once again. He then turned to Jacques. "Why don't you go and get us some wood for the fire. Don't get lost."

"Yeah, Zack, make sure he doesn't get lost." Zack reluctantly stood up along with Jacques and went off into the woods. Max finally had some time alone with his long-lost brother.

"Has your Xylonite activated?"

"My what?" Max asked.

"Your Xylonite."

"What the hell is that?"

"Oh geez, okay. Have you noticed that when you're mad or in danger, your eyes start to see things more rapidly? You start to calculate things faster; you move more quickly. This is a skill that the family has passed down for generations, and its controllable."

Cody's eyes turned bright yellow. "When I'm in these eyes, I never miss anything. I receive information and react almost instantaneously. It's sort of a biomechanical hack in our genetic code. It can allow us to see in low visibility, locate sound waves, see farther and see more details, and sometimes there are some random extras, but only if you're really lucky. You can imagine what kind of advantage it gives us against our opponents. One who is well versed in this knowledge can be quite deadly."

"One such as yourself."

Cody smiled. "It's really simple to turn on. Just remember that feeling and they will activate. Any time you were full of rage or in great danger."

Max took a second to center his thoughts on the memories of when he was annoyed and angry with his guardians when he was a kid. He looked back at Cody to see him shaking his head.

"Whatever you thought of was too weak. You need true rage. A time you were desperate. A time when there was no one to help. A time when you felt rage surging in every neuron in your body at once."

Memories of his first encounter with Xaldoruks flashed into his mind. He thought back to his mission on Tronk when Genesis was in danger. He felt all of those emotions again, from the shock of seeing her hurt to the anger he felt toward his enemy. He opened his eyes and turned to Cody.

"Did it work?"

"Interesting. Yours are yellow. Same as mine."

"Really?"

Cody activated his Xylonite and his eyes turned yellow. "We are a rare breed, you and I. Do you know what this means? We are bound to have great power given to us through these eyes. These aren't just rare; this is the color of the first Xylonite activated by a woman named Eveliya Blaze. Legend says she was able to destroy whole planets with just a blink of her eyes."

Max's eyes went back to normal. "How did you learn all of this stuff? You didn't have the data file, and Mom and Dad were dead. How did you learn about any of this stuff?"

Cody's eyes returned to normal as well. "The Roark and Smith parents."

Max stopped for a second. He heard familiar names but knew that it couldn't be the same people. "What? Zack's parents?"

"Exactly."

"No, that's impossible. You weren't there at all. I would've remembered you."

"I was there. I was there from the very beginning."

"No, you weren't! I have no memory of you anywhere."

"Memory is just mind data. Like the data file, it can be corrupted and erased."

"They wouldn't do that to us. None of us remembered you."

"Then they played the façade well. If you don't believe me, ask them yourself. See what they say."

Max stood up in disbelief. "Then when did you leave? Why did you leave?"

Cody stopped and paused for a second. He sat back down near the fire and looked up to the green-clouded sky.

"It was to keep a promise."

"What was the promise?"

"That's between me and him."

"And the Smiths and the Roarks just let you go? You just walked away?"

"Those guys," he chuckled. "They just let me go. They didn't even try to stop me. Nobody really minded that I left. Nobody except the UPA, but they were just mad 'cause they lost their best recruit in centuries."

"Best recruit?"

"I got the rank of Elite Sandshark only months after I joined. But you start to learn something when you get high enough in the ranks. Nobody really cares about you, just your product. You'll learn it the same way I did."

Max stayed quiet for a minute and tried not to believe what Cody had said about the UPA. Instead he moved to another topic.

"Another question: what are you doing here?"

Cody looked at his little brother, thinking hard about how to answer that. "Jacques and I are in search of something. We need to find a crystal somewhere on this planet."

"What for?"

"Now that answer I keep to myself."

"Did you get a gut feeling to find it or are you using some form of detection?"

"Did you feel something?"

"When I was looking for you, yeah."

"I think that's something we share, too. Since you and I share the same blood, I bet that was just our instincts telling us how to find each other."

"I feel that same feeling when I'm looking for Genesis, too."

"Genesis?"

"She's our sister. She's the reason why I came to find you, as a matter of fact. She's seriously hurt. She probably won't be able to see again. We need you to get back to the UPA and heal her."

Cody sat quietly as if he were ignoring the notion. Max waited for an answer. "Tell you what: you help me find this crystal we're looking for, and I'll go and heal our sister."

Max smiled and went back to eating.

Later that night everyone was asleep around the dying fire. Zack started to hear some voice whispering to him. He woke up and looked past the fire. There was a woman with blond hair, dressed in a white robe who was looking at him through the strands strewn over her face. Zack stood up quickly ready to fight, with his hand hovering over the hilt of his Blade. The woman turned around and started walking toward the mountain nearby. Zack didn't feel a threat from this woman, but was confused.

"Who are you?" he asked.

The woman didn't answer. The area began to fill with a thick fog. She kept walking farther away, and soon Zack lost sight of her. He burrowed through the fog, and he was at the mountain, but the woman was gone. He looked up to a tall cliff at the mountain and saw her there. Zack started climbing the mountain to reach her. He got a deep cut on his hand from one rock on the mountain but kept going. When he reached the cliff where she stood, he found that she was at the mouth of a cave. He walked toward her, and she simply turned to the cave.

"You want me to go in here?" he asked her.

The woman pointed to the center of the cave. Zack couldn't see anything. She walked into the cave. There was a pool of water in front of her across which she walked. She stood in the middle of the pond's surface and turned around. She opened her mouth, and it turned into a dark hole. It kept getting wider as she screamed and then exploded into shock waves.

Zack ran back down to the campsite and woke Max up.

"Max, you have to follow me," Zack said insistently.

"Why? What's up?"

"Well, the creepiest thing just happened to me. There was this lady, and she led me up this cliff and then went to the center of this lake in this cave and then exploded."

Max stared at him for a second. "Are you sure that wasn't a dream? Because that sounds like some dreamtime stuff."

Zack showed his bloodied hand. "I didn't dream this up. We should investigate this, dude! This could be where their crystal is."

Max looked back at Cody sleeping. He thought about how good it would feel to earn his brother's respect like this. He nodded and woke them up. They all headed to the cave that Zack had visited.

The four guys stood at the mouth of the cave, looking out to the pond in the middle of the room. Max held a flame to light the way.

"This is where you saw it?" Cody asked.

"Yeah, she stood in the middle and just blew up."

"Anything weird about her blowing up?"

"Well, she blew up. Is that not weird enough?"

Max put his foot into the lake. He immediately got shocked and pulled it out. "What the hell is up with this?"

"Zack, try walking in," Cody suggested. Zack stepped his foot in with no shock coming to him. Cody stepped in after him. Max followed him with Jacques right behind. Zack followed the pool of water leading into a river that flowed deeper into the cave. There were blue lights pulsing along the walls of the cave.

"So what's with this crystal anyway," Max asked. "Why do you need to find it?"

"It's an ancient artifact. It's called Prazks. It's a shock crystal. I'm sure you've heard the legend of the Orchaic Crystals?

"Vaguely," Zack said. "They're some all-powerful crystals that the first Terrascopians used to rewrite human genetics, right?"

"It's more than that. It's said that when God created the universe, He created thirteen elements to keep the world in balance. And in order to keep these elements stable, the crystals were created to keep a balance between order and chaos. Now the fun part of this story is that Lucifer, God's own fallen angel, decided to use these crystals against God. They had an epic battle among the heavens in which Lucifer was brutally beaten. And with a powerful hit that broke the barrier of space and time, God smote Lucifer down to Earth to be damned. He then took the crystals and hid them on Zapheraizia. Water, fire, lightning, ground, wind, telekinesis, nature, physical ability, sound, time, space, light, and darkness. These are the thirteen elements that govern the universe."

He pulled out a cylindrical container that held a red crystal in it. "This is the crystal of fire. We found this one earlier. That's part of the reason why I believed the noobie when he said he saw a woman guide him here. A similar situation happened to me when I got this one."

"Yeah, I have a name. It's Zack."

"Yeah, I like 'noobie' better."

Max stepped in. "So what's the element for this crystal?"

"We're hunting the lightning crystal. Should explain why the apparition came to him."

Zack turned around to him. "So because my power is lightning…"

"You're the only one who can syphon off enough electricity to get the crystal. Lucky we ran into you, kid." Cody pointed behind Zack, and there was the crystal floating over a podium. Cody patted him on the shoulder. "Go get it, noobie."

Zack walked slowly toward the podium. Cody, Max, and Jacques stayed behind. By the time he was halfway there, he got hit by large amounts of lightning energy from the natural nodes in the walls. Zack stopped a bit and just absorbed the energy. It slowed him down even more, and made his movements heavy. He was brought to his knees trying to take in all the excess energy. Max started to run after him, but Cody stopped him before he got past him.

"This is something only he can accomplish alone. You can't help him."

Max backed up and watched as his best friend's power was being put to the test. Zack stood up as the shock waves were still hitting him. He pressed forward and started to gain momentum. Another pair of shock nodes activated and hit Zack hard, but he powered through them. He was only a few feet away from the crystal. Another bolt hit Zack in his back. He fell into the water and let the shock nodes hit him. Mustering up all the energy he had left, he jumped up and grabbed the crystal. The crystal started to shock him with all its power. He pulled the crystal with all of his strength from the podium. When it released from its position, Zack yelled as all the excess energy blew a hole in the top of the mountain. The cave went dark. The only light present was Max's flame.

Zack sat on his knees, just holding the crystal to his chest. He looked at it and started smiling. "I got it." He said softly to himself, enjoying the victory. He got up and started walking back to the group, holding the glowing crystal above his head. "Guys, look! I got it!"

At that very moment, Zack felt the crystal being lifted from his hands. He looked up and saw Cody soaring above him, snatching the crystal away from him. He landed on top of the podium and put the crystal in a small container.

Max was shocked. He turned around and saw that Jacques had his hand right above his head. Max moved out of the way as the hand slammed into the water. Before Max could blink, Jacques used his other hand and tried to catch him again. Max moved off to the other side and saw that there was another hand waiting to crush him. Instead, Max jumped to his head and kicked him hard in the face and turned back to Cody.

"Well, it's been fun, kiddies," Cody said, saluting them. "But I'm signing off. Feel free to build a statue of me in my absence if you miss me." He jumped through the hole that Zack had made and a flame jet stream boosted him upward. Max ran after him and tried to do the same thing. He projected himself upward and went up after Cody.

He reached the top of the cliff by the cave entrance. The green sky had changed to an orange nebula shining in the day. As he crawled out of the hole, Max spotted Cody staring off into the distance.

"What are you doing, Cody?"

"Isn't it beautiful, the world we live in? So much to see, so much to gain from it."

"Cody, what are you doing?"

"Come on, little brother, now you're just asking stupid questions."

"What about Genesis? What about our sister?"

"She's your sister. Not mine. Why am I responsible for what she's done? She's never been of any consequence until now; why is that my problem? I don't even remember having a sister. As far as I know, you're just making that up to bring me back to the UPA."

"I'm not. She needs you. You were the best. The UPA will be overjoyed to have you back."

"I'm not getting sucked back into this war, not when there's a bigger one coming."

"Don't you get it? She needs you. I need you. The UPA needs you."

"Don't *you* get it? I ran away from all of that! I'm the one they don't speak of because I did the one thing forbidden among the ranks of Elite Sandshark. I'm the fallen Sandshark. And do you know what? I'm not sorry. All the people who have died in this war, they're no longer my responsibility. I escaped. I'm not going back. I'm never going back. I have power—oh, so much power now. I don't need the UPA on my back anymore."

A violet flame materialized in his palm. It elongated and curved at the end. The flames shook off and a scythe with a skull at the base of the Blade appeared in his hand. It had bones all over it and writing on the Blade.

"Whoa, what is that?" Max stepped back cautiously.

"Oh, do you like it? It's a gift from the Grim Reaper himself. His scythe."

"How did you get that?"

"The same way you get anything from anyone in the universe. You pry it from their cold, dead hands." He activated his Xylonite, and his eyes turned yellow. They both looked up and saw the nebula clouds start to circle above their heads. "Look, brother. Do you see? Even the sky knows what's about to transpire here. It feels the potential greatness of this moment and has come to watch." He started laughing and pointed his scythe at Max. Max activated his Xylonite and materialized his Blade.

Cody kept laughing maniacally. "You're a fool, little brother. Now witness the true power of fire."

A burst of violet fire erupted from him and surrounded Max. The scythe's Blade had fire burning on it. Cody launched toward Max and swung at him. Max saw the attack coming and blocked it. Cody kept swinging at him, and Max either dodged or blocked the attack. His Xylonite recognized Cody's patterns in close-range attacks. Max backed up to put some distance between Cody and himself. Cody smiled and started twirling the scythe above his head. Once he had it spinning fast enough, he launched it at Max, and a chain materialized from his hand that connected to the end of the scythe. He waited until it reached Max's distance and swung it at him with the skull side forward. He then spun the whole chain above his head, spanning the whole battlefield, and then launched it again at Max. Max kept jumping and ducking, realizing that he was in a worse state than when he was in close combat. He tried to make his way closer to get a shot at Cody. Cody reeled the chain back in and started spinning again with the Blade in front this time. He launched it faster at Max, who didn't have time to dodge. He blocked the sharp end of the Blade with his right arm. Cody smiled and yanked on the chain, pulling Max in harshly.

Max thought about aiming his Blade toward Cody but didn't have it in him to potentially kill his brother. Cody punched Max in the gut when he got close and in the scythe's grasp. As he cringed, Max jerked his head back, hitting Cody's. Max backed up and then swiftly kicked him in the head. He picked up his Blade and swung it at Cody, who blocked it in time.

The two exchanged blows. Max swung his sword again, sending a lot of power through it. It collided with the scythe and pushed both warriors back. Max was nearing the edge of the battleground where the ground dropped sharply away over a cliff. Both Cody and Max gathered their power in their right palms and launched it at each other. Cody yelled, "Fusion cannon," and a powerful burst of purple flame collided with Max's stream of fire. The attack kept pushing Max closer and closer to the edge. He cut off the attack and jumped over the edge, just narrowly dodging the cannon breaking through his attack. There were branches hanging out of the rock of the mountain. Max grabbed one of those branches and hung there. He looked up and saw Cody hurtling toward him. Max swung into the trees nearby. Cody followed him.

Max jumped through the trees, trying to escape. Cody quickly caught up and engaged. Max fell out of the tree and rolled over. Cody jumped down to his level.

"You know, little brother, you're not half bad. Glad somebody taught you something in that hellhole."

Max just panted, trying to catch his breath. "You know those powers that each Xylonite has?"

Cody ran and knelt down to him eagerly. "What? What is it?" he asked incessantly. "What is your Xylonite power?"

"*This!*" Max smiled and looked at him. Cody just stared into his eyes waiting for something to happen. At that moment, Max poked his eyes. While he was dazed, Max grabbed a large, heavy stick of wood and clobbered him on the head, knocking him out. Max gathered his breath and stood looking down at his brother, disappointed at what he had found. He kept looking at his brother's pockets, knowing what he was about to do was a bad idea.

Zack made his way out of the cave, still trying to gather energy. As he got down the cliff and back to the campsite, he heard Max coming from behind.

"Run, man!" Max screamed at him, hurrying down the mountain.

"What? Why?"

There was a burst of purple fire in the distance, erupting high enough that Max and Zack could see it.

"What is that?" Zack asked.

"My brother." Max ran, and Zack followed. They headed back to the ship. As they proceeded they could feel heat waves behind them.

"That can't be good," Max said.

"What the hell did you do to make him so mad?"

Max thought about it. "Uh...I beat him."

They made it back to the ship and hopped on. Immediately Zack prepared the ship and it lifted off through the trees. Cody, completely enraged at his defeat, arrived too late. By the time he reached their landing site, they were already long gone into the sky.

"Well played, little brother," he muttered. He walked off into the forest.

Max sat in the chair as they exited the V-Nebula. He looked over at Zack, flying the ship.

"I'm sorry, Zack," he muttered.

"Sorry for what?"

"I totally dragged you along for this stupid endeavor. The best part is you saw it coming the whole time, and I didn't listen to you."

"Well, I'm not going to say that I told you so. But I did."

Zack laughed, trying to lighten the mood. He looked over at Max who was sulking and staring out the window. "Look, it's not like it's all your fault or anything. I'll be honest. I was eager to meet this guy, too. This is someone who was such a star and was known by so many people that we know—yet not a single one talks about him. I guess now we know why."

"You didn't know about him before, did you?"

"What? No, first time I heard about this guy was when you dragged me here."

"Don't lie to me."

Zack turned to his best friend, feeling a bit threatened. "I promise you, I'm just as shocked as you." Max turned back around and gave a small sigh. "Why do you ask?"

"Our parents have been keeping secrets from us."

"What?"

"Cody was there in the beginning of our childhood."

"How?"

"I don't know. He was there the whole time. But we're missing those memories. I'm assuming Tyra and Genesis are as well. If what he said was true, that means they altered our memories."

"Why would they do that?"

"One of many questions to be asked, brother."

He stared out into space for a bit.

"Still, can you imagine him, though? Cody may be a bit older than us, but he must've been only thirteen or fourteen by the time he left. How could he have that much power at such a young age? He had enough power to make his way in the universe by himself..."

"That must have hardened him a lot."

"Explains why he didn't care to help Genesis at all."

"Well, that's all he knows. With too much power comes a lack of empathy. When you learn to rely on yourself only, you forget how to rely on other people."

Max looked at his arm and found it was still shaking. He clenched his fist and shook it off.

"Anyway, let's head back to the UPA, return the ship, and try to forget that this happened at all."

"Except you're going to tell Genesis, right?"

Max thought hard about it. He put his hand to his head. "No," he said with certainty. "She doesn't need to know."

"And thus the secret lives on."

"What would telling her do for her? She would probably be better off not knowing."

"You know, just because you're her older brother doesn't mean that you need to decide what's good for her."

Max scowled at his friend.

"But hey, it's your call, I guess."

Zack got far away from the nebula. He engaged the jump to sonic light speed toward their home.

They landed the ship back at the same hangar and left through its front door. It was still night and close to dawn. Max was a bit calmer but still had a sense of worry about him. Zack patted his back.

"Hey, this wasn't even a mission, dude. Cheer up! Genesis will be fine."

Max's eyes widened as he remembered something. "You're right, Zack," he said with a more upbeat tone in his voice. "She will be."

"Okay, what's on your brain?"

"Well, it was something I picked up from Cody. It may be enough to save her eyesight."

"Well, what is it?"

Max put his finger up and paused for a second, looking at the ground with a lot of focus. "You know what else I just remembered?"

"What?"

"We snuck into the hangar to steal the ship. We just walked out the front door. Isn't that a bit…conspicuous?" At that moment, several agents on motorbikes and jeeps drove up to them, pointing flashlights and guns at them. Max's smile disappeared.

Max and Zack stood at the center of the room. Max waited for the platform to move with a slightly smug look on his face as he got his story straight in his head. Zack, sweating profusely, was a bit more worried about how he would explain his side of the story. The platform started to rise. As they emerged from the floor of the council room, they saw twelve chairs floating high in a circle. The room's background looked like the room was traveling through the cosmos. They both stood with Luand right in front of them, a mild smile on his face.

"Well, well, well," Luand began. "What do we have here?"

"These two are accused of stealing and using an unauthorized ship and traveling to dangerous reaches of space with it," Risare said.

Luand looked at both of them. "Seriously?" he said in disbelief. "We are waging war on an enemy that is never-ending, and we're debating the matter of a simple joyride?"

Another Sandshark appeared in his chair.

"Apologies, master. I had some issues to take care of." He looked over and saw Max in the center of room. Max glared at him, a bit disappointed that he called Luand 'master.'"

"Battlux," Luand announced. "So nice of you to join us. Max, not sure you've met the newest addition to the council, Battlux Comatis, my apprentice." Battlux smirked at Max. "We are 'apparently' discussing the issue and/or punishment of these two for taking a joyride in a UPA ship."

"Yes, I'm fully aware. I read the case file." He got up from his chair and floated on a platform around the two."

"Frankly, my fellow Sandsharks..."

"I'm listening," Max coyly interjected.

Battlux glared at him again. "Fellow councilmen, these two have clearly shown a disrespect for the rules and regulations that we hold for the stability and safety of the UPA."

"Oh, please stop BS-ing this," Max called out. "If taking a ship is damaging to the stability of the UPA, then I think you have another issue to deal with."

Zack elbowed him.

"And as you can see, a clear disregard for the authorities who outrank them. These are not the characteristics of a Sandshark, but of a child. You know this. I know this. They mock the name by acting this way. Therefore, I move that these two be stripped of their rank and brought back to basic, where they understand the meaning of the word *respect*. Because clearly these two skipped that class." He floated back to his chair.

"Fair point," Luand stated. "Chaos Flame, let's see if you can top that?"

"Watch me," he said under his breath. He cleared his throat and began his monologue. "Lavish ladies and generous gentlemen of the Elite Sandshark Council. Battlux may be right. I may be a bit crass, maybe too casual, and a bit witty, dashed with a little bit of sexy. But I'll bet every single one of you is the same way with each other. I'm no different. The only thing Battlux has really pointed out is that I am Terrascopian, or more traditionally, human. Second, notice the pointed angle of his argument. He wants me not only to be stripped of my rank but also taken back to basic? Seems a bit harsh for a matter of a mere test ride, which, by the way, was a bit bumpy and not at all fit for service in a mission. You're welcome. Anyway, I would like to add that we received information that someone was hurt and in danger. We took the initiative and responsibility as Sandsharks to go and help them before the situation got worse. And it is in our power to do so. Yes, it was an unauthorized mission, but it was a success. The mission was productive, and we returned the ship the next day. As Sandsharks, we did fulfill our duty."

Luand smiled. "Well, I'm thoroughly swayed. Chaos Flame and Volt Storm, you are both cleared of this situation."

They both bowed as a platform extended behind them. The two started to walk back down the hall. Before they were able to leave, Luand called them back.

"By the way, did anything specific happen on the mission that we should know about?"

Max paused, trying not to make eye contact with him. "No, sir. Nothing else."

"Are you sure?" he asked again. Max knew that Luand knew something.

"Would you like a report of everything that happened?"

"That won't be necessary."

Max nodded, and they both left the room.

The two sat in his room after the meeting.

"I will never doubt you again!" Zack chuckled. "I can't believe you talked him out of punishing us."

"I don't think it was all me. Luand didn't seem like he was going to punish us anyway. I think it was more of a test. He definitely knew more than he let on."

"What makes you think that?"

Max pulled two cylinders out of his back pocket. Each contained a glowing crystal.

"Max, what are those?"

"Stuff of legend, Zack, stuff of legend."

"How did you get these?"

"Knocked out my brother, took the crystals and ran."

"Oh my god! You think Luand knew you had them?"

"At least he would think I would tell him about them."

"Why didn't you?"

"If we gave them the power, they wouldn't give it up. They would just lock it away, and we'd never see it."

"That's true. Also was it just me or was there a bit of 'hormonal tension' between you and Battlux? What was that about?"

"He just rubbed me the wrong way as soon as he arrived."

"Is it because he was trying to get you demoted or because he's Luand's apprentice?"

"What?"

"Dude, it was incredible. When he said 'apprentice,' it looked like you found out your crush had a boyfriend. You're not subtle with it. You've always eyed that spot."

"Can you blame me? He gets to train under Luand. Bet even my brother can't say that."

He saw the sun rising through his blinds and jumped up and out of the room.

Tyra sat next to Genesis, who was starting to wake from her comatose state. Her eyes were still bandaged, but she started to move.

"Hello?" she whispered.

"Genesis?"

"Tyra?"

"Yeah, it's me. Relax!"

"Why can't I see? What's going on?"

"Gen, you were permanently blinded on the last mission. The doctors can't seem to return your eyesight, even with the most advanced technology. You won't be able to see again."

Max barged into the room. "Tyra, shut up! Gen! Glad you're awake. Good news. You're going to be able to see again."

"Max, is that you?"

"Look, I know it seems bad now, but I know how to fix everything."

"How?"

"It's an ancient trick that only you and I know how to do."

Zack looked at Max, concerned.

"All right; what is it?"

"It's called the Xylonite. It's an ocular program that we inherited in our genes. It's unique to you and me. If you can activate it, you'll be able to see."

"Max, wait," Tyra said. "You're not making any sense. Where did you learn this? How do you know?"

Max paused. "Long story. I just did a lot of research, okay? Think you can do it, Gen?"

"Tell me what I need to do."

"Okay, this may be a bit painful. Activating it the first time will take a lot of energy, so concentrate. Focus all of the energy in your eyes. It will feel like your eyes are burning. It's like a wall you have to dig through. You can't let up or give in to the pain. Think hard about the worst pain you've had and embrace it. It's hard, but you can do it."

"Okay. I'm ready," she said eagerly.

Max held her hand tightly. A few minutes passed, and no one spoke; she remained still. Suddenly her heart rate increased dramatically. Genesis tightened her grip and started screaming. She held her hands to her eyes. Zack rushed to her, but Max held him back. She kept rocking and screeching more loudly as the seconds passed. A medical team rushed into the room and commanded the three of them out.

"Keep fighting, Genesis! I'm here! Keep pushing!"

The medical team shoved the three out of Gen's room and closed the door, tending to Genesis, leaving her cries as the last thing they heard.

6 CRYSTALS

They waited for days, always returning to the locked door of Genesis's room to see if she had gotten better. The longer it took for her to get better, the more Max started to feel guilt. He kept sitting and waiting outside, hoping to hear some word on how she was doing. Zack began to grow restless as well. Tyra watched the boys tap their feet and become increasingly impatient. Just as Max was about to barge in again, a doctor emerged from the room.

"You may see her now," he said, giving Max a smirk.

Max, Tyra, and Zack all rushed in. Genesis was still in bed, sitting upright. She unwrapped the bandages around her head. She flipped her eyelids and saw her brother staring right at her.

"Welcome back to the world of the living, sis," Max said. Genesis smiled and launched a hug at Max. Tears dripped down her face. "Okay, we need to see if it worked." Max backed up and looked straight at her eyes. He saw that her irises were a sparkling blue with gold highlights. Max grinned. "Welcome to the club, sis. Your Xylonite has officially come in."

Genesis giggled again. "What club? Isn't it just you and me?"

Max looked at Zack, who was violently shaking his head signaling not to bring him into this. "Uh, exactly. That's what makes it so exclusive." He kept smiling, trying to pass it off as one of his jokes. Tyra looked suspiciously at the two of them. Genesis sat up and prepared to leave.

The four walked out of the hospital. Genesis and Zack walked ahead, talking for a bit, while Tyra snatched Max and held him against the wall.

"You know how much I hate being left out, right, Max?"

"What do you mean?"

"You and Zack know something that you're not telling Genesis. Now you can keep it from her and that's fine, but not from me!"

"Tyra, this is one thing that doesn't really concern you this time."

"Oh, please. If you can trust Zack with it, you can trust me. You tell me all your secrets before you tell him. What makes this so different?"

"It just is."

"Max, I'm not giving you a choice. What happened during your little excursion?"

Max twisted his face and gave a sigh. "Zack and I found my brother. His name is Codysseus. We were trying to bring him back to the UPA to help Genesis, but he didn't want to come. He almost ended up killing both of us." Tyra let go of his shirt. "Genesis doesn't need to go looking for him, nor does she need to know he didn't care. If there's a right time, I'll tell her, but until then, please keep this to yourself, okay? And I don't want to say his name all that much, either. I don't want to know what would happen if it resurfaced here."

Tyra crossed her arms for a minute, feeling split between two of her best friends. She reluctantly nodded.

"There's more, too. Have you heard about the Orchaic Crystals—thirteen crystals that control the thirteen elements of the universe? Well, they aren't so much legend as you think. I can't get into it right now, but remind me to tell you about it later. I need to help Zack with something else right now. Can you go and take Genesis to the Reactivation Hall and sign her back into the computer for me?"

He turned around and approached Genesis and Zack. "Genesis, I've got something special planned for you. After you're done getting reactivated, get ready, because tonight's going to be fun."

Hidden in the darkest shadow in a distant corner of the universe, Xaldoruks stood in his headquarters examining the progress of the war. Below his balcony was Zamx, bobbing his head through a seemingly infinite number of books. With each page, his foot tapped harder, itching for some sort of action.

"With all due respect, master, why am I studying these texts when I should be out there winning this war for us?"

"Patience is my father's virtue, and I am pleased to see your lack of it. Unfortunately, it is imperative to my plans. The events that follow must take place precisely when I schedule them. As for your scriptures, darkness is equal part brain and brawn. You play like you're a dark master when in truth you know nothing. The ancient texts, the sacred rituals, the untold power of black magic—it all is a mystery to you, isn't it? You must understand all aspects of darkness to meet your full potential. As you are, darkness is merely a tool you borrow. "

"I was born in darkness."

"Which makes it that much more disappointing that you know nothing about it. Understand these texts and absorbing your counterpart will be easier than breathing. There are a lot of dark secrets you must unlock before doing so."

"Fine. If you don't mind me asking, what exactly are you doing right now?"

"Deciding where our next target will be. It may be one of our last."

"What do you mean?"

"As you know, this war is about to come to a sudden end soon. This next target will be my way of making it easier. If we're able to complete this next mission, it should crush any hopes held by anyone not brave enough to witness the final battle."

"So we want the strongest and bravest to only become even more brave and not to mention determined when they fight us? Why?"

"You know what I say: 'bravery is the kindest word for stupidity.' Arm yourself, apprentice. We're heading to Vacalon."

Max, Zack, Tyra, and Genesis all sat at the café table, laughing about their adventures. Max looked at the clock and saw it was 1:45 a.m.

"Geez, it's about that time again."

"No!" Genesis sighed. "Can we stay just a bit longer?"

"Sorry, Gen," Zack said. "But I have an assignment early tomorrow."

"Well, sucks for you!" Max laughed.

"What? You don't?"

"I'm finally using my vacation days. I'm taking a week off to make sure Genesis's transition is smooth."

"Max, you don't need to do that for me," Genesis said.

"Don't worry; I'm not. That's just the excuse."

"Why now?"

"Well, the week after is our break; I managed to get myself a longer one."

"So you manage to avoid all of the most difficult missions?" Tyra teased.

"Yep."

"All of the toughest battles before the year's end."

"Yes."

"Even the greatest challenges ever, and you won't be a part of them."

Max realized the grave mistake he had made. "Damn it, Zack, why didn't you tell me the best missions would be happening now?"

"Sorry, bro," he laughed. "But now that you're not taking any missions, I get to complete them and look incredible. I no longer have you as competition. All is fair in love and war."

"Lord knows we're in war now…"

"Okay," Tyra said, standing up. "I'm going to leave now 'cause I know we can talk about this all night."

She stood up and left the group. As she was about to exit the building, she saw a figure hidden in the building's shadow. She stepped closer to it.

"Kevin?" she called out. He was sitting tucked in a corner, looking dazed.

"Hey," she said, getting his attention. "You all right?" he remained quiet. "I just wanted to say good job on the last mission. I heard it wouldn't have been a success without you."

"What are you doing?" Kevin snapped.

"Making conversation?"

"Well, stop it! I'm sure you have better things to do." He

turned away.

Tyra sat next to him. "Yes, I do." He remained quiet. "Did I do something to make you hate me, because it seems like I did?"

Kevin kept his back to her.

"Kevin, you've got to let me in sometime. Or at least someone."

"Why?" he snapped. "Why do I 'have' to let you in?"

Tyra paused. "We're teammates."

"Does that really matter these days?"

"To me it does. I don't call just anyone my teammate. For me, you have to earn it."

"What have I possibly done to earn that?"

"Are you kidding? You've saved my life more than your fair share of times. You're someone I can thoroughly rely on."

"That wasn't for you; I'm just doing my job."

"That's what I mean. Out of everyone I work with, you're the only one who manages to keep his emotions in check. Kevin, you've had my back for a long time and…I've come to trust you a lot. I hope at some point you can feel the same about me."

Looking at her, he saw something in her expression. The only word he could find to describe it was *honesty*. Just as she was about to leave, Kevin stopped her.

"Tyra, I…trust you. In fact you're the only one I can trust…It's just the rest of the world that I can never leave my back turned to."

"Why is that?"

He caved in again. He was about to retreat to his room when he paused for a moment. He extended his hand to her.

"Maybe it would be easier to show you why."

She smiled and grabbed it as he led her to his room.

Xaldoruks's ship had come out of sonic light speed to an orange planet. As the ship flew over the planet, the people looked up with cold eyes. The cities were circular, with roads leading to the other cities and arenas in the center of each. The cities even went into the sky, reaching beyond the clouds and linking together like a spider's web. The planet's network spread far and wide but met at the largest city. It was gigantic and had a towering castle at the center of a burned, orange landscape. The sky was a lighter hue than the ground but grew dark red where it met the horizon. The air tasted like iron on the tongue.

Xaldoruks's ship landed right outside the largest city. As he walked out, he was met by the Royal Army of the Vacalonians. The soldiers wore golden suits similar to Roman armor, hardened and made denser than most metals. All parts of their bodies were covered, leaving no flesh exposed. At the front was their king, wearing a stern and unwelcoming frown. He held a gold staff in his hand.

"Well, it sure is nice to taste that blood-soaked air," Xaldoruks said in a friendly tone. "Is that O positive I'm tasting? Don't tell me you've killed off another blood type again, Garacolon."

The man stood in front of him, unchanging in his expression. "Xaldoruks, what are you doing here?"

Xaldoruks smiled and walked up to him. "Just checking up on my favorite warlord."

"My people haven't fought any of your forces. We haven't helped the UPA no matter how much they beg, nor have we interfered with any of your senseless conquests."

"Well, you should know all about senseless conquests, right?"

"I've kept my end of our bargain. Now you must keep yours. Leave and stay as far away from this planet as possible."

Xaldoruks's smile disappeared. He leaned in while the king struggled to stay stationary. "Why are you so afraid of me?"

The king started to sweat a bit as he mustered the strength to respond. "A king knows no fear."

"But I do. Hell, I practically invented it. I can't find another word for the vibes you're giving me other than fear and dread."

"Please, you clearly know not of what you speak."

"Of course I don't, because every fearless man greets an incoming ship with an entire legion of his best troops behind him. Clearly this isn't fear. What kind of 'most feared and vicious race alive' would you be if you all were equally fearful of one man?"

"You and I both know...you're no simple man."

Xaldoruks smiled.

The king stepped up to Xaldoruks. "I will not hesitate to unleash my strongest and most ruthless warriors on you right now. I will burn you where you stand, and I will do it without fear if you do not leave right now."

"Well, see, you could do that. But I really don't feel like starting a war right now."

"Now who is afraid?"

"Oh, please don't mistake my willingness to let you live for fear. I truly have no fear at all. I'm trying to prevent the sudden disappearance of your entire race."

"Xaldoruks, you are vastly underestimating our planet's power."

"Obviously you haven't begun to fathom mine."

"So it is war, then?"

"If you really want to get it off your chest."

The king retreated through his forces. Xaldoruks smiled a wide grin and turned back to his ship.

Tyra walked into a dark room lit by candlelight. There were books along all the walls and stacks of them filling most of the space. Spare pieces of scrap paper were scattered around with polygons drawn on them. It had an odd smell of a sedative, which calmed her nerves a little too much for her to feel comfortable. The atmosphere was just warm enough that she felt the constant need to lower the temperature. She wanted to leave immediately but knew that Kevin wouldn't take too kindly to that. Thus she stuck through it.

"You have so many books in here," she said, complimenting him. "It could almost rival our library."

"Please, excuse the mess. I've been reading a lot."

"Yeah, no kidding."

Kevin dug through a mountain of books and picked up one from the stack. He opened it to a page that had a picture of scientists around an operating table.

"That guy at the front of the table is one of my ancestors. He was one of the original Terrascopians who terraformed the planet. You see my family was in charge of the genetic experiments that brought superpowers into the Terrascopian genome. Here they're operating on a patient—probably the first patient to ever receive these powers. All of these books here are their research. All the formulas, equations, and results of experiments that lead to...well, us."

Tyra looked back at the picture. "What are these stones?"

"Well, while the Terrascopians traveled from planet to planet trying to find a home, they kept finding these stones that held great power. As they picked them up, they used them to help change the genetic code. Only a handful actually survived the procedures, and eventually their genes outlived the humans without the genetic change. It was survival of the fittest, and some people got some cheat codes."

Tyra flipped though the book and found a bunch of graphs and charts. She kept shaking her head. "These don't make any sense. Why is everything so inconsistent? You can't possibly get any honest data from these."

"These anomalies are caused by the stones. They cause all sorts of chaos and unpredictable eventualities."

"You can't honestly believe that."

"On the contrary, it's one of the only things I'm a hundred percent certain of."

Tyra heard a whisper next to her ear. She turned around and saw no one there. "You're sure we're the only ones in here, right?"

"Of course, you're the only other person besides me and Supreme Elite Sandshark Luand who have been in this room."

"I thought I heard a voice."

"What voice?"

She turned back in that direction and saw a box slightly glowing on the shelf. She approached it and gently opened it. The whispers suddenly disappeared. There was a bunch of junk and trinkets with a bright blue crystal shining through them. There was a clear crystal next to it as well. She grabbed both and went to Kevin.

"What are these?"

"I don't know. They've never actually shined like that before."

"Do you have any idea why?"

"I haven't actually even thought about that box for years."

"You wouldn't mind if I took them, would you?"

"That's fine. I'm not particularly attached to them, nor are they important to me."

"Thank you." She put them in her bag.

Kevin started to withdraw again.

"What's wrong?" Tyra asked.

"I've never given anything to anyone before. This is new to me...I'm not really sure what comes next."

"Well, I'll have to thank you again for letting me be the first. You know, people think you're so hard and scary, but you're one of the sweetest people I've ever met."

Kevin finally cracked a smile and made a noise that sounded like single gentle chuckle. "Tyra, you are much kinder than I ever thought."

The cities blazed against the night sky. As the cities burned, the capital fought to the last man to defend against the Negative forces. Xaldoruks's army conquered city after city, destroying and consuming its citizens, as it got closer to the capital.

The king stood atop his castle watching the carnage unfold. Growing increasingly frustrated, he yelled as loud as he could at his potential failure. He turned to his wife, who was standing in front of a holographic projector of the events taking place outside.

"Our forces are being destroyed. We won't last much longer under this siege."

"My king," his wife said, trying to sooth him, "you will win this battle as you always do—standing with your troops and facing the enemy."

"But with an enemy so endless and so skilled, you may not want to watch your husband attempt to triumph against it."

"I will always be by your side."

"Listen, if things get rough, I need you to leave. There's an escape pod that leads off the planet. Only if it is the last resort will you contact the UPA."

"I already told you I would never leave you!"

"Please." He put his hand on her belly. "There are more important things that you need to protect right now." She looked into his eyes and felt it would be the last time. Fearing this, she kissed him.

"I love you."

The king tried to hold back tears. "I love you, too."

As they embraced, the queen looked over to the rocking chair and saw a figure rocking back and forth slowly.

"How sentimental." The king turned to the source of the voice. There he saw Xaldoruks sitting with his legs crossed and a knife in his hand, picking the dirt from under his fingernails. "No, please, continue. This is cute: you and your wife together in love. It seems like every being he created is capable of love. Maybe it's to keep you in line. I don't really know. To me it seems like a weakness. Oh, look at your faces. Obviously you disagree. Don't worry. I'll show you what I'm talking about."

The knife then turned into a Blade and he launched at the couple. The two pushed off each other, and the queen summoned her Blade. The king struck at Xaldoruks's back, but he moved away before he made contact. The two continuously attacked him, trying to push him to a corner. Suddenly the queen pushed her king into a hallway.

"Go! I'll be right behind you."

"Claradine, no!"

"This is not a command from your queen but from your wife. Get the hell out of here!" she yelled. The king scurried along the hallway, escaping to the lower levels.

Xaldoruks started to laugh. "You shouldn't have left us alone. Now I can really have my fun."

"I do not fear you, creature."

"Spoken like a compensating child."

"I am Vacalonian. We know not what fear is!"

"Well then, time to widen your vocabulary."

The king ran through the corridors of the castle. As he made it to the ground level, he tried to run through the front door to get more troops to assist him. When he got to the steps of the castle, he saw Xaldoruks holding his wife by the hair with her arms and legs tied together. He pressed a Blade to her neck.

"Don't hurt her."

"Oh come on, Garacolon. Don't be so naïve. I'm going to completely destroy her. Now I just want to point out that you brought this upon yourself."

Behind him the gates to the castle opened. A strapping youth rushed in and stopped just behind them.

"Mother? What's going on?"

Xaldoruks looked behind him. "Well hello there. Garacolon, it's rude not to introduce me to your son!"

"Unhand my mother, you fiend!" the boy yelled as he came charging at the two of them.

"Stop right now, Karolon!" Garacolon yelled.

"But mother!"

"Do as your father commands!" she yelled at him. The boy stopped in his tracks.

"Oh, don't listen to them," Xaldoruks shouted. "Release all that anger and come at me."

"Karolon, if you value your mother's life, you will not move from that spot."

"Now, that is impressive," Xaldoruks chuckled. "You trained him to be totally whipped and subservient. I'm sure he'll grow up to be just like his father."

The king called out in a loud, booming voice. "That is enough! I will not sit and allow you to diminish my family! We will end this war before it begins. I challenge you, Xaldoruks, to a Final Battle."

"Finally!"

"In one week's time, you and I will fight to the death in the duel arena for the fate of the planet."

"Eh, see…I'm a busy guy. I've got a lot to do next week. Can't keep still, you know, with waging war and whatnot. So how about in…twelve hours?"

"Impossible, ritual states each side gets one week to complete the preparations for the match."

"Okay, well, let's see if I can motivate you a little bit. Your wife will be staying with me while you wait your little week. I'll wait for twelve hours in the arena. For every hour you keep me waiting, your wife will get a large gash or a beating…depending on how I'm feeling at the moment. So now that I know you're listening, another change will be made. Instead of it being one-on-one, it will be two-on-two. You and your son versus me and my own son."

"You have a son?"

"Did you think it so impossible? So remember—you and your son, twelve hours. Don't keep me waiting. If you do…" He raised the sword to the queen's belly and slowly moved the Blade through her flesh. She struggled to keep herself strong until a scream escaped her lips. The men cringed in horror of their family being brutally tortured.

"Well, well, look at that. I can play her like an upright bass." Xaldoruks looked the king straight in the eye. "Tell me love isn't weakness now."

Then with the shadows surrounding him, he disappeared into

the night.

Max was putting on his pajamas and shutting down his systems when, without warning, he heard his door open. He whipped his head to the door and saw Tyra there.

"Tyra, as much as I love the idea of you barging unannounced into my room, knocking is a gesture that has lasted this long for a reason."

"Max, I need to talk to you."

"Oh, don't tell me. We're breaking up again. Sorry, that's what I remember the last time you said those words."

"Seriously, Max, focus. It's about a specific crystal you mentioned."

"I already told you all I know about the things."

"Max, I found two of them."

"Ty, chances are you didn't. These things are powerful, not to mention rare. There are only thirteen in the entire universe. You're not likely to find them so easily. They're hidden in some dangerous and well-guarded places." Max sat in his chair and turned to his desk. Tyra opened her hand in front of him. Max stared at the glowing crystals.

"Like the UPA base?"

"Where did you find them?"

"The one room no one but two people have ever been in. Well, now it's three."

Max crawled under his bed and picked up his other two crystals and showed them to her. He picked up the blue crystal from Tyra, and the glimmer started to fade.

"What happened to it?"

"Max, I haven't the slightest idea what this is."

"Where did you get these again?"

"It's a long story."

"Summarize it. Summarize the half hour it took to find some of the most powerful crystals in the universe."

"Well, on my way back to my room, I met up with Kevin. I think I befriended him. He's a lot gentler than people think he is. Anyway, I went into his room and…"

"And?" Max asked impatiently. "Ty, please tell me you didn't."

"No! Of course I didn't. Anyway, why would it matter to you?"

"Just keep going with the story."

"He told me how his ancestors were the experimenters from the history books. When I looked over at this box he had, I was drawn to it. So I found them, and he gave them to me."

"Did he know what they were?"

"He described rocks that sounded an awful lot like what you told me but didn't seem to know that these might be them."

"Well, let's keep it that way. If these glow brightly with specific people, then I'd better take that blue one. You take the red one, just in case."

"What about the other two?"

"I'll give Genesis the yellow one and Zack the clear one."

"Do you think it's safe to give your sister one? You may have to tell her about your brother."

"I'll just say I need her to take care of this for me. She won't ask why."

"I think you should talk to Kevin yourself."

"Doesn't he hate me?"

"He might, but when I was connecting with him..."

"What?"

She took a moment and just looked at Max. "He reminded me a lot of you."

Xaldoruks stood in the middle of the arena with the queen in one hand and his Blade in the other. Zamx circled around impatiently, waiting to fight. The queen struggled to stay strong as the wounds to her body started to ache.

"Where the hell are they?" Zamx yelled.

"I did give them twelve hours to decide to come."

"This is ridiculous; you messed up this time! They're not going to come. I mean, what's stopping them from just blowing up the arena while we're here?"

"Garacolon. He's too traditional to even think about blowing up this arena. Even if they wanted to, we still have their queen. They want to minimize damage to her as much as possible. That's how I know they'll come. They'll meet my demands whether they want to or not."

Suddenly they looked up and saw people trickling into the stands. They continued to come in from all sides until the stadium was completely filled with the screams of the Vacalonian people. From the other side of the arena emerged the king and his son. The two observed the queen in the hands of this madman with huge cuts and bruises all over her body.

"What the hell? We came here four hours earlier than you requested. What the hell is this? You said you wouldn't hurt her."

"I absolutely said no such thing," Xaldoruks said, scoffing. "I said that I'd give you twelve hours, and for every hour I'm waiting, I'll cut her. I've been waiting for eight hours—therefore, eight wounds. As for the rest…I got bored. Did you not hear me say I was going to destroy her?"

"You fiend."

"Oh, you're too kind. Zamx, hold this." He threw the queen to him, yanking her hair. He turned to the screaming crowd. He raised his hand in the air and sharply brought it down and the crowd was silenced.

"Ladies and gentlemen of Vacalon. My name is Xaldoruks. I am leader of the Negative army, destroyer of races, invincible by birth…I have come for your world. To my left is my apprentice, Zamx. In his hands is your queen." He turned to them. "Get rid of her." From Zamx's shadow a dark portal emerged and swallowed the queen whole.

"What have you done to her?" yelled the king.

"Your queen is in another castle for now," Xaldoruks said with a slight smirk. "You'll get her back if you win this fight. Now the stage has been preset. No outside help for either side is allowed. If someone does interfere, whomever it was that they were trying to help is automatically killed and so is the helper. Are the rules understood?"

The two men nodded.

"Good. Now, here's what's going to happen: first, the young ones will fight each other."

The king nodded, and his son marched into the center. Zamx scoffed.

"Seriously?" the boy said. "This is supposed to be my training exercise?"

"Make sure you finish this quickly," Xaldoruks commanded.

"I have a fight I would like to get to."

"I only promise to try," Zamx said, bowing his head. He walked over to meet his opponent. The crowd started to chant something softly in the native language. The son looked at Zamx, obviously welling up with much anger. Zamx kept shaking his head and looking back at Xaldoruks, wondering if he was actually serious about this. The chanting got louder. Everyone's eyes were on the referee sitting on the sidelines. His arm went up and the chanting ceased. Everyone held his or her breath, waiting for the final movement.

The referee lowered his hand, and the fight began.

In the blink of an eye, Karolon rushed past Zamx and crashed right into the wall. Zamx rolled his eyes. As Karolon pulled himself away from the wall, he summoned his Blade and charged at Zamx. Zamx, however, put his hands in his pockets and kept dodging the hate-filled swings. He then started teasing the boy.

"Geez, you clearly don't know how to use anger. What kind of warrior doesn't know how to use his own anger? They must have gotten you right out of your crib. Seriously, this is a joke. I mean, fiercest race in the universe? I've had craps that scared me more than you do."

With each jeer, Karolon only grew angrier and more reckless. Zamx easily found an opening and kicked him in the groin. As the son cringed in pain, Zamx turned to the audience and presented himself to them as they all booed him.

"Zamx!" Xaldoruks yelled at him. The Negative cringed and turned to Karolon. He realized he was enjoying himself too much. He turned around and saw his opponent tower over him with his Blade already on a descending arc toward him. He hit the ground so hard it cracked, throwing debris into the air. The air cleared, and Zamx had disappeared. Zamx then came rushing at him, and Karolon met him at a cross-Blade.

"Let me let you in on a little secret, buddy," Zamx whispered. Karolon felt a piercing pain through his chest. He looked down and saw a dark Blade going though his chest. He looked behind him and saw Zamx holding the Blade. He felt another piercing pain through his leg. Then, Karolon's own shadow had risen from the dirt to stab him in the back. One after another the Blade's shadow continued to strike his body. He was brought to his knees, coughing up blood.

Zamx backed away from him a bit. "Well, enough of the posers. Will the real Blade please stand up?" Karolon looked at his father and saw him standing still at the sight of his son about to be defeated. The Blade sliced the son's head off with ease. The head rolled off in front of the king, and the body collapsed. Zamx said nothing and walked back to his master's side.

The king stared at it, feeling so much rage spinning in his heart. He looked up to Xaldoruks and saw him drawing his Blade. The king marched to his opponent and forcefully tapped his sword out of the way.

"You massacre my people. You belittle my family and made us look like a joke. You have mocked me for the last time, Dark Lord. You will die at my hands."

"You always were all talk, Garacolon. You never could deliver."

With a mighty roar, the king swung at the devil. Xaldoruks dodged each vengeful swing. He laughed and scoffed as he glided away from his enemy's attacks.

"This is laughable. You expect to defeat me going on like this? You play like you're this king to which the planets should cower when you yourself have no power at all. You rule worlds by just the mention of your name. People say they have other loyalties, but their true allegiance is to you. You are the main power that really pulls the strings in this universe. You do this all out of people's fear of your whims. You cannot say you don't know the definition of fear. You use it religiously to control your people. Shall I take that away from you? Shall I show them your true colors?"

Xaldoruks materialized another Blade from the original, caught the king's Blade with them, and shattered the Blade into pieces. The pieces remained suspended in the air as the king fell to the ground with his eyes wide. Suddenly all of the fragments pointed and launched at him, leaving him with thousands upon thousands of tiny cuts and scrapes. His whole body screamed in pain. The king's authority had been taken from him. The man kept inching away from Xaldoruks, who kept approaching with his two Blades. Xaldoruks took a step forward, and the king stopped with tears running down his face, mixing with the cuts on his body.

"Kiss my boot." The king crawled over to him and kissed it, begging for his life. Xaldoruks kicked him off and addressed the crowd. "This is your king, ladies and gentlemen. This is the man who rules over you with a fist of steel. Look at him now. How far he has come, groveling at my feet. This is the man none of you could conquer. This is the man who has threatened countless planets, killed millions, and destroyed worlds...kissing my boot." He stabbed the king's head and pushed it aside. Darkness emerged from under his feet and spread quickly throughout the stadium. The crowds screamed in terror.

"Sh, sh, sh!" Xaldoruks whispered as the crowds fled. "Just let it happen. It'll all be over soon."

The next morning, Max went to the library to get information on the Orchaic Crystals. He searched all over the history section of the library, but was unable to find the books he was looking for.

"Run artificial intelligence program Lib-Seeker," he said.

A small computer-generated woman appeared in front of him.

"Hello, Chaos Flame Sandshark."

"Nice to see you again, Seek."

"I haven't detected your presence in the library for a long time."

"Oh, you know me. I've been busy."

"How may I serve you, Chaos Flame?"

"I need you to find all reference files on the Orchaic Crystals."

The program took a moment and then reappeared. "Apologies, but the references you seek have been corrupted"

"Corrupted? What do you mean? All of them?"

"Rebooting search procedure...Apologies, but the references you seek have been corrupted."

"What about 'Orchaic'?"

"All data relating to the term 'Orchaic' seem to be corrupted to the point that retrieval would be futile."

Max sighed and sat in a chair, feeling frustrated. He remembered what Cody said about the crystals being the thirteen elements of the universe and how God and Lucifer fought over them during the beginning of the universe. Max then got an idea.

"Lib-Seeker, find me the revised Genesis story."

A grid appeared over the aisle and targeted the file. Max

picked it up and read it.

The whims of mortals ran rampant and uncontrolled, breeding ignorance into existence. God said "Let there be knowledge and intelligence sown into this space and may peace be brought to all." And so it happened, the world was filled with God's gift. Then the mortals fought over higher matters instead of untempered quarrels. The powers of Chaos flourished in an endless cycle of destruction.

God then descended from the heavens and said "There can be no Chaos without Order, and no Order without Chaos. This realm is not prepared for the grace that they can offer. Let there be thirteen stones with all the power and strength of the elements, each with a portion of Chaos and Order to lock these powers away. No one may wield such power but I. The power of Orchaos is mine alone to control. As God set them to his side, he ascended back to the heavens with the power of Orchaos.

God sent His thirteen children to guard the thirteen stones: Jesu was given Hilgyt, Mar was given Yetranu, Joph was given Itaxerrin, Mak was given Ennoxrif, Lu was given Nixsoc, Jea was given Chypscyr, Mateo was given Potexlam, Michel was given Prazks, Abham was given Ralnacx, Mosea was given Qazua, Elibe was given Nelcoczy, Gabriel was given Ezpacs, and His oldest child Lucifer was given Sendrakxs. Each of the angels were thankful that God had entrusted them with such responsibility. God then said, "I trust you with these treasures. You are to guard them, protect them… but do not ever use them." All of His children respected His wishes. All except Lucifer. Lucifer was mesmerized with the power Sendrakxs. He fell victim to this darkness. His brothers and sisters, upon learning of his disobedience, rejected him and called him 'Xaldoruks', the celestial word for "Dark Soul".

God had continued creating the Universe. Lucifer observed that even though his father had temporarily controlled Chaos, He still had trouble containing it. He saw it was the only kind of power God had not been able to defeat. He lusted after the power for himself, the power to defy God.

God had begun creating Earth, His perfect planet. For this He required the power of the Orchaic stones He had given His children be returned to Him. Each angel, even Lucifer, obeyed their Father and returned the stones. Each day He used the stones to create this new world. When God rested on the seventh day, Lucifer saw that the stones were unguarded. As he reached to grab them, God awoke and struck his hand away. Lucifer rose with darkness in his heart and defied his father, attacking Him. He finally obtained the stones during the fight and continued to strike his Father. God quickly forced them into a pocket of time, as he tried to protect the universe he created. The conflict bounced throughout time as Lucifer kept fighting back. Fortunately, God's power was far greater than His son's. As He struck His son, the stones were scattered all across the corners of the universe. God spoke, "My son, my oldest son. You have defied me. You have betrayed me and tried to destroy me. You have committed the ultimate act of treason. You will be banished from this realm and never shall you return." With another strike, God banished Lucifer from His realm sending him hurtling towards the Earth. His fall destroyed the large amounts of life on the planet causing many large species to suddenly become extinct.

Now among the land of the mortal, Lucifer prowled the ends of the Earth and lived for eons of years among God's creatures. As he lured them with his temptations, he gained more power. In his following, he attracted all manner of vicious and fearful creatures to him. Slowly he was contaminating the perfect land God had intended to be Paradise.

After eons of living on earth, he one day approached the garden named Eden, and found two creatures, a man and a woman, of similar likeness to his original form. They were just instructed by God to enjoy the fruits of the garden but not to touch one tree. The two agreed and went about their ways.

Lucifer went to the woman in the form of a snake and tempted her with the fruit of the forbidden tree. "There is incredible power in these trees," he said to her. "One can know all the wonders of this universe as God does. He wants you to remain weak by only giving you Order. Chaos he keeps for himself so you will never deny him. Learn to live by yourself. Learn the power of Chaos." When she trusted Lucifer, she bit into the apple. Her purity was lost and her knowledge of the universe expanded. She shared this with the man, both robbed of the balance inside them. God came to them and saw what had occurred. When they blamed the snake for their disobedience, God restored it to it's original form revealing Lucifer.

"My son," he said unto him. "You have disobeyed me for the last time. Must I now take that which is most precious to you?" With one word, God had taken Lucifer's power. He was then only able to walk the Earth for all eternity.

The seething dark angel scoured the earth. For all of time, he was forced to watch his Father's creations go forth and multiply. His desire to go home became an obsession. He cast himself apart, yearning for a way to escape his prison. While he studied, he discovered the Orchaic crystals could restore the power lost to him. He despaired when he discovered, too, there was no way to travel the cosmos yet to obtain them. He waited for humanity to take to the stars. Soon enough, humanity had forsaken their Earthly home, and sought refuge on another planet. Traveling with them, Lucifer was able to return to space, closer to redemption and his Orchaic Crystals.

The human race settled on a planet Zapheraizia. As their technologies evolved, Lucifer soon was able to travel the stars and search for them himself. On the many days and months the journey took, he successfully found all thirteen of the crystals. He returned to Zapheraizia, at Final Destination Tower, where he enacted his plan to return home, the Celestial Realm. He summoned all manner of dark demons and vicious creatures to terrorize the planet.

A heavenly light opened in the sky. Once again, God had emerged. Outraged at the incessant disobedience of his banished son, God spoke no words to him. He only struck him down repeatedly. However, Lucifer fought back. The two deities fought across the universe. Once again. Like before, he was no match of the might of God. God took the stones and scattered them again. He bound Lucifer in his own darkness in the core of the planet. With that final act of God, Lucifer and his plagues were never seen again…

"Is this the only file on the story now?"

"Affirmative. All other references on this topic are corrupted."

"My guess is this file was out of the library when the data was corrupted. But this is the UPA official library. How can so much data just be corrupted like that?"

"Cause: Unknown. Library security system working at one hundred percent capacity."

"Whoever or whatever corrupted this data probably wouldn't want this file to still be accessible. Can you delete my search history?"

"Apologies. Cannot perform your directive at your current rank."

"Enter code 723, Delta, Sigma, NALUD."

"Code recognized. Primary directive confirmed. Search history for the past twenty minutes has been deleted."

Max began to leave but paused and walked back.

"You wouldn't happen to know where Kevin is, would you?"

Kevin sat at the top of the base looking out at the city whirling around him. The wind blew through his body. Max opened the door and approached him.

"Kevin?"

He opened his eyes but didn't turn back to him. "Max," he said. "I figured it was only a matter of time before you visited me."

"What makes you say that?" Max kept thinking about what Tyra had said, warning him not to mention it.

"Okay, seriously, dude, if you're going to hide information from me, at least have the decency to not scream it in your head."

Max was stunned. "You can hear my thoughts?"

"Not so sure now. You may have blown my eardrums out. Learn to quiet your mind. Otherwise you'll reveal all your many secrets."

"Stop it, Kevin."

"So many thoughts."

"Stay out of my head."

"The things you're most ashamed of…"

"*Get out!*"

Kevin turned around and walked toward Max. "You don't want the war to end either, do you? You enjoy the bloodshed."

"*No*," Max snapped. "The bloodshed needs to stop."

"Don't lie to yourself, Max. I know what's in your mind. You like your life right now. You're afraid that if the war ends, so does your lifestyle."

Max backed off and turned away. He took a breath and turned back around to Kevin. "I get to use the power I've been given to my full potential. My power isn't destructive here. I save people, entire countries—even entire planets. I don't want people to die. That's not it. But there's so much excitement in my life right now. I just don't want the fun to end."

"Well, I guess you don't need to worry about that. None of us are nearly important enough for the war to end in our lifetime."

"That's the other thing…I want to be the one to end it. Can you imagine being the one to end the multimillennial war? My name would be immortalized in history for sure."

"So that's it? Fame? That's your motivation?"

"Yeah, I guess. Why?"

"No reason. I just never thought you cared about it so much."

"Well, fair enough. It's more than that, I guess. I mean there are other reasons."

"You don't have to explain anything to me, Max. I, of all people, am not going to judge anyone, if that's what you fear."

"What about you? Why do you not want it to end?"

"Well, it's…never mind."

"No, tell me. What is it?"

"Well…It's to avenge my father."

"What happened to him?"

Kevin paused. He sat down on a nearby pillar. He took a small bag of a mashed powder-like substance. He poured it into a small napkin from his pocket, rolled it up, and stuck it in his mouth. Max sat with him, lit his thumb, and lit the end of the napkin. Purple smoke started to come out of Kevin's breath. Max coughed but stayed on the smoke-filled roof.

"When I was a kid, I had a…uh…difficult time making friends. My father was a very skilled alchemist. He had such a knowledge of minerals and substances. All he needed to do was snap his fingers and one thing would turn into another – well, not literally- but he even had a private study of all his top-secret materials. I ended up being in one of his experiments, but it's not what you think. I volunteered so Dad could keep his job, and I was successful. My natural powers were amplified, but it didn't last long. I was called a lab rat, and it angered my father more than anyone. He despaired because he didn't want me to be lowered to the level of a test subject. Anyway, a few years later, one of Dad's alchemic reactions didn't work, and instead of his telekinetic power growing rapidly, he grew more curious about the world. He had seen something that made him think he could unlock it. He wanted to know everything and wanted to know it all at once. Some people would call it insanity, and maybe they're right, but my father was *not* a mad scientist. People started looking at me differently because of what my father did, and in time I started to resent him and his damn experiments. My mother was so worried about him. He became aloof and lost touch with reality. His condition got so bad that he tried to experiment on her. When that happened, she packed our stuff, and me, and left him.

"As we were leaving, I looked at him, and the man I adored seemed no more. A few weeks later, Dad was all over the news, and he was experimenting—or what the news said—attacking everyone. The local authorities came and shot him on live TV. During the investigation they came to the conclusion that his condition had gotten worse due to loneliness. And that haunted me 'cause that means that it was my fault. He died because I wasn't there. I killed my father. My mother told me never to be like him, and I promised I

144

wouldn't." He stood up. "This is something Tyra does not know. I'd appreciate it if you didn't tell her this story."

He reached into his pocket and pulled out a vial with blue liquid inside it.

"What is that?" Max asked.

"This is one of the many secrets my dad never released to the general public or to the government. I don't intend to, either. He found out that it increases the mind's abilities and potential so it can help enhance their power. It allows mental access to the power cells in the body and increases their reproduction rate, allowing you to use more of your natural-born ability."

Kevin extended his arm to him.

"Dude, why are you giving this to me?"

"There's something else I saw in your mind. You have a ravenous and frighteningly unquenchable thirst for power."

"What? No I don't?"

"Whatever you say; I'm not the one you're lying to."

Max looked away from him.

"Look, I'm trusting you with this. You don't have to use it. But keep it safe."

"Why me?"

"Well, looking at the history of my family's research and involvement, your family has assisted mine on multiple occasions."

"What do you mean?"

"Well, when my father was taken away, apparently someone by the name of Codysseus Blaze helped keep this vial a secret."

Max clenched his fist and took the vial.

"I take it you didn't know that?"

Max forced a smile. "No, I didn't know that. There are a lot of things about my family that I don't know that apparently everyone else does." He stood up and looked over the edge of the roof. "It's about time I got some answers. And I think I know exactly who can give them to me."

7 GIFTS FROM THE PAST

The wind blew violently. The cold knocked on every door in the city. Nature's own blockade barricaded every house, and the skies were severely blinded with hail, rain, and snow impaling every poor soul stuck in this Zapheraizian blizzard.

Max stayed inside his room, looking out the window. He put his hand on it and jolted back from the cold as it quickly ran through his body. He walked over to his thermostat and turned it from 148 degrees to 180 degrees Fahrenheit. He put his hands on the heater and took in the heat. He went back to the window. In the distance, he saw, just barely, a light that quickly descended into the darkness.

Zack had his things packed in suitcases that were being loaded onto their shuttle. He sat in the hangar waiting for his friends as everyone else was talking to each other about their families like little children.

Max walked out into the hangar with his suitcase in hand and a burgundy sweater on. He had on winter boots and a scarf around his neck as if he were already outside in the snow.

"Max," Zack said as he walked up to him. "It's literally ninety-eight degrees in here. You don't need all those layers, man."

"You know I can't help it. As long as it's cold outside, everywhere I go I will feel like I'm freezing. I've never been able to take it like you can, Tyra." Tyra walked up behind Zack wearing a short skirt and a tank top.

"Well, I don't know about you, but it's anything but cold in here."

"Well, it sure isn't warm."

"I don't get it," Zack interjected. "Year round you are okay; when it comes to warmth, you're just like everyone else, but come winter and *bam*! Everything is cold to you. Your sister does the same type of crap, too."

Max threw his suitcase on the stack being loaded and went into the shuttle.

"So, who's house are we heading to this year?"

"We're going to Zack's, since it's bigger," Tyra said. "We're going to try to have both my family and Zack's family over."

"Fair warning, bro—we may have to sleep in our bunk beds again," Zack said.

Max smiled. "I don't care too much where it happens, just as long as I get to spend my birthday with my friends. And besides, I'm glad that all of the parents will be there. There is definitely something I want to talk to them about."

"What is it?" Zack asked.

Max looked at Zack. Suddenly he knew exactly what it was and began to worry. "Come on. Do you have to bring this up now?"

"If not now, then I never will get the chance."

The ship was loaded. Max, Zack, and Tyra all sat with Genesis on the shuttle. The hangar window opened, and the blizzard came rushing in. The shuttle shot out into the blinding snowstorm and passed over all the major corners of the city. It had been a long time since Max and his friends had seen it, given how busy they had been with their war. It seemed like a completely new place to them. The snow covered all the buildings while the vehicles flew above them, lighting the sky like stars. The trip seemed long, and with each passing moment, both Max and Genesis shivered in their coats. The storm just kept pelting the glass as if it were trying to get them.

The ship made its rounds around the city, dropping off operatives at their homes to celebrate the holidays. Finally, the shuttle reached Zack's house. Each person's suitcase came out from the floor. Max paused before leaving the shuttle, afraid to touch the snow. He looked up and saw Tyra in front of him, reaching out for him. Max smiled, grabbed her hand and set foot on the snow, watching it melt under his feet. He finally got into the house and was greeted by Mrs. Roark.

"Oh, Max," she shouted with great joy. Max turned to her,

and the smile disappeared from his face. "I haven't seen you in such a long time. How've you been?" she said, cradling him in her arms. She gave him a hug. Suddenly, she felt her body temperature drop quickly.

"Max, sweetie, you're taking my heat."

He jolted back. "Oh, jeez, I'm sorry! I'm just cold, you know."

"Oh, you poor baby! Here, let's get you to the fire."

Mrs. Roark led the group into the warm living room with a blazing campfire burning in the middle. The rest of the Roark and Smith families sat in the living room with snacks and wine on the table. Tyra ran to her parents and gave them a huge hug. She turned to the girl next to them and gave her a cold look.

"What is she doing here?" Tyra asked. "I thought you wanted this to be fun."

"So glad to see you again, sis," the girl said.

"Andrea, I don't feel like busting into your emo train wreck right now."

"Yet you obviously felt the need to take it from me."

"Well, guess who wore it better." Tyra walked away, and Andrea turned her head.

The rest of the group poured in and greeted their parents. Tyra embraced her parents while Max joined Zack in embracing his. Zack looked up and heard two familiar voices.

"Arthur? Tyler?"

The two emerged from their room and walked out to the balcony upstairs.

"Hey!" the two yelled. Zack ran to them and jumped at them. They both gave him a noogie.

"I thought you were stuck in the Infinity Circuit Systems."

"We were," replied Arthur.

"But we came," added Tyler.

"We saw."

"And we conquered!"

"I see you two still have a joint brain," Genesis called out.

"Oh, come on upstairs, Gen. We got a machine we've been working on, and we need someone to praise us for it."

Genesis giggled and ran upstairs with the boys to their room.

Max saw her as the door closed. As soon as she was gone, he

made his way to Zack's father.

"Max," the older man said with a firm handshake. "Working at the UPA at the rank you are and to be so accomplished at your age—well, let's just say it's no surprise. I'm really proud of you, son."

Max stared back at him, trying to keep a polite smile. "Why would you say that it's no surprise?"

Mr. Roark smiled. "Well…it's in your blood."

"I'm glad you bring up blood. I've just been wondering lately: is it possible that there is someone other than Gen and me we should probably know about?"

Mr. Roark was silent for a second. "Well, not that anyone knows of. All that information would be in the data file."

"Which conveniently is unavailable."

"I don't care for your tone, Max. What are you saying?"

"I'm just saying it's very odd that it just disappeared like that."

"Max, this is completely unfounded. You're smarter than this. You are much smarter than to believe I took your family's data file. We don't have it."

"Oh, I know you don't. I do. Yeah, I found it on another planet quite a distance from here. When I got back, I looked through the thing and found something I probably should've known for a long time now."

Mr. Roark wiped his brow. "Max, you would've been better off if you hadn't discovered Cody existed at all."

Hearing him mention Cody's name quickly riled up Max.

"You didn't have the authority to do that at all!" Max yelled.

"If you lived in my house and were under my protection, then yes, I did!"

"Why didn't you tell me I had a brother?"

"You've never met him. You don't know what he's like! We needed to keep him as far from you as possible."

"But I have! I used the data file to find him. And I met him."

"Tell me. Did he seem like the proper role model for a child?"

Max paused for a second. "Don't try to justify it! All this time I've been under the impression it was just my sister and me left. But it's not even like I didn't ask you! You constantly and deliberately lied to us!"

"What would you have done if you had this knowledge? Maybe fantasize? Constantly think about him until you ran away, too."

"So instead you kept lying to a child! So much so that you erased not just mine but all of our memories of him."

"Max, it's about time you grew up and realized that parents lie to their kids all the time. Did you know Santa Claus and the Easter Bunny aren't real, either?"

"So how exactly did it go down?"

"What?"

"How did he run away? Did you even try to stop him, or did you leave the front door unlocked and wide open?"

"How dare you even think that?"

"What? You kept him a secret for so long. Is it ludicrous to think that you didn't care or even want him? You're lucky Genesis doesn't know. Otherwise you'd have both of us infuriated."

There was a moment of silence. The both looked up and saw everyone staring at them. They looked up at the balcony and saw Genesis standing there. Max started to run to her, but she ran back and slammed the door to her room. Max looked back at Mr. Roark.

"I think it's time for the kids to go upstairs until dinner is ready," Mr. Roark said.

Max backed up, grabbing his bags, and walked up the stairs to his old room. The rest of the gang followed. From the upstairs balcony, Max gave Mr. Roark a cold stare.

"You know, there's something you have to realize," Max said back. "We're not kids anymore."

Max and Zack were on their bunk beds. Max was lying on the top bunk looking through the sky window above the room. He stared up into the night sky, as if he were looking for something. Zack just sat on the bottom bunk with his legs resting on his suitcase.

"Hey, Max," Zack called. "What *did* Cody say to you—about how he left, that is?"

Max thought back for a moment. "He said he was keeping a promise. He wouldn't tell me to whom, just that it was something he swore to do. He told me he left when he was thirteen, that he asked to leave, and our parents just let him go without a fight."

"I see. But they seemed pretty eager to get us out of there, don't you think?"

"Oh definitely; they're probably getting their stories straight about Codysseus." Max jumped down from his bunk and started pacing across the room. Zack looked up at him.

"What's up, dude?"

"It's Genesis." Max sighed. "Something isn't right with her."

"I told you. Keeping this a secret from her would only backfire on you!"

"Oh, shut up!"

"Hey, don't take your stupidity out on me!"

Max sat on his chair and sighed again. "She's never going to forgive me, is she? Won't even listen to me."

"Why do you say that?"

"She'll go into her silent treatment mode."

"Go apologize. It can't hurt."

"On the contrary it may do just that. She may think it's pompous and arrogant and go all 'how dare you say that to me' on us."

"'Us'? No. You. Not us." Max paused for a moment, then walked out of the room. He went over to Genesis's door and knocked hesitantly.

"Genesis?" he called out. "It's me. Let me in. I want to explain. Can we do this without a door in between us? Please?" He didn't get a reply. "Genesis?" Max waited for a bit and then slowly headed back toward his room. He heard the door to Genesis's room open. Max walked over as she stood by the door.

"Look Genesis. I want to apologize. Okay?"

"What the hell were you thinking? Did you just hope that I wouldn't find out?"

"I was going to tell you at the right time. I just wanted to protect you for now. But our 'parents' weren't going to tell us at all! They're the ones you should really be mad at."

"You know what? Maybe. But the one I put all of my trust in, the one I tell everything, the only one who I thought I could take on the world with, lied to me. Tell me: which do you think is the more unforgivable sin?"

"You can still trust me. I thought I had hope when I found out we had a brother. But when I met him he wasn't exactly trustworthy, and I just didn't want you to have your trust destroyed, too. I was just trying to protect you."

"You know, I'm not as mad at our parents for not telling me as I am at you for doing the exact same thing and trying to bust them for it. Not to mention the fact that you met him and didn't bring me. Don't you see it, Max? You're the world's biggest hypocrite! Our parents kept him a secret from us so that we wouldn't get hurt trying to find him or find out about his abandoning us, but you did the exact same thing trying to keep me from him, too! You don't have a right to baby me, Max! You may be my older brother, but you are not some watchdog for me! It was fun having you around to protect me for a while, but guess what? I've outgrown it."

The two stared each other down. Max stepped back a bit and exhaled, not knowing how to continue.

"Genesis. I will do anything for you to trust me again. I truly am sorry!"

She paused for a moment to see if he was truthful. "There is only one thing I want."

"Anything."

"Give me the data file."

Max stayed silent. He looked down and saw Genesis's hand ready to receive it. The longer it lingered, the worse Max felt. He looked up at her and slowly shook his head, backing away.

"You can't even give me that. Wow. See, this shows me that you are just all words. Who else are you hiding from me?"

"Genesis, you and I know damn well what you're really going to do with it if I give it to you, and I cannot let that happen."

"Just give it to me."

"No."

"You want me to trust you, don't you?"

"Yes, but not like this."

"How can I trust you if you can't trust me?"

"Because you're immature, impulsive, and can't handle anything on your own!" Max yelled.

Genesis's eyes inflated and her body exploded with anger.

"Get out!" she yelled, repeatedly pushing him out. She slammed the door behind him and started sobbing. Max turned around and banged on the door trying to get back in.

"Genesis! I'm sorry. I didn't mean to say that! Please!" Max stayed quiet for a second. From the other side of the door, he could hear faint sounds of sobbing. He lightly hit his head on the wall.

The next morning the sun was out, the snow was glistening, and everyone was outside. They frolicked in the snow, enjoying it like small children again.

Max stood at the sliding door watching his friends play. He took his hot chocolate from the table he was leaning on and sipped it. Zack showed up next to him with his own cup of chocolate.

"How'd it go?" he asked.

"Well, it went not great at all."

"What? What happened?"

"I tried, man. I tried explaining myself, and she called me a hypocrite."

"Which you are."

"But she did give me a chance to make it better."

"Then why didn't you take it?"

Max turned to Zack and looked him in the eye. "Zack, she asked for the data file."

"Did you give it to her?"

"Are you insane? No, I didn't give it to her."

"I don't see why not."

"If I were to give her the data file, she would use it to find Codysseus herself. Do you really want that girl to meet the man we barely got away from by herself?"

"Fine, fair enough. What else happened?"

"Well, I told her no. She kept insisting. I kept rejecting. Then—on my way out—I may have called her immature and inadequate."

"What the hell is wrong with you?"

"I don't know. I just snapped. I didn't even know I thought that, but...it was weird."

"Geez. Now I know what Tyra's talking about. You really are an idiot."

"I know. I just wish I could fix this, and that Gen knows that I'm on her side."

"Are you sure? Or are you hoping she's on yours?"

Max leaned back with his arms crossed. There was a pause between them. Zack got up and left to go outside. Max stood with his hot chocolate steaming in his face but not sipping it. Andrea came up to him and leaned on the table next to him.

"Why aren't you out there?" she asked.

Max turned to her. "Why aren't you?"

"I'm wearing black. White obviously isn't my color. Too much of it will make me sick."

Max chuckled.

"Your turn."

Max remained quiet, thinking to himself. She looked back at the snow and grabbed her hot chocolate. "That's a stupid reason," she said. Max turned to her with an eyebrow raised. "I can read minds," she said. "Yours reminds me a lot of his."

"By 'his,' you mean my brother's, right?"

She closed her eyes, smiled, and bit her lip. "Yes, I do mean Cody."

"How close were you to him?"

"Well, the twins and I were to Cody like Zack and Tyra are to you." She started to reminisce. "We were four of a kind. We all loved to hang around the neighborhood. The twins would play tricks on each other. Cody would play tricks on both of them, and I was the pacifist. They would always playfully get into fights and ask me to settle them. And once I showed that I sided with someone, that person would always start instigating. We were so happy together. And Cody...I really did love Cody. He was so cute and fun. But he always cared for his annoying little brother."

Max perked up after almost falling asleep. "Wait—what?"

"He loved you and that bratty sister of yours. I think even more than me. He was everything to me but always put me behind you. It got so bad I almost was driven to the point where I hated you so much for stealing my time with Cody. But later on, I was robbed of it by another thing, the UPA. Both the twins and Cody wanted to go, but that was just not what I wanted to do. So I saw him even less. He put himself in tons of danger, and when I saw him, I wanted him even more to stay and be with me. He kept talking about this guy called Luand, who kept stopping by even before they joined."

"Uncle Luand," Max said. "I remember him visiting. Wait—did he actually train under Luand?"

"Would you quit interrupting me?" she snapped. "Yes, he kept talking about how he received special training from Luand personally. Now I know why he was so happy. Anyway, Cody's happiness didn't last long. One night, six years after your parents died, I saw him packing up all of his clothes and tools. I stopped him. I asked 'Where are you going?' At that moment, I felt so much darkness in his thoughts. His eyes were yellow. His stare was so dark. He looked so...so...attractive. I begged him to take me with him, but he kept saying, 'No, I can't take you with me. I must walk this road by myself.' That he was keeping some promise to someone he really respected. I thought then he must not love me. He must be in love with someone else. After that, I heard a conflict with the parents, and that's a part you know now. Then I never saw him again."

"Funny," Max said. "He said the same thing to me about some promise he's keeping. But he didn't seem to be talking about another girl."

"Really? Well, I guess it doesn't matter now. He's probably galaxies away from wherever you met him."

Max was tempted to tell her how he found him, to show her that he wasn't completely lost, but held back, fearing that she might steal the file herself just to find him. She looked at Max and leaned back in, creeping toward his hand.

"You know something, Max?" she said, grabbing his right hand. "You look a lot like him." She leaned into him. Max pushed her away and stepped away from her.

"Yeah, funny thing about that," he said. "I'm not him. Besides, your sister..."

"My sister? Oh, please don't tell me you're still on this."

"Tyra's..."

"Only ever going to see you as a friend. A really close brother, if you will."

Max looked out at Tyra playing in the snow.

"Still...I know anything involving you would make her mad...It's a bit sensible to say angering her wouldn't be a wise career move, right?"

She crossed her arms and turned to the wall. He looked back at his arm.

"I'm determined to do whatever it takes to find the power to be stronger than my brother."

Andrea lifted herself from the table. "No matter how hard you try, you'll never match Cody's strength. He's like a machine— only gets better and better. If you feel like you're in his shadow even though he isn't in your life, it's because he's the best and he won't ever lose that title." She started to walk away, then suddenly turned back. "You should go outside. Your friends look like they're having a lot of fun."

"Andrea," Max said. "Since you're so skilled at reading minds, I'm sure you have the ability to manipulate things in them, correct?"

Her smile disappeared. "If I trained my skills, I suppose, yes."

"You could erase or change people's memories, couldn't you?"

"Yes, I could."

"Did you have something to do with my memories being erased?

She smiled, rolled her eyes. "Please, if I could do that, I would've messed with all three of your heads a lot more than I did." She walked out of the room, and Max looked back outside where his family and friends played. He looked back into his cup of chocolate and went back upstairs.

It was Christmas Eve. Everyone was excited. The whole group walked home at night from the church after celebrating the Christmas Vigil.

"Ugh!" Zack proclaimed, stomping through the snow. "I hate having to go to church before Christmas. It takes up my time to be excited about Christmas."

"Well, think of it this way, little brother," Tyler said.

"Now you don't have to go to mass *on* Christmas," Arthur finished.

"Oh, yeah," Zack said with a smile. "You know this year I'm going to kick your ass at the games."

"Don't get too excited, boys," Mrs. Roark said. "Tomorrow morning we're all going to early morning mass."

The three of them collectively groaned.

Max and Tyra followed behind them, chuckling. Suddenly, Max stopped in front of the graveyard next to the church. Tyra walked back to him and stared at what he was looking at. There were graves in the ground, but there were a bunch of hovering crosses above them that represented more people. The floating crosses were made of the remains of the individuals they honored.

Tyra shook Max's arm. "Max, what's wrong?"

He just kept staring.

"What's going on?" Zack asked.

Max remained quiet. Finally, he spoke. "Hey, you guys. Do you think I should visit them?"

"Who?" Tyra asked.

"My mom and dad?"

They both looked into the graveyard.

"You know what?" Zack said. "Now would be as good a time as any to find out."

The three of them looked around carefully at the vast ocean of graves. Eventually, they came upon an archway. Over the top there was a sign that read, Sea of Blaze. Max's anxiety began to build. He cautiously walked through the graveyard skimming each name, looking for two specific ones. He felt as though each grave was inspecting and evaluating him. The mere atmosphere of the graveyard intimidated him. Zack and Tyra kept looking as well on the upper levels. There was a Rockertus, a Royettebus, Cathelina, Benjourno, Boveria, and many more.

Tyra passed one of the gravestones and saw that it read, Venitorimus Blaze, Master of Orchaos.

"Hey, Max, do you know a…" She turned and saw him on his knees. She walked over to him but gave him space. She could barely make out what he was mumbling. Zack showed up soon after, yelling for Max. Tyra stopped him before he disturbed Max. She tried hard to listen to what he was saying.

"Hi, Mom. Hi, Dad. It's your baby boy, all grown up now. It's hard to believe that it's been almost eighteen years. I'm twenty now. Well, I just turned twenty yesterday so… I can't remember anything about you or most of my childhood…just some bits and pieces." Max kept wiping his eyes. "So…what is there to talk about? Oh, I joined the UPA. Following your footsteps, Dad. Had a lot of missions; some went well, some not so much. But I always learn from my mistakes…based on what I hear about you guys, I think that's something you would've been proud to hear. Oh, I met my brother for the first time. Yeah, he turned out great. Genesis is turning out okay. She's a bit mad at me right now, but it's nothing that can't be fixed later. You know…it's weird talking to you. Well, I say talking; I'm really just talking to a gravestone hologram. I don't know. Having a symbol of you guys right in front of me, it almost doesn't mean anything to me. You guys are stories. Just stories. That's all you've ever been. Well, I guess that's all we all are in the end. I guess what I'm saying is that this isn't enough. You guys just being here represented by a rock and a hologram, is just not…But I guess that's why I'm here. That's why Genesis is here. We're here to make you proud, to make your stories continue. I promise we won't let you down."

Max started to cry and shook his head. He sniffed his nose, picked himself up, and wiped the tears from his face.

"Okay, let's go!" Max said.

"You okay?" Tyra asked.

"Never better," Max said with a smile. "Now come on. Which way is home again?"

Christmas morning everyone got up and met downstairs. For a few hours they all agreed to forget their frustrations with each other and enjoy Christmas morning as a family—all except Genesis, who stayed locked in her room throughout the festivities. As the excitement died down and everyone veered off to enjoy their gifts, Genesis remained stationary. Zack went up to her room with a small box in hand.

"Genesis," Zack called out. "Gen? Come on. You've got to come out sometime. Come on, you missed Christmas morning. That's the best part of the trip!" There was no reply. Zack sighed and placed a box from his pocket at her door. "Fine, stay locked in there. I just wanted to make sure you at least got my gift for you. Merry Christmas." He started to walk away. The door then opened. He looked back and saw Genesis picking up the gift. As she went into her room, she left the door open. Zack smiled and walked back into the room, closing the door behind him.

"You going to open it?" Zack asked.

She unwrapped the box and saw a necklace in it with the most beautiful diamond that shimmered without direct light. Her jaw dropped. She was speechless in its glow. She looked back up at Zack, who was smiling.

"Zack," she said struggling for words. "This is…this is too much!"

Zack was already behind her, putting the necklace on. She looked in the mirror and smiled. She jumped at Zack with a big hug, thanking him.

"Feeling better?" Zack asked. She nodded. "Look...I don't think you should be mad at Max."

Her smile disappeared, and she stepped back. "Did Max tell you to do all this?"

"What? *No*! I promise! Max doesn't even know I'm here. He's too proud to ask me to do this. I'm just saying I don't think you should be mad at him." She rolled her eyes. "Look, I don't think he should be mad at my parents, either! Okay, yes, I get that you both deserve to know about your family, all of your family. But you also have to see it from their perspective. Both you and Max are powerfully driven by the things you find important, nothing more so than family. If they told you about Cody back then, you both would most likely have run away to find him, and then we'd lose you! Max kept it from you because he knows how important family is to you. Family is sticking by each other, caring and loving each other. Most importantly, family is helping each other when they need it. Cody...Cody was not family. I've met him; he wasn't the kind of guy you would want to meet or even consider family. Max didn't want your vision of family to be destroyed. He's never going to get over the fact that you're growing up and you're not as naïve as you were. It's a form of love, not cruelty."

"Well, Max needs to get over it. I'm done playing this child that everyone needs to care for!"

"You know, Gen...I can help you with that. I can help hone your training. I've been training with Max for a while. I know how I can..."

"Wouldn't that defeat the purpose of me being independent?"

"Don't confuse independence with not asking for help." He grabbed her hand. "You don't have to do this alone. We're here for you. Use us."

Genesis smiled and hugged him gently.

Max sat in front of the fireplace with a blanket Zack's mom had knitted for him around his shoulders. He stared into the flame as it stared back at him. Tyra was passing by and spotted him. She walked over and started petting his head.

"See anything good in there?" she teased.

"Hey, Ty," Max said, smiling.

"Why do you like staring into fire all the time?"

"I don't know. It's just...when I look into it, I can find a soothing rhythm in how it burns. It calms me, helps me find some kind of peace. Helps me forget whatever is bothering me."

"So, something's up. Do you want to talk?"

"Wasn't that what we're doing? Talking?"

"No, not what I mean."

"Hey, have you stayed in your pajamas this whole time?"

"Max, stop trying to change the subject."

Max twisted his face and sighed. "Tyra, there's nothing to talk about."

"Oh, okay. I guess I'll go then." She got up, ready to leave.

"Wait..." He said, calling her back. "Seriously? You're going to 'ultimatum' me like this again?"

"Until it stops working, yes."

Max smiled and laughed a little bit. "Fine, you win. But don't get too confident; it's just because I like your company, okay?"

"Whatever helps you go to sleep at night," she said, joking. Max kept smiling as she looked at him. "So what's up?"

Max's smile disappeared. "Genesis wasn't here for Christmas...at all. How mad do you have to be at someone to miss one of the best parts of the Christmas season? Sure, you got presents and all that, but come on. Even I put my anger aside for the day. She's always loved family time and now..."

"Max, she just needs to blow off some steam. She's never mad at you forever."

"She's never mad at me at all! I don't know what to do? I've never screwed up this badly before."

"Well..."

"Excluding...you know..."

"Yeah. Max, you made a mistake; you're full of them. Trust me, you're a dumbass. But you two are as thick as thieves. In the end you'll always support each other."

"It's just...I really don't want her to be as distant as Cody. She's all I have left. If she's gone I truly have nothing."

Tyra grabbed his hand and looked at him reassuringly. "You have me."

The two stared at each other. Max grabbed her hand back

and smiled. A grin snuck onto her face, too. Both of their hearts started beating with more force and power. The fire felt warmer. Tyra placed her hand around his head as his arm caressed her waist. They came closer, and the tension became palatable. From a distance, Max could hear people talking. Though he was curious, he was too engulfed in this moment. Just as he was about to kiss her, he heard the words "...Codysseus a secret." He leaped from Tyra, who was left confused, and stepped behind the wall of the next room. Tyra walked up behind him.

"So that was a typical Max shutdown. I don't know why I even..."

Max covered her mouth as the voices in the other room became clearer.

"We left this topic a long time ago," Zack's father said.

"Well, we couldn't see this coming at all," his wife said, trying to comfort him.

"You keep saying that! This isn't going to happen, not in my house!"

"No. We agreed that if we tell him that we would tell him together."

"Darling, what's there to tell? He already knows what we did!"

"Yes, he does," Tyra's mom said softly. "But I read his mind. He doesn't know why." She turned to Andrea. "Andrea, dear, you saw it, too, didn't you?"

Andrea nodded quickly, not making eye contact with her.

"Well, the kid is SOL, because I'm not telling him why." Zack's father crossed his legs like a stubborn child, folded his arms in the chair, and pouted. Tyra's father stood up.

"Regis, look, don't be a juvenile about this. The kids know they have a brother. We might as well tell them what really happened—tell them the truth so that they won't hate us."

"You make this sound like it's so easy." He stood up from the chair and walked to the window in the kitchen above the sink. "Do you guys realize how much he looks like his father? From his nose, to his eyes, to even his hairstyle, it's almost like Max is Marcus. Marcus trusted me. He wanted me to make sure his kids were safe if he ever was gone. That's why I—no, we—took them in. I made him a promise beyond promises, and I couldn't stop Cody. And he left.

And now you're asking me to go to his only other son and say that I failed at the most important promise of my life? No...I'm sorry, but no."

"But it wasn't just you, Reg." Mrs. Smith came up. "None of us could stop him."

"It wasn't your fault alone. We were out of practice. We didn't know how to work together without Marcus and Sarah on our team." Mrs. Roark walked behind her husband. "But you fought the hardest of all of us. You tried to keep him here. Just...he trained and prepared for that day. We were caught way off guard."

He remained quiet.

"Regis, if you think it was your fault, don't. Okay?" his wife said, comforting him. "You have to let this go."

He turned to his wife. "Okay...Okay, we can tell him the truth," Regis said, wiping the tears away.

Andrea rolled her eyes and coughed. "So that's great. Glad you got your weird long-sought catharsis, but there's one other huge problem with telling the squirt: the fact that Luand told us not to! Are you forgetting that little detail? He made it a rule. We don't talk about Cody ever!"

"Andrea, honey, I'm sure it won't matter now. Max already knows about it."

"I'm sure, yeah, but I don't think you're aware of what this situation is psychologically doing to him."

"Oh, we are aware."

"Uh, no, I don't think so. Luand has looked at this 'group' for a long time. You guys may not have noticed, but I did. He manipulated each one of you like a chess piece, affecting your emotions and your actions from his great tower. All except me. He only needed me to erase Max's entire memory of Cody. After that I no longer served a purpose, but he definitely needed Cody and he definitely needed Max. Mom, you looked into his mind, but you didn't see everything. There was a lot of anger toward you, but in that anger there was a lot of untapped...something. I couldn't make it out so I don't know what it was, but it was scary. What if Luand wanted Max to feel this way for something? What if he forbade you from telling him because he has some big plan? I don't know. He was always invested in their family. Maybe he's planning something."

They all looked at each other for a moment. After a long

silence, they all reluctantly realized she was right.

"Okay," Regis agreed. "Fair enough. We'll leave it to Luand in his wisdom." He sat back down, and there was a moment of silence.

Max backed away and returned to the couch in front of the fireplace, completely flabbergasted. Tyra ran back to him.

"Max, are you okay? That was a lot you just heard."

"You know…all the time I'm being pushed around and jostled back and forth whenever I bring it up. I can never get a straight answer. Until now. This was Luand's entire plan. He's the one who has all the answers And he's going to give them to me!"

8 TRUTH

5023 FD. It was the New Year, and the shuttle had arrived to take the group back to base. As everyone said their good-byes, Max smiled and shook Regis's hand calmly. He entered the shuttle, and they flew off. Tyra sat next to Max as he stared in front of him, deep in thought. Concerned about Max's reaction to the news he had heard on Christmas, she kept trying to take his mind off it. Max was too lost in his thoughts to really notice.

Upon arrival at the base, Max went straight to his room. Finally, in a more familiar place than his childhood home had become, he lay down and tried to actually relax on his bed. Every time he closed his eyes, he became suddenly restless. Every thought running through his brain managed to lead to Cody. He needed his answers. He got up from his bed and bolted out of the room. Max kept zooming through the halls. Tyra caught him passing by and grabbed his arm.

"What are you doing?" he said, shocked back into reality.

"Max, I'm just worried about you. The news about Luand and your brother could mess with anyone's head. I just want to make sure that you're not going to do anything stupid."

"Ty, look, I'm fine. Yes, the initial reception of this info was pretty big, and it had a huge shock factor, but I'm okay. I can handle it. I'm not even going to see Luand, okay?"

"Promise me..."

"Easy. I promise I'm not going to see Luand today."

"No," she said. She took a step closer to him. "The ones we

used to make."

Max stared at her, feeling some force pushing him toward her. He turned and left her there alone.

In the Elite Sandshark Council room, Luand sat in his chair. His eyes closed as he floated around in the void with a light ring under him lighting the room. The other empty chairs floated around him. A wind blew into the room and revolved around a single chair. As the wind passed, it left behind Battlux sitting in his chair. He looked up at Luand.

"Master," he called out to him.

Luand's eyes remained closed.

"He's still in his pre-meeting state. This better be productive this time," said another voice. Then suddenly another Sandshark appeared out of nowhere. She flipped her hair and looked at Battlux with a roll of her eye.

"Reduya," he said in a mocking tone. "You're early today. What? Did the world seem to be slightly more significant than your hair?"

"Save it for the meeting, Batty. You don't want to get all of your 'useful commentary' out before we start, do you?"

Rocks formed in another chair at the end of the room. Another girl sat in a chair. Then another person appeared at another chair. One after the other, they all appeared in their chairs until all twelve were full. At that moment Luand opened his eyes. He looked around the room.

"Zeiliz, Tzocy, Iramint, Aenlan, Risare, Hopejs, Salelabi, Lagimil, Reduya, Mysame, Battlux, and myself. All twelve are here. Thus we begin the Sandsharks meeting." As he said this, the dark room lit itself, and stars started to appear in the room. The room seemed to move through space into a nebula surrounding a sun.

"So, what is the thrilling topic of discussion today? Pollution in the Fifth-X Nebula or taxes on the corrosions?" Iramint asked.

"Why do you talk?" snapped Aenlan. "Don't waste time."

He shrugged his shoulders. "I'm just trying to lighten the mood."

Zeiliz's chair moved up. "We need to keep discussing this war until we find a solution to this hell of a problem."

"You know, generations of Sandsharks have started meetings

the exact same way, and we haven't come up with anything. Everything we've tried has been tried centuries before and probably will be again centuries after," Hopejs said in despair.

"Yeah, I have to agree," Tzocy added. "Generations of Sandsharks have tried to find some sort of magical golden bullet for this war, and here we are eons later and it's in the same place. The likelihood of us being the generation to solve this is one in 490,323."

"You and your statistics, TZ," Reduya commented. "Always so inspiring."

"Well, your comments aren't exactly making our hearts leap with courage either," Risare said.

"Enough!" Luand spoke up. "You can talk about your little dramas later. Tzocy, you had a proposition to discuss."

Tzocy nodded. His chair moved forward a bit.

"Well, destroying bases isn't working. They only rebuild another one on another planet, and though they may terrorize the planet, it isn't stopping the problem. We're hitting the problem where it appears, not where it starts. So I propose that we move all our forces into searching for where the Negatives are getting their orders."

"Right," Aenlan scoffed. "Because the Negatives are so willing to tell us exactly where Xaldoruks is, that will be a piece of cake while other planets are destroyed by the Negatives."

"This could work. On Darod a few months ago, we managed to capture a Negative and study it. We've already confirmed that Negatives have some shred of their mortality left, especially the strong ones. They're able to adapt. If we put together a special team specifically to find ground zero, it can accompany every mission, study the Negatives further, and analyze the information after the mission is accomplished."

"Oh yeah, every mission is so successful that we wouldn't possibly need to worry that our *best* agents will be taken from other and more difficult missions for this supplemental role."

"Okay then, Aenlan, you got any better ideas?"

"I have another option to present to the council," Lagimil grunted. "Look for the areas that have the highest concentration of Negatives, send me there, and destroy the base."

"As much as we thoroughly enjoy your pride and arrogance, Lagimil, you don't have enough power to destroy the base, and that plan to find ground zero isn't credible enough since Negative energy can generate itself pretty quickly, making a number of places seem like ground zero," Hopejs said.

"Okay, but this isn't the dark ages. We have the technology to detect any slight anomalies. I'm sure every outbreak cannot be uniform."

"Yeah, and besides, why not let the guy tear something up?" Iramint teased. "The man is a freaking tank. If it weren't for Luand, Lagimil would be our secret weapon."

"You know very well why. What about that Chaos Flame kid?" Zeiliz asked, interrupting. "He seems to be pretty successful in his missions. Maybe he should lead another?"

"Yeah, 'cause we all know that he's Luand's little pet project," Iramint said, scoffing.

"Funny how all of us aren't allowed to have favorites, but top dog gets to play puppet master," Reduya said.

"Well, how good is he?" Hopejs asked.

"He's a few years behind his...brother, but still."

"You think he'll follow in his footsteps?"

Iramint crossed his arms. "I don't know about you, but I don't plan to associate with another thirteenth member of the council anytime soon."

"You know he'd know what to do to solve this, Ira," Mysame said. "We had the most productivity with him on our team. He had ideas no one would ever lay out!"

"Well, unfortunately he's not here, okay? He left us, and betrayed us, and if we ever see him, we need to shoot on sight! Understand?" Aenlan yelled. Everyone was quiet.

"So how are we going to end this war?" Salelabi inquired. Everyone in the room looked at each other. Battlux cleared his throat and moved to the center of the room.

"If I may, comrades, I agree with Tzocy that attacking the local bases is a strategy that is getting quite old and tiresome. It doesn't get us anywhere. Negative bases keep appearing on planets, some of which we have already cured. In order to prevent these bases from spawning again, I suggest we place the planets we control under tight security where everything is monitored. We need to make sure that any Negative activity is eliminated immediately. Furthermore, I suggest we put forth legislation that states to all other governments that if Negative forces invade their planet, the Universal Protection Agency has the right to come in and take formal charge of the situation, putting more planets under our safe control. If we stop the forces from spreading, we may close in on ground zero. As for Maximillion Blaze, despite his success in his assignments, I must say, regardless of popular bias, I do not trust him. His men don't always come back from his missions. He acts too much like his brother. He's too powerful for us to control. Eventually he will follow right in his footsteps. He's already broken many rules and gotten off scot-free. His arrogance is too great and makes him unpredictable."

"You're one to talk about being arrogant," Reduya commented.

"My point remains. I don't like how fast he's advancing. He became a Sandshark far sooner than average, not unlike another young prodigy we know."

"That's partially your fault, Battlux," Salelabi said, interrupting. "It was your plan that got more than half of the Elite Sandsharks we had killed, which forced us not only to look at colonels and generals to fill their space but anyone we could get. And you can't even blame them for passing, too. We decided to grade and accept them on a much smaller and easier test than the actual test. The fact that they passed is not surprising."

"Yes, but you saw the grades. Maximilian Blaze scored above the average for even the smartest colonels," Zeiliz retorted. "Had we given him the actual test, he would have still passed."

"But you are missing another important piece of information. He didn't win the exam; it was the other kid, Zactavious Roark, who became the *Elite* Sandshark. I don't see you worrying too much about him. If anything, he's closer to resembling Cody than Max."

"All I'm saying," Battlux said, chiming back in, "is that there is definitely a seed of darkness in him, and I don't want to bring him close to us so that we suffer another blow like Codysseus. We shouldn't be so quick to trust him."

"Just like we were so quick to trust you?" Aenlan countered. He looked at her, and she glared back. There was silence in the room for a moment.

Battlux continued. "Moving on, my last suggestion is a bit of a stretch. After we prevent the spread of Negative forces, we will eventually close in on ground zero; however, that may take a lot of time. I have reason to believe that ground zero resides along the outskirts of our galaxy. So to put an immediate end to this war, we need to take affirmative action. I've looked up the statistics, and the total population of the 360 degrees of outskirts in our galaxy is about one three-hundredth of the population of this city alone. The fact that there is so little presence there and that it is so isolated means that it would be the perfect place for ground zero. So we should place subspace bombs and plant them around the galaxy and…"

"Stop, Battlux!" Luand roared.

Battlux stopped midsentence. His chair retreated from the center of the ring as Luand circled around the room. He looked at Battlux. "I will not take a chance and endanger that population."

"Yes, but sir, it's only a small number of people who would d—"

"Enough!" Luand shouted. "I will not attack my own people with a subspace bomb, Battlux."

"Wait," Mysame said, tuning in again. "I missed that briefing. What's a subspace bomb?"

"It's a portable trap hole."

"More like a black hole," Iramint added. "It detonates and sucks in everything within its radius and sends it into subspace. Its radius is unpredictable in size."

"I will not doom the people in the outskirts of the galaxy to a hell worse than death. Those people are just as important as the people in the main city."

"Are you kidding me?" Battlux argued. "A few hundred people spread out among the vast perimeter of the galaxy are a generous estimation. Nobody knows anyone who is there, and if they all disappeared, no one would miss them."

"Battlux," Luand roared, "my decision is final on this subject."

Battlux backed down with a cold look on his face.

"Yes, sir."

"I think that Tzocy's plan would be most effective. Make sure you assemble a team of your best strategists to analyze the information we are looking for from the Negatives. We'll find it and feed it to them to decipher. Also, Battlux, you were right. Taking control over those systems would prevent worlds from falling into Negative control again. We'll draft and train people on each world to fortify our defenses as we widen ourselves. Have someone work on that legislation. When it's done begin enforcing it. What's the word on the crystals?"

Everyone looked around at each other.

Battlux sat up, exasperated. "We are working on locating the rest of them now, sir, but we believe the Negatives are hunting them."

"Good; keep me posted. This meeting is concluded."

"Oh, thank god," exclaimed Hopejs.

With a flash they all vanished—all except Battlux and Luand. The room returned from its beautiful colors and stars to a black background with a light ring under them. There was a long silence. Then Battlux spoke up.

"Master, I…"

"Battlux," Luand said, cutting him off. His chair floated in front of him. "I have to say I'm disappointed in you."

"Sir, I merely suggested the quickest and most logical solution to the problem at hand. Isn't that what you taught me?"

"No! I taught you how to quickly devise a plan that would cause the least amount of damage. Subspace attacks? All of your suggestions today were those of a mindless ruler with no regard for his people. I'm warning you, don't you dare use this war as an excuse to test your experiments on innocent people."

"Information is key: if we used the bombs, maybe we could further understand the extent of their power, maybe even learn how to use subspace as a power source altogether. All kinds of power could be at our fingertips."

"I've heard enough," Luand said, turning away from him. "See to your assignments, Battlux. You have a lot to learn before you succeed me in any way."

Battlux stood up in his chair and bowed to Luand. "Thank you, sir."

The same wind picked up and swiftly carried Battlux out of the room. All of the chairs in the room lowered to the ring. Luand stood up and walked to the center. A smile creased his face.

"I could get you in a lot of trouble right now," he said.

Max suddenly appeared in Battlux's seat with his legs crossed. "Well, you know me: can't stop finding trouble."

Luand turned around. "Clever, quick, resourceful, and

stealthy. You're getting better and better every day."

The smile disappeared from Max's face. "Like my brother?"

Luand's smile disappeared as well. "Have a good break, Max?"

"You personally trained Cody, didn't you?"

"I did." Luand looked away, paused, and looked back. "I saw potential in him that I didn't want to go to waste."

Max nodded and turned away.

"Why the sudden interest?"

"I want you to train me."

Luand paused. There was a silence and great tension between the two of them.

"Why?"

"Why not?"

"I'm a busy man."

"I have potential, don't I?"

"You're so sure?"

"One hundred percent—now more than ever."

"What makes you think I want to train you?"

"Because I'm another chance. A chance to get it right."

"Assuming I feel guilt for getting it wrong."

"I know I can handle it."

"You don't even know what you're up against."

"I know I can handle anything he can."

"Anything *who* can?"

"You know who."

"Why don't you cut the crap, kid, and tell me the real reason you want to train with me?"

Max swallowed and paused. "I want to be stronger than my brother."

Luand looked into Max's eyes and saw the same determination that he had seen in Cody years before. His smile returned to his face. "A month from today, meet me at my ship on Deck 51 at four in the morning."

"What? Why a month from now?"

"You're going to want to prepare for the greatest challenge you will ever know."

Max grew more excited.

"But let me give you fair warning. When I train people, I

don't go easy on them in any sense of the word. I train for results and for drastic and permanent improvement. This training will easily be the toughest training you will ever go through in your life. I'll see you in a month."

Luand then disappeared. Max sat in the chair, wondering what he had gotten himself into.

For the next month, Max did nothing but train his body, trying to make his attacks more potent and his movements quicker. He practiced using his Xylonite and became more skilled at controlling it. He didn't understand what else he could do to become stronger. He kept going over the same routine, all the while thinking of all the questions he wanted answered. To him this was more than a training mission; this was the moment the truth of his past and future would be revealed.

The month passed. Max stood at Dock 51 waiting for Luand. The ship had not yet arrived. Max stood there impatiently with his heart beating loudly in anticipation. His thoughts raced, every possible scenario of what could happen passing through his head. Finally, Luand arrived at the dock with a grin on his face. He saw Max's serious look.

"Dude, relax," Luand said in a laid-back tone. Max was caught a bit off guard hearing such a relaxed tone coming from such a commanding spirit. "You're full of anxiety. Patience. That's definitely something you need to learn."

"Well, I'm sure I'm going to be learning a lot from this."

Luand looked at him and patted his shoulder. "I think you may actually survive, Max," he said in a comforting voice. "But that doesn't mean I won't stop trying to kill you."

Max saw the transport shuttle arriving and his heart sank. Deep down he knew there was no going back. The two of them got on the ship and took off.

Max sat quiet and motionless while Luand sat eating away at the copious amounts of food stored on the ship. He kept looking at Max and trying to make casual conversation, but it didn't seem to provoke him to move at all. It was like this the entire thirty-six-hour trip. An awkward silence between the two polluted the stuffy shuttle. Max was trying to prepare himself mentally for whatever would happen when he got off the ship.

Before he knew it, the ship stopped, and so did Max's heart. Luand picked up his gear and walked off.

"We're here," he said, trying to prompt Max to move. Max eagerly grabbed his gear. As soon as they were off the shuttle, it retreated into the atmosphere. Max was very uncertain of where he was. He looked around and saw that it was barren. There was nothing around him. There were barely any trees, and where there were, they were dead. The entire landscape was dead. There were a few mountains in the distance, but they were all dead as well. There was no sign of life or civilization anywhere.

"Where are we?"

"This is Limbo. It's a void planet."

"Void planet? I thought those were only theoretical—what would happen if a planet were to naturally be destroyed."

"It was. This is in theory the first planet. Eons of civilizations lived here until it all just died. There is no life, nothing to harm here. It's also on its own time stream. Sixteen days on Zapheraizia is one year here."

"And this is where you train?"

"Yes."

"Wow, I figured you needed a large area like an island or a continent, but you need an entire planet?"

"It's safest if I do it like this. I hope you know I've been waiting for this for a very long time. I've been hoping you would be ready soon. And now you are."

"So you did want to train me? Why?"

"You're my Chosen One."

"Wait—is this one of those 'sole survivor, savior of the world' kind of things?"

"Max, your vanity knows no bounds."

Max's smile faded away.

"I have chosen you to, in fact, be the one to set the universe right because I believe that you are the only one with the power and the potential to do so. You are strong, fearless, and unusually flexible in more ways than you know. However, your problem is you are too egotistical and vain. You are driven by greed and pride. You look only to yourself yet you pretend that you fight for the greater good. You don't want to end this war because it harms people; you want to end it for the fame."

"That's not true."

"You're not lying to me, Max."

"I care about everyone this war affects."

"But what did you tell me before we came here? What was the reason you wanted to train with me?"

There was a silence for a moment. "I wanted to be stronger than my brother."

"And there it is: the newfound source of your greed. You constantly obsess over power—a power you tell yourself you can use to end the war and save people. The reality is you seek power so you can outshine your brother. You're jealous of the attention he's given. The wrong things motivate you. In order for you to be ready for what you need to do, your outlook must be ready as well."

"Okay, fine; what's next?"

"Your darkness."

"What?" Max's heart stopped for a moment.

"Your darkness has manifested itself in more than one incident. And it's getting stronger, isn't it? The problem is that you don't even know you're doing it. Your mind shuts down when it takes over. The last time you used it, you killed a man."

Max's eyes widened. His heart started beating. He didn't want to be exiled like the rest of the dark users. His mind began to race with millions of possibilities of what could happen. He took a moment to quiet his fears, unsure of how he would be punished. "Can you cure me?"

Luand sighed and stood up. Max followed him.

"Max, if I am going to train you, you must understand something completely, and it will change your view of the world as you know it."

They started walking.

"Okay then…"

"'Balance applies to everything'"

"Doesn't seem too mind-blowing."

"It means exactly what it sounds like. Everything in the universe needs to have a balance. For something to exist, its opposite should exist as well in equal measure. Everything must be even for there to be peace. The UPA fights to protect this balance, correct?"

"Yeah, we do."

"Wrong."

"Wait—what?"

"The UPA fights for one side of the balance."

"Yes, we fight for the light, for the good."

"Light is one side of the coin. What do you think the other side is?"

"Well, it has to be darkness."

"Yes. You see, darkness alone will destroy and dominate. It tends to want to destroy everything and rule through fear. Now light alone seeks to protect the universe from the darkness, and in order to do that, it tends to want to control it so that the darkness cannot get its hands on it."

"So what you're saying is that light is just as bad as dark?"

"Mind blowing, right? This is the first step of your training. You have to stop seeing the world as black or white, but instead as black *and* white. Everything you know and everything that was taught to you by the UPA is pure light. Pure light is a closed-minded view. This is called Malevolence, the state of pure light or dark. Light seeks to control, where darkness seeks to destroy. This is our true enemy, and the entire universe is plunged into its grasp. As long as this war continues, the scales of light and dark will continue to polarize. For as long as this war has been waged, people within the UPA's control have lived in protection, but they live in fear as well."

"Fear? Fear of what?"

"Of darkness. More broadly, they fear change. They are so fixed in their beliefs that they don't even want to think about the possibility that they may be just as bad as darkness."

"So if light and dark are just two sides of a bad coin, then who are the good guys?"

Luand smiled. "Now you're asking the right questions," he said, looking up. "The answer is the Truth: a balance between light and darkness in one human body."

"Light and dark working together in one being? Is such a thing possible?"

"Think about it like this. In a beautiful picture, you don't just have all white or all black, right? It's not interesting. The best pictures have harmony between the brightest lights and the darkest darks. The dark complements light just as light enhances the dark so that the picture becomes beautiful."

"It's just that it seems so impossible that such opposites can work in conjunction with each other."

"I'm not the only one. There are others who know the Truth as well—the other students I've trained—and they are masters of both light and dark, as I am. Years ago I gathered and preached this to a group of opened-minded people and created an organization called The Truth."

"Where are they now?"

"I don't know. It's been so long since I've seen them. They are probably spread out across the universe by now."

"Why didn't you tell this to the council? The UPA? The whole planet? Why wasn't this Truth revealed to the general public?"

"Because as I said before, people are living in fear. The planet of Zapheraizia is so engulfed in Malevolence that it would shun and turn on anyone who presented anything other than what it believes is true."

"And I'm supposed to fix it? That's quite a plateful, isn't it? Fixing the universe?"

"If it's too big of a task I'm sure my other apprentice can handle it."

"Other apprentice? You mean Battlux?"

"Yes. You two took quite the liking to each other in our little hearing. I'm sure that if you wanted to back out, he would be more than happy to fulfill this destiny."

Max remained quiet.

"Doesn't feel so good knowing that you're not on the pedestal that you think you are on."

"So how do I train myself to harness this 'Truth'?"

"You learn to balance the light and darkness within your heart. That's why we are here. This planet has a balance of light and dark within it."

"But all I need to do is master it. Easy."

"It should be—but not quite. You see, Max, there's another reason why you are uniquely apt for this mission. You have two darknesses: heart darkness and blood darkness."

"What?"

"Okay, I'll explain this as clearly as I can. You know the Orchaic Crystals? The elements they represent were the basis for the powers we have now. Thanks to a fusion of manual and natural selection, we enhanced the human genome to create power cells that hold the genetic code for the thirteen original powers. As we are human, we've managed to evolve into the different versions of them. In this, the dominant gene normally would be the most active and would manifest itself. Very rarely, the recessive power will be more active and even more rarely both dominant-dominant and dominant-recessive powers will coexist. The power cells are multiplied and used to hold both powers in check. Now you clearly have fire down. That's your active trait."

"Of course. Both my parents were pyrosharks."

"Not quite. No one told you. Fire was a secondary gene to your father. He had two powers active. It was only he who held it in his family."

"What? What was his second power?"

"His dominant gene power was blood darkness. When you were born, you received two dominant genes for fire and one dominant gene for darkness. The strength of your fire genes as well as your willpower suppressed the darkness for a while, but now it's unleashing itself in bursts, and if you don't learn to manage and control it, it will start to explode like an eruption that can be contained no more."

"That can't actually be true."

"The dark bursts you've been having ever since you arrived at the UPA are not the darkness from your heart. They're your genes activating."

"So I'm bad! I'm permanently stuck in this 'Malevolence' thing?"

"Max, listen to me. Something else you need to understand is that not all darkness is part of Malevolence."

"Okay, now you are really starting to confuse me."

"The dark bursts you've been having are your blood darkness, meaning that it's in your genes to have it. It's exactly like your fire in that it doesn't mean you are in Malevolence. This is the equivalent of the lumosharks at the base. Their powers are light just as yours are dark."

"So I'm okay?"

"Well…kind of. Stay with me, here. The other darkness that resides in yours and everyone's heart is what is harmful. This is heart darkness, and since your dark powers are starting to manifest themselves, it's almost making it easier for the heart darkness to plunge you into Malevolence. If we are going to unlock your full potential and use your dark abilities to your advantage, you must learn to differentiate the two darknesses.

"Okay, so darkness and fire are from my blood powers, and I need to balance the light and dark in my heart. Because of my own blood darkness, my heart darkness has a catalyst to get to me and throw me into Malevolence."

"*Yes!* Now you get it." Luand stepped away from him while Max stood still. "Okay, first thing we need to take care of is your hand-to-hand combat."

"What's wrong with my hand-to-hand combat?"

"Well to put it lightly, it's absolute crap!"

"Are you kidding me?"

"No. You need to be able to react quickly and increase your natural skill. I assume your Xylonite has activated by now and you've been using it, yes? Forget about it. What skills do you use when you fight?"

"Well, I have my natural skill, and I guess I've been using my Xylonite skill more."

"Exactly. Your Xylonite helps you. You train using your Xylonite as well, I would assume?"

"Yeah, so?"

"So, you're only training your body when you're in a specific state. Your body will only be as strong as you are when you train. Say that you are unable to use your Xylonite in battle. How screwed would you be? See, your friends don't have the Xylonite to train with. So their natural abilities excel while yours stay put. You may think that you're the strongest of your friends, but really you are the weakest link. You are actually dragging you friends down when you work together on a team."

"So what do I have to do?"

"You have to last ten minutes in a fight with me without using your Xylonite."

Max paused. "Okay then, bring it on."

Luand laughed and moved back. "Oh, we are going to fix that arrogance of yours right up." Without a signal, Luand launched a fast and huge energy blast of light. Max jumped out of the way. He looked back and saw the blast continue to the mountain. When it hit the mountain, the whole structure of the mountain burst into raw energy, causing a huge explosion. Max's eyes widened. He looked back at Luand to find him over him. "Never let your eyes off the opponent," he said as he hurled his fist to the ground.

Max rolled over and dodged it. Max tried to trip him, but he jumped a fair distance away from him. The dust from his landing on the ground flew into the air and rushed around Max. He couldn't see a thing. His eyes were irritated. He couldn't see normally, and the temptation to use his Xylonite grew stronger with each passing moment. Suddenly another blast came out from behind him. He heard Luand yelling at him. "Resist the temptation." Another blast flew past him. Max kept dodging. He started to run in one direction to get out of the smoke. When he finally managed to see something, Luand appeared in front of him and slugged him in the gut. Out of breath, Max grabbed his stomach in pain. Luand picked him up by the neck and threw him back into the dust cloud. Max struggled to get up. He felt a punch from behind. Then another. Then another. They became quicker and more potent as time progressed. Finally, Max fell to the ground, completely out of energy. The dust started to fade away. Luand approached him.

"Two minutes and twenty-four seconds, Max." He gave a big sigh. "Oh boy, we've got some work to do. Your stamina is outrageously low. Did you train at all?"

Max struggled to get his words out. "You didn't tell me how to train. How was I supposed to know that it was wrong?"

"Okay, rest up, kid. We've got a lot of ground to cover. I want you to meet me at that mountain."

"Where are you going?"

"I've got to go train myself. I can't have you holding me back."

"How long do I have to rest?"

"As long as you like. This is your training time you're sleeping on. You decide how much you get out of it. No matter what you're thinking, there's no getting off this planet for another year."

He walked away. Max lay on the cold, hard ground. He looked up to the gray sky until his eyelids became too heavy and he fell asleep.

Max found himself standing at the top of a skyscraper

looking out onto the city. He felt the breeze on his face as the sun set over the horizon. There were two red spots in the clouds. They progressively got bigger and brighter. Everything else began to grow dimmer and darker. The shadows around him began to close in. The eyes began to give shape to a body of some monstrous creature. Claws and wings began to form. It was a beast Max had seen in his dreams before. The foul breath polluted the air again. A giant dragon appeared in front of him. The two of them looked at each other for a long while. The moment lasted for what seemed like forever.

"You called me," the dragon said. "That's a new trick for you."

"You are the darkness inside of me?" Max inquired.

"I am the darkness that resides in your heart. Your darkest desires are my being, starved by the light you hold so strong."

"Well, I'm going to need both of you to work together if you can."

"The light is not a malleable force. It will destroy me, as I seek to destroy it."

"Yeah, well guess what? We're all in the same being, and control isn't going anywhere, so we're going to have to cooperate."

"You are so naïve, boy. You think my power is so easy to tap into?"

"I have no doubt that you're going to try to take over my body. That's why I'm ready to find a balance with you."

"Why balance? You enjoy new things, new experiences. I could easily give you my power, all of it. There would be no strings attached. All of it would be yours to use as you please."

"So much power that I wouldn't be able to help myself, right? So much to use that I would just have to find a place to use it— essentially starting chaos instead of preventing it. That is the string that is attached."

"And what is wrong with chaos? Chaos is the thing that keeps the universe moving. Without chaos, there would be no motive for advancement and creativity. Life would be at a standstill. And let's face it: you humans hate being idle. You would find your way to chaos soon enough, and it would and shall reign. You try to capture something that's too abstract for you to grip."

"Because the moments without it are worth fighting for. The moments without worrying that you will be destroyed the next day are something that can set anyone's mind at ease."

"But I can see into your heart. I know you better than you know yourself. That mask you wear every day in order to fit into society can only take you so far. I see your true nature. It says that you hate standing still. You hate a lazy day because you want to exercise your power. You can't even sit still for a single moment because you know there is something you can be doing. You hate sitting still." The dragon opened its mouth, and a dark orb floated out of it in front of Max. "So move."

Max stood there with the orb floating in front of him. The temptation was extremely hard for him to resist. He could see all the things he could do with that power. His arm started to reach for it, but he tried to hold back. His arm was fully extended with his fingers around the orb. A small flame formed in the palm of his hand. Then without warning, a giant blast of fire emerged from Max's hand, destroying the orb and obliterating the dragon. Max lowered his hand and started to walk away.

When he turned, he saw Tyra, glowing and sitting on a bench. He walked and sat next to her.

"What are you doing here?" he asked.

"I'm here to congratulate you," she responded.

"For what?"

"You defeated the darkness. You know how to keep him at bay." She leaned closer to him.

"Well, uh…thanks." He started to get nervous as if he were a kid having a crush again.

"Come on; I'll take you out to dinner." She got up and reached her hand out to him. Just as he was about to grab it, he stopped himself.

"What's wrong?" she asked.

Max's smile disappeared. "One: Tyra wouldn't take me out to dinner…ever! She always makes me pay. Two: you don't smell the way she does. You're not her."

"Max, this is a dream; things aren't going to be the same as in the real world." She reached to grab his hand, but he still retreated.

"No, this is something else, something worse. Something's telling me not to touch you!"

"Why?" she asked, getting more and more frustrated. "Why won't you be with me?"

He kept backing up. "I'm not going to fight you!"

Tyra grew brighter and her face more beastly. "Then you will burn in the light!" She grew into a giant demon with light shining from behind her. She rushed toward him in a quick blitz.

Max opened his eyes, again with Luand sitting over him. He sat up, holding his head in confusion.

"What happened this time?" he asked.

"You just fell asleep."

"How long this time?"

"I'd say a couple of seconds in the universe, a couple of hours here."

"Well, you would not believe the dream I had."

"I think I would, since I tailored it."

"Well, first what hap—" Max stopped and looked at him. "Wait—what?"

"Well, not the whole thing, but parts of it."

"You can control dreams?"

"Ha, ha; indeed."

"Well, can you explain to me what the hell my dream was about, because I had a dragon and Tyra?"

"Oh, so yours is a dragon? Haven't seen one of those in a long time. That was the manifestation of your darkness. It was everything about you that resides in the shadows. And then you should've seen someone you trusted above all others. They were your light. They were supposed to tempt you in a way different than the dragon tempted you. Luckily you refused both the light and the dark, so you successfully passed your second test."

Max felt a stupid grin appear on his face that he couldn't help.

"Now that I know you can resist both, you need to let darkness in. Your heart is shrouded by light. In order to balance it, you will need to accept your darkness for what it is. Once you are able to let it reside in your heart, you may become unstable, hostile, and a bunch of other lovely emotions. Eventually the light will calm you down. When this happens pay close attention to everything. This is what the Truth is about—understanding both sides of a story. These choices will be forced upon you in your dreams. For now, resist the light."

"No rest, even in my dreams?"

"They will be on you constantly while you're here, but should ease up after a while when you leave. You don't want to rest for too long or too often. Now hurry up! We have to continue to the next part of your training." Luand pointed to the top of a faraway mountain. "You are going to climb that mountain and meet me at the top."

"When?"

"Now."

"What?"

"See you." In a flash he disappeared. Max released a sigh and started running toward the mountain.

The distance alone drained Max of energy. There weren't any threats, twists, or turns, just a desolate wasteland surrounding him. He looked up and saw a giant light ball floating about in the sky. When he got to the mountain's base, there was a note at the bottom left there for him.

Get to the top of the mountain by the time the light ball reaches the bottom.

P.S. Don't rest or you will not make it.

Frustrated and yearning for a break, Max mustered up his remaining energy and climbed the mountain. He had only gotten a few feet above the ground level by the time he thought he couldn't go on. The light ball was descending, and he had no energy left to climb. Nevertheless, he kept pushing. Inch by inch he kept moving. Hours later, he struggled on the final rocks that impaled his hands and feet. Pushing himself up, he rolled onto the flat surface of the mountaintop, where Luand waited patiently.

"Well, hey, you actually made it in time. We will be doing an exercise in close combat next. You won't be allowed to move your body from your stance. No advancing or retreating. This will teach you to be more grounded in your fighting."

"Brilliant," Max said, still struggling to catch his breath. "How long until we do that?"

"We're doing that right now."

"Please, I need to rest. I have no energy."

"Well, I guess I can easily call the ship and send you back to base."

"Fine, fine; I'm coming." He stumbled to his feet and

wobbled over to where Luand stood.

"The objective of this game is simple. Make me lose my footing and don't let me push you off the mountain. You have the first move."

Max took a breath. Just as he was about to get into his stance, Luand chopped him in the neck. Max fell to his knee and struggled to breathe.

"I thought you said I have the first move," he said, choking on air.

"You took too long." Luand kicked him in the gut, blowing out more wind from Max's body.

"That's not fair," he said, barely able to form a sentence.

"Yeah, I'm sure your enemies will abide by the rules." He picked Max up and punched him over the edge of the mountain. He rolled down and landed on an outcropping on the side. Luand walked back to the center of the mountaintop and waited again.

Max started coughing, struggling to regain his breath. Angry with his mentor, he climbed the mountain again. Max reached the top, feeling all of the same pains and struggles from the first time. He saw Luand standing waiting for him. Still out of breath from his climb, he approached.

"Why didn't you go easy on me, at least for the first try?"

"Your enemies won't give you the courtesy, so why should I? I'm not going to coddle you like everyone else in your life has. Also, since you've never tasted victory in this exercise, you'll work harder and won't stop until you achieve it. Now...you have the first move."

Max took a breath and Luand went for the chop again. This time Max blocked it, then was hit in the gut with his other hand. Pushing Luand back, Max then immediately moved behind him. Luand turned around and attacked again, this time flipping Max back to the side he was originally on. Then with one finger, Luand pushed Max back down the mountain.

He climbed again with a bit of anger in his stomach.

"We will do this all day until you complete your objective."

Max walked up and got into his stance.

"The first move is yours."

Max didn't give Luand time to finish delivering the word before he launched a punch to his head, which he evaded. Proud of the swiftness of the attack, Max smiled but was brutally punished an instant later.

"You celebrated," Luand said, chastising him. "Why were you celebrating?"

"Baby steps. I attacked."

"Max, if you celebrate every time you take a baby step, you will not complete this training and all of this will have been for nothing. Stop thinking the world is your playground where you get a pat on the back for breathing correctly."

Luand kicked him again. And Max fell off the cliff again.

Try after try, and failure after failure, Max continued to attempt to complete this task. With each attempt he was more fatigued and the angry flame in his body raged. His anger fueled his attempts after he grew increasingly frustrated with his failures. The climbs back up the mountain ceased to be what really drained Max because he was so focused on the fight.

After what seemed like hundreds of attempts of fighting with no energy, Max punched the wall of the mountain in frustration. He looked at the hole he left in the wall and came to a realization. He took a breath and climbed back up to the mountaintop. Luand stood in his spot, and Max approached him once more. There was a calmness of breath this time. The two just stared at each other for a moment.

Then without warning, Max launched at him with a stream of attacks. Luand dodged each one with subtle movements of his head and upper body. Then Luand started attacking back. Max mixed a combination of blocks and dodges and counters while his feet remained fixed to the ground. The two moved at blurring speeds, each trying to knock the other over. Suddenly they introduced feet into the game where they started attempting to trip each other, but each dodged the other. It was like an intense game of chess in which each person had to think several maneuvers ahead of the other. Finally, Max saw an opening and pushed Luand's gut. With a slight pause in his movement, Max went for a punch to the face. The hit connected, and the fight stopped. Luand's foot shifted a tiny bit to maintain his balance. The two stood still with Max's fist still in Luand's face. He removed Max's hand and stepped away.

"Exercise complete." He walked away, and Max smiled. Suddenly his body collapsed. All of his limbs were paralyzed.

"Luand!" he yelled. "What's happening to me?"

"Relax; you just passed your energy threshold. You pushed yourself way beyond your natural limit for an extended period of time. Now that your body isn't in constant motion, it's realizing that it needs immediate rest and has shut down. You'll be fine." He walked back over to his limp apprentice. "But before you completely knock out, let's review. What did you gain from this?"

"Well, I'm definitely faster and more comfortable with my feet."

"Think more abstractly."

"Anger?"

"Yes. You experienced frustration in this exercise. Your failures got to you, and you responded with rage. You relied on your anger to give you power, and though it did give you strength, your technique and your speed suffered. But only when you saw your anger and controlled it did you succeed. This is the Truth. You took your heart's darkness and balanced it with your heart's light. Power fused with control. Only then did you succeed. Now that you've been there and you've seen completely what anger can do to you, you know how to counter an opponent stuck in that mindset." He walked to the edge of the mountaintop, looking out at the tops of trees in the distance. "When you are rested, go to the forest. The next step to your training lies there." He then jumped off the edge. Max took in his break and recharged.

A few hours later, he walked over to the forest. The trees were all dead and thick, clustered against one another. There was a clearing with a circle of empty space and a tree stump in the middle where Luand was meditating. Max crossed his legs and sat across from him.

"You have tasted what your heart's darkness can do. Now you must taste your blood's darkness and know the difference. The heart's darkness is mostly harnessed when you seek power while you partake in the seven deadly sins: wrath, pride, greed, lust, gluttony, sloth, and envy. With a drive strong enough, any of these can plunge a heart into darkness. This is going to be extremely difficult since you are not a very patient guy. In this exercise you may fall into sloth, envy, or pride, in which you will activate a dark energy. This, however, will not be your blood darkness. You will have to stay here and listen for it."

"Listen for it?"

"Yes. For your firepower, you didn't need to listen all that hard because you were more open-minded and a blank slate, but now your heart is still imprinted with Light Malevolence, not to mention you have fire already as a power, so accessing your blood darkness will be hard the first time."

"I thought you said it was pushing its way out. Shouldn't I just wait for it then?"

"We could, but that would be a large waste of time, and you wouldn't be able to hold on to it. This way you can begin to access it regularly."

"Well, how long will it take?"

"I don't know."

"Well, what am I listening for?"

"I don't know."

"You know, this is a great teaching method."

Luand got up from the stump and placed Max on it.

"I'm not trying to mess with you. This exercise is very personalized. How long this takes and what you are hearing is different for each person."

"Give me an estimate, at least."

"Well...if you're lucky, the process may only take a matter of three months."

"Three months?" Max said, shocked. "What the hell am I going to do standing here for three months?"

"Listen. Seriously, you need help in the listening department."

"What am I going to do for food?"

"This planet, although seemingly dead, nourishes the body so that it has no need for food or water. That's another reason why this is the perfect training ground. Now get to it. If you ever need me, I'll be on the other side of the planet training, so don't come whining to me if you get impatient. You have three months to listen for your darkness or you're sent back to base. Don't push it, or it will not come. Good luck, kiddo."

With that he teleported before Max could ask another question. Max closed his eyes and started to listen for something he didn't understand.

Hours went by, and he couldn't hear anything. He couldn't hear any voices speaking to him or anything even hinting at darkness. After a while he started to think that this was only a way to get rid of him so that Luand could train on his own. He grew more and more frustrated as he had no idea what he was listening for. He could feel himself getting angrier and calmed his mind. He sat there quietly with his eyes closed.

He spent the first month sitting quietly, not once moving from that spot. His mind was awake the whole time, sitting and focusing. With a month of constant attention to his power, his mind started to drift, but he didn't think anything of it. Slowly, as his thoughts grew more gleeful and further away from his task, he finally started to drift into sleep. He then felt something and woke himself up. He looked around and realized it wasn't the right darkness. Luand said it would happen. Sloth had a hold of him. He woke himself up and tried to keep his mind on track.

After seemingly endless hours, his legs started to get numb. He couldn't feel his feet anymore. His neck was stiff and his arms were frozen from lack of movement. Max didn't dare move them because he was afraid he would destroy all of the progress he had made. So the statue continued to sit still, clearing his mind every so often.

He started to think about his brother and how powerful he was. He thought that if he were tasked with it, he would have completed the task already. Angry and jealous, Max grew even more impatient. Though he tried to fight it, his thoughts kept revolving around him. He opened his eyes, got off the stump thinking he couldn't take it anymore, and went for a walk.

He walked through the forest aimlessly, just happy that his legs had moved after weeks of being numbingly stationary. The trees seemed to never end around him. Then faintly, as if from nowhere, he heard a noise coming from behind him. It was jazz music playing in the background quietly. He turned around and saw a door. Without thinking, he opened the door and was in a black room with a light on a piano. No one sat at it, but the keys were playing by themselves. Max moved his hand along the piano and sat down. Holding his fingers above the keys, he attempted to play along with them. When he hit the first key, he opened his eyes and was back at the stump.

A dark aura surrounded Max. His stone-stiff face cracked a smile. He listened to the music and heard what it had to say. Suddenly and without warning, he started to sink into his shadow. He couldn't get out. He kept sinking quicker and quicker as if it were quicksand. His face was soon covered, and he was scared. He didn't know how to stop it or where, if anywhere, he was going. He sunk into his shadow, and it disappeared from the spot, leaving only an empty stump in the dead forest.

Luand was busy training hard on the other side of the planet. He was about to attack multiple doppelgangers when suddenly a black spot appeared in front of him on the ground. Max suddenly rose from it, confused and bewildered. He turned around and saw Luand, looking just as confused as he was.

"Did you do that?" Max asked.

"Do what?"

"Bring me here."

"No, but I've got one good question for you. Why are you not on your stump?"

"I think I did it."

"Did what?"

"Harness it."

"Darkness?"

"Yeah."

"It's been a month and a half… You have three!"

"Yeah, but I felt it."

"But that's impossible."

"Well, then how did I get here?"

"How *did* you get here?"

"I don't know. I thought you did it."

"I didn't do it."

"Well unless the planet did it, I think I did."

"How'd you do that?"

"Darkness."

"What?" Luand walked up to Max and examined him. "Well, I will admit that I did expect you to exceed expectations because, let's face it, you always do, but I gave you at least two months. You did it in one and a half."

"Is that good, or do I have to marinate on my stump some more?"

"No, no, that's good. We can move on to the next phase."

"What's the next phase?"

"I get to teach you some tricks."

A number of months passed. Max eagerly learned each technique and rehearsed it religiously. He rarely rested, and when he did, he trained himself in his dreams, balancing both temptations of light and darkness. Max kept fighting and sparring with Luand each time, not using his Xylonite. He felt himself getting better. After seven months, Max was ready for his first real test.

Luand stood on one side of the field while Max stood on the other. Max had his hand on his Blade ready to attack. Luand called out to him.

"Okay, Max, what are the rules again?"

"Use the dark-based attacks to last ten minutes in a fight with you, switch between melee and swordplay, do not use Xylonite."

"Good. You have the first move."

Max vanished in an instant, reappeared behind him, and attacked. Luand dodged to get some distance while Max closely followed. They kept close and fought right in each other's faces. Max unexpectedly tripped and fell. Luand took advantage of that and tried to knock him down before he hit the ground. He then felt the ground crumble from his punch, but there was no Max. He looked up and saw he had teleported a safe distance away. Max threw circular shadows at Luand that flew at sonic speeds through the air and circled Luand. Max created a giant portal next to him. He punched into it, and his arm reappeared through one of the floating shadows surrounding Luand. He kept punching and kicking through the portal, and Luand kept blocking his attacks. Then Max jumped through the portal and launched at Luand and threw him off balance for a bit. Max ran toward him and grabbed his Blade. Luand materialized another Blade out of nowhere. The two clashed swords and exchanged blows. Max kept laughing out of enjoyment. For a while Luand was amused by his laughter until he didn't stop. He kept laughing. Soon his laughter didn't sound playful; it sounded demonic and insane. Luand backed away and saw that Max's shadow aura was out of his control. Heart darkness had taken control.

Max created a shadow thread from his wrist and connected it to his Blade. He then launched the Blade at Luand. He jumped out of the way as the Blade barely missed him. Max pulled on the thread, forcing it to swing back to him. He kept spinning it above his head and launching it at Luand. Luand suddenly vanished. Max turned around and saw him approaching from behind. He quickly sank into a shadow portal below him and reappeared behind Luand. He then leaped at him, trying to grab him, while Luand dodged. A circular ring facing him appeared in front of Max. As his arm went through it, a large demon's hand came out on the other side, grabbed Luand, and threw him across the decaying field. Max laughed maniacally.

Luand stood up once again and glared at Max. "Okay, Max," he said. "You're out of control. I'm ending this now!" Luand disappeared again. Max couldn't figure out where he had gone. He turned around and saw him holding his throat from behind. Suddenly, Max felt all of his dark energy being drained from his body. He started to feel light-headed, then dizzy, then drowsy until he finally collapsed, unconscious and defeated.

He woke up and saw Luand sitting next to him, eating. It was dark out, and there was a fire in front of him warming some food. He held his head in pain as he slowly sat up.

"What happened this time?" he said in a daze.

"You disrupted the balance of power in your body," Luand said. "The darkness became too powerful for you to control, so it controlled you. All of your rage, anger, insanity, and irrationality personified and took the form of your darkness. The only way to prevent you from being consumed by it completely was to take some of your darkness and give you some of my light."

"Your light is inside of me?"

"Yeah. It'll balance out your darkness until you're ready for it. For now, eat."

Max grabbed a chicken leg, and before he took a bite, he found something funny. "Wait—I thought I didn't need to eat while I'm on this planet."

"Just because you don't have to doesn't mean you shouldn't. Think of it as a treat."

Max smiled. "So I guess I failed the test, right?"

"Yes, but failure is better than success. When you succeed you don't learn nearly as much as when you fail. For instance, you learned that you still need to differentiate your blood's darkness from your heart's darkness. In the heat of battle, it's understandably difficult to master, but you must get it."

"So I have to wonder, the legislation that exiled all of the people with darkness to the outskirts of the planet and our galaxy, the dark users—what do they use? Heart darkness?"

Luand remained quiet.

"Right?"

"Just eat, okay?"

"Luand…you wanted me to know the Truth. Don't you think it's time you told me?"

Luand sighed. "They're blood darkness users, like you."

"Why the hell are they exiled? They're just like me; why are they being punished for something they can't help!"

"Because that is what Malevolence is, Max—irrational fear. It was assumed that anyone who used darkness of any kind was an associate of Xaldoruks and therefore was on the wrong side of the war. When they were initially exiled, all those years ago, the leaders were afraid. Any form of darkness suffered from ignorant fear. After that, it made it practically impossible to fix."

"But why specifically darkness? Why was that power chosen to be bad?"

"Back when the first Terrascopians arrived on Zapheraizia, you know that they created thirteen different powers accidentally when trying to make humans more adaptable to the planet. You know of the Orchaic Crystals, the same crystals that you and Zack found on your little encounter with Codysseus."

"Wait—how do you know about that?"

"The thirteen original powers were derived from those crystals: fire, water, electricity, nature, wind, physicality, land, psychic, sound, time, space, light, and darkness. We humans evolved as we always do, More and more powers began to branch off of the original thirteen. For example, from the psychic crystal, telekinesis, hypnosis, and mind-reading abilities branched off. From water crystal, ice-controlling abilities and water kinesis were derived. From Sendrakxs, darkness was created. It's a power just like any other, but it became rare after the purge was issued. The force that created the Negatives and plagued the universe with this war was darkness. They spawn from the heart darkness of the universe itself. With this knowledge the government demanded that all dark users be purged from the planet. The senseless slaughter over the decades almost wiped out the whole lot of them. Though the act was dismantled, the ones who remain are in hiding in fear that something like it would happen again."

"And no one can help them? No one can even try to make peace with them?"

"Now you see why this world is rotten. I can only keep it from getting any worse for so long. Light is obsessed with control, and the council now thinks that if we control more systems, there will be more protection, but that's not how it works! That's how the military came to make all the decisions. It all needs to stop. But I can't do anything in my position, believe it or not. That's why I'm training you."

"And the dark user that created the Negatives so many millennia ago was considered to be the first Xaldoruks, right?"

"First. Last. Only. Whatever you want to say."

"Oh, come on, you can't honestly say that it's all the same guy, can you?"

"Max, you do know what Xaldoruks translates to."

"'Dark Soul,' often used in reference to the devil."

"And you think that's just coincidence?"

"No, it's rhetoric. Whoever these people are, they pass down the name devil to instill fear and keep it going."

"Max, the Sandsharks of old and the Sandsharks now are fighting the same person, same body, same soul. Trust me."

"Impossible. That means he's lived for thousands of years."

"The stories are real, Max. You know the Genesis story, how the name was given to him, and the first use of the Orchaic Crystals together. Throughout this war, we haven't been fighting an organization passing the name down from one person to the next. It's one being, who's lived longer than a few millennia."

"No way. I can't believe that."

"Max, the reality is we are fighting the dark angel himself."

"Oh god, I'd rather him be an organization. That way I at least know that he can be killed. But an angel? An actual angel? No, no way. We're fighting a force of nature, Luand. You are sending us to our deaths! This is a being beyond us! How can you knowingly let us march off into a battle we can't hope to win?"

"Because there is hope to win. Just because he is an angel doesn't mean he can't be defeated. It is possible to kill him. We've been close before. He's been brought to his knees more than once. I've done it, your brother has, and now you will."

Max saw his opportunity to ask questions about his brother.

Something in him kept pulling him back.

"Luand, I've searched for answers, but no one seems to want to give them to me. I want answers about my brother."

"Sure, Max; what do you want to know?"

Max was a bit confused. After all the evasive answers and people dodging the question, he was about to just tell Max anything he wanted to know? Suddenly all of his questions disappeared. He couldn't decide what he wanted to know about him.

"Your brother was one of the brightest and strongest, as I am sure you know. It was a huge loss when we lost him. I trained him like I trained you. He was an incredibly skilled tactician and strategist—even earned a place as the thirteenth member of the council. We thought he was the one who could actually end the war, but his position was short-lived. After learning everything about the Truth and the nature of Malevolence, he thought that the UPA was beyond salvation and that Malevolence was an invincible condition of the world. Of course he's wrong. I noticed how strong a bond you and he had, and I knew that if you knew he left, you would eventually follow. So because of this, I requested that he not be spoken of at all. Even had your guardians wipe your and your friends' memories of him to keep you from searching. But even this I knew wouldn't last long. Somehow you would find out about him and lose control of your anger at someone, either your guardians or me. That spark of anger would be your gateway into understanding the Truth."

"So all of this was your plan. You manipulated me that much?"

"I prefer the term 'directed.'"

"I'm assuming that's why my data file was missing?"

"No. He managed to break into the vault and steal his data file so no one could follow him."

"Wait—you're saying he stole the data file?"

"Yes."

"That's a bit odd."

"How come?"

Max hesitated to continue.

"A while ago, in the attack on Darod, I encountered a unique Negative. This one took my likeness and was far stronger than a normal Negative. He's actually the one who gave me the data file back."

"A Negative."

"Yes, one who was exactly like me in the way he walked, moved—even his voice was exactly like mine. More importantly, he fought like I did as well."

"A Negative clone." Luand furled his eyebrows and lost himself in deep thought for a moment. "It's probably nothing to worry about. But Max, here's a bit of friendly advice: Don't try to compare yourself to your brother. It's great to have competition to push yourself, but don't do it to the point that you constantly become jealous."

"What will you do? Have a mentoshark force him out of my brain again?"

"No, Max, you're too strong to have your memory adjusted like that. Just don't think about him. You'll find yourself stronger than him a lot faster if you don't."

There was a beeping coming from Luand's pocket. He picked up the device and checked what it was. His eyes widened and he shot up.

"We've got to go."

"What?"

He called the ship down from orbit.

"Luand," Max called out. "What's going on?"

"I'm sorry, Max, it looks like I have to cut this training short."

"Why? What happened?"

"Before we left, I sent the order for the UPA to find ground zero—where all the Negatives are getting their orders. They found it. There is a short window of opportunity for us to take it. We have to go now! We'll finish our training some other time. Do not forget what I taught you here—all the techniques, all the power you obtained. Remember it. But do not use your blood darkness."

"What? *Why?*"

"You are still not ready. Your blood and heart darkness are not clear to you yet. I can't risk you falling into Malevolence—or worse, the darkness of it. If you fall into your darkness and you're at the UPA, I can't protect you. For now, lay off it. Remember, as mortal beings, we must be mindful of our seven deadly sins. But the ones you personally must watch most are pride, envy, and greed. Balance them. Remember the Truth. When we return, I will continue your training, and you will master it. But remember, Malevolence can always be trumped by the truth. But for now, let's see your fighting skills in the field, shall we?"

The ship had arrived, opening for them. The two boarded and left the planet for Zapheraizia, hoping the next step in the war would be one of the last.

At the UPA, a special team was gathered to prepare for an assault. There were several members of the council—Battlux, Aenlan, Iramint, and Zeiliz—along with Tyra, Genesis, and Zack. They all sat behind the circular holograph table. Battlux had begun.

"I have chosen you three Sandsharks because of your specific skill sets and your adaptability in situations. This mission, until we get there, is a bit in flux. Once you have received all of the information, you will propose tactics to infiltrate and complete the objective. I'm very much counting on you three."

"Four," Luand said, bursting in with Max following closely behind. "Four people on your team. Max is going with them." Everyone saluted him, and he signaled them all to stop.

"Sir, with all due respect, this team is specific to this mission. We can't afford any extras."

"Battlux, have you made plans yet?"

"No."

"Have you started to speculate approaches?"

"No, we..."

"Ah, let me finish. Did you even give them the information they need to make a plan yet?

"No, sir."

"Well then, you're able to add one more person. Plus, Max is very close to this group. He should be able to increase their adaptability."

"Yes sir," Battlux said, submitting.

"Max, I'd like you to formally meet Battlux. He's my current apprentice."

Max extended his hand. "Pleasure to meet you."

Battlux looked at it and then shook it. "Pleasure's all yours."

Max sat down and smiled at his friends. When he looked at Genesis, she didn't look back. Battlux then dimmed the lights and began the presentation.

"Our target is a castle in the capital of Regnos 7. It has had the highest concentration of Negative Matter being produced that hasn't yet been materialized. According to reports the planet has been reduced to scavengers. Thus it doesn't make sense why this castle has such uptight security. The whole thing has sensors that prevent any of our vehicles from getting anywhere near it. But because Negative Matter is somehow being shipped out from here, there most likely has to be a way in. That's why we came to you…four. We need a way into the castle and a way to neutralize the production of Negative Matter. Preferably permanently."

Max spoke up. "Well, look at the structure of it. It looks the same as the base on Darod. Why not surround it and treat it the same way? The vehicles will keep their distance and attack from afar."

"Now, if we wanted to waste our resources and alert them to us, that would be great, but unfortunately we can't. We are trying to keep this a covert mission. Since a lot of our forces are off trying to find other potential targets, we're keeping this one small. Not only that, but it's not just the castle that's shielded; it's the entire planet. There is a force field shielding it from all entry or escape. There is only one spot in that shield that is potentially vulnerable, which they use to export the Negative Matter, but we don't have the time to try to find it."

"So there's no way to get under it and drill up somehow?" Zack thought aloud.

"You see our dilemma?"

Genesis raised her hand but then retracted it. Aenlan noticed and looked at her. "Did you want to say something?"

Genesis stuttered. "Oh, it's nothing."

"No really. Do tell."

"Well, I was thinking. The ships can't get into the planet's atmosphere, right? So they don't. What if we launched the team from space right on top of the castle? If their defense is looking for us, the one place they probably aren't looking is up."

Iramint laughed. "Launch a team from space into the atmosphere? Are you crazy? No one can dive that way and survive; that atmosphere is too dense. You'd burn upon entry."

"Perhaps, but don't we have digging suits that are built to withstand great amounts of sudden pressure and go through high-density matter?"

"Yeah, but would they work like that?"

"There's no reason they shouldn't. Once we're there we ease up on the landing on the top tower. We enter through the window and snake our way to the bottom of the castle, where we take care of the Negative Matter."

"What about an extraction plan?"

"Teleports?"

Battlux interrupted. "You can't do that. The shield prevents all forms of escape. Once you find your way past the shielding, the only way out would be to exit the atmosphere the exact same way. We don't have any equipment to do that."

"Okay, fine," Genesis said. "We bring the teleports anyway and split into two teams. One goes to destroy the Matter and the other releases the shield, also allowing people all over the planet to leave and get help. We teleport back and mission accomplished, right?"

The council members looked at each other and smiled. "Sounds like a fair plan. You're in charge, Genesis."

"Wait—me?"

"Yeah, your plan, you lead. Don't let us down. Get ready to deploy in a few minutes. We need to go ASAP." The council members left, and Genesis was still frozen. Tyra started to congratulate her.

"Genesis! This is the first mission you're leading! Congrats." A small grin snuck onto Genesis's face.

"Yeah, congrats, sis," Max said patting her back. She gave him a cold look and marched off.

"You heard the man. Get ready to deploy in ten minutes," she commanded.

Max sighed. "She's still mad at me?"

"Yeah," Zack said, walking behind him. "Don't worry; it won't be for long." He ran ahead, leaving Tyra and Max.

"So where have you been, lately?"

"I was uh…training with Luand."

"Really? How was that?"

"Oh, you know…pretty okay."

"'Okay'? 'Okay'? You have private, concentrated training time with the leader of the UPA, and all you can say about it is 'okay'?"

"I mean, what do you want me to say? It was intense. I

learned a lot. I'm a better Sandshark because of it."

"Okay, that's fine. Did you get the answers you wanted?"

Max had a warm smile on his face. "Yeah, yeah, I did."

"Well, I was hoping you would let it go. Maybe Gen will, too." The two walked off to the hangar and boarded a warship.

Upon coming out of sonic light speed, the warship reached a giant red planet covered with fog. The team had gotten their gear on when Battlux arrived at the deployment room.

"The schematics of the castle have just been uploaded to your screens. Fusion Ember, you're the captain. You guys are going to deploy into two teams. I assume you have that decided."

"Yes," Genesis confirmed. "Tyra and I will go and disable the force field while Max and Zack go down deeper and neutralize the Matter."

"Wait, Ember," Max called out. "When did we decide this?"

"We didn't. I made the decision that would best suit the mission. Any problems with that?"

"Anyway," Battlux continued, "when you see the castle, hit the red button on your suits. This will cushion your impact and slow you down enough so that you can land. Good luck."

The four turned around, and Genesis started the countdown. Once she hit zero, they were sucked into the void of space.

There they were weightless, drifting closer and closer to the planet. Slowly they started to pick up velocity. Their bodies had weight again, and they hurled toward the planet like rockets. They each put their hands in front of their heads and cones formed as they started to spin through the dense atmosphere. A few moments later, they saw the castle towers cuing them to each hit the red button, and they started slowing down. The suits started blowing a lot of air below them, and they landed softly on two different towers. Zack and Max signaled to the ladies that they were going in. They smashed a window open and jumped into the castle. Tyra and Genesis did the same.

Once inside Max and Zack deactivated the suits and walked out the door. When they walked out they faced the inside of a gigantic chimney that was currently functioning, blowing a foul smoke right into their faces. They hooked their grappling hooks from their belts to the edge and jumped down the chimney. When they got closer to the bottom, they saw a light burning. Max threw a fireball to knock the fire out and landed. The two kept moving in search of the Negative Matter generator.

Genesis and Tyra snuck around the castle, scoffing at how little security there was inside.

"Why isn't there anything here?" Genesis asked.

"Well, either we aren't anywhere close to anything that needs protecting, or they are just so confident that they underestimated us and thought we couldn't get in. I'll tell you, the second one is going to help me sleep better."

"I hear that."

"Are we going in the right direction?"

Genesis brought up the schematics in front of her. "Yeah, we're on the right track."

"Let me ask you. Are you still mad at Chaos Flame?"

"Ugh, please tell me he didn't ask you to ask me, too."

"Oh no, he wouldn't let me do that."

"Funny, you're the second person to say that to me in the exact same context."

"And trust me, I know all about hating that guy. It's just, how long are you going to keep this up?"

"Look, Winter, honestly, I'm not mad at him. I get why he did it. But that's not what this is about. All his life he's seen me only as his little sister. Now, I'm not a child anymore. I'm more than just his little sister. I'm a pyroshark now. I'm leading a mission. He has to follow my orders now. It's time he stopped seeing me as a damsel in distress. The best way to do that is to not treat him like a brother."

Tyra sighed. "You know he only protects you because it's built into him. He can't help it. It comes with you being the only blood relative he's got. On some subconscious level, I'm sure I would want my sister to care about me at least a little bit. It's good you're growing up, but just don't leave Flame out in the cold forever, okay?"

"Now that you bring it up, what happened between you and Andrea?"

"She wasn't a good older sister. That's what happened. All my life she would shoo me away like I was some annoying fly. And maybe I was; I was young and idolized my older sister. So what? But she didn't see it that way. She saw it as me trying to take over her life. So she chose to keep me out of as much of it as possible. I got this brilliant idea to emulate her gothic, emo style to show that I wasn't good at it. But then I started to like it. I felt comfortable. I identified with it. It freed me to be who I am. Which only made her hate me more. I'm not going to apologize for being who I am. She can deal with that."

"Is that it? There seems to be more than just her not liking your style."

"You're right. I did something to her that she would never forgive me for. But that's for another time. I think there's something up ahead."

They came up to a door with a bunch of controls in it. "This is probably it," Genesis said, sitting at the computer. She started hacking away while Tyra watched the door. Suddenly there was a huge power surge throughout the entire castle. "Done. Our part is finished."

"Did this seem a bit too easy to you? Something this important is never this poorly guarded."

"Well, I don't want to stay to find out." She called Max and Zack. "Fusion Ember and Crimson Winter to Chaos Flame and Volt Storm: our mission is complete. Repeat, the force field is down. How are you on your end?"

"Well, we have suddenly come down with some heavy concentrations of Negatives. We're going to need one of you down here. We think we're close to the source."

"Finally," Tyra exclaimed, drawing her Blade. "It's about time I sliced something up. I'll go down and assist them. You can call it in and teleport back up." Tyra started down the hallway.

"Fusion Ember to warship."

"What's your status?" Battlux responded.

"Winter and I have completed our part of the mission. The shields are down. Chaos and Volt are currently engaged and are close to completing the second objective. I'm sending Winter to assist them."

"Negative, Ember. You will abort the second objective."

"What? But the mission isn't complete."

"You will abort."

"May I ask why?"

"We have alternative ways of dealing with this that will take less time and get you out of there sooner. Tell your team to teleport back."

"Sir, you can't. At least not yet."

"Why is that?"

"The uh…shields are still lowering. We have about fifteen minutes before they're completely neutralized."

"Fine. Have your team out of there in fifteen minutes." Battlux hung up the call and went to his captain. "Prep the subspace missiles."

"Winter!" Genesis called franticly. "We have fifteen minutes to get out of here."

"What? Why the time limit?"

"They say they have alternative ways of dealing with this. I think that means they're going to nuke it right next to a civilian population."

"Volt. Flame. Did you hear that?"

"Yeah, I heard it," Zack responded. "Leave it to Battlux to cut things short like this. I knew he was no good. Okay guys, listen: we're at the door of the objective. Winter, what's your ETA?"

The Negatives they were fighting suddenly froze into ice with a Blade sticking out of one of them. The Blade shot out and sliced them all into ice shards.

"About three seconds."

"Whoa. Anyone else feel that chill in the air?" Max teased.

"I'll teleport back to the warship to see if I can buy you guys any more time." Genesis hit a button on her suit, and she flashed back onto the warship.

Max stood at the door trying to fiddle his way through. Finally growing frustrated with it, he took a deep breath, raised his hands to the door, and watched it melt into a puddle of metal.

"Whoa, dude!" Zack said, amazed. "When could you melt stuff like that?"

"Comes with training."

There was another deep elevator shaft. The three hooked their grappling hooks onto their platform and dropped to the bottom. Upon landing, they entered another giant room. Each stood in awe of what they saw. Their jaws dropped, and they froze in their feet.

Genesis marched up to Battlux at the bridge.

"What the hell, Battlux? Why are you cutting my mission?"

"Because this was always the plan. I didn't need you to destroy the Matter generator. I needed you come up with an idea to get rid of the force field."

"Why?"

"Subspace missiles."

"What?"

"Tiny black holes contained and used as weapons."

"You're going to set black holes onto a civilian population? No way Luand authorized this."

"Well, good, because he doesn't need to. When the black holes are done they will leave nothing. No proof of anything."

"There are *people* down there."

"Collateral damage."

"You can't do this. This is my mission."

Suddenly Max's voice was heard on the bridge. "Chaos Flame to warship."

"We read you, Chaos Flame. If I recall you were given specific orders to evacuate the field."

"Yeah, look: we found something far more important than the generator."

"What?"

"We   found   all   of   the   Orchaic   Crystals."

9 FEAR

Max, Zack, and Tyra just gazed in awe at the magnificent view of the Orchaic Crystals. All of them circled a gigantic pot with a black crystal floating above it. There were streams of energy flowing from them into the pot. The room was filled with light as the power from the crystals enclosed the trio.

"Volt, can you shut us off?" Max asked.

Zack sent an electrical current through his communicator and fried the communication for a moment. "We're down."

Max stepped up and was amazed at the sight. "These are the rest of them. These are all nine of the crystals we don't already have."

"They must be harvesting all of their power to make the Negative Matter," Tyra concluded. "This is where it comes from."

Max heard a rumble from above them. He snapped out of his hypnosis and pulled a bunch of capsules from his pocket. His head started to feel a bit heavy, and his body felt like it was getting squeezed.

"All right, the crystals are what generate the matter. Easy solution: pick up the crystals and teleport back to the warship before they blow us up." Max ran into the ring of crystals. All of a sudden he felt the pressure grow thicker until he collapsed. Zack and Tyra ran to his assistance, but as they called out to him, there was no reply. As Max slipped out of consciousness, he could hear his friends under attack. The battle started around him, and he couldn't do anything to help.

On the warship, Genesis pleaded with Battlux.

"You can't fire those missiles—they are still down there!"

"No, you child, that's not why we can't fire. They just said they found the Orchaic Crystals."

"What are they?"

"Orchaic Crystals, or the Eternal Crystals, contain power this universe hasn't seen since its creation. They are the evolutionary jump—what gives a mere human the powers of an angel and gives an angel the powers of a god."

"And the team found them?"

"This expedition may have just turned the tide of the entire war in a far greater way than we ever hoped. We can't afford to lose them."

"So the missiles won't be fired."

"They must. This is my only chance. I'll give them twenty-five more minutes for them to get here. Then, Orchaic Crystals or not, subspace will devour them."

Max floated in a void. As he opened his eyes, he saw a vision in millions of small flashes. He saw two sides of what seemed like a war. He saw the UPA along with a bunch of his comrades on the other side of him. He stood next to his brother and sister with a bunch of warriors behind them. The two sides began to charge at each other, and he watched his friends get crushed and shot down. As he fought, a being appeared behind him with a sword and swung for his neck. Max opened his eyes and was brought back into reality; his face was still buried in the floor.

He looked up to see that Zack and Tyra were hopping from wall to wall, chasing something. Zack kept shooting lightning shots at it, and Tyra kept trying to contain it, shooting ice from her double-edged hunter Blades. The light in the room was dimmer. He looked and saw that the Orchaic Crystals were gone from their suspended position. He noticed there was glow from Zack's bag and assumed the crystals were in there.

Max stood up and slowly assessed himself. The creature saw this and then turned around to Zack and Tyra. He opened his palm, launching tentacles and trapping them against a wall. He leaped from the wall and opposed Max. He looked at him and laughed while Max slowly wobbled to his feet. This time he had a plan on how to confront him.

"You again."

"Did you miss me?" Zamx replied.

"You're too late. The crystals are ours. Without them your factory for Negative Matter is history. This war is coming to an end."

Zamx's warm chuckle broke into a full-blown laugh.

"Oh please," he said. "You're right. This war is coming to an end, but not because you managed to get your hands on some worthless rocks. We've gotten all of the power we could from those things. Might as well find a lake and skip them."

Max gave him a cold look as he pulled himself together. "Then why are you here?"

"Well, I was bored and needed to stretch my legs. I wanted to play with your friends because god knows you get more than your fair share of time with them. And finally I came for you."

"What do you mean?"

"I mean the destruction of the reality you know. The universe will be ripped apart and recreated in my lord Xaldoruks's image."

"Negative, you mean. Lucifer won't mind if I disagree with that plan."

Zamx's smirk disappeared and reappeared on Max's face.

"Ah, did I touch a nerve? There are plenty of stories about who your master is. People call him the worst thing to happen to the universe; they call him Satan. But men like you and me know the truth—that all those names people call him aren't as metaphoric as people believe. He truly is the thirteenth angel, isn't he? The fallen star damned to scrounge around with the rest of us mortals. And this plan of his to rip apart the universe and recreate it in his image is what, in the end? Is it just a way of crying out to Daddy? Forgive me for saying, but it seems just a bit childish, to say the least. Yeah, that's what it is. This is just a child trying to say screw you to his old man. So much carnage, so much work, because of some daddy issues."

Zamx's laugh returned but more malevolently and disturbing than before, as if it were piercing Max directly. "You know, Max, I have to commend you for having as much balls as you do. Even with this knowledge, you still dis him like he's just another kid on the playground. But he's far more than that. He's a god now."

"Well, it's actually quite calming. If the devil is real, then that must mean God's real too. Sets my soul at ease a bit."

"There is no God, only Xaldoruks. Only darkness. Soon the

entire universe will know this to be law."

"How? How is this going to happen?"

"Well, the first part of the plan involves you. You should be honored. After millennia of war, you are the key that brings it to an end."

"I'm assuming you mean in a way that's less then pleasant."

"I'm sure you've noticed that you and I are the same. Same look, same voice, same everything—except for one minor detail in the looks department. Our right arms are different."

"Your 'master' ripped off my right arm."

"Yeah, funny how that worked out. You see, once he ripped it off, he didn't just toss it. He used it to his advantage—to see if a Negative could be forged as its own being. And with your DNA, he managed to create one—a Negative that could sustain its own life and not just feed off another."

"So you're saying that…"

"Yeah, say hi to your arm," he said, waving his right hand at him.

"You bastard!"

"Ah, ah, ah. Let me finish. Because we are of the same flesh and blood, we are eternally linked. However, my life force isn't purely independent. This arm isn't mine. It's still spiritually linked to you. So no matter what happens, if you die, I die. Also the opposite is the same. If I die, I'm taking you with me. So in order for me to be truly independent and eternal, the pieces must become one again."

"Great; hand over my arm."

"Your soul and mine must fuse into one, fueling the collision between positive and negative, creating a being that can sustain life eternal among mortal men. This is the state where I will inherit the universe and claim its rule in my hand. But in order for any of that to happen, your light must give way to darkness. Your power must clash with mine, and your mind, heart, and soul must submit."

"There is only one minor flaw in your plan," Max said. "What if I don't fight you?"

Zamx started to walk around to him. Max moved in the opposite direction until they were walking in a standoff.

"See, Max, you and I are total opposites. I am darkness and you are light. It is destiny that you and I are to fight. There is no way for you to not fight me." He pointed to Tyra and Zack. "Every time you try to leave or refuse to fight, I will squeeze the life right out of them, and I will make you watch them die."

"Ah, I see." Max dropped his wit and spoke with more bass in his voice. "You should know—I may not be as bright a light as you think."

Zamx scoffed. The two stopped in their places.

"Well, now that the lecture is over, let's move on to the demonstration." Zamx drew his Blade base, and the darkness summoned the Dark Sanctuary Blade. Max drew his Chaos Blade. Zamx jumped at Max and attacked from above. Max swiftly blocked and countered, trading blows. The battle had begun.

Meanwhile, Zack struggled to get out of the tentacles. Tyra had hit her head hard on the wall and gone unconscious. Zack kept pushing and pulling while the tentacles only got tighter around them. He realized he was making it worse. Zack concentrated and felt the pulses from the tentacle at regular intervals. He started to send shocks into the tentacle and, slowly but surely, he was getting through.

Max kept fighting Zamx. However, despite his training with Luand, he ended up running out of energy really quickly. Starting the battle off with so much force took its toll on him. He was doing more dodging than attacking, and every attack he made, was failing.

"Come on, Blaze," Zamx shouted. "You're dying on me. You can't be tired already. *Give me more!*" Max just kept panting. "Release your chains and come at me with full force…or do you need some motivation?" He extended his arm and clenched his fist. The tentacles around Zack and Tyra tightened. Max shot back up.

"Okay! Okay!" he said. "I'll play your game. He extended his right arm and pushed the glowing blue shoulder button. Fluid started going down the tube and into his arm and body.

"Now I'm ready!" He took the Chaos Blade and found new energy to keep going.

Tyra finally woke up. The tentacles started to tighten more frequently. Zack tried to send stronger pulses. But it still took too long and Zack started to panic.

Max stayed on the offensive, attacking from the top, side, and behind. He even resorted to throwing fireballs. But still he grew more and more tired. And the more he grew tired, the more he grew frustrated and angry about his own inabilities. The angrier he became the sloppier his moves and attacks became as well. He fought hard against the temptation to use his Xylonite and focused on defeating his opponent.

Zamx made it worse by egging him on.

"Geez, dude, you're so pathetic right now. What the hell happened to all that sweet talk? I could spar with a fragile puppy—it'd be more entertaining than you." He knelt down to Max, who was trying to catch his breath. "Do you know what your problem is? You're fighting your impulses. Your heart is telling you to not let me get away with it, but your mind is getting in the way, keeping you from harnessing the strength you need to defeat me. It's keeping you weak, bud. You have to ignore it and channel that energy and thought into one emotion. Rage. Jealousy. Pride. Anything. Charge at me with it and see how much more powerful you feel."

Dark auras started to flow from Max. Hatred started to take shape. More of his emotions started to form by means of dark energy. Max kept remembering Luand's words and tried to fight back. But it was too late. He had tasted his heart's darkness once before, and Zamx's taunting made him crave it again. He had no control anymore. He hungered for his heart darkness.

Zamx smiled.

"That's it, Max," he said. "Can you feel it? Now give in to it. Give in to your lust for power. Let your gluttony for it hunt it down. Let your envy take control of you. Protect your pride with power. Let your greed be your instincts. Let sloth relinquish you from your burdens to the light. Let your wrath be your power. And then unleash it all at once!"

In one strong and powered yell, Max released giant waves of darkness that stretched throughout the area. Dragon wings grew out of his back. His teeth grew sharper and his left hand's nails did as well. His right arm grew in size to match the other arm. His eyes turned into an eternal pit of darkness. The darkness inside him had finally been unleashed.

Zamx was pleased. He had a satisfied look on his face as he put away his Blade. But then the smirk disappeared. There were too many strong pulses that kept coming. He hadn't expected the dragon wings to manifest. As he felt each pulse coming from him grow stronger than the last, he started to back away slowly.

Max spoke to him in a demonic voice. "Where do you think

you're going, Zamx?" Zamx looked back. "I'm not done with you yet!"

Max opened his wings and flapped them in one strong and hard stroke. A strong wind struck Zamx and launched him into the air. He opened his eyes and saw that Max was right in front of him. But a second later, he was behind him. Max punched him and moved to a different place multiple times. He thrashed him around the room until finally he knocked him to the ground. Max gently landed on the ground while Zamx lay in the seat of rubble made by his fall.

Max sent power to his Chaos Blade. Zamx summoned his Dark Sanctuary Blade and sent power to it as well. The two ran at each other and clashed swords. Max attacked and ran right through Zamx's defense. Every time he attacked, Zamx could not block. Finally, he mustered up the last of his power and barely defended himself from the immense flow of darkness coming from Max. However, this didn't faze Max at all. He held one hand behind his back and laughed maniacally. He then hit Zamx's gut and shot a direct burst of a jet stream. Zamx traveled a long distance and rolled on the floor.

Zack still struggled to get out from his contained state. However, Tyra kept watching Max fight. She suddenly was appalled at who her friend had become.

Zamx picked himself up off the floor. When he turned to look at Max, he was kicked onto the floor. "Come on, Zamx!" he said. He kept kicking him into the hard tiles. "You act like you're so tough, don't you? What was all that talk about?" Max held his head to the floor and kept smashing it. He flew up, leaving him in the ground and held his sword with the edge facing Zamx. He stood there floating, his eyes closed and thinking about how he could be rid of Zamx for good.

Zamx just lay there half-conscious, motionless, and smiling, waiting for death to take both of them. Just as he was about to strike, Max heard a voice crying out to him. He opened his eyes, turned, and saw that Tyra was screaming at him from the floor of the room next to Zack, whose left hand was completely numb.

"Don't do it, Max," she yelled. "Remember what he said. If you kill him, you'll kill yourself."

Max dropped the Chaos Blade and grabbed his head in pain. With so much confusion in his head, he fell out of the air. He took regular breaths. When he opened his eyes, he saw he was back to normal. He felt a shooting pain in his left arm, and his right was functioning but in terrible condition.

Zamx picked himself up to his feet. He laughed at Max loudly, grabbing his attention.

"Well, looks like I really did underestimate you, Max! You were right. You're not as bright as I thought. I'm curious to know how this little ability will help future events to unfold."

He turned to the wall and opened a dark portal.

"I'll see you a lot sooner than you'd like."

He walked through the portal and disappeared. Max ran over to Zack and Tyra.

"Are you all right?" he asked.

"We're fine," Tyra answered. "Don't worry about us. What about you?"

"Well, my left arm is bruised badly, and my right arm could use repairs, but other than that, I'm fine. What about you guys? Do you still have them?"

Zack took off his bag and showed the crystals inside it.

"All right, let's go." Max headed to the door, but Zack and Tyra remained still.

"Wait, Max," Zack called out. "What the hell was all of that? Where did it come from?"

Max turned around slowly. "It's nothing, okay?"

"Nothing? Really? What we saw out there was not you! It was something…well, dark."

"Don't worry; you won't see it again. Now we've got to go."

"It's what he trained you to do, isn't it?" Tyra spoke up.

Max remained silent.

"You picked that up with Luand. Why? Why would he teach you something like that?"

"It's not what you think, okay? All you need to know is that the rules of the world that we enforce, that we are told are true, are not as black and white as you may think."

"What does that mean?" Zack yelled at him.

"Do you really want to discuss this now?"

"Yes, Max. Why are you dark? Why are there wings out of your back, and why is this something I'm just discovering now!"

"Zack," he said, grabbing his friend's shoulder. "Please. Trust me. This wasn't a secret that I've had for long, okay? Luand taught me some of it, but he never finished. That's why I was out of control. I wasn't supposed to use it yet until I completely understood it. When I do I will tell you, but Luand is still our leader. He wouldn't teach me anything I wouldn't need for the better. Please, can you accept that?"

Zack looked into Max's eyes and nodded hesitantly.

"Great, now can we get the hell out of here?"

They each hit the teleports on their suits, but none of them responded.

"What the hell?"

"They must've broken when we were on the wall and you were fighting Zamx," Tyra said.

"So we're stuck."

"Oh my god," Zack said, freaking out. "We don't have time to get out to the top. What the hell are we going to do?"

"Zack, calm down," Max yelled. "We can figure it out. Everything has an exit point."

Tyra spotted the portal that Zamx had gone through.

"And I think Zamx just left us one."

"The portal? Who knows where it will take us?"

"It's better than staying here, facing a certain doom." She grabbed their hands and ran for the portal. It started to close slowly. Running faster, the three made it into the portal at the last second.

"Time's up! Fire the missile," Battlux ordered. The captain and his men prepared the guns to fire. Genesis only looked out to the planet using her Xylonite. She focused her eyes to the top of a tower and saw that Max, Zack, and Tyra were there.

"Battlux, you can't do this. I see them at the top of the tower. If they haven't teleported, then that probably means they can't. Their gear is probably damaged. We have to retrieve them."

"There's no time left. We've spent too long on this mission; we need to move out."

"No, look for yourself: he's just on top of that tower. Zoom in on our target. They're waiting for us! Look! We can grab them, fly out, and then shoot your damn missiles. Please do not just leave them there."

Battlux looked off at the planet. Genesis could see the

faintest of smiles appear on his face. Then he said "Fire." The warship launched a subspace missile at the castle.

The portal took them to the top of the tower of the castle. They looked up to the sky and tried to communicate with the ship but were unable to.

"How are we going to get back to the ship? Are they picking us up?" Tyra asked.

"I think we were lucky that we haven't been blown up yet," Max concluded. "If they were planning to shoot something at this castle, it would be on its way right now."

"Great; so how are we getting out?"

Max kept smacking his head, trying to think. "Okay, okay. Idea. Technically speaking only our teleports are broken; our suits are still functioning. So we can actually shoot up the same way we came down, right?"

"There is that matter of gravity pulling us back," Zach said sarcastically.

"Yeah, but I have wings right now. What if I were to fly us back to the ship?"

"Could you take us both?"

"I haven't used these for too long, so I'm not sure. But I could definitely try."

"But that wouldn't work anyway," Zack interjected. "In order to break the atmosphere of any planet you'd have to be going at a rocket's speed. We can't just cruise through to the ship."

"Damn it! You're right." Max kept smacking his head. "Okay, another idea. I can burn molecules in the air to launch us up like a rocket! If you guys hold on tight, we can break through the atmosphere."

"But then we'll be in space. There's no air to burn in space or to push us with your wings."

"We'll have to take the chance."

"If it's the only plan we've got, let's go."

They all put their helmets on, and Zack and Tyra grabbed onto Max tightly. Max started shooting fire at his feet, and the three blasted off into the sky, using his wings to keep him going straight. As they soared higher into the sky, a metal object passed them on its way down.

"What was that?" Tyra asked.

"That's probably the missile they were going to shoot at us."

The missile hit the castle, but there was no explosion. A light sparked from the castle, and then it started to cave in on itself. All of the pieces of it were sucked into a black-and-purple ball growing from the center. The trio looked back and saw the reaction. Max suddenly slowed down and was unable to move quickly.

"Max!" Zack called out. "What's happening?"

"It's a black hole!" he yelled back. "It's sucking up all the air so I can't get out fast enough."

"Max you have to go faster! We'll be killed by it!"

Max furiously tried to push himself, but nothing new was happening. Zack then remembered that their suit had jets built into their back and their shoes. He signaled to Tyra to turn them on. With the extra boost, Max started to speed up again, pushing them away from the black hole and toward the ship.

"Zack, link us up again."

Zack sent electric bursts though his communicator, setting up the link again.

"Ember! Ember! Come in."

Genesis, on the verge of tears, leaped at the sound of her communicator.

"Flame?"

"Open the launch door at the bottom of the ship!"

The trio had just left the atmosphere and gone into space. Max's fire went out, and his wings started to freeze. It was up to Zack and Tyra to aim them at the ship. Genesis ran to the ship's launching room and opened the hatch. At that moment, Max shot out of space into the wall of the room. Genesis closed the door and filled the room with air, immediately running to Zack and helping him up. Max breathed heavily and stirred as he watched his sister ignore him still.

"Don't worry; I'm all right," he said, trying to get her attention. "I just did something amazing again. Just another morning for Max Blaze." He was about to fall on his side but was caught by Tyra who helped him back to his feet.

He turned to the door and found Battlux staring at him with a crew standing right behind him.

"Battlux!" he shouted. He started to walk toward him.

"Mission accomplished. The shield has been neutralized; the Negative Matter generator has been disabled. But I'll have you know that it was thanks to me. And we didn't need your stupid missile to clean up! What the hell was that?"

Battlux remained quiet.

"That was a subspace missile, wasn't it?"

Battlux stared him down, but Max gave him an equally harsh look.

"Do you have the crystals?" Battlux asked in a commanding tone.

Max looked back at Zack.

"Give him the bag, Zack." Zack walked up and handed his pack to Battlux. Battlux looked inside, confirmed the contents, and passed it on to his captain.

"Arrest the Chaos Flame Sandshark. Put him in a containment cell until we get to headquarters."

The soldiers pointed their guns at Max and apprehended him. Max struggled and fought back. Zack moved to Max's aid but was apprehended, as were Tyra and Genesis.

"What the hell is this? I just got you the crystals. I completed the mission."

"Look at those wings. They are obviously of dark origins. According to the law of the Universal Protection Agency, I am forced to arrest and contain you. I'm only following orders."

The soldiers took a shock collar and stuck it on his neck, sending large bolts of lightning through him. As he went unconscious, the wings disappeared. They took him to a cell while the other soldiers released Genesis, Tyra, and Zack.

"I hope that you will do the same thing if you are in my position."

"You can't get away with this," Tyra warned. "You're at fault, too. If Max goes to jail, we tell Luand about your 'subspace' whatever."

Battlux walked back to them. "You tell Luand about my little experiment, I make sure something worse than jail happens to him."

Max was transferred from the ship to his cell in the bottom of the prison building. He sat in the cell with an invisible screen lock keeping him in while he banged his head next to the cold, hard steel platform they called his bed. Staring into the wall, he could almost hear people on the floor above.

He felt a lot of anger surging through him. Every time he thought about breaking out, he kept hearing Luand's voice telling him that being angry wouldn't help him. He went back to listening to the steady beat of his head banging against the bed singing a lullaby to himself. He tried to remember where it was from. Concentrating on it, he could tell it was a woman's voice singing to him. It was gentle and calming. He knew this was what his mother sang to him as a child. He smiled and continued humming.

Another person was being escorted to the dark cell next to him. He kept yelling, "I'm innocent, I tell you. Honest. I didn't do anything. I just walked downtown and then...nothing. I don't remember a thing, I swear." The guard just threw him in the cell, hit a button, and left. The man didn't see any bars keeping him in. He got happy and ran for the entrance full force but was inexplicably beaten back hard into the wall. Max stopped his lullaby for a moment.

"If it were that easy, don't you think everyone would be out of here by now?"

The man turned around and tried walking toward him, but was beaten hard to the other invisible wall on the opposite side of the cell. "What the hell is this?" he said. "I need to get out of here!"

Max chuckled. "Good luck with that."

"Well, excuse me for not giving up hope in this crappy cell."

Max turned his head to the man. "I haven't given up hope," he said, offended. "I know how to get out of this thing from the inside."

"Really? And how is that?" the stranger asked.

"I work here. These are classic invisible counter walls. They are designed to take the power of the prisoner, magnify it, and counterattack if they try to escape."

"If you know so much about these cells, why aren't you breaking out?"

"Well, that wouldn't make me look any less guilty, now would it? I have to let them think I believe in this judicial system." He turned back to the front of the cell. The man turned back as well. The two stayed silent for a while.

"Your power is physical strength?" Max asked.

216

"It was until some cloaked guy walks up to me, grabs my arm, and leaves this mark on me." He showed Max his arm. It had markings in the shape of a handprint. "Ever since then, I've been blacking out at the end of the day and waking up to everything being a mess. I always have to run from planet to planet, but then I black out, and the cycle repeats again. The same thing happened in downtown, and now I'm here. And all of this was because I have to give some kid named Maximillion Blaze some message from the guy."

Max looked up. "What did you just say?"

"I have to give some kid named Maximillion Blaze some message from the cloaked man. He said he'd be able to read the marking on my arm."

"Let me see your arm again."

The stranger presented it to him. Max looked at it and couldn't see anything but the handprint mark. He then used his Xylonite to look at it. After he activated it, words appeared:

The end is near. Enjoy the final battles of the war!
Love ZMX

Max turned and scoffed at it. "It's a stupid message, probably. I don't think it's anything your recipient needs to see."

After about a week of pointless conversations and idle waiting, Max thought about the war and how much bloodshed had been caused. Haunted by thinking of all the lives that gave themselves up for the battle, he got on his knees, folded his hands, and just sat in silence. Reflecting on every life he had encountered, he silently opened his mouth and said, "Thank you."

The guard came back for the man and opened his cell door.

"Well, good-bye, my friend. Looks like my fate is sealed." He got up and headed for the stairs with the man. "Before I go, kid, what's your name?"

Max looked at him and shook his head. "My name's not important. It's everyone else's you have to think about."

Another week passed, and Max grew more and more numb after being locked in the same place for so long. Realizing it was just like the stump in his training with Luand, he tried to listen to his dark powers. He noticed a shadow come in front of him.

"Zack?" Max called out.

"Close, but no cigar," the voice said.

"What?" Max said, confused.

"Never mind."

Max opened his eyes.

"Luand," Max said, feeling a shred of relief. "So the formal interrogations begin? Okay, so what is the story you've been told?"

"You were trying to attack the troops while you flew into the ship holding Zack and Tyra hostage. You tried to steal the bag of Orchaic Crystals from Battlux and attacked your own sister. You were a complete tyrant and almost destroyed the ship. Of course, Zack, Tyra, and Genesis told me their story, which is much more reasonable. My only question for you is why did you not follow my orders about keeping darkness away for now? I told you something like this would happen."

"It wasn't my fault completely. Remember the Negative I told you about in training? He showed up again. Turns out he was born from the arm that Xaldoruks severed from my body on my first day. He's trying to get me to join with him into one being so we can be the perfect balance of positive and negative."

"Using a Negative that can live by itself and a Positive with enough trained dark power that it would be strong enough to withstand the procedure. Since he was born of your arm, your genetics are the same and your body wouldn't fight the union. Damn, that's clever."

"What? What is?"

"Remember how I said you were my chosen one? Well, it turns out you are Xaldoruks's as well. He's trying to create another body for himself. By balancing his own negative power with a positive template, he can use his darkness to take over the perfect host body and be able to live on for eons more with more power than before."

"So, Xaldoruks is trying to get to me?"

"Oh Max, I do apologize. By training you the way I have and showing you the Truth, I've endangered you far more than I should have. He's going to try to draw you out, make every attempt to make you fall into your Dark Malevolence. And he won't ever stop." Max sat back and felt ultimately helpless. "I am so sorry about this—all of this. I just wished the world wasn't so stuck in its ways. I dreamed once that the war was over and that people were accepting of other people. Everyone knew the truth, and people only fought to defend it. Darkness and light coexisted in perfect harmony, and the suns rose on a clear future for everyone."

"You're starting to sound like that Michael Lex Queen guy from Earth seven thousand years ago."

"You mean Martin Luther King Jr."

"Right, him."

Luand stood up from his chair. "You'd better think up your counterarguments, Max," he warned. "Your trial is tomorrow. I'll try to help you as much as I can, but if it's not enough for the council, I'm out of ways to help."

Max nodded and got to work and Luand left.

"Maximilian Blaze!" Luand announced. Max stood in the middle of the ring of council members floating in their high chairs, with a moving background of the universe flowing by. Max felt just a bit too familiar with his position.

"You have been brought here by the order of ventushark Battlux to report some form of use of darkness on a mission led by Genesis Blaze, the Fusion Ember. Do you deny these charges?"

"No."

"Well, that's all we needed, right, master?" Battlux interjected. "He clearly isn't denying it; therefore, I move to abide by the rules of the agency in requesting he be decommissioned immediately."

"What?" Max said, shocked. "Decommissioned? That's completely uncalled for."

"In accordance to the laws that we have," Luand announced, "Battlux is correct. Decommissioning you would be our next action."

"That's completely unfair. He's only trying to get rid of me because I know what he did that was illegal on that mission."

"Sir," Battlux said with haste, "I implore you to decommission him right now!"

"Silence, Battlux," Luand said. "What is it he actually did?"

"He launched an illegal subspace missile at a civilian population without Genesis's authorization and more importantly, I'm sure, without yours."

"This is an outrageous accusation," Battlux said.

"Check the coordinates where the castle used to be. You'll find a perfect crater where the event occurred."

"Max, we've already checked the castle's location.

Unfortunately, due to the nature of the subspace technology, it is impossible to know whether or not a subspace device was used, much less if it were used by Battlux."

"There were plenty of witnesses. Everyone who was on the warship when the missile was fired."

"Everyone on that ship denies that a subspace missile was fired."

"That's ridiculous! What about Zack and Tyra? Even Genesis, the leader of that mission. Her word has to have some weight."

"You are correct that they all argued in your defense. However, this council knows how close you are to each of them and since they're the only ones who argued for you, the validity of their word is put into question."

"Oh, come on."

Luand stared at Max for a moment. Max shrugged, and Luand shook his head, disappointed. "Because of your use of darkness, you would be decommissioned and exiled. However, since we are not from the dark ages, and the last time we had to use this ruling was millennia ago, I think that it is necessary to update these laws."

"What?" Battlux said, shocked.

"You used the reported dark wings to rescue not only yourself but your friends as well from some unauthorized missile that destroyed the castle. If you can use this power from the surface to launch yourself into space, it must be an incredible power you have. You seemed to showcase many of the strengths this power has. Perhaps this is an ability to open our eyes to. Iramint, I want you to monitor Maximilian Blaze and put him on surveillance. If we can know the power of this darkness and make sure it is truly benign, perhaps we can have a thirteenth Sandshark class again. So Max, you will be granted your freedom, but you will be surveyed from now on. Do you accept these terms?"

"Absolutely."

"Sir," Battlux said. "I believe you're letting your connection to the defendant cloud your judgment.

"It is true I know Chaos Flame well. And it's because of this that I know what he is like and I can discern what really happened. This session is over. You may go."

Max vanished from the room. Luand leaned back and addressed the council again.

"How are the crystals?"

"Safe and contained. All nine are powerless, but we will find the other four. They may be able to restore power to the rest of them."

"Don't waste your effort. We have all we need. Continue searching for targets and return to your assignments."

With that, they all disappeared, leaving Battlux and Luand.

"Sir, what the hell was that? You merely left him with a warning. Twenty-four-hour surveillance?"

"You're lucky I didn't switch you two out and start prosecuting you! Using subspace missiles on civilian populations? Do you really think I'm naïve enough to not notice something like that? Have you lost your mind?"

"Nobody can trace it back to us. If anything they'll just blame the Negatives. It's their technology. We just need more information on it. How else will we get that if we don't test some things out?"

"What happened to you, Battlux? You've fallen so far so suddenly. First it was your obsession with subspace technology. Now, it seems, it's Max. You are dangerously close to being replaced."

Luand then disappeared, leaving Battlux by himself.

"How would I know? I feel like it's happened already.".

10 PHASE 1

Eyes followed him everywhere. It was three weeks after his release, and the hammering stares weighed him down. He couldn't even be in the lounge without being treated like an outsider. His miraculous evasion of punishment from the council, a feat he was extremely proud of, seemed suddenly wrong. Tyra, Zack, Robert, and Kevin were the only friends he had left who would still talk to him. They all sat at the lunch table in the cafeteria with the web of eyes revolving around them. As people orbited their table at a safe distance, Max grew more uncomfortable as the moments passed by.

"Max," Tyra called out, trying to pacify his agitated state, "don't think about it."

"When the entire base is scolding you with no words, it becomes really hard." He finally broke after a while, unable to take the pressure. "I need some air." As soon as he left, people instantaneously flocked to the table.

A girl with fluffy, curly hair showed up. "Why are you still hanging around with that freak?"

"You mean the person you had a crush on three weeks ago?" Tyra said.

"But he uses darkness. You do realize how taboo that is?"

"To save us!" Zack commented. "It was only once, and if he hadn't, we would all have died. He saved our lives."

"So? It almost doesn't seem worth it. It's because of people like him that the Negatives are even around. Now we have one of them in our ranks? It's disgusting."

"Yeah," yet another said. "I have to agree. I think I'd rather be dead than be saved by darkness."

"Come on, guys," Robert interjected. "Are you listening to yourselves? This is our friend. What's so bad about darkness anyway? He's the same guy that you guys hung around before. Now suddenly you're shunning him."

"Are you an idiot? Darkness is the enemy of light. It disrupts the balance of the world, and we need to make sure we can keep the world under control. That's why every dark Terrascopian born is rejected to facilities to be watched. I guess he must have gotten away."

Zack jumped up. "That's because we're afraid of them for something only Xaldoruks did. Just because the worst of them did something this bad doesn't mean all of them are evil."

"Zack, we have plenty of good reason. It's not fear. It's safety. Seriously, I feel we should just decommission him right now!"

"Okay, now you're getting ridiculous. Max has saved lives countless times, including yours, and now you want to thank him by getting rid of him. If he could, he would rescue any one of you right here and now, even after what you said about him. He's not bad!"

"You watch what you say, Zack!" the girl said, snapping back. "It almost sounds like you're defending darkness."

"Yeah, if that were the case, you'd have to be decommissioned, too."

Zack remained quiet. The two opperatives left the table. The tense air was palatable and there was an awkward silence.

Tyra spoke to Zack. "That was a lot of nice things you said back there."

"Yeah, well, don't get used to it. As much as I want to defend my best friend and refuse to have him badmouthed, I'm still not comfortable with the idea that he uses darkness."

"I'm struggling with it, too. But the fact that Max uses it isn't what disturbs me."

"What does?"

"What if what we've been taught has been a lie the whole time? Darkness was supposed to be the absolute enemy, and yet here we have been working with it this whole time. What else isn't true? Or what other facts are out of date?"

Kevin stood up from the table and turned to Tyra. "I think

Max is showing us that it's okay to stand out, even in ways that aren't socially accepted. Perhaps if he can do some serious good, like win a major battle or show the world his merit, he can bring a new kind of harmony—one no one expected."

"Well, Kevin, you have telekinetic powers. If you can see the future, tell us. Does any of that happen?"

Kevin smirked and walked away.

A UPA fighter ship came out of sonic light speed and stopped at the planet's orbit. Sitting at the wheel was Zamx with dead soldiers at his feet. He hit the communicator screen. It sent out a hologram to the center of the ship showing Xaldoruks. Zamx got out of the chair and knelt before his lord and master.

"My lord, I have done as you asked and commandeered the UPA ship. I am now orbiting Zapheraizia. How would you like me to proceed?"

"Take the item out of the cylinder in your bag and ingest it. Think of the face of the driver, then descend upon their headquarters."

"Master, do you mean I—"

"Yes, my apprentice. You may begin Phase 1."

"With pleasure, my master."

The communication cut off. He did as he was told and picked up the cylinder. He picked up a large purple egg. It cracked open, releasing from it what looked like a small octopus. He stuck it down his throat. After he swallowed, the tentacles began crawling out of his mouth and emerging from the side of his body. They wrapped around his head and his arms until none of his body could be seen. The tentacles then molded together and began to take the shape of another individual.

He got back into the driver's seat and flew the ship to the planet. Bypassing security at the orbital stations, he descended upon Zapheraizia.

He flew the ship into the hangar and hid the bodies of the two dead soldiers in one of its closets. As he walked out and headed to the bunking dorms, his appearance changed. His hair became long and fiery, his shoes became heels, and his eyes became misleadingly gentle. His figure became thin and curvy, all wrapped in a leather outfit. As he walked through the door, he saw Max coming from upstairs. The two looked at each other.

"Hey, Ty," Max said.

Zamx stayed quiet.

Suddenly Max's Xylonite activated on its own. He felt something was wrong with the girl he had just passed. He looked at her, but she looked normal. She waved at him, and he waved back, giving a quick fake smile. She continued on upstairs. Max went outside with a vexed look on his face.

Zamx kept searching through the upper cabins of the building but couldn't find it. With every dorm he entered, his anger grew, but he tried hard to keep it in check so as to not blow his cover.

He came around a corner and saw Tyra wandering about, looking for Max. He hid behind the corner and thought about how to proceed. Tyra knocked on many doors asking whether or not anyone had seen Max. With every door, she got only rude remarks about him and a slammed door in her face. She continued down the hall and saw Max at the end.

"Max?" He remained quiet. She ran to him but didn't hug him. "Where the hell have you been?" she said, with a commanding boom in her voice.

He barely opened his mouth. "Hi."

"Are you doing all right? I know how you get when you're by yourself for too long."

"Well, I think that's just it. I need some time alone."

Tyra shook her head and grabbed his arm. "Max, we've been getting to know each other a lot better lately. And I know you. Okay? Don't shut me out now. Something's wrong with you. It's all over your face."

He yanked his arm out of her grip and started walking past. "No, seriously. I'll be fine on my own."

"Well, fine. Be a pariah. See if I care," she said sharply, walking the other way. As he turned away from her, an abnormally large smile crept onto Zamx's face.

Max went back inside and found Zack talking to a few friends. When he arrived, his friends evacuated. He ignored them and addressed Zack.

"Have you seen Tyra?"

"Not since the café."

"I passed her earlier and something's not right."

"Did your Xylonite activate or something?"

"That's how I knew something was up. She looked fine, but still."

"Well, maybe you're losing your touch. It's probably nothing."

"What about Gen? Have you seen Genesis?"

"Yeah, that reminds me. I need to talk to her about something."

Zack bolted up the stairs.

Max gave a deep sigh. "Okay, you go check on Gen, and I'll just…Oh, whatever." Then he ran off to the dorm rooms. It didn't take long for him to find Tyra sitting in the lounge, reading a book with a vexed look on her face.

"Max," she said with a lot of attitude. "I thought you wanted time to yourself?"

"I said I needed some air," Max said.

"Look, I tried to reach out to you, but you didn't seem to want it, so it's too late now."

"When did you do that?"

"In the hallway upstairs, a few minutes ago."

"But I haven't been up there yet." He stopped and paused. "Tyra, do you remember waving to me on the main stairs this morning as I was going outside?"

"No. I was upstairs looking for you."

There was a moment of pause.

"Ah, shit!" He grabbed her hand and ran out of the hall.

"Max, what's going on?" she shouted.

"Keep your voice down, Ty!"

"Well, I would if I only knew what's going on."

"There's an extremely skilled shape-shifter in the base. I have a hunch about what they're here for, but I'm not sure. We need to find Genesis. Tell her to check on the Orchaic Crystal I gave her, and you do the same."

Zamx began to grow very impatient. He was really tempted to blow the entire base into the sky instead of checking all of the doors. But he kept his anger under control for fear of the scanner discovering his Negative energy. He calmed himself and continued searching the rooms.

Max ran to his room really quickly and checked the box under his bed. He shifted his Koratoric Cube over and found the Orchaic Crystal still sitting there.

Genesis was sitting on her bed facing the window, reading a magazine. She heard a heavy knock on the door. Confused and startled, she opened it. To her surprise, Zack stood at the door, panting and out of breath.

"Zack? What are you doing here?"

Zack tried to catch his breath.

"I...just...wanted to...talk about...something."

"Um," she said, still caught off guard by the visit. "Okay, just let me get my coat, and we can go eat while we talk. I'm a little hungry."

"Okay."

She went back in and got her coat and came out and grabbed Zack's hand. He started to blush. Just as they were walking down, Max and Tyra came down the hall.

"Max, don't worry," Zack called out. "Genesis is okay. The shape-shifter didn't get to her."

Max nodded and started back the other way. "Okay, great. Take her to a safe spot and go check..." He paused and turned back to Zack and squinted his eyes in suspicion. "How'd you know about the shape-shifter?"

"You told me about it."

"I only told Tyra, and I only suggested that something was wrong with her to you." Zack's eyebrow twitched, and his face furled into a frown. He grabbed Genesis's arm.

"Gen, get away from him."

Genesis tried to, but he tightened his grip.

"Come on, Max, you can't seriously be accusing me? I simply asked around and came to the conclusion that it was a shape-shifter."

"I told Zack to keep it a secret," Max said.

"Come on, Max, when have I ever been able to keep a secret?"

"All right. I'm just going to stop your bullshit right here. I never actually told Zack any of this so..."

Max snapped his fingers and sent a tiny fire bolt to his head.

Zack's head exploded but put itself back together.

"As I thought," Max said. "Not human."

They glared at each other for a while. "That's a very interesting shape-shifting technique. You changed not only your appearance, but also your brainwaves and genetic makeup. Only extremely small flaws revealed you." Max snarled. "Now, why don't you show us who you really are?" Max grabbed his face and tore it from his head, dropping the creature that hatched from the egg on the floor. Zamx's true face was revealed. Max was stunned. In a blinding fury, he charged at Zamx.

Zamx then whipped his arm, and a telekinetic pulse pushed Max back.

"Sorry, bro, but we cannot do this now. Don't worry, though; this is only the beginning of the end...at the place where this all began. So it will finally end, and we shall begin anew."

Zamx raised his arm to the ceiling, blasted it open, and flew through the hole. Max jumped after him and grabbed his leg. The two flew around the base as Genesis flailed in Zamx's clutch. Max kept trying to pull Zamx down. Zamx ended up crashing through the ceiling of the lobby and onto the floor. When he hit the surface he lost his grip on Genesis, and she went flying away from him. Tyra and Zack came running down the stairs. They saw Max and Zamx opposite each other. Zamx roared at Max, and just as he was about to charge at him, he heard a screeching in his ear. He stopped and held his head in pain. Xaldoruks's voice rang through his head.

"Zamx!" he yelled. "Do not confront him. Take the girl and return to me. I swear to you, fail to do this and your existence will remain incomplete!"

Zamx screamed, "No! No! I must be complete! Please, okay? I shall obey my master." The screeching in his head stopped. He gave Max a cold look and held out his arm in Genesis's direction. She was stirring and trying to get focused to attack. His dark arm extended further and grabbed her body. He then blew the front door open and flew out. As Max ran after them an unrelenting rage burst from his heart. The wings shot from his back again, and he took flight.

Above the clouds Zamx flew, holding the squirming Genesis in his dark hand. Out of nowhere, a flame shot out from underneath the clouds. Another one followed. More kept coming. Finally, Max shot out and attempted to tackle Zamx, who dodged him just in time.

Max circled back and shot at him like a human bullet. Zamx kept going and saw as he turned around that Max was following dangerously close. Max turned and saw a figure in the far distance. In less than a second, a ship rammed Max out of the sky and into the ocean.

Zamx landed on the ship's wing and looked down at him and laughed. He put Genesis in the back, got in, and flew off with Max's sister. Max rose to the surface and swam to a nearby patch of land and watched the vessel soar off. He realized that he had used the last of his energy chasing Zamx. He clicked a button on his belt and teleported back to base.

Once inside, Max saw that everyone was cleaning up from Zamx's attack. He walked around and saw the mess. He then saw Zack and Tyra near the main stairs. Once he started running to them, a bunch of Sandsharks tackled him to the floor.

Battlux walked up to Max. "I figured you'd betray us, but I never thought you'd do it by yourself. Always thought you would get some of your Negative pawns to help you."

"You're dumber than you look if you think I did this," Max commented. Zack and Tyra immediately ran to Max's aid.

"What are you doing?" Tyra yelled at him.

"The kid has gone too far, attacking the main base of the UPA. I'm using this to take you out."

"Are you an idiot?" Zack shouted. "Max was the only one who made an effort to save the base!"

"As far as I'm concerned, your argument is completely invalid, seeing as how you are a biased party. I cannot take that information. I have several eyewitnesses who claim Max was the one who grabbed Genesis and flew off after destroying the base."

"Well, if you'd kept asking," Tyra said with her anger flaring, "you'd find that there are unbiased people here who are willing to claim that Max saved the base from the shape-shifting being that looked exactly like him."

"Ha, I doubt that's the case. Max is a dark user. I'm sure most of these lovely people would like to see him go. What more proof do we need than the eyewitnesses? I'm just doing what the people would want. But if you have a better way to handle this situation that is fair and legal, share it. Perhaps have another trial for Mr. Blaze here and now after this fiasco?"

Max spoke quietly under his breath. "We don't have time for another damn trial. They just took my sister."

Battlux turned around and addressed Max. "Who has your sister? Where?"

"Zamx, damn it!" he screamed. "The guy who attacked us! I have to go get her, now! She's the only family I have left. We have to get her now! Who knows what they'll do to her."

"Get her from where?"

"I don't know, but I have to start looking!" Max started to scream louder.

Luand walked in, and the rest of the council followed. He looked at Max crying out with his head to the floor. Luand looked at Battlux.

"Sir, this child has attempted to attack and destroy this branch of the UPA. He also seems to have an accomplice that has kidnapped his sister."

Luand looked back at Max and gave a great sigh.

"Release him," he said to the soldiers holding him down.

"What?"

"Battlux, you must think I'm a fool."

"Sir, what do you mean?"

"You know as well as I do this wasn't Max's doing. I'm sick of you complaining to me, acting like a childish tattletale. "

"But sir…"

"You and your damn jealousy. This obsession with destroying Max has gone on long enough. It's time you met me in my office."

"But sir!"

"Now!" he yelled.

Battlux reluctantly stepped away.

"Max, I'm going to want to talk to you as well, so stay put."

Max nodded and sat at the stairs with his friends.

Battlux and Luand stepped into the council meeting room. They didn't get into their chairs. Luand merely stood at the door and finally confronted his apprentice.

"You are expelled from my training."

"What?"

"This ravenous jealousy you have is eating your soul. You're too engulfed in your ways for me to teach you anything."

"This isn't fair."

"You're right. There's more. As long as I lead this planet to the future, you will never be on the council again. You will never have enough power to advance. You will never lead this organization."

"You can't do that!" Battlux yelled, outraged.

"Pride and jealousy are your most prized possessions. They only grow for each rank you gain. Expect an official notice in the coming weeks."

Luand opened the door and left the room, leaving Battlux defeated.

Max stayed on the stairs as he was told. Luand came up to him, and they took a walk around the building.

"So tell me," Luand whispered to him, "was it him?"

"Yes, it was. The counterpart from before."

"He's getting more active and far more arrogant."

"No kidding. Infiltrating the base like this takes guts, especially for a Negative. The thing is, this time he looked like he wanted to fight me but was held back by something."

"Or someone."

"You think it was Xaldoruks who pulled the leash?"

"It would seem so. Breaking in here, he had to have a purpose. Fighting you wouldn't help achieve that purpose."

"My question is why did he take my sister? It doesn't make any sense."

"He's trying to get to you."

"What? Me? Why didn't he just take me?"

"You remember why he wants you. You and your Negative are supposed to become one body in darkness. They're trying to evoke rage out of you. You would defend your sister to the last breath. Just remember that when we get her, you have to keep your cool."

"So we're getting her?"

"Of course we are," he said with an assuring grin. "But first we need to figure out where they took her. We'll need every resource we can get our hands on." He glared at Max for a moment.

"I knew you knew I had the crystals in the first place."

"It's time to turn them in. We may end up needing them. Is there anything he told you that would hint at where they would be?"

"I think he said, 'This is only the beginning of the end. Where this all began, so shall we.'"

"So this is definitely their last play. All the cards are on the table now. Max, I want you on the team to figure out where the final base is. Tell them this clue and don't stop searching until you find it."

Max saluted him with a giant grin of determination and ran off to find his sister.

The flames roared around her as she floated weightlessly in an empty room. She struggled to get the stench of decaying corpses and rotting organisms emanating from under her out of her nose. Invisible shackles were squeezing her arms and legs, allowing only her head to move. A pool of blood covered the floor. The door to the cell opened and Zamx walked in, shutting it behind him.

"Hey," he called out. "Still alive in here?"

Genesis looked up at him with eyes that looked dead already.

"Just making sure that you're not dead yet."

"Very generous of you. That could almost be mistaken for kindness."

"Oh, don't make that mistake. Killing you would be too easy, not to mention a gift compared to what we have in store for you. We just don't want you to miss out on the fun." Zamx started giggling with the thought of it.

"Why? What's the point of all this anyway? Why kidnap me? What value do I have to you?"

Zamx's laugh stopped. He looked at his right arm. "It's not us you have value to, but the one who's going to rescue you."

"I assume you're talking about my brother—the one whose face you stole." Zamx remained quiet. "Well, sad to say, but you kidnapped me at a bad time. I've sort of been shunning him lately. Based on the way I've been treating him, I doubt he even cares I'm gone."

"Don't sell yourself short, bait. Just because you've been ignoring him doesn't mean that he won't bend the universe to find you. I gave him a clue as to where we are. If he can crack it, then he'll be here soon enough. Then he and I will become one."

"Why is it so important that you and he become one?"

"He and I are the battle between light and dark. Lord Xaldoruks wants his successor to be powerful. As I am now, I am not at my full potential. I'm only half. With Max fused to my body…"

"What? You will be *all* powerful?"

"More than that. I'll be eternal! I will inherit this universe as my own. And I will no longer be bound by any rules or restrictions. I will be my own."

"What do you mean?"

Zamx sighed. "Never mind. Just shut up and sit quiet."

Zamx turned around and headed for the exit. Just before he got through the door, Genesis spoke.

"You don't have your own emotions, do you?"

Zamx stopped in his tracks. He turned back around. "What did you say?"

"You can't feel on your own."

"I have my own emotions," he said under his breath.

"Only based on Max's emotions."

"I can feel all I want," he said, suddenly agitated. "My thoughts are my own. My actions are my own. And my opinions you can be damn sure are my own. I can hate and want, be angry or proud. For example, I know I hate you a lot more now."

"Only because Max loves me."

"I follow and worship Lord Xaldoruks out of respect."

"Only because Max fights against and despises him."

"Just shut up!"

"And you can't even come up with a snappy comeback. Oh yeah, you're the opposite of my brother all right."

He remained quiet, trying to ignore her.

"Is that the real reason why you want to fuse? How can you live like that?"

"Easily. So my emotions tend to be negative in nature. What do you think I am? These negative emotions, these feelings—they are what empower me. Just as you feel stronger when you help someone and relieve pain, I feel stronger when I inflict it. My emotions make me stronger. Incomplete as we are, we Negatives are the enhancement of life throughout the universe. Your life force empowers us. The world you hold will be ours as our birthright. We will declare independence once and for all from this 'god' who created you."

"And the sad part is that as independent as you are, your existence purely revolves around us. Even if you become one with

Max, you'll still be dependent on him to exist on your own. Your whole world that you want to declare independent is built on what we are. You may have a heart and a mind, but the one thing you can never forge for yourself, the thing you have to take from others, is a soul."

"A soul?" Zamx scoffed. "What exactly is a soul?"

"What?"

"You have one, right? So what is it? What is a soul in scientific terms?"

Genesis thought about it. "You can't. You can't define a soul scientifically. In those terms a soul doesn't even exist. It is the essence of one's personality, which manifests itself as a state of mind that affects our choices."

"Spoken like a pawn of the government. You think too literally. If that were the true definition of a soul, then we Negatives would have them. No, the true definition is much more complex. A soul, as Lord Xaldoruks and I have come to understand it, is the spiritual principle of life, feeling, or thought regarding emotional aspects of human nature—or in other words, the source of life. You don't realize it, but that is what runs you beings. Not the heart or the lungs, but the soul—the one thing that any being has yet to completely explain. Lord Xaldoruks discovered something on another planet when he once searched for the orchaic crystals—a blue, flowing gel-like substance. It had the power to augment one's abilities, and it gave him the power to animate Negative Matter, give it a personality, and make it live. But not complete it. From scratch Lord Xaldoruks discovered the basics of a life form considered to be the basis of a soul, a negative soul. But it wasn't finished. The Negative life wouldn't stimulate itself on its own. It would only live for a short time, then die. Lord Xaldoruks, soon after, came up with the idea of finding another life source. So eventually, he started feeding Positive life forms to the Negative test subjects. They lasted a little longer, but a Positive's life can only sustain a Negative for so long. So his goal was to somehow link a Positive being's life force to a Negative's life source without killing it. This led to him linking the Negative half soul to the Positive complete soul in the hopes that the half soul would become complete. That portion of his plan didn't work. But he found a way for us to live, but only as long as the human lives and vice versa. This is the law I live by. The Negatives' spawn is pure energy that latches on to a life form and takes over its body and takes various forms. But I am the first unique Negative, one that can succeed the greatness of my master." His watch started to ring. "Looks like my time is up here." He turned his back and headed for the door.

"He's going to kill you," she said. "And you know that. In the end it's not worth that."

He smirked at her. "You're so cute!"

"Why?"

"You think I'm going to take it without a fight. If Lord Xaldoruks tries to absorb me, I'm not going to just let him."

"You really think you can take on your own master by yourself?"

"He promised me a kingdom to rule. By blessing or Blade, it will be mine. Besides, Max will be inside me if my master does intend to fight me."

"Now you're the cute one."

"Why?"

"Because you think Max is going to take it without a fight."

"With you, Genesis, he just might." He exited the room, leaving Genesis to worry about Max's future as well as her own.

Moments had passed, and Genesis couldn't find a way to free herself. All she could do was float in the ring of fire and wait for someone to help her. As she let the thought of her rescue set in, she violently rejected it. She felt this was the perfect way to show that she could survive on her own. She looked around the room for something that might free her from her invisible shackles. Over by the door of the room, she saw what looked like a switch. Since she couldn't launch any projectiles at it, she resorted to spitting at the switch. She kept going at it for ten minutes straight. When she was just about to give up on this tactic, she spat out a bit of fire that latched on to the switch and burned it out. Not expecting this turn of events, she fell on top of the pile of corpses. She was finally free. She picked herself up, jumped over the ring of fire, and walked out the door and searched for gear.

Xaldoruks sat in a chair looking at the images on his surveillance screens. Zamx walked in.

"How's she doing?" he asked.

"She's fine; she'll last long enough for the UPA to find us." Xaldoruks turned around and went back to his work. Zamx turned back as well but paused before attending to his work. "My Lord," he muttered, "how will you benefit from my completion? It seems very selfless of you, if you don't mind me saying."

"When a good thing comes to you, do not question why it came about. You may just have it taken away."

"I just wonder. What's going to happen to me when I do become complete?"

Xaldoruks paused. "You will inherit the universe, of course. I will most likely die with my father when I confront him soon after your union. So you will need to succeed me."

Zamx nodded and hesitantly turned around in his chair. The alarm sounded, and a screen turned on showing a view from a monitor outside the cell. They saw Genesis in a room with a bunch of defeated Negatives, grabbing her gear. She looked at the camera and shot it down with a ball of fire. The screen went to static. Zamx clenched his fist.

"How did she escape? I just checked on her." He ran to the door.

Xaldoruks stopped him. "Wait, Zamx," he said. "I grow increasingly impatient and bored. Let her wander around for a while. You can play with her as you wish, but remember she remains alive. Then send her to the lunar room."

Zamx grinned.

Genesis strapped on her utility belt, grabbed both of her Blades, and equipped herself with some of the tools and weapons from the Negatives around the room. She got to a door and carved a hole in it with her Blades. Behind the door was an entire hallway filled with Negatives. She unstrapped the Blades from her wrist and launched at them, knocking them down one by one until none were left. By the time she was done, she was out of breath and exhausted. She heard more Negatives coming from around the corner. She noticed an air vent above her head. She shot it open and then jumped off the walls and into the vents before the Negatives turned the corner. Scared out of her mind, she tried to find an escape route.

She found her way to a spot above Xaldoruks's chamber. He merely sat in his chair in silence. After everything she had heard about him, the vicious and brutal things he had done, she didn't see anything so odd or threatening about him. Genesis carefully continued on through the ventilation system.

She came across a room with hundreds upon hundreds of weapons and machinery. With a small wrist knife, she carved a hole in the vent and fell through it. She found herself in a large room with an array of weaponry and machine parts. In the center was a giant machine. She looked around it and realized the amount of power it contained.

"This must be…" she said to herself as the fear inside her increased.

"Intriguing, isn't it?" said a voice in the distance. Genesis summoned her Blades and prepared for a fight. Zamx emerged from the darkness. "So much power in one machine. Yet it failed to pass the test."

"What do you mean?" Genesis asked. She noticed Negatives were closing in on her from all directions.

"Right now, you're in the junkyard. What you see here are the prototypes to the device that can transform the universe into the haven it was meant to be. Don't worry; the real thing is much more powerful."

She looked back at the machine.

"But…" she muttered.

"You still feel its power now, don't you?"

"Yeah, this thing is powerful enough to destroy the known universe."

"Yes, but our known universe is never the whole universe. The universe is expanding constantly. The Big Bang is still occurring. We needed to find a way to suppress the expansion."

"How exactly do you plan to do that?"

"Well, you'll see soon enough."

Before she knew it, Zamx had summoned his Blade and launched at her. The two had a small battle as the circling Negatives closed in. Tides shifted back and forth. Genesis started to grow increasingly furious. Her Xylonite started to glow. Zamx smiled.

"What's wrong, Genesis?" he said, taunting her. "Your attacks seem to be a little bit half-assed. Are you getting angry, maybe? Maybe you're just getting weaker. I wonder if Max will come to your rescue like he did last time?"

Genesis got angrier. She charged at him. Her moves became

more powerful but also grew sloppy and slow. Their Blades crossed. Zamx smiled widely beyond what his face would allow. His eyes grew to an enormous size. His teeth grew extremely sharp. She looked at him and saw a vision of Hell itself.

"I think it's time I finish this. It's been fun, tiny human, but this is game over," he said.

Genesis threw a smoke bomb on the floor from her back pocket and vanished. She jumped over the ring of Negatives down a hall full of mirrors. She blindly kept turning, trying to escape him, but quickly lost her way. The mirrors kept changing and moving around. Zamx's voice echoed through the reflections.

"You're trying so hard to fight your helplessness," he said. Genesis tried to cover her ears and not listen. "You fight because you don't accept who you are: a damsel in distress. You're nothing but bait for the real fish to bite at. You've been babied for too long. The time you were supposed to use to get better you used to hide and be protected. Now you're just an anvil weighing your friends down. And because of you and your weakness, your brother's soul will die!"

Genesis kept screaming and ran faster. She arrived in a room with a glass ceiling. The pale moonlight shone through almost as brightly as a sun. This room was different than the others. It looked like a ballroom. She gazed across the room and saw a figure dressed in formal attire. Uncertain of what was coming toward her, she drew her Blades. The figure stepped into the light. It was Xaldoruks himself.

"Beautiful, isn't it?"

"Let me out of here right now."

"I'm afraid I cannot do that." He waved his hands. Suddenly, the Blades in Genesis's hands felt scaly and slimy. She looked at them and saw two giant snakes in her palms. She jumped in fear and dropped the reptiles. She looked back at Xaldoruks. He was holding his hand out, offering to dance. She refused to take it. At that moment, she heard the snakes hissing their way toward her again. She jumped again, but this time into Xaldoruks's hands. She looked into his hypnotic gaze and grew oddly comfortable in his arms. A waltz suddenly started to play in the background... and the two began to dance with the music.

"Why have you continued this?" Genesis asked.

"What?"

"This war. Why have you decided to further the fighting? What's the point of this entire thing? What are you trying to prove?"

Xaldoruks looked off for a moment. "Perfection," he responded. "The universe is so imperfect. I've lived in this dimension long enough to see its full extent. Tell me, why would a god who is said to be so perfect create such an imperfect universe? The answer is simple. This god who created it is not so perfect. His decisions are careless. Why not create a new universe, one that can be perfect? I guess that would be one reason. At least that would be a reason to give me some shred of humanity, wouldn't it?"

"Well...I guess."

"Now it's my turn. You never answered my question from earlier."

"Question? What question?"

"It's beautiful, isn't it?" He looked up at the sky.

"What is? Our moon??"

"Yes. The Kendozia moon. Did you know that moons actually emit dark energy? Every night, the moon takes in the light energy coming from the sun and reflects it back to the planet as dark energy. It's why the darkness users are so active in the slums at night. It's a perfect example of imperfection."

"How?"

"The darkness users terrorize their area due to the dark energy emitted from the moon. Later on the light energy ruins the chaos that ensues by putting creation into it. The dark energy does all it can to destroy, but it's always blocked by creation. There is always a cycle: destruction and creation."

"The destruction you find beautiful."

"He creates a universe bent on destroying itself, yet he will never let it complete its task. It is constantly regenerating. The cycle keeps the universe in a constant state of stationary evolution."

"And you seek to move us forward? How?"

"By destroying the light energy. Darkness will shroud the universe in nothing but dark energy. The universe will finally complete its goal of self-destruction. Everything in life has a chain that keeps you from your ending. Even you have one."

"Me?"

"The human race. You would've met your end eons ago, but no. You continue on and breed. You continue the chain."

Genesis backed away from Xaldoruks. "Let me out of here, now."

"Your purity is what continues the species." Xaldoruks tackled her to the floor and held her hands down. She screamed for her life. "Like I said, creation replaced with destruction."

"We've been looking at the same data for weeks," screamed Max. "Why can't we find it?" Max paced around the planning table with holograms of the known universe. In the room with him were Luand, Battlux, and Zack, as well as a few other members of the Sandshark Council. The room was dark, letting the glow of the hologram light it up.

"Okay, let's just look at all the information we have one more time," Zack said, hoping to calm Max down. "We've turned in the Orchaic Crystals we had so we have all thirteen; however, all but a few are close to completely drained of their power. We know that they want us to attack them, and we know that they plan to end the entire war with this battle, so we know to use all our force with this one. We also know that Max is important to them somehow, so keeping him away from them is important. We also have the Negative's words: 'At the place where this all began...so it will finally end, and we shall begin anew.'"

"We don't have too many clues, do we?" Luand said.

"That's not good enough. We can't stop there," Max exclaimed. "We can't just look at the direct clues."

"Relax, Max, we'll get there in time," Luand said, trying to calm him. "Tzocy, work on the pattern-recognition program. Identify all of the targeted planets and try to find justification to access their data. That should help us. Max, take a rest."

"What?" Max said, shocked at the notion. "No, I'm fine; I need to help."

"Son, you've been here for days on end. I think you deserve at least twenty-four hours of rest. I'll extend that time if I must."

Max was about to argue the point, but Luand gave him a stern face that stopped him in his tracks. "That's an order."

Max sighed and saluted him. "Yes, sir," he said. He walked out with a peeved look on his face.

"Volt Storm!" Luand called.

Zack hurried to him. "Yes, sir."

"Assist Chaos Flame on his assignment. Make sure he doesn't enter this room."

"Ordering me to take a break as well, sir?" he said, while still fighting fatigue.

"Chaos is very impulsive. He won't stop thinking about this. Trust me, he needs a break much more than he cares to admit. I need him in his best condition."

"I'll make sure he relaxes, sir."

Zack walked away to follow Max. He thought about Genesis and how good she made him feel when she was around.

Max sat at the window in front of the building on the fifteenth floor. Zack walked up to him and looked out the window to the Final Destination Tower.

"She's hurting, Zack," he muttered. "I feel it. She's being tortured. Just barely alive."

"She's strong," Zack said, trying to ease Max's mind.

"She may be the strongest girl in the galaxy. I'm still not comfortable with my baby sister being subject to the devil's whims."

They both looked at the tower.

"Don't worry, bro. We'll get her back." Finally, a smile emerged on Max's face. Finally glad to see a grin on his best friend, he continued to admire the tower, to get him to think about something else. "Isn't it incredible that that tower has survived thousands of years of wars?"

"Hard to believe that thing is five thousand years old. It's just about as old as the war itself."

"Yeah, she's a relic all right. This is where our new understandings began. We may not have been born there, but we as an evolved species started with that first landing. We saw the universe for what it was, and it all started with that first rocket."

"Remember when we used to visit that place all the time," Max said, reminiscing

"We'd have those adventures all up and down the tower."

"And at the end of the day, your dad would still insist on teaching us that this was the place where the Terrascopians began."

"In the end it was for the better, right?"

"I guess so." Max suddenly paused, then looked up. "That's it."

"What?"

"Come on, we have to get back to the lab."

"But I was under orders to keep you out of there." The two ran right to the lab door. Max put his thumb on the lock pad, but it didn't open.

"Oh, come on." He hit on the com-link into the room. "Luand! Luand! Open up!"

"Aren't you supposed to be on that twenty-four-hour break? It's barely been twenty-four minutes."

"No, I figured it out! I know where the base is."

It suddenly got quiet. Luand opened the door slightly.

"How then?"

"Let me in, and I'll show you why."

Luand open the door, and Max marched to the hologram.

"Zamx has been giving me clues ever since that mission on Darod because he's trying to get me ready for whatever they're going to do to me. They've been preparing me for this battle."

"So what? We know that already," Battlux said impatiently.

"Zamx said, 'At the place where this all began...so it will finally end, and we shall begin anew.'"

"We've already checked the center of the universe, and nothing is there."

"You're thinking too literally. The place where we as the Terrascopian race finally began. It's the same place the first Terrascopians landed on Zapheraizia. It's the one place on the planet that is most significant to us, the one place that we use to remember how far we've come, the place where their view of the universe finally expanded —where worlds begin."

"You mean to say that our enemies' base of operations..."

"Has been staring us in the face whole time. It's Final Destination Tower!"

"Max, that's a huge speculation." Luand said.

"I know, but I'm a hundred percent confident. We can't waste any time. We have to attack now!"

"Sure, but first we have to investigate, evaluate, come up with a plan."

"What? Oh, come on, this is no time for protocol. We need to go now!"

"Max! You will calm down. You will wait, and you will accept it. Understand?"

Max's mind was still pumping adrenaline through his body, itching to run over. He took in a deep breath. "Yes, sir."

"I know it's hard to wait. If you are a hundred percent sure, we have to evacuate the capital."

"We need to move as soon as possible."

"Keep a level head, Max. This is what they want. They want you to lose control. You have to promise me to keep yourself in balance. Remember the Truth."

"I assume you don't want me using my dark powers now, right?"

"Your powers are unstable but may be useful. Use them only as a last resort. Your life is most important. You can always return from Malevolence, but you cannot return from death."

"So are we going to prepare for battle?"

"As soon as the city is empty."

It was a foggy day. Residents of the city evacuated, and the streets were deserted. All of the buildings were empty. Only Final Destination Tower looked over the UPA building as if the two structures were about to face off against each other.

Max stood on the roof of the main building next to Tyra.

"You ready?" she asked him.

"More than ever. Genesis doesn't deserve to be in pain anymore, especially not because of me."

Tyra looked at Max and gently punched him in the arm. "I'm giving you one job. Don't die, okay?"

Max smiled. "I only promise to try."

Tyra's light smile disappeared, and she walked away.

Luand walked up behind him.

"You joining the fight this time, sir?" Max asked.

"Of course," he said. "This very well may be the final fight of the war. I wouldn't dream of missing it."

"It'll be great to fight alongside you. I'll get to see what you're like in the field."

"Oh, no you won't. You'll be busy."

"Doing what?"

"Leading this battle."

"What? Why me?"

"Your plan, your sister. You're the leader."

"Luand…I can't lead the entire agency into this battle."

"That's not why I gave you command. This is your sister. No one will fight to save her harder than you will. You fight to save her. Leave Xaldoruks to me."

"You sure you can take him down on your own? I could back you up."

Luand remained quiet and then smiled. "This battle will make you famous, Max. You'll be immortalized in history if we win."

Max shook his head. "I don't care about that anymore. Genesis is in trouble. No matter how hard they try, this battle will not be made about me. This battle is for the countless men and women who have lost their lives in this damned eternal war."

Luand smiled even more. "All I wanted to hear."

Max smiled and jumped off the side of the building.

Zamx approached Xaldoruks, who sat in his chair staring down at the empty city.

"The stage is set and the machine is in position," Zamx reported.

"You've done well, my friend," Xaldoruks replied. "You will be greatly rewarded for your efforts. For today you become complete and obtain a power stronger than any other has ever known."

"You really think he'll come?"

"His pride and wrath will bring him to us. His dark desires will be his undoing in more than one way today."

A camera beeped, and displayed Max emerging from the fog and standing in front of the tower.

"He has arrived. Let him in."

Max stood ready at the door of the tower. Suddenly aware, he felt a strong dark presence around him. He was about to knock on the door when it suddenly opened for him. Knowing they were expecting him, Max was happy that his assumption was correct. From the familiar base of the tower he walked up the spiraling steps to the top. He arrived in a big empty room with no ceiling. Across the room he saw Zamx, leaning against the wall.

"Oh, so glad you could make it! I was starting to worry."

"Impressive, Zamx. I must say you've impressed me. How long have the Negative detectors orbiting the planet been hacked to give us false information?"

"We've been here for quite some time. Maybe since your encounter with my father."

"Oh, that reminds me. Where is dear old Dad?"

"Probably putting the finishing touches on your sister."

Max felt the last comment touch a nerve in his body. He fought hard to keep himself under control. "Let her go. And maybe I won't kill you."

Zamx laughed. "Don't make idle threats. You can't kill me because our souls are linked together. Not to mention you don't have the stomach to kill someone. Well, consciously anyway."

"Maybe I don't, but I know a good group of people who are willing to try." Max pointed out toward the fog. Zamx looked and saw millions of soldiers with a large assortment of vehicles, robots, and weapons. Every single being in the UPA had come out to fight.

Zamx only chuckled. "You think you're so clever, don't you?"

Four doors to the tower's base opened. Negatives started flooding the streets by the millions. They charged toward the UPA soldiers. Zamx grinned. "I guess both of us like to be prepared. The one thing in this life we share."

The soldiers engaged their enemies. Max drew his Chaos Blade, and Zamx drew his. The two launched at each other with ferocious attacks. The final battle had begun.

11 RE:GENERATION

UPA soldiers fought for their lives against the countless Negatives storming the city. Great beasts rose from the ground as breathtaking robots confronted them. Battalions and starships kept coming from the base to the battlefield. Luand stood at the top of his base watching the carnage unfold. He put a mask on and turned back to his elite squadron.

"You ready for this?"

"Yes, sir!" they all responded.

"Let's move out."

From the top of the base Luand and his squad jumped down and flew into the battle on gliders. They all shot at the field, taking out a large chunk of the Negatives approaching the city. Once Luand had arrived on the field with his organization, the squad covered his landing by eliminating all the Negatives in his area. He summoned giant robotic claws to his hands and with a wide swipe he sliced all of the Negatives within the radius of his attack. He kept charging forward and was amazed when he saw the entirety of the UPA fighting together as one.

Zack was fending off his own set of Negatives with a few members of his team. They kept closing in on him as he struggled to push them back. Tyra and a few members of her squad fought their own groups of Negatives, holding their ground. Max's and Zamx's power surged with each blow they dealt each other. The ring of their swords resounded through the entire battlefield. Max tried to move quickly and pinpoint his opponent's weaknesses while Zamx fought at varying tempos, switching often from attack to defense.

"Very good," Zamx said with a laugh, clearly enjoying himself. "I almost thought this would've been too easy."

"Where's my sister, Zamx!"

"All in due time, my brother. Focus on the task at hand. You need to give me your all."

The two were stuck in a Blade lock, each pushing on the other and trying to gain the upper hand. Max felt something wrap around his leg. Without warning he was tossed across the floor and into the wall. Max looked up and saw an octopus tentacle emerging from his back. However, it looked different from the ones he had seen before.

"How'd you like my new tentacles? Interesting how darkness manifests itself. But then again, you would know all about that, wouldn't you?"

Max stood up, and his wings emerged from his back. Zamx's smile disappeared.

Max then flew above Zamx and swooped in with his Blade to attack. Zamx pulled him down and struck at him. As Max narrowly escaped, he countered and fought with an assortment of attacks. He used everything from his training with Luand—from fire attacks to blood darkness attacks. Max pulled no punches in this fight. However, because of his extra effort, he paid no attention to his stamina and started feeling fatigue quickly. His movements slowed, his fluidity became rough, and his attacks became weaker.

Finally, Max lost his balance. Zamx swung with a very powerful and swift strike. Max caught himself and lifted his Blade in time to block.

Max activated his Xylonite for the first time in a long while. The ability seemed new to him. Each attack that was thrown at him Max was able to dodge. He stayed on the defensive for a while until he could gather some energy. Every time he saw one, Max went for the opening. Zamx, however, dodged with ease as well and slithered back to the offensive. With his frustration increasing with every failed attempt, Max began to take the offensive more and more. He tried to keep calm, but he still couldn't accept his failure to harm Zamx. Soon he found himself only on the offensive while dark aura surrounded him. He was using more dark attacks, but they quickly melded into heart darkness attacks. This only fed Zamx's excitement. Max's power continued to rise, and slowly he lost control. This time he realized it and he realized he had to end this fight quickly before he got worse.

With one swift stroke, Max sliced Zamx's chest with a cut not deep enough to kill, but deep enough to seriously damage him. Zamx fell to his knees, and Max relaxed his powers. Relieved that he remained in control, he sighed and caught his breath, as he was sure he had won.

"Luand," he called in on his communicator. "Luand, the tower is secure; feel free to come in. It won't be long before Xaldoruks comes. Volt Storm, Crimson Winter, leave your squads at the front. You're helping me defend the tower."

Max heard the faint sound of laughter behind him. He turned around and saw Zamx laughing himself to hysteria. Max's sigh of relief evaporated as his opponent's laughter robbed him of his victory.

"What's so funny?"

"Tell me, Max, how are two things put together in this universe? The answer is simple. They clash. The two objects must collide and be compatible. You were trying so hard to keep a cool head, but you slipped up. You let your frustration get the better of you. Your heart's darkness bled out, and it was with this darkness that you struck your winning blow."

"What?" Max screamed. Zamx continued laughing as he stood up.

"We are finally compatible. We will be one!"

Tentacles shot out from his back and grabbed Max. Max struggled to get out but fell to his knees. Zamx walked over to his constrained counterpart.

"You'll never enter into my soul," Max said furiously. "I've trained with both light and darkness. My body can repel you from any direction."

Zamx chuckled again. "You really are a dumbass."

"What?"

"There are three internal forces in a positive being. The mind, the heart, and the soul. Together they allow for a human being to function mentally, physically, and spiritually. Because they work together, they must always be connected. They always have a way of influencing one another. Now, every being has a spark of insanity, that unyielding nerve in your head that whispers to you to push someone if they're at the edge of a cliff, or turn around and pull the trigger on a comrade just because you can. This is the tiny bit of hell that sits in your mind untouched—the hell inside your head. I can follow this spark of insanity in your mind directly to your heart, whose darkness will propel me to your soul. Have a nice dream. You'll be in it for a while."

A bright light flashed at the tip of Zamx's finger. In that flash Zamx was gone, and Max just lay on the floor.

A figure walked up the steps to the same floor and walked right past the unconscious Sandshark. "Chaos ensues, and it shall be greeted with destruction."

Zack and Tyra both tried to make their way to the tower. Zack was hiding behind a mound. Tyra ran behind the same mound, trying to escape a few savage Negative beasts tailing her.

"Running away?" Zack said, teasing her. "Definitely not like you."

"Shut up," Tyra snapped. "I'm trying to save my energy; you should, too."

"Please, I'm a freaking powerhouse," he said. "The only way I could run out of energy is if I die."

"Which, if you're not careful, could be soon."

"Weren't you running from something?"

"Beast-like Negatives. Obviously Xaldoruks has been busy since our last battle. They're like dogs, but they can't smell and are nearsighted. But they make up for it with their ferocious sense of hearing."

"So what do we do? Shield-shocker?"

"Shield-shocker sounds good."

Tyra created an ice shield around them. Zack got up and shot a bolt of lightning through a small hole in it and watched as it expanded and disintegrated all of the enemies on the other side. Tyra then took down the shield and they both got up and ran for the tower.

They were once again hindered in their approach. A giant amount of Negative Matter started to form in front of them. It grew larger and kept expanding until it formed into an insect-like creature. It was tall with only one wing that spun around the axis of its body. It had huge eyes, and below it were octopus tentacles. The body was thick but narrow. It had six legs and one large tail with slimy Negative Matter oozing out.

It lifted its tail. Zack and Tyra separated as the slimy limb slammed to the ground. Zack circled the beast, trying to cut the base of its limbs, but his Blade wouldn't go through. Instead, he climbed onto the beast from the limb and made his way up. In midair he shot a lightning burst in the beast's eye. The next thing he felt were the suction cups of one of the tentacles pulling him back and hurling him toward the ground. Tyra managed to surround him in snow just in time to break the fall. He looked around and saw Tyra standing with her double-edged Blade in front of her. The air around her circled her Blade.

"Tyra, what are you doing?" Zack asked.

"Shut up," she snapped. "I'm trying to focus."

Her eyes opened. Her Blades suddenly were both covered in ice that curved at the end. She pulled back her right fist, and a long line came from it. She aimed straight for the beast's head. As it looked at her, she exhaled slowly and released the arrow. It went cleanly through the beast, and in a flash it was completely frozen in a thick block of ice. Then it shattered, showering down like snow on the now empty battlefield.

"What the hell was that?" Zack asked, very perplexed.

"Just something new." They looked at the tower door and prepared themselves.

"They probably just don't want anyone interfering with Zamx and Chaos Flame."

"Well then, they are really going to hate us."

They ran up the stairs to the top of the tower. When they burst through the door, Tyra stopped and froze in her place. Zack looked at her, and she looked back. They saw Max unconscious on the floor. Zack immediately ran to him in a panic.

"Chaos? Max, wake up!" he shouted frantically. He checked all his vitals and made sure he was breathing. Since everything checked out and Max still was not responding, he kept imploring Max to wake up. Tyra simply kicked Max as she passed by.

"Leave him alone, Volt. Flame will be fine. He always is. Keep your head, will you?" Tyra looked up and saw a man looking out of the window. She cautiously moved closer to him. "Besides, we have bigger problems on our plate."

The man didn't seem to acknowledge their presence.

"Hey," she yelled at him, but he didn't turn around. "What did you do to Max?" But there was still no response. She lifted her Blade, pulled back her arm, and released an arrow again. It stopped just before it made contact. Dark aura surrounded the arrow and shattered it.

"Now that's just rude," said the man. He turned around. "Didn't your parents teach you better manners?"

The two of them stood in fear. They remembered the face back from the first day when he fought Max. All of that childish fear resurfaced and they were frozen in their place. It was Xaldoruks.

Max floated with his eyes closed, unsure of where he was. It felt familiar, but it wasn't the tower.

"Where am I?" he asked. "Is this a dream? Can I wake up? What happened? I remember, something...but what was it?" He opened his eyes. At that moment he descended onto a marble floor. There were seats on each side of him and columns that held up a higher level. There was a stained glass window with odd designs letting in warm, bright colors onto the center of the floor. On the walls were characters of a language Max had never seen before. He looked behind him and saw there was no door. He was standing in the darkness while the other half of the room was ablaze with light.

"What is this?" he asked again. "Some kind of church?"

"This is the room that your soul manifested as our battleground."

Max turned around and looked for the source of the voice. He saw Zamx approaching from the far end of the room with a casual stride and a sickening smile. "This is where your heart and mind meet. How interesting that it chose this, of all places. Tells you a little bit about yourself, doesn't it?"

Max just gave him a cold stare.

Zamx looked at the walls. "Do you know what this language is? Probably not. Then I guess you'll never hope to know what it says."

"Why are we here, in my soul?"

"Our union is still under procedure. See how there is one half of the room is flooded in the light that that window is providing? See how your side is shrouded in darkness? That should give you a hint."

"I have to kick your ass a second time, don't I?"

"That pride is what will get you killed, you know."

"Quit it," Max snapped. "My friends are waiting for me. I just want you out of my soul, and I'll be on my merry way." The both summoned their Blades and launched at each other.

Zack and Tyra were about to confront Xaldoruks. They stood Blades in hand while he stood leaning on the wall with his arms crossed.

"Do you know what it's like to be promised something so magnificent and so wondrous that it was all you could dream of? You were told that you had to perform a task. It was a simple task—one that could be performed with absolute ease. So instead you choose to go a step further to impress people and show them just how much better than them you really are. Yet you are punished over and over again for merely being superior. You soon decide that you need no approval from them. You just need to take what is yours. They will never give it to you. They are afraid. You're afraid, too. You both fear weakness. You fear being useless and fragile. But it's more than that." He began to move closer to the two. "You, Tyrishana, fear vulnerability. The last thing you want is to become useless, scared, fragile, and weak. You fight so hard to bury your weaknesses both physically and emotionally. You see your feelings as weaknesses, too, don't you? All this energy is just to bury them in your work, being 'professional' because you refuse to face the fact that you are vulnerable. You are weak. You live in denial, girl! You, Zactavious, fear failure. You were pushed to a position for which you weren't ready. You have responsibilities you'd never dreamed of nor aimed for. You know that his leadership will lead to the death of many, and you don't want to face his future. He doesn't want to live with that. You want to run! Be free from that! From responsibility! You're scared of it! Fear runs your world."

Xaldoruks turned back around. Zack and Tyra struggled to put what he said out of their minds. Just as they were about to attack, they felt an odd dark energy behind them. They turned around and saw Max standing upright with dark aura being emitted from his body. His skin had markings all over him, and his eyes were a hollow yellow with no pupils.

"Max?" Tyra said. "What are you doing?"

He didn't respond.

"Max cannot hear you right now," Xaldoruks said. "He's just a puppet. While Zamx fights him in his soul, his body is just a corpse, and now it's one consumed by his heart's own darkness. Have fun with him. Consider him a sneak peek of the new Max you're about to meet."

Max walked toward them and summoned both his Chaos Blade and Zamx's Blade. Zack tried to reason with him as they backed away from him.

"Max, buddy? This isn't you, okay? We don't want to hurt you."

"Oh my god, could you sound any more clichéd?" Tyra said trying to focus on a better way of getting to Max.

"Really, Tyra? You want to do this now?"

At that moment, Max jumped in between them and struck both of them. He jumped toward Tyra and swung at her. She rolled over and kicked his chest, pushing him to Zack, who caught him in a full nelson.

"Come on, Max! Snap out of it!" Max flipped under Zack, throwing him to Tyra. As the two got back up, grabbing their Blades, Max's flew into his hands. He ran to them and started attacking both friends simultaneously. He blocked and attacked each swiftly, making it impossible to land a move on him. He pushed them both back in the same direction.

While they were still dazed, Max let go of his Blades, and dark attachments connected him to the handles of each one. He spun his Chaos Blade above his head like a propeller. The two looked at Max and saw him launch the Blade toward them. They jumped out of the way just in time. But then they saw another attack coming. Max then launched the second Blade. Zack and Tyra kept dodging attacks, trying to get closer to Max. Max kept swinging and launching his Blades at them. Zack moved in a series of flashes and got close enough to tackle him to the floor. Max's face remained emotionless.

Zack screamed at him. *"Max! You have to wake up!"*

Max kept shooting fireballs at Zamx as they bounced off his Blade and into the walls and the columns. Zamx started to close in. With each blow Zamx could feel Max's fatigue growing. The walls of the room began to fade.

"You're running out of time, Max," the shadow teased. Max knew he was right. He started hearing voices in his head telling him to hurry and to wake up. Max knew that was exactly what he needed to do. He grabbed his Blade with his other hand and pushed Zamx back to the front of the church. Max stood in the shadows of the room and gathered dark energy to fire at him. When he did, Zamx raised his hand and absorbed the energy. Max fell to his knees exhausted. Zamx slowly walked up to him.

"I'm not sure I want to join my body to this. Why weaken myself? It doesn't matter. My powers will be balanced at last inside a complete body."

Max hated it, but he had to admit it. He was beaten. There was nothing he could do to fight back. All his energy had been taken from him. He could barely stand. The walls of the room were fading and disintegrating. The light started to grow dimmer. He closed his eyes, accepting his fate. A voice from a memory came into his head. Faint, but powerful. It called out to him say "Find the balance. Find the Truth!"

With a roar, the room materialized again. Max felt a surge of energy course through him as the darkness in the room began to balance itself. Max suddenly tripped Zamx and grabbed his own Blade trying to strike him before he got up. Zamx defended and ran back to the stained glass at the front of the church. Max rushed and followed behind him. Zamx jumped from the glass to a pillar and kept jumping from object to object as Max followed closely behind. He reached the back of the church and blocked Max from tackling him. Max landed and rushed at him again. The two exchanged blows. Their Blades crossed and were locked, trying to force the other to give in. Max then punched him in the gut and kicked him toward the window. While he was in the air, he paused at the line where light and darkness met. Both light and dark auras twisted around him and collected in his hands. He then extended his arms and launched this energy at Zamx. The beam pushed Zamx out of the window, shattering it into pieces. Max fell to the floor.

Max had Zack pinned onto the floor with both Blades crossed above his neck. Tyra struggled to get up, and Zack was defenseless. The mindless Max began to lower the Blades onto

Zack's neck when suddenly his Xylonite activated. He started screaming, and he jumped off his friend. Zamx's Blade disappeared, letting the Chaos Blade fall, but Zack caught it before it could kill him. A dark light was bursting though his forehead. Then Zamx flew out of his head and to the wall, immobilized. Max just kept panting, completely worn out from the events in his head. Tyra ran up to him and slapped him across the face. Then she held him tightly. Zack gave a giant sigh of relief. Max, still barely aware of what had happened, hugged her back.

"All right," he said, slowly getting up. "Who's next?" He grabbed his Blade from the floor and faced his friends. They all turned to Xaldoruks, who remained in the same position the whole time.

"Did Luand show up?" Max asked.

"Luand?"

"Just watch out for him, okay?"

Xaldoruks removed himself from the wall and started walking toward them.

"The cycle must be broken. Your world is constantly in pain and then it regenerates. You remain stationary. The universe must finish its task. It seeks to destroy itself, and so the perfect universe shall do just that. The reformation of the universe where chaos is order will be the world that the new generation will form. This will be enough for me, enough to prove that I am right. I will show you the world you seek so dearly."

He summoned his Fallen Blade and stood with a smile on his face.

Max stood across from Xaldoruks next to his best friends, Chaos Blade in hand. In his mind he felt sheer terror. It was the same terror that he felt when he first faced him when he was a child. He put his hand to his mechanical arm. Fear returned, shaking his every fiber. He had barely survived last time, and this might just be his final act. He remembered his weakness when he couldn't stop the volcano on Plasia. He became more and more unsure of himself as the seconds rolled by. How could he win against Xaldoruks, the devil himself?

Zack grabbed his shoulder and gave him a comforting grin. There was the answer. His fear had been controlled, and his confidence reassured. With no sign that Luand was coming to save them, he approached his enemy. With each step his resolve to protect everything he loved grew stronger. He saw only himself and his opponent. The walk became a brisk run, and with a swift strike, the prophetic battle had begun.

The two exchanged blows quickly, each more powerful than the last. Max felt his body weakening faster than he normally did. His body hadn't yet recovered from the last battle with Zamx. With all his power, he pushed through it, remembering every maneuver he learned. Shockingly, Max lost his footing again, and Xaldoruks took the opportunity as soon as it presented itself. He launched attacks even faster, forcing Max to dodge and back up. He rolled, jumped, and flipped his way around Xaldoruks's sword like a monkey. Xaldoruks continued to attack with his Blade pounding as Max struggled to dodge each attack.

He was pushed back against a wall, and just when he thought he was defeated, out of nowhere, Zack appeared from above and swung his Blade at Xaldoruks. Xaldoruks jumped back just in time to dodge it and retaliate against Zack. He launched a sudden wave of dark energy that blew both Max and Zack off their feet. He then went in closer for the killing blow to get rid of Zack.

Max screamed at Zack, "*Move!*" He pushed him just in time to miss Xaldoruks's strike. "Go! Run!"

Zack took his Blade and ran around behind Xaldoruks. Max jumped over him and tried to attack from behind, only to be blocked by a seemingly omnipresent Blade. Zack attacked from over Max's head. Xaldoruks spawned another Blade from the original one, blocking Max to block Zack. Max then continued pushing him back, letting Zack play leapfrog off him to continue the barrage. Max threw a few fireballs at him while Zack kept pushing him back. Max then fell through a portal that led to the other side of him, and the two lunged at him. At that moment, Xaldoruks pushed both of them in the opposite direction. As he flew back, Zack shot a bolt of lightning past Xaldoruks to Max, who caught it with his right arm and redirected it to Xaldoruks. The dark lord was finally hit.

Both Max and Zack looked to Tyra and saw that she was charging her arrow. They jumped out of the way, and suddenly a brisk, icy wind blew through her hair. The arrow broke through the air and hurled toward Xaldoruks. He moved his head slightly, and the arrow flew right by him. He looked back at her, and she was already in front of him with her Blade. She kept her attacks quick and directed. She knew she couldn't give him any chance to attack her back. Xaldoruks kept dodging and blocking her barrage.

Max and Zack simultaneously attacked him from behind. Suddenly, the two found their legs grabbed by Xaldoruks's shadow. It then rose from the floor, took the three-dimensional shape of Xaldoruks and threw Max and Zack at the wall. It turned around and hit Tyra with a pulse of dark energy. The shadow walked into Xaldoruks and shifted into an extra-large suit of armor around him. He started to levitate, and his swords went into the armor's hands. The arms and Blades then split again, giving him four Fallen Blades to use. He stood there with his arms crossed while the armor was ready to fight. He wore a huge grin as he mocked them, saying, "Look, no hands."

The three Sandsharks circled him cautiously trying to locate a weak spot. They looked at one another then jumped Xaldoruks simultaneously. Unfortunately, he was able to block each attack launched at him. They grew more and more frustrated by this impenetrable defense while Xaldoruks only sat and scoffed. Suddenly, his arm pushed Tyra out of the way. Zack threw his sword in the air as he ran toward his target, but he was pushed away by the same arm. Max jumped before the arm could reach him, grabbed Zack's flailing Blade, and stood in front of his opponent's four Blades.

Max ran toward Xaldoruks as his Blades kept swiping at him. He put all his energy into his feet, and he appeared in front of the large opening through which Xaldoruks was watching. Xaldoruks's smirk disappeared. He moved back and started dodging more than blocking. Max kept attacking with both Blades. He grew more methodical and intensive with his attacks as he detected that Xaldoruks wasn't as confident as before. Then with a great burst of stored dark energy, Xaldoruks knocked him back, and his Chaos Blade fell out of his hand.

Tyra's Blade was right next to him, so he grabbed it and ran back at him. He jumped high and started attacking hard with the power his friends' swords gave him. He felt no fear anymore, as if his friends were still standing alongside him. Xaldoruks fired an energy blast that struck Max hard, pushing him off balance. As he lay on the floor and struggled to get up, his body, to his surprise, refused to move. It was stiff, and he couldn't fight back because it had run way past its normal exhausted limits the same way he had when he climbed the mountain with Luand.

Xaldoruks then pinned him to the ground with three Blades. The fourth Blade was ready to strike him, pointing right at his face. Time seemed to stop. No more combatants were able to fight.

"This is the best the universe has to offer?" Xaldoruks said, scoffing. The Blade moved away from Max's face, and he pulled back the Blades pinning Max down.

He heard Xaldoruks mutter, "I actually wish Luand were here instead."

The divided Blades returned to one sword, and he walked out of his armor and to the center of the room. A machine rose from the floor and pointed at the sky.

Max mustered up what little energy he could to get a grip on his Blade. He knew he needed strength but was reluctant to use it. Realizing there was no other option, he mustered the last ounces of energy he had left and lifted himself off the ground. He felt his heart's dark energy start to surge through his body. His body grew sturdier, his grip was hardened, and his eyes burned with an anger he'd never felt before.

Zack looked up and saw Max losing control and throwing rationality away. He tried to stop him, but before he was able to move, Max had already started running toward his target. He jumped high into the air, holding his Blade over his head. A small speck of sunlight managed to break through the clouds to hit his Blade so that it reflected right into Tyra's eyes. She looked up and saw Max suspended in the air. His Blade fell to the floor with a ringing clatter of metal. Blood ran down Xaldoruks's Blade and dripped on the floor. Max's eyes remained wide open in shock. All his dark energy disappeared. Tyra just stared in awe as she saw Max impaled by Xaldoruks's Blade. Tyra couldn't find a single thought that could comprehend the sight she beheld. Her heart started to ache, and several truths she had always denied to herself became clear. The only thing she could think to do was scream.

Max's vision started to blur, and his body twitched. He fought with everything his body would allow to get the Blade out of his chest. Xaldoruks pushed him off the Blade as Zack and Tyra watched the corpse of their best friend fall to the floor at the hands of the devil.

Zack's heart kept beating louder and louder as the realization of his friend's murder set in. In a righteous fury, he ran for his Blade and charged at Xaldoruks, screaming, "You bastard!"

A dark pulse blew him back into the wall.

"You see this?" Xaldoruks said to Tyra. "You see your friend's corpse. Look! This is the truth of the world you live in. Death and destruction are always here. And now I can see it in your eyes. You wish to halt it. You wish to continue the cycle. Right now I see your feeble little minds trying to figure out a way of reversing this destruction and bringing him back. That is your flaw. This is why the universe never reaches its goal. You seek to stop destruction. That is why I must stop you. The cycle must be broken. And by the power of the crystals, it will be."

He moved to the machine. The whole floor elevated to the sky. The machine activated the power of the Orchaic Crystals it held within and shot a dark laser into the sky, creating a layer of black and purple clouds above the planet. The fighting on the battlefield stopped as everyone looked up at the darkening sky. The black clouds moved over the UPA building and spread quickly in every direction.

Tyra looked at Zack. "Did we fail again?"

Zack looked at the sky as a tear ran down his face.

"Yes, Tyra," he whispered. "We failed."

Xaldoruks only laughed. His new world was finally in his grasp. He stepped away from the machine and saw his Negative spawn below grow larger and stronger as the battle continued.

"Father, oh Father, can you hear me up there?" he yelled at the sky. "You created a world so far from perfect that I'm afraid you left me with no other choice but this. Banishing me at the beginning of time was your mistake. I've seen all of the flaws in your universe. I shall show you what this universe needs to be. I will show you the world of darkness…"

He was cut off when the laser suddenly stopped. He turned around and saw the machine explode, shoving him off his feet. Completely confused, he sat there in disbelief. Too many emotions for him to process filled his body. He looked to the sky and saw the spread of darkness cease. He turned around and saw Max's corpse. He looked toward Zack and Tyra, who sat astonished. Filled with rage he rushed at Zack and clutched his entire neck in his palm and squeezed it.

"You know, that machine was not an easy thing to destroy. It's not like you just shoot a torpedo into an exhaust port two meters wide. That had the power of the Orchaic Crystals defending it! Now, my question to you before I ravage your body and use what remains as a foot stool is, how did you destroy it?" Xaldoruks squeezed his neck harder. Zack coughed up blood, struggling to respond.

"That wasn't me!"

Xaldoruks grew more frustrated as his confusion grew.

"That just wasn't the answer I was looking for!"

Zack remained silent while struggling to breathe. "I'll make sure you die a very agonizing death. Oh, don't worry! The universe will be right behind you." Xaldoruks threw Zack off to the side. Zack grabbed the edge of the platform before he fell off. Xaldoruks approached him and stepped on his hand.

"What will you do now, human?"

Then Xaldoruks felt something disturbing. A light started to shine. Xaldoruks turned around and saw Max, still alive. Max grabbed his blood-soaked Blade and turned around.

"You're not done with me yet, Lucifer!"

Xaldoruks summoned his Blade once again and launched at Max. Max did the same and tackled Xaldoruks in midair and off the side of the building.

The two fell, hurtling toward the ground. Then Xaldoruks pushed Max away from him and floated back to the top of the tower. Max, covered in an array of light, flew up right behind him. Their Blades clashed and sparks flew above the battlefield.

Xaldoruks repeatedly struck at Max. Only anger filled his heart. Too many things didn't make sense about what was happening. Out of all the millennia and eons he had spent planning, he could never have foreseen this outcome.

"This sure is a surprise!" he yelled, as he kept striking Max's Blade. "Tell me, why the sudden spark of life? Max, what's gotten into you?"

Max chuckled and shocked Xaldoruks back.

"You really want to know?" Max said, teasing him. "It was only a theory, and I honestly didn't think it would work, but I have in my possession all thirteen of the Orchaic Crystals. I used the four you didn't drain to destroy the machine, releasing the energy you stole, back into the other nine crystals. Then with each one fully powered, they pulled me back from my near-death state."

Max charged a bolt of light from his hand past Xaldoruks. The shot then imploded on itself, pulling Xaldoruks in.

"What is this?"

"An opening to the void space outside our universe—also known as a white hole."

Xaldoruks struggled to keep himself from falling in.

"This war is over, Lucifer," Max said, remaining unmoved by the white hole. "You're at your limit. I'm clearly stronger than you, so why not just end it?"

Xaldoruks shot darkness into the white hole, and it exploded. The two recommenced the fight. Max fought more vigorously than he could ever imagine. There was no fear, no pain—only power. The balance in his heart made perfect sense. He threw white holes all around Xaldoruks so he could be pulled apart and end the fight. Xaldoruks sent a dark pulse and destroyed them all, causing an explosion that hid him from Max. Immediately after the explosion, he launched at Max, grabbing his head.

"You have all thirteen?" he said, smiling. "Even Sendrakxs?"

Max felt a huge pain in his body. It felt as though his life was being sucked away from him. The Orchaic Crystals were losing all of their power. Max screamed in pain. Xaldoruks then released him, and he fell back to the floor of the tower, where the crystals fell out of his pocket. Xaldoruks had more power than he had ever had before.

"This world…will know darkness."

A big sphere surrounded him.

Max struggled back to his feet and looked up. As the sphere started to dissolve, he could see some sort of creature coming out of it. It formed into an enormous snakelike dragon with yellow eyes. It had six tails, all of different animals, and six wings keeping it in the air. Arms grew from the creature's sides and grabbed the buildings around it. As it landed, the planet quaked in fear. Max stood in awe of the great beast Xaldoruks had become as he spread dark energy throughout the city.

From the UPA, ships shot out toward it, ferociously showering it with attacks. None of the shots seemed to affect it as it continued to destroy the city.

Max fell to his knees and grabbed the Orchaic Crystals. Xaldoruks spread his own darkness throughout the battlefield. The Negatives started to spawn and grow continuously stronger and faster, killing more forces by the minute. Max looked out at the battle. He looked around and saw the ruined state it was in. Everything he knew was being destroyed.

With each move Xaldoruks made, more of the tower crumbled. The floor under Max collapsed, and he fell directly into the bowels of the tower. He pushed the debris off and looked up at the darkened sky. He turned over and saw Genesis curled in a corner. Max ran to her.

"Genesis," he said, holding her in his arms. She didn't say a word. She didn't seem to even notice that her brother was there with her. She only shivered in terror, mentally broken.

"What did he do to you?" Max held his sister close and looked up, watching the sky grow darker.

"I'm sorry, Genesis," he said as a tear fell down his face and dripped onto hers. "I tried. My backup plan didn't even work. I thought...I thought I was strong enough to do this. I just didn't know how out of my league this battle was."

He looked up to the blackened sky. Raindrops fell on his face. "God must really hate us to let this happen. I'm out of tricks. I'm out of clever comebacks. I'm...I'm just out."

Raindrops dripped from Max's face onto his sister's. A tear from Max's face dropped right into her eye. Her Xylonite flashed, and she finally moved, looking at her brother. She raised her hand and softly smacked his face. Max grabbed her hand and squeezed it tightly.

"When did you start giving up?" she muttered. "There is always a way to win."

"Gen, he has the power of all thirteen of the Orchaic Crystals. He's taken the powers of a vengeful god for himself. He sets the rules now. I just don't know how to fight that."

"Since when did you decide to follow the rules?" she said, and Max smiled. "Remember, you don't have to do this alone. We're here for you. Use us."

At that moment he remembered something from his training with Luand. He expanded his wings from his back and carried Genesis up to the top of the tower. He found Zack and Tyra, and he saw that Zack had a huge wound in his shoulder. Tyra was working to patch it up. Max looked back at the battlefield and saw how many bodies had piled up. He sat Genesis down with his friends.

"How you doing, bro?" he asked Zack.

Zack coughed and braced for the pain as Tyra wrapped his wound. "Well, this is easily the second-worst gash I've ever had in my arm."

Max lowered his head. Just as he was about to apologize, he felt Zack's hand slap him across the face.

"What the hell was that for?"

"Don't you dare say that you're sorry. This is something we all agreed to do. We knew what we were getting into."

Max smiled. "You're right; this is our story, our destiny. Still doesn't mean you had to slap me." Zack slapped him again. "What was that for?"

"That's for making us think you were dead."

"I thought I was dead. It's total luck I'm still alive." He stood back up, only to be slapped by Tyra. "What's with the slapping?"

"I was mad too...and it looked like fun when he did it. Not to mention I gave you one job, Max. One job: don't die."

The three of them laughed together and remembered how good it felt. They then looked at the monster in the distance destroying the city.

"Xaldoruks really won this one. " Zack looked up in despair.

"Not yet," Max snapped. "We can't let that happen. There is one last thing we can try. It's a long shot, and it's not going to work...but it's the only thing we've got left."

Max proceeded to tell them his idea. Once he was done, he flew off, calling the rest of the forces on the battlefield to fill them in. Zack and Tyra picked up Genesis and carried her down the stairs.

Xaldoruks destroyed many buildings of Zapheraizia's capital. Each of his wings expanded and crushed several giant monuments. He opened his mouth, and a large blast exploded from it and decimated the other half of the city. Just as he was about to continue his rampage, a large burst of energy destroyed one of his wings. He turned around and saw that all of the UPA's cannons were aimed at him. Every active force of the UPA charged at the beast's feet and started to attack it. Xaldoruks stood there and shook his head at his enemies' futile persistence. Suddenly he felt a cold spear pierce his cheek. He looked over and saw a glimmer in the distance. Tyra had shot one of her ice arrows at him.

Suddenly a large wave of attacks from the entire UPA aimed for that exact point, allowing him to actually feel the pain. Tyra shot another arrow at him and the forces on the ground started to attack that as well. She kept shooting arrows until he was covered in ice. Though all the operatives on the ground and on the buildings attacked with all their strength, Xaldoruks broke through the ice with a mighty roar and charged another blast in his mouth. A few of the members tried to run away before the blast had a chance to hit them. Just as the blast was about to launch, several controlled nuclear explosions detonated at his mouth. The ball of dark energy imploded in his mouth before he had a chance to attack.

Max stood on a cliff in the far distance, observing the fight with his Xylonite. He sat down in despair.

"It's just as I thought: Tyra needs to penetrate the armor with her arrows and then a series of attacks break through. There are still two levels of armor before we end it. How do I get to those?" He got up and shrugged his shoulders. "Well, I wasn't thinking before; why start now?"

He centered his focus on himself, and he attempted to harness the Truth once more. However, the harder he tried, the more he got nothing. His power was failing him. Then he thought of Genesis and all of the torture she'd had to endure. He then thought about all of the friends he had lost that day. He thought of all the planets he had seen destroyed, all the pain he had seen, and the families they had left behind to join the UPA. He remembered Luand's words, and they kept ringing in his head.

"Malevolence can always be trumped by the Truth."

He opened his eyes and he was in a wide field, sitting with his father on a bench under an incredibly large tree. He looked up and saw his father's dreadlocks that he liked having around him. He kept hearing words, but they were just a blur. As he focused in on the sound of the voice, words started to take shape, and he listened.

"...And finally there's pride, definitely the most dangerous. You'll be so confident that you think no one can stop you...and I want you to be confident, son, but...look, you're a kind boy who cares for the people who care for him. People will boost your ego, I have no doubt, but...uh...Honey, I don't know if he's even listening.

Oh, all right. Max, just know that you are loved. Always fight for the people you love and who love you. With them, you're never alone. Your mother and I will always be here for you. We'll never leave you. You see, we're a part of your mind, heart, and soul."

A tear ran down his face. When he opened his eyes again, he saw streaks of light and dark energy circling him in a perfect balance. His wings emerged again, and he jumped down the cliff, Chaos Blade in hand, and launched toward the monster.

Tyra was shooting arrows at Xaldoruks when she heard Max's voice on her communicator.

"Winter, I'm on my way. We only have one shot at this; make sure everyone's synced. When I say 'now,' everything has to happen, okay?"

"Roger that."

She called Zack to see if he was ready and then called the UPA attendants commanding the cannons. Max held his Blade ready, concentrating his energy into it, and with a quick gust, he soared across the sky at breakneck speed.

At the UPA, several dozen people were monitoring the fight. One of the scanners sounded an alert. The attendant at the chair addressed the commander.

"Sir, we have something a great distance away going supersonic toward the battle." The commander looked up and realized what it was.

"Good lord, that's the signal. Divert all power to the cannons and make sure everyone is aimed for the same single point." He got onto his phone and called Tyra, still firing arrows at Xaldoruks.

"Winter, we've just received a report that he's gone supersonic and is heading toward you now."

She called Zack. Zack called to his brothers, who confirmed their position on the field. Tyra cued Kevin and Robert to begin their phase. They both signaled their troops to shoot several giant hooks from the top of several buildings to the center of the monster. Tyra called back to Max.

"Max, we're ready," he heard on his earpiece. Kevin's and Robert's troops pulled at the armor to tear it apart. Xaldoruks roared in pain as its core was ripped open. Max stayed focused on his target. Tyra kept shooting several arrows at it. She then saw the armor on its chest fall and a glowing light emanate from it. She yelled into the communicator.

"The chest is exposed!"

Once he was several miles away from his target, Max yelled, "*Now!*"

The twins activated the shock grid they had set up around Xaldoruks's feet, preventing him from moving. Tyra shot a large arrow right at the beast's center. Not a second after the arrow made contact, the UPA fired its largest and most powerful cannon at the exact spot, leaving a hole in it. Following up rather quickly, Zack fired his strongest shock cannon at the same spot. Just before it made contact, he caught a glimpse of Max shooting through the sky.

Max aimed his Blade. Without slowing down and without mercy, he soared toward Xaldoruks, but just before the Blade made contact, odd markings started to glow red on it again. Max flew right into the center of where the relentless barrage was taking place, emerged on the other side, and completely stopped in midair. He held his Blade in place and did not move a muscle. The monster had frozen stiff. The battlefield was completely silent. No one dared to move. Then all of the Negatives in the battlefield started to disintegrate. The monster started to as well. All the dark energy it emitted was slowly dying until only Xaldoruks's true form remained.

All he could do was laugh.

"You really are trying to be quite remarkable, aren't you? You fight and fight for something you've never known, for a state of permanence that you so dread. You are quite amusing."

Max turned around. "You're done, Satan. The universe is finally rid of you, and peace is restored."

"Restored? That implies it was there in the beginning." He kept laughing. "Max. Oh, Max, don't you see? Your world has never known peace, and it never will. There's nothing to restore. In fact, the only thing that you've destroyed…is the one thing you tried to save."

He looked down and saw his body start to disappear. He looked back up and smiled. "I will look quite familiar."

With those last words, Xaldoruks disappeared into the air. Max couldn't feel the dark pressure he had felt all his life anymore. There was no bit of Xadoruks left behind. Yet he didn't feel like he had won.

He felt the pain in his shoulder and fell from the sky onto a nearby building. He lay there looking at the darkened sky and rested. When he opened his eyes, he saw Tyra staring down at him. He smiled and tried to touch her face. Before he could, she kissed him. Before he could process what had just happened, he grabbed her close and kissed her again.

"It's the classic boy-gets-girl ending," he said, joking. "To be honest, I didn't think you would actually be so stereotypical." She pushed away from him.

"Okay, you're never getting a kiss again," she said, teasing. Max followed her, begging to be forgiven. He then stopped and realized that it was over. The whole war was over. The legendary stories of everything he had known in his life had ended. He felt overwhelming amounts of joy. He knew that the universe was safe after being in turmoil for so long. However, deep down in the part of himself that he kept ignoring his entire life, he was sad.

The soldiers celebrated their victory. The five-thousand-year war had finally ended with them as the victors. A number of soldiers went into the tower and picked up Genesis carefully. Max found a rover, and he and Tyra headed back to the UPA main building. As they drove by the piles of bodies of individuals who had died during the fight, they realized the true cost of their victory. They managed to pick up Zack on their way. Max thought back to the beginning before the fight and thought about every detail of it.

"You know what my main question is throughout all of this? Where was Luand?"

"Why would you wonder that?" Zack asked. "Didn't he let you fight Xaldoruks because it would be poetic, or something like that? He'd say something ridiculous like that, right?"

"Well, he told me to focus on getting Genesis and to save Xaldoruks for him."

"He gave you one job, and you blew it."

"Oh, come on, you really think he's going to reprimand me for this?"

He slowed the rover down and approached a large crowd that seemed to be focusing on something. Max got out of the rover and broke through the crowd to see what it was that everyone was staring at. Tyra and Zack followed closely behind him. The closer he got to the center, the greater the pain in his stomach became. Just before he got to the middle, he realized the absolute last thing he would want to see was Luand lying dead on the battlefield. Max, scared of the possibility, quickly dismissed it from his mind, assuring himself it could never happen.

He blinked once more and stood struck by awe. His heart sank, and he took a deep breath as he saw his worst fear become a reality. He turned away, almost refusing to accept it and saying it was just a joke. He felt tears trying to emerge, but they couldn't. He held them in as if not to give Luand the satisfaction of besting him once more. He was tired of crying and instead yelled.

He burst through the crowd back to the rover, and Tyra rushed after him. Max hopped into the driver's seat, and Tyra slammed onto the door.

"Max, what are you doing?"

"This isn't fair. Luand didn't deserve this—not at all!"

"Okay, great. So you need to exact revenge, but on who?"

Max moved, agitated, knowing there was no one left to avenge Luand. Everyone had been defeated and the battle won. He kept banging his head on the wheel of the rover.

"But I didn't know!"

"What would you do?" Tyra yelled, trying to snap him out of his newfound rage. "Would you like to defeat Xaldoruks again but with the anger from Luand's death? Is that what he would want? For you to win out of revenge?"

Max clenched his hands and yelled again. He stepped out of the rover, fell to the ground and rested his head on Tyra's leg. Tyra knelt down and held him.

EPILOGUE

Max stood on the ruined floors of the UPA. Zack and Tyra stood among the rubble. Max looked out of the building at the ruined city in which he once lived, now completely destroyed by war. A gentle wind started to blow at them as the endless black and purple clouds shifted.

"This is it," Max muttered. "This is what we were fighting for. Luand wanted this more than anyone. It's not fair he didn't get to see it."

"A universe without Xaldoruks?" Zack said, walking behind him. "The universe hasn't seen this yet, has it?"

"Almost makes me wonder if destroying him was the best thing to do."

"It was," Tyra said. The two turned back to her. "A world that's constantly dying due to the whims of a dark angel isn't the world I'm willing to accept."

Max smiled. "Too bad the cost of the new universe was the one who wanted it the most. Somehow I think Luand knew we'd be the ones to end it—that these Sandsharks would be in the final battle."

"What makes you say that?"

"When we were training and we'd take a break, he kept referring to us as the Re:Generation, as if we were going to return the universe to what it was."

They all smiled.

"The universe already feels less safe without him," Zack said.

"What is the council going to do without him?" Tyra asked.

"Well, they've prepared for this—sort of. The council will have to elect a new leader if Luand didn't name the successor in his will. But until then, they'll continue to make decisions by voting."

"It will take forever for them to make any decision."

"Well, they've already made their first."

Tyra walked to him. "What do you mean, Zack? Why don't we know?"

Zack sighed. "The council was deciding on what to do with the rest of the UPA as we are. They can't rebuild the HQ where it is, not with this darkness surrounding about half the planet. Until we're able to reverse the effects, we'll have to find a new HQ, and until they find a new location and rebuild HQ, we're moving. Now, even though we lost more than half our members during the battle, we still outnumber every other base. We can't all move to another location and stay together."

"So you mean…"

"They're taking fractions of the remaining HQ members and sending them to other planets. They told the Elite Sandsharks today, and I can only imagine they'll tell you soon."

"Well, it doesn't have to be that bad," Max said, trying to be positive. "We can still stick together."

Zack shook his head. "They're separating us based on our skill sets. Max, since both you and I are powerhouses on the battlefield, we won't be stationed together. In fact, most of the Sandsharks are being sent to different planets to balance teams to finish the job."

"Finish what job? Didn't we all finish the job?"

"Look, when Xaldoruks said he wanted to create a new universe, he meant it, and not just this planet. This man was creating a new reality. He had the same machines on other planets. Some of them went off when he started this one, but others still haven't yet. If there's any chance to fix what he has done, it will be first done by destroying the machines. That's the mission for all of us as of now."

Tyra grabbed Max's hand and squeezed.

"When are we leaving?"

Zack looked away from Max and then turned back. He started to walk past them. "The assignments have already been made. I'd start packing what we have left if I were you." He walked down the hall.

Max held Tyra's hands. "Just as we were about to be something amazing again."

Tyra smiled and nodded. Max saw something peculiar emerging from her eyes. He didn't know what it was. Tyra tried to ignore it and straightened Max's collar. Finally, a single tear slipped. It was the first tear Max had seen from Tyra since they were kids. He held her close to him. He didn't want the moment to go.

Max went back to his room and started packing. The room he had known for seven years was no longer a safe place for him to be. As he took his belongings off the walls, he felt more and more out of place while still so unsure of his future.

Under his bed he found his Koratoric cube still flashing. He stared at it and remembered each time he looked at it and couldn't understand it at all. He started moving the twelve-by-twelve cube, not expecting anything out of it. When he moved the last corner into place, he realized he had solved one side of it. Without even thinking he had gotten farther than he ever had before.

He felt something unlock, releasing some sort of power. Suddenly the cube's face began to shine brightly.

ABOUT THE AUTHOR

Steven Gondré-Lewis (Gondré) presents his debut novel, which was over ten years in the making. He is a budding playwright, actor, and singer who hopes to use his talent to connect with others in a transformative way. Growing up in Bronx, New York, he spared no opportunity to let his imagination run wild as a very young child. Books and movies like Star Wars and Harry Potter were influential in helping his imagination to flourish. He still enjoys those and many other classics to this day. While attending school in Montgomery County, Maryland, his creative ideas only continued to flow. By the time he was nine, he had formulated the first ideas for Max Blaze and began writing little scraps of the story and drawing sketches of the characters on notebooks and loose paper. From those days, the environment surrounding the people of Zapheriazia went through many changes evolving into the story with which you've been presented.

His family is very proud of him -- a young, bright, African-American young man who has produced this incredible work and seems unstoppable.

Made in the USA
Coppell, TX
02 July 2020